ROAD W. Depeyster
Road to Boston
Lane
Delancy
Mr Dayokney
Bowery
Grand
Great Square
Street
DIVISION STREET
Mr Jones
Degrushis Rope Walk
Mr L. Rutgers
Mr Thyuder

Salt Meadows

GORLAR'S HOOK

CROWN Pᵗ OR

R I V E R

S O U N D

O R

O R

Rapalie
PART OF LONG OR NASSAU ISLAND
Ramsens Mill

B A Y

ALSO BY COLIN HARRISON

Risk

The Finder

The Havana Room

Afterburn

Manhattan Nocturne

Bodies Electric

Break and Enter

YOU BELONG TO ME

YOU BELONG TO ME

COLIN HARRISON

SARAH CRICHTON BOOKS

FARRAR, STRAUS AND GIROUX   NEW YORK

•

Sarah Crichton Books
Farrar, Straus and Giroux
18 West 18th Street, New York 10011

Chapter 1 of *You Belong to Me* originally appeared, in slightly different form, on the website *RealClearLife*.

Library of Congress Cataloging-in-Publication Data
Names: Harrison, Colin, 1960– author.
Title: You belong to me : a novel / Colin Harrison.
Description: First edition. | New York : Sarah Crichton Books / Farrar, Straus
and Giroux, 2017.
Identifiers: LCCN 2016032802 | ISBN 9780374299477 (hardcover) |
ISBN 9781429944625 (e-book)
Subjects: LCSH: Triangles (Interpersonal relations)—Fiction. | Psychological fiction. |
BISAC: FICTION / Thrillers. | GSAFD: Suspense fiction.
Classification: LCC PS3558.A6655 Y68 2017 | DDC 813/.54—dc23
LC record available at https://lccn.loc.gov/2016032802

Designed by Abby Kagan

Our books may be purchased in bulk for promotional, educational, or business use. Please contact your local bookseller or the Macmillan Corporate and Premium Sales Department at 1-800-221-7945, extension 5442, or by e-mail at MacmillanSpecialMarkets@macmillan.com.

www.fsgbooks.com
www.twitter.com/fsgbooks • www.facebook.com/fsgbooks

1 3 5 7 9 10 8 6 4 2

For Sarah, for Walker, for Julia

The city changes faster, alas, than the human heart.

—BAUDELAIRE

YOU BELONG TO ME

Her story, his trouble, begins in desire. He was walking
with Jennifer Mehraz, in a rush. She'd been late to his office, and he'd
waited in the lobby until the last minute, then three minutes more
until she arrived, swishing in wearing a blue summer dress. "Oh, Paul,
I couldn't get a cab—" And so on. We must hurry. Now they were cutting
through Rockefeller Center, where the Friday lunchtime crowds were
out, men in their shirtsleeves, women letting the September sun hit their
legs, eating their expensive sandwiches, phoning, texting, watching and
being watched. They didn't much see him, but they definitely noticed
Jennifer.

"You can just go right in?" She took long steps in her heels, the wind
pushing against her dress. "You don't need a ticket or something?"

"Only if you're bidding."

"Will you bid?"

Paul nodded. "Absolutely."

"Will you *win*?"

"I'd better."

She hurried to keep up. "Do you always win?"

"No. But I rarely lose."

They crossed Forty-ninth Street, passing the limo drivers parked at the curb, smoking in the time-wasting, disconsolate way that they do, and entered the Christie's plaza.

"Just follow me," Paul told her as they pushed through the glass doors of the auction house. He collected his white bidding paddle at the desk and they proceeded to an elegant theater, where he found two seats for them a third of the way down and close to the aisle—he preferred not to be too far forward, so that his competitors wouldn't sit behind him.

Around them sat the crowd one sees at Christie's: rich people or their playacting representatives. He'd been going for more than twenty years now, ever since his days as an associate in an elephantine law firm seven blocks away, wondering how long it would be before he was fired for laziness or incompetence. The Christie's staff had seen him often enough through the years that they would quietly nod; he was, however, merely another pilgrim to the house of treasure, where the wonders of the world passed by every day, miracles owned by kings, emperors, presidents, moguls, thieves, fanatics, and visionaries, often never to be seen publicly again in the same century *or ever*. He wasn't so interested in Picassos or Elizabeth Taylor's jewels or the occasional Stradivarius. The latest Leonardo da Vinci manuscript or Qing dynasty porcelain bowl left him cold. There was one thing for Paul, and one thing only—old maps of New York City. He was a collector, had been since he was ten years old. How many maps did he own? Too many to count. Most worth not much and few worth quite a bit. And that day at Christie's some superb maps were going on the block, including one he'd tracked for years.

Jennifer watched as the tuxedoed auctioneer adjusted his microphone; meanwhile several wealthy older women inspected her from the row behind. Perhaps they were there to see their own heirlooms sell. A number of the old New York City fortunes had been wiped out in recent years, not that the world cared much or should. It seemed, however, that the women disapproved of Jennifer—Too blond? Too much leg? Too much shoulder? The diamond on her finger too glitteringly huge?—and scrutinized the both of them closely, wondering if she were Paul's young wife or a mistress. The city was full of mistresses, though few people cared to note that fact. And perhaps Paul looked the type—a bit of the boulevardier, the charming lout lucky to still have his hair, they were probably thinking, a worldly squint in his eyes. But definitely not loaded. Has *some* money but not big money. Shoes not quite good enough, and that watch looks cheap. Rumpled and wrinkled, his best years already behind him, their appraisals made with practiced and devastating accuracy. Yet the women's scrutiny seemed more focused on Jennifer; they could sense that she was not born into the world of money but had pushed or pulled or moaned her way into it. Or maybe they studied her coldly just because she was young, as once they had been and were no longer.

Jennifer was checking her phone. "Ahmed says hello."

"Where is he?"

"Somewhere on the Atlantic Ocean."

"When does he get home?"

"Sunday. Then we have the benefit the next night, remember?"

"I bought my tickets."

"But you'd rather not go?"

He hated everything about fancy dinners, including the beginnings, middles, and ends. But Jennifer and her husband were his neighbors across the hall, having become one of those wealthy young couples who kept up a busy schedule, with corporate socializing and charity events three nights a week when Ahmed wasn't zooming off to do yet another deal.

"Well?" she prodded.

"I used to go to these things, back in the day."

"And?"

"The shrimp is usually pretty good."

She leaned against him, and he smelled her perfume. "Paul, you might have actual *fun*, you know . . . Maybe you'll see an old flameroo." She took the white numbered paddle from his hand and gave it an experimental wave, her gold bangle bracelets clanking softly. "Will Rachel be there?"

"She will, indeed."

"Right, she can't let you float around *unescorted*."

Jennifer flashed him a wicked little grin that pierced him completely. Then again, he had been pierced completely by women any number of times and yet had lived to tell the tale. After his second divorce, he'd bounced and bumped his way from one woman to another. He seemed to have lost the marriage knack; it hadn't been pretty.

"Wait, who are *they*?" Jennifer pointed at a trio of fussy-looking middle-aged men just arrived, whom Paul recognized as cold-blooded antiquities dealers from Paris, Shanghai, and Dubai. "They look sneaky," she said. "Pretending not to be."

She wasn't quite as wide-eyed as a year earlier, when she and Ahmed had moved in across from him. Learning fast, as you do on the way up. Ahmed was elevatoring toward the top, having graduated from Yale at age twenty and from Harvard's business *and* law schools at twenty-four, now a hybrid financier-lawyer. Serious high-powered intellect, no doubt about that. Full of himself, a world-beater in a city full of them. He had turned down *three* attempts by Goldman Sachs to hire him. Now thirty-two, Ahmed jetted around the globe doing deals, fronting the money for much older men who preferred to remain unseen. Paul had studied him, from an oblique angle. Maybe that was why he'd agreed to go to the wretched benefit, to watch the newest players in the theater of wealth and ambition, with Ahmed one of the fresh leading men. In effect, Ahmed was no longer working for one entity but several at a time, straddling the liquid intersection point of investment banks, energy companies, and sovereign governments. He was already making a boatload of money. He didn't like Paul much, and considered Paul's branch of law—employment and immigration—tedious small-ball, more or less akin to the manual labor done by the uniformed service workers who cleaned his office each evening. Was Ahmed wrong? No, not at all.

Oh, but the *real* reason he doesn't like me, thought Paul, is that I understand his wife better than he does. Paul knew where Jennifer came from, understood what her last few freckles and faintly nasal Pennsylvania accent *meant*. He doubted Ahmed had ever seen her hometown of Reading, having grown up in a rich immigrant Iranian family in Los Angeles, where the Mehraz family now owned a regional bank and a great deal of commercial real estate. He seemed in a hurry to be the first Iranian-American senator or governor, for which an American-born wife was a prerequisite. But those positions would come years from now, long after his fortune had been banked, his reputation made. Tall and slender without being delicate, his black hair brushed straight back, Ahmed looked both elegant and powerful. And as he aged he would appear even more so. Older men had already started to fear him; Paul had seen as much at the parties, the men watching Ahmed's eyes for a sign of approval, the invisible wires of their anxieties yanking their weathered faces into a grin at his smallest conversational niceties, or nodding when there was no reason to nod. Yes, when the old men fear the young men, take notice, pal.

The auction was announced. He reminded Jennifer they were required to turn off their phones so as not to be able to communicate with confederates in shill bidding.

She handed him the paddle. "Better take this away from me before I do something outrageous," she said playfully. "Would you've left without me if I hadn't shown up at your office?"

"Yes."

"Really? But I'm your *date*." She gazed at him, and he saw in her bright eyes a swirl of sexual amusement and yet confusion about her place in the world. "Really?" she repeated.

But he was scanning the crowd for competitors, noting some fellow worshippers as well as a smattering of local investors who speculated in rare maps or bought them for their business clientele, rare maps now seen as a legitimate hedge against inflation in the same way that collectible coins or fine art were bought to diversify investment portfolios. They all knew one another in their fiendish little world, these greedily obsessive hoarders, these fetishizers of ancient ink and paper; they saw one another at the map collecting societies, they trailed through the overpriced Manhattan galleries, asking casually if the runners had found anything interesting in the estate auctions in New England, the South, the Midwest. Whether anything extraordinary had turned up. As it *always* did, sooner or later!

What drove such fanaticism? The end of paper. People had long collected maps, but now the world felt a great silent death transpiring. It was said that one of the oil-soaked Saudi princes had lost his head and was buying up any and all maps of the Middle East, any document showing land from the Suez Canal to the far shores of Oman. Price no object, of course. Millions upon millions. Had even quietly approached the British Museum for its priceless military maps of Arabia, and may not have been rebuffed. So, too, were the young Chinese moguls buying up maps of China, especially the eastern coast, where so much had changed over the last thirty years—rivers moved, shorelines filled in, mountains pulverized. American collectors from the West tended to like the huge multicolored maps of Texas, with its shifting borders, and interior regions marked as the territories of Apache or Comanche Indians, and most especially, the various maps prior to 1740 that showed California as an island. But across the world, the common element was the demise of paper. Now maps were pure digital information, pixelated sat-photo hybrids, ever more brilliantly interactive and throbbingly detailed. Zoom in, zoom out. But no matter how dense they were with glittering up-to-the-minute information, these maps were not tangible. No practiced hand had made them. No weak-eyed wretch had pressed an irregular sheet of rag paper upon an ink-rolled copper plate. Paul couldn't touch them or feel them; continuously updated, they preserved *nothing*.

Against this onslaught of time, he collected maps of New York City. Was it because he had spent his life there? Oh, Paul, he was just fifty now, old enough to be haunted by memory late at night, alone in bed and listening to the sirens rush away in the far streets, old enough that some of his maps, those few from the late twentieth century and beyond, represented landscapes where he himself had once stood. A boy attending public school in Brooklyn, riding the graffiti-slathered subways in the 1970s. A young college student at Columbia panting after the Barnard girls. A freshly minted lawyer, putting in the long hours, still interested in keeping his shoes shined. But for the most part, the New York City frozen in his maps had been long lost to time and to all living memory. He could only console himself by inspecting them closely with his magnifying eyeglasses, made for surgeons, 6X, ordered from Germany. He would gaze at such maps, then lift his eyes to the window and see what had become of those same places, the glass city built atop the iron city built atop the brick city built over wooden structures held together with oak pegs and four-sided iron nails. For that is what New York is, a never completed masterwork, torn down even as it is resurrected, each minute populated by a different swarm of humanity streaming in and out through the bridges and tunnels—

—which was how Jennifer Mehraz had first appeared in New York City. Still Jenny Hayes then, she'd arrived from Pennsylvania on a Greyhound bus that passed through the Lincoln Tunnel, her luggage consisting of a battered duffel and a backpack. Reading was an unremarkable small city, but deeply American. He'd been there. Yes, sir. Poor and old, the factories empty or torn down. Surrounded by cornfields and new subdivisions. It had a minor league baseball team and men who fixed tractor-trailers and obese retired people eating breakfast at McDonald's. And yet from time to time a stunning and privately troubled girl grows up in a place like Reading, and only slightly less frequently does she leave to seek her future in Los Angeles, New York, Las Vegas . . . the big towns, where the light and noise, the distant mountains of money, are to be found. The more beautiful the girls, the more volatile their destinies. The world always has uses for them, especially ones who have no advantage other than their beauty, no education, no money, no family . . . who have already measured the distance between themselves and desperation. He'd met a number over the years, especially between marriages I and II, and had seen how tough and lonely they often were. Carrying around big holes inside, marked LOST FATHER, MOTHER BIPOLAR, BROTHER SELLS SYNTHETIC HEROIN, or some such. He and Jennifer had discussed how she'd grown up, and he'd wondered if her desire to talk to him was due to her awareness that the walls were quickly going up around her, that year by year she would be more completely defined by Ahmed's identity and wealth and position, carried ever that much farther away from where she'd come. Her mother had been a town beauty who'd married the wrong man a couple of different times. Jennifer never spoke to her now. And it was this past, she'd admitted, that she tended not to describe in detail for Ahmed, because doing so made him look at her a certain way. She'd learned to tell people she'd "studied at Penn State" before coming to New York to look for work. Technically, this was true, but there was an unexplained gap of almost three years between the time she arrived in New York and the day she'd met Ahmed. Did Ahmed know much about those years? Paul's guess was no.

"You ready?" Jennifer asked him, watching the auctioneer confer with various aides and assistants.

"First the French and British maps."

For sale was the entire Hingham Collection, accrued over more than one hundred years, initially by a British sea captain and then by the captain's son and grandson. The American heirs, it was said, had squandered their considerable inheritance in all the usual ways (stock market myopia; pharmaceutical existentialism; penile dementia; the wretched euphoria of alcoholism) and a few less usual ones (the self-important funding of incomprehensible art films; the dona-tion of weighty sums to religious charismatics), and had been forced to sell off the many hundreds of maps in the collection, the total value of which exceeded $60 million, according to the pre-auction estimates. Old Captain Hingham, long of beard when alive and utterly dead since 1904, had purchased maps in all of his ports of call, said the Christie's program, around Europe, of course, Africa, India, the Asian coastal cities, Australia. He'd rolled them up in clean sheets of Japanese rice paper and slipped them into surplus brass artillery shells he bought from the British navy and expertly sealed them with muslin and wax against the invasion of moisture, light, insects, or curious human fin-gers. Each long brass shell was labeled with the particulars of the map's age, dimensions, provenance, and purchase price. When he returned twice a year to his seaside cottage on the North Yorkshire coast, he placed the maps and his captain's logs (also sealed with wax) into a re-cessed space in the bone-dry stone cellar. And that is where they stayed, unopened and stacked like wine bottles in an angled mahogany lattice, as his son and grandson, both in the British merchant marine, kept adding to them without ever looking at what was already there. It wasn't until the late 1960s that the great-great-granddaughter retrieved

the hundreds of maps stored beneath the house, revealing a spectacular collection. Old Captain Hingham had amassed something for just
about everyone, including half a dozen maps of old New York.

But Paul was only interested in one. It was about a hundred and
fifty years old and had long fascinated him: the private, oversized map
of Manhattan printed by D. T. Valentine. From the period of 1841 to
the early 1870s, Valentine, a fastidious, portly man who parted his hair
down the middle, assembled a spectacular annual volume called the
Manual of the Common Council of New York. These were small, thick
books compiling the statistics of the burgeoning city, with reports on
the progress of its construction, and were distributed to wealthy businessmen, politicians, and other notables, who often had their names stamped
in gold on the spine. The yearly volumes were lavishly illustrated with
hand-colored engravings depicting scenes from the city as well as folded
maps representing New York of both the present day and the past. Paul
had dutifully acquired a copy of every one.

But D. T. Valentine had commissioned a private, oversized version of
his vertical representation of the island of Manhattan, one on which
he noted and hand-colored the exact locations and names of saloons,
brothels of fine reputation, churches, schools, firehouses, insane asylums,
and cemeteries (including those reserved for Negroes, Quakers, and
Jews). Most maps of the period were no larger than two feet by three
feet, but this beauty stretched forty-one inches wide by sixty-four inches
high. Two examples were known to be in existence: a less ornate version
held in the New York Public Library and the second in the Hingham
Collection, bought for three dollars in gold in 1887, when the contents
of Valentine's personal effects were liquidated. The map's cartouche
featured an Indian and a worldly New Yorker in a top hat sitting on
either side of a globe, upon which a golden eagle and a beaver perched.
The waters of the Hudson and East Rivers were replete with representa-
tions of the major wooden sailing vessels of the day, and the docks of the
East Side were each labeled by the shipping lines they serviced. Where the
burgeoning metropolis reached the bucolic edge of the countryside—
somewhere around present-day Ninetieth Street—Valentine could not
resist inscribing what remaining farms existed on the isle of Manhattan

as well as representing where their orchards stood, rendering tiny apple trees in rows. Paul even knew how many, having counted them while poring over the high-resolution scan of the map that the auction house provided; its clarity and detail were virtually pornographic.

There were specific reasons why he craved this map, each more mentally toothsome than the next. First, the map was rare, complete, beautiful, magnificent, and was desired by every major New York City map collector. Yet the same could be said of perhaps a dozen maps appearing on the market each year. Second—and of signal interest to those same collectors—the map was so large that Valentine had ample space to annotate the map as he saw fit. This meant that he recorded, in his quill pen (the blue ink of his minute letterings tinged with violet), on certain streets the comings and goings of personages whose travels he deemed worthy of documentation. Such as a line of faint dashes through the Bowery thus inscribed: *This route walked by M*^r*. Charles Dickens of England on 1*st *visit to U. States, 1842.* Ten blocks north, along the edge of Cooper Union's Great Hall, read the notation *A. Lincoln speech given here Febry, 1860.* Last, Valentine's hand identification of the names of various saloons, bars, inns, and houses of ill repute included, at the corner of Bleecker and "Broad-Way," a saloon owned by a W. E. Reeves, Paul's great-great-grandfather, whose own records had amounted to no more than a worthless, mouse-nibbled sheaf of papers. Fantastic. *Irresistible.* Oh, did he want—

—such a pedestrian word, *want.* Useless in these circumstances. He desired and needed and required the oversized map, he *craved* it; he fevered for it, he felt that it was already rightfully his; he wanted to touch it and smell it and possess it, to run his finger along its stiff edges. He had felt such possessiveness before—with women, and during legal battles. He was not, at heart, decorous and civilized, no matter how he appeared. His ostensible refinement went only so deep, and beneath that there was something else, harder, meaner, a man governed by impulse and need rather than prudence. His second wife, who was in no way shy about her opinions, said to him, "Paul, you *look* nice, but you are actually a fucking bastard." There'd been no point in disagreeing.

Now the auctioneer announced himself, and the first of the Hingham maps, an enormous 1753 *Plan de la Rivière Seine à Paris*, was immediately displayed, to general applause. A spectacular map with the Jardin des Tuileries drawn in detail as well as the twelve bridges across the Seine listed in a numbered key. If you were a Parisian, how could you possibly resist? The bidding began slowly, then accelerated in ten-thousand-dollar increments until the pretenders were winnowed out.

"Wow," said Jennifer. "The French were—"

"The best mapmakers of their era," he said.

"So beautiful," Jennifer whispered, glossy lips an inch from his ear. "But not for me."

Two numbered paddles were being waved from either side of the room, and the auctioneer consulted with the staff on the phone with the call-in bidders. It was then that Paul noticed a stir, a disturbance, in the gallery of expensive hair and clever eyeglasses behind them. Eager to see if any of the Manhattan dealers in front might make a play for the Paris map, he paid no attention. Until he heard Jennifer make a noise—a little strangled cry.

She had turned to look down their row of seats. Standing in the aisle four patrons away was a large young man in desert-colored soldier's fatigues. He was tall and hawkishly handsome in a blond, sun-beaten way, and he stared down at her expectantly. Aggressively. As if he knew her well. His large hands looked calloused. He didn't react to the curious stares from the auction patrons who'd noticed him, including the gaggle of disapproving women behind them.

"How did—?" Jennifer whispered fiercely, seemingly aware of the exact distance the man had traveled to this place, or even what he had overcome to be standing before her. She stood, weakly, it seemed, and glanced at Paul, her eyes clouded by both an unnamed grief and an inability to resist an even stronger feeling. Paul waited for her to offer a word of explanation.

But Jennifer said nothing and squeezed awkwardly past the four seat-holders to the aisle, not bothering to apologize, and collapsed against the man. His arms enveloped her, his chin atop her head, but he did not close his eyes during their embrace and instead swept his gaze aggressively across all those who witnessed them, particularly Paul, daring anyone to intervene. Paul waited for Jennifer to look back at him, but she did not. They left together then, Jennifer fetching in her blue summer dress as she leaned against the man, needing or wanting his support like one who is intoxicated and does not expect to recover anytime soon.

He sat mystified, the minutes flicking by, no longer thinking about where he was or what he was doing, searching his conversations with Jennifer for any reference to this unnamed man. He was not a brother or a cousin, Paul was sure, despite the similar coloring, for she had folded herself into the man's arms in a much different way, with intimate familiarity. And how did he know she was here? Jennifer had walked straight from her apartment to Paul's office. She had not expected him, for her reaction showed her surprise. One doesn't just happen upon former lovers—if that was what they were—in a place like New York. The city is too big, the chances for coincidental contact too small . . .

It was then that Paul heard the auctioneer announce the next item, and he instinctively consulted his catalog. Had he really not been paying attention? Had the Chinese already battled for Captain Hingham's Shanghai maps? The D. T. Valentine map had just gone up—*My god, I have to be more alert!*—and for the next few minutes he waved his paddle with reckless insistence, eager to just buy the damn thing, overpaying if necessary, and not interested in the thrill of competition. He had been looking forward to having Jennifer next to him as he won this fabulous map, and now she was gone, leaving him irritated and perplexed by her disappearance. He kept his paddle aloft. The other serious bidders—three collectors and a dealer—saw his fanatical determination and gave up. Going once, twice . . . *Bang.* Sold to the tall man with the scowl on his face.

Later, after Paul had signed the papers that specified the buyer's premium atop the "hammer price," and stood to go, a corpulent young man stepped forward.

"Mr. Paul Reeves?"

"Yes?"

"I work for Robert Gibbs." A prominent estate attorney who tidied the piles of money left behind by wealthy people. "We had reason to think that you might be at the auction today."

"Well, here I apparently am."

"Mr. Gibbs instructed me to find you and let you know, in a highly confidential manner"—the young man leaned forward—"that the health of Mr. James Stassen is not good, that he is, ah, *failing*."

"James McKinley Stassen?"

The young man quietly nodded.

Paul felt suddenly alert, electric with alarm. The owner of the Stassen-Ratzer map of New York? Was it possible? Unseen in thirty years? Hand-colored copperplate engraving, 47⅜ by 35 inches? Commissioned by the British Admiralty in 1766, the Ratzer was the finest map of an American city made in the eighteenth century and was extremely rare. Created by Lieutenant Bernard Ratzer, military engineer in the Royal American Regiment. Stassen's copy had a singular history, and had accidentally appeared in the blurry background of a black-and-white photograph in a *Life* magazine article from the early 1940s about Manhattan society women. Paul had a copy of the article in his files. The Stassen-Ratzer map. Worth a *thousand* rare Valentines!

"I didn't realize he was still alive."

"It's expected that Mr. Stassen will last—well, not too much longer." The young man handed Paul a business card. "Mr. Gibbs would take it as a great favor if you would contact him at your convenience . . . But sooner rather than later."

Now it was Paul who kept his voice low. "The potential sale is to occur before Stassen dies?"

"Mr. Gibbs will explain the particularities."

He took that as a yes. "Tell your boss I'm impressed he found me. I'd like to meet him Monday or Tuesday?"

"Mr. Stassen is having a medical procedure in his apartment early next week. The soonest would be Wednesday morning at nine."

"Fine, fine," said Paul. "I'll be there."

"We propose you meet at Mr. Stassen's residence."

Because that's where the map is, thought Paul. "Okay."

The man produced a piece of paper. "The address, on Park Avenue. Mr. Gibbs will meet you in the lobby at nine."

Paul folded the paper into his pocket. "Assuming, of course, Mr. Stassen doesn't leave us before then."

He walked home to Sixty-sixth Street, trying to enjoy his capture of the Valentine, but distracted by the fact that the Stassen-Ratzer was in play. What was wrong with him? He had followed the Valentine map for eight years. Now he had it! And so what! Could he feel no satisfaction? Was he such a materialistic idiot that he already needed the next acquisition, the next *confiscation*? This is truly an illness, he thought, I'm a goddamned, pathetic map *junkie*, a middle-aged man who hoards old pieces of paper. But . . . but no!—*no*, the Stassen-Ratzer map *merited* such psychic distress! . . . If the rumors, the rare glimpses, reported over the years were true—and maybe they weren't!—but if they were, then it was not just *any* map of New York City, it was Halley's Comet and Michael Jordan and Sophia Loren and John Lennon and Angkor Wat. There was one, *only one*. Could he afford the Stassen map? No. Not possible. Well, yes, but it would hurt mightily. He'd have to mortgage his apartment. Or sell off holdings. But that took time. This was a different situation; the seller would demand payment quickly. As the sole owner of his law firm, Paul could draw on the firm's credit line. Certainly irregular, yet not quite illegal. But doable. A little paperwork to adjust and sign. Maybe he would will the map to the Smithsonian, the only proper thing to do. BEQUEST OF PAUL REEVES. Had a nice egomaniacal ring to it. Why hadn't Stassen done that? Impossible to know. He found himself sweating through his suit, striding faster than necessary, pressing forward as if genuinely rushing to get somewhere. Then, there he was, turning the corner to his apartment building, a fifty-eight-story stack in which each floor was shaped like the letter U laid flat and contained two mirror-image apartments, the elevator arriving at their intersection.

"Afternoon, sir," muttered Parker, the doorman. Paul thought his

YOU BELONG TO ME · 17

navy-blue uniform was ridiculous and suspected Parker did, too, the effect being to compress his personality within his starched jacket and striped pants. But now Paul wondered if he caught a glint in Parker's eye—a shard of savage amusement that he knew he'd better keep to himself. Which, a second or two later, he did, his expression melting into the disinterested formality he usually displayed.

The elevator stopped on the forty-seventh floor. Jennifer and Ahmed's apartment, 47-E, stood to the right, and Paul's, 47-W, to the left. They would stay in their three-bedroom only a little while longer, he surmised. It wasn't grand enough for their rising station, and within a year or two, perhaps after a first child, they would inevitably move to a much larger place, Central Park West perhaps, or the new building on Fifty-seventh Street, where the penthouse had just sold for no less than $120 million to the daughter of a Russian oligarch. He noticed that their front door was open, about an inch, as if someone had intended to shut it but had been distracted. This happened from time to time and usually meant Jennifer had dashed down to the lobby to greet a friend or retrieve a delivery. He took a step toward the door, noticed no lights on in the apartment, and listened a moment. Nothing. He turned toward his own door a few paces away.

His apartment had once been a similar three-bedroom but he had converted it into a one-bedroom with a large display gallery. The building was designed so that all of its apartments would catch the morning light through their eastern windows. The two legs of the U were a mere forty-five feet away from each other, and when the light was just so, one could gaze directly through that space into the large plate-glass windows of the mirror-image apartment across the way. In the morning the eastern apartments could look into the sun-washed western apartments and in the afternoon the western could look into the eastern. But not in Paul's case, for these windows were located along one wall of his map gallery and he'd installed slatted louver blinds on all of them, virtually eliminating the penetration of sunlight into the room.

The reason was simple. Sunlight damaged maps, especially those that were brightly colored. Although all of his maps were framed with ultraviolet glass, he was distrustful that this offered full protection. So his private museum remained hidden from the world. He had installed floor-to-ceiling display walls and his maps hung there undisturbed. They were laid out according to strict chronology, and one stepped into the room at the middle of the seventeenth century—the period when maps of New York City were first made, often drawn by hand with pen and ink—and reached the present era at the end. There were a few blank gaps in this progression, places he expected someday to fill. Oh, he *was* happy now to have the Valentine map! It was quite an experience to walk past these maps one after the other. He saw time. He saw *what had happened*. Would that he owned every map ever drawn of New York! Merely to posit that idea made him a little crazy; to have every map would be to have *all of it*, every block and street and lane and alley and crooked road—and such possession would only be godlike, for no such collection did exist, or could. The closest would be the complete holdings of the New York Public Library, and although the curators there had access to this near-infinity, they did not *possess* it. The maps did not *belong* to them. They did not have the legitimate power of destruction. They could not burn the whole lot, as Paul could with his collection, were he ever mad enough to do that. For the collector collects to *have*. To own, to worship, to possess—to say this is mine and no one else's.

Because the windows of his map room were always shuttered, the occupants of the other apartment across the way had long ago lost their inhibitions in front of their own windows. He rarely took advantage of this vulnerability. However, guided by instinct or curiosity, now he proceeded to the farthest window—the one directly opposite Jennifer and Ahmed's bedroom—and, perfectly hidden in shadow, gently pulled down the slat at eye level.

He saw them.

The tall blond soldier was atop Jennifer, her long legs lifted high around his waist, her arms clasped around his shoulders. The late light was sufficient to see the undulating ridge of tanned muscle that ran along either side of his spine, the lifting buttocks that sank and rose and sank again, driving himself into her. A movement neither too hurried nor too slow. Paul watched them with affection for their youth and urgency; he had been that young, that vital, once. We all were, no? Or will have been? But if he gazed upon their copulation with a kind of sentimental reverie, he also could not forget certain lessons learned and unlearned and learned again at great cost in his own life, as one who had batted around in the city for decades now, seen men and women regularly wreck their lives while guided by the astonishing conviction that they were doing just the opposite. That they had it all figured out, that they knew what was up, that the reward was worth the risk, that the secret wouldn't be broken, that one's own heart was knowable. Yet there Jennifer and her soldier were, in the grip of great glory and hidden happiness, and although he was glad for them (how can we condemn lovers, really?—is it possible?) he wondered if the moment was yet an ominous beginning, certainly for Jennifer Mehraz and her husband, but perhaps even for himself as well.

He dropped the slat . . . but lifted it again. He had to see, of course, see all. Now Jennifer's arms rose in the air above the soldier, splayed wide, open to him, receiving whatever might come next. As he loomed above her, she reverently licked the thick curve of his neck. That she was beneath a man not her husband in the expensive vault that her husband had bought—the front door still open, no less—was apparently far from her consciousness. The seconds passed; the big soldier thrust again and again until a last convulsion ran through Jennifer, and then through him. Jennifer lifted her forehead against the man's chest—Paul imagined he could hear her cry out—and then they were done.

He gently let the slat fall, and stepped back into the darkness of his maps, which seemed gathered about him in silent witness, each a different, frozen face of the city that had held innumerable lives.

Decades tumbling on decades.

Wish and dream, trouble and desire.

2

Ahmed wasn't sentimental about the view, the sight of lower Manhattan rising up out of a gloomy Sunday dawn as the great vessel slipped toward the Verrazano-Narrows Bridge five miles south of the island's tip. Yet British and French and German tourists stood clustered at the foredeck taking pictures with their phones, huddling with cups of coffee, the sun just above the horizon to the east. His four Japanese companions were still in their staterooms communicating directly with their colleagues in Tokyo, though it was now evening there. The deal was done, the documents revised and transmitted back and forth among Tokyo, New York, Dubai, and London almost continuously. As luxurious accommodations went, the RMS *Queen Mary 2* was unquestionably fine, but for physical isolation, its transit across the North Atlantic couldn't be beat. Once you were heading west from England, beyond helicopter range of the Royal Navy, that was *it*; the only way off the 1,132-foot ship was to take an endless swim. You and your counterparts were stuck there together and so you had better negotiate. The fact that they had hit heavy seas added some urgency to the conversation, and when the captain explained in his droll British accent that the ship was equipped with the latest turbine stabilizers fore and aft and that there was no reason for "undue concern," the Japanese bankers became more compliant. They were, after all, going to get paid, collectively and individually, so long as a deal went through. Their Tokyo bank had possessed the foresight in 1986 to buy from the then bankrupt Russian government, for the equivalent of 900 million yen in gold bars, the deepwater drilling rights to a huge quadrant near the Lomonosov Ridge within the Russian Arctic sector. It had been a nearly clairvoyant purchase, based on the work of an ancient Japanese climatologist who predicted that the future retreat of polar ice would not only make the region accessible to deepwater mining technologies but also to shipping routes certain to open between Russia and North America, allowing for faster and cheaper trade between those continents. By the early years of the twenty-first century, Russia had realized its mistake and had initiated a series of controversial seabed claims into international Arctic waters and had even mounted a scientific expedition that sought to prove that the Lomonosov Ridge was in fact an extension of the Russian landmass—a laughable notion, but one did *not* laugh in the faces of the Russians. The rise of Vladimir Putin from a slippery KGB bureaucrat to a stone-faced dictator bent on restoring Russia's primacy on the world stage meant that Russia would make further exploitation of the quadrant by any other nation costly, if not impossible. With the ongoing weakening of the Japanese economy, the bank decided to cash in the value of the drilling rights when the fluctuating price of oil made them look most valuable. The bank didn't have the capital to develop the rights, nor the stomach to fight with Russia for access to the waters, nor with Canada, which had also claimed sovereignty over the region.

Ahmed's job on behalf of his consortium was to get the Japanese bankers to cut their price in half by explaining how few international companies could successfully do business with Putin. Translation: If you don't sell to us, you might not be able to sell to anyone else—and then where are you, with unhappy shareholders and capital locked up when you need it elsewhere? So for the first day of the trip, while the other passengers inspected the lesser Renoirs for sale or enjoyed seaweed facials in the ship's spa, Ahmed had expounded on the general political weakening of the Russian oil oligarchs, the West's unwillingness to lend to them, the technological problems associated with developing the deepwater crust, including the best risk-management estimates of an ecological disaster, and, not least, the gathering consensus by oil company geologists that other quadrants in the region might be more promising. The bankers' English was pretty good, but the conversation slowed at times as the Japanese translators caught up. He'd been careful to be deferential to the oldest Japanese executive, Mr. Yamamoto, always waiting for him to enter and exit the room first. And by addressing Yamamoto primarily, as a sign of respect. In the end the Japanese bankers had come down by thirty-one percent, which was enough, and had thrown in a half-built casino they were financing in Macau, subject to approval by Beijing. Ahmed hadn't seen the casino coming, and it was a shrewd move that immediately caught the fancy of his bosses, none of whom knew how difficult it was to run a casino in China, let alone make money from it in an overbuilt, intricately corrupt Macau. But no matter, the deal was done, hands shaken, bows exchanged, the translators and secretaries double-checking the language, the papers signed. The Japanese men had celebrated with a round of champagne late the previous evening, the lights of the New Jersey coastline not yet visible, but Ahmed had not joined them, for he had received some unpleasant news.

Now he took out his handheld device and studied again the frozen still shot from the apartment house security camera: his wife standing close, too close, to a tall American soldier in the building's elevator. From Jennifer's height, five-foot-seven, he estimated that the man was six-foot-three, very broad across the shoulders and chest. Had seen a lot of sun. Low body fat, judging from the musculature of his neck. Who was this man? Ahmed burned to know. How had Jennifer been so careless? The only explanation was that she did not care whether she was discovered. Or perhaps she was so carried away by passion that she had forgotten to be careful. It was an important distinction and one he intended to draw. Their apartment had no internal security cameras; was that a mistake or a mercy? In their next apartment, he would have them installed as part of the remodeling.

He heard the excited cries of other passengers and looked up. The misty blur of the Statue of Liberty had emerged and some of the tourists were moving to the port side to photograph it. Why? The statue no longer meant anything; it was a sentimental relic from a lost age, when France was a world player and could afford to send great gifts across the ocean. France was now one of the fading museum states of Europe, a second-rate economic power with no oil, fatally expensive labor costs, and a population of angry, marginalized Islamic immigrants who would in time destroy its famous culture, which protected the very freedoms they would never have enjoyed in their original countries. He watched the looming statue become more distinct by degrees, eliciting a stream of camera flashes from the passengers. The Manhattan harbor no longer meant much, either. The channel was not deep enough for the world's largest ships, and the skyline couldn't compare with Shanghai or Singapore. The new World Trade Center was respectable enough, yet was just another symbol, really, for it was a historical certainty that the money would ebb away from New York as it had drained from Paris and Brussels the century before. That is, if another massive hurricane didn't doom it first.

His corporate phone worked on the ship and in every country. But the one Ahmed took out of his pocket was a local one that had just come into range of the cell towers of lower Manhattan. He switched it on and dialed his cousin, who was expecting a call this early on a Sunday morning.

"Yes?" Amir answered.

"You find out how long he was there?"

"A couple of hours."

"Did he leave alone?"

"Yes."

Ahmed remained alert to the fact that Paul Reeves had also been with Jennifer that same afternoon. Reeves liked her, it was plain to see, and Ahmed knew that Jennifer did not mind spending time with Reeves. "Did my neighbor have anything to do with it?"

"Doesn't seem so."

"Why is that?" he snapped.

"Hey, *relax*, Ahmed. She apparently walked to his office building, met Reeves in the lobby downstairs, then they walked to the auction. The guy she left with must have been following her all along."

"You know who he is?"

"No."

"Do you know *where* he is?"

"No."

"The phones?"

"Nothing, no calls either way."

"E-mail, anything?"

"Not so far as we can see."

"They have to be communicating somehow." His cousin was silent. "Just keep watching her."

"If they find him?"

"Let me know. He will show up again sooner or later."

"Okay."

"Can we have someone follow Reeves, too? I want to find out what he's doing."

"We can do that."

"Just please make sure you are using our people." The Middle Eastern security companies all had connections in Paris and London and New York and could initiate professional surveillance within a day. The billing would go to Ahmed's French banker, who would pay it using an Algerian account that Ahmed replenished once a year. All the electronic transfers would take place outside of the U.S. and avoid American banks and EU regulations. He was acutely aware of the necessity to avoid any personal controversy that might attach itself to his company.

"How's our uncle?" he asked now.

"Up and down. The pills keep his heart steady."

The old man lived in Palm Springs and sat next to the pool most afternoons, worrying about the family spread across the world, each day reading the printed editions of the *Financial Times* of London, *Le Monde*, and two of the many Iranian newspapers published in Los Angeles.

"Please keep this thing about my wife between us."

"Of course, Ahmed."

He hung up and watched Manhattan approach. This is the old world, he thought. But the next new world is being made now, in the melting

Arctic cap—the deep-pocketed oil companies quietly knew *much* more than the UN, or the CIA, or the university climatologists—and in a generation the whole zone would be populated by millions of people, most of them working for resource-extraction companies like the ones he did business with, even as the fiscal strength of the world kept migrating to China, India, Brazil, Indonesia. The United States, meanwhile, was steadily fracturing into two populations: those few who had enough money and those many who didn't. Vast sections of the country were economically dead, its inhabitants hypnotized by the Internet, zombied by pharmaceuticals, illegal drugs, and Christian-identity babble, the family structure destroyed by successive decades of divorce, job loss, and domestic violence. Most of the baby-boom generation had no money for retirement, and the great howling sound coming from the next decade would be the millions of old white people living hand to mouth, increasingly infirm, demented, and politically irrelevant. Meanwhile the Latinos would be spreading inexorably, the re-Conquistadores, eventually electing a Latino president while the black underclass sank further behind, no other race interested in helping them now—sorry, but it *was* true—statistically a shrinking percentage of the population. In a generation, America would be run by the remaining elite whites, native-born Asians, the Jews (of course), the relatively few successful Latinos and blacks, and a sizable sampling of Indians, immigrant Chinese, and all the bright foreign students churned out by the Ivy League who had decided to stay. This was a truth you would hear no American politician utter, because it had history in it, and no one, especially the politicians, had any answers when it came to the constant pressures of history. He had learned from his father and uncle about how nations changed relentlessly. They had been successful builders in Tehran in the 1970s, favored by the Shah, and had the foresight to establish secret Swiss bank accounts as young men. The Mehrazes had been Westernized—spoke and read English, wore business suits, stayed clean-shaven. Bell-bottom jeans, Camel cigarettes, Johnnie Walker Black, and American muscle cars. (Had his handsome father, now dead twenty years, had sex with Western women on his trips to Switzerland? There was no doubt.) When the revolution came in 1979, and with it the rise of the Islamic fundamentalists, his uncle had gotten everyone in the immediate family out of the country, much to their confusion and protest, and they ended up first in Turkey, where Ahmed was born, then London, and then years later in Los Angeles, where so many expatriate Iranians landed and where his mother still lived. It had been a precarious journey for a proud family. They had not gotten all of their money out of the country, but enough of it to start over. With their European bank accounts and their international connections, the Mehrazes had built up business, Ahmed's uncle trying to find the right combination of enterprises to create wealth. Importing, little apartment houses, then luxury goods for a while, then long-haul trucking, but that involved organized crime and biker gangs, then speculation in California commercial real estate—they hit the cycle perfectly, sold out at the top in 2006—and finally commercial banking and property development. Money that made money that made even more money. Nobody in the Mehraz family had to work so hard anymore. But his uncle had always said, think around the corner, try to see what is coming before anyone else does. So it was that Ahmed, whose bandy-legged grandfather never left his village in Iran, could now be standing on the promenade deck of the *Queen Mary 2* as it sailed into New York, having just completed a $719 million private deal. He wished his uncle could see him now. But Ahmed was losing his family, he knew. They did not really understand what he did. They were Iranian, but he was not, not exactly. He had gone to boarding school, spoke French better than he spoke Farsi, had finally become a naturalized U.S. citizen after college, dreamed in English, understood the American legal system, felt a residual allegiance to Islam but didn't practice it, and had married an uber-white American woman who had probably lied about her past. Yes, Jennifer had lied about herself in some important way. It made him furious, but the fact that she lay just beyond his psychic grasp was alluring, too. Jennifer knew that if she wanted to she could walk out of their apartment, out of their marriage, out of *his* identity, dropping it in the doorway like a discarded coat that no longer pleased her, and meet someone with nice cuff links at, say, the bar in the Pierre Hotel on the other side of Central Park, and start a new story line. She was a selfreinventor, and would be, so long as she stayed so attractive, ten years more anyway. That was the loaded pistol she kept with her and it thrilled him, kept him motivated, made him possessive. Maybe they would have children, though he didn't have time now to be a devoted father. He wasn't sure if Jennifer wanted them, either. The topic irritated her, perhaps. *A man and a woman are not married until they have children*, his mother had said to him many times, dark eyes burning. *You can argue with me, Ahmed, but it is true.* Which meant *You can still leave her and marry a nice Iranian girl, with long dark hair and dark eyes and big hips. We are Iranians, we are smarter and better educated, and our culture is eight thousand years old. Your ancestors fought Genghis Khan in the thirteenth century. The Persians had already conquered Asia when New York City was only a village of stick houses. We are a sophisticated and elegant family that accepts the differences in people, but we do not want our family* whitened! *Please do not disappoint me.* His mother had been the more religious of his parents, insistent the old ways be kept. She'd also been unknowingly medicated with beta-blockers on the morning of Ahmed's wedding, his uncle secretly dissolving the pills into her tea in the hotel breakfast.

Now he dialed Jennifer. "Did I wake you?" he asked.

"I was making coffee."

He would listen to every syllable for a lie. "What's up?"

"Well, Friday I went to an auction with Paul. He was there to buy a map, of course."

"Did he get it?"

The slightest hesitation. "Yes, yes, of course."

"Yesterday?"

"Yesterday I looked at some apartments for us, that big one on Fifty-seventh Street. We have the benefit at the hotel tomorrow night. Paul and his girlfriend are coming, remember?"

"She's the one who wants him to marry her?"

"Yes, but I doubt he will."

"Does he usually discuss his romantic status with you?"

"No," Jennifer answered. "Just a feeling I have."

"You miss me?"

"Of course!"

Ahmed wondered. Had she had sex with the soldier? It was a reasonable conclusion. But maybe not. Maybe he didn't have enough facts. He would proceed methodically. Like a case history in business school where the initial interpretation of the optics is logical but utterly wrong. The right new input suddenly changed the interpretation of the data. He would go at her tonight, try to sense any hesitation on her part, any distance. And reclaim her. *You are mine*, he whispered to himself.

But maybe I do not *really* know my wife, Ahmed thought. It seemed quite possible. Likely, even. After all, she did not really know her husband.

3

She was too smart, too successful, and too old to get a Brazilian, right? It was what boy-crazy girls did, not professional *women*, no? After all, she had a successful ad agency to run, a zillion clients and their very special insane-omatic problems, and employees who all wanted to be promoted every three months. Wasn't *that* painful enough? Meanwhile, the agency's owners demanded larger profits, the web designers wanted to be globally famous artists, and she, Rachel, only wanted Mr. Paul to pay better attention to her. And a Brazilian wax, according to the pop-up ad for a certain idiotic women's dating-advice website, was the way to get a man's attention *and keep it, girls!* Please. *Please!* It was not that at age thirty-eight she didn't appreciate the procedure's aesthetic intentions, the polished tidiness of the flesh, the managed femininity, the need for *definition*. And certainly when she was younger the prospect of a mere bikini wax had created the tingling anticipation of all that would soon follow: the drinking, the meal, the wobbly collapse into the cab, the anticipated bedroom activities. She had been really rather skilled at the bedroom activities, took pride in her technique, and now she didn't do it quite enough anymore and feared—no, she secretly knew!—that the falloff in frequency would only continue as the years ticked by. Replacing sex with yoga—it was happening to women all over the city. And then *someday*, just when you didn't know it, *you'd had sex for the very last time in your life.* So now just thinking about a Brazilian was infused with bitter ironies: the wasted energies of her youth, the unending expenditure of hard-earned money in the pursuit of romance, the illusion of control over the untamed, indeed hairy, complexities of life. And besides, Mr. P. would not notice, or care, really. She could waltz in front of him with a clever little downward arrow and he wouldn't see it. Half the girls in the gym lasered off all their hair *permanently*, achieved a sort of lurid adult-sized prepubescence or *whatever*. A bald twat, just looming there. Would he notice *that*? What was wrong with him? His mind was elsewhere, at all times. She wondered why she bothered . . .

Why? Because he *was* eligible. Because she wasn't getting any younger. Because she could still have children, if he would just *get on the bus*. Because he still had a full head of dark hair, just a touch of gray near his ears. Because he was, uh, wealthy. Not "rich" in New York terms, but wealthy enough. Secure. Somewhere between ten and fifteen million, all in. Plus the map collection, whatever *that* was worth. But was he a little unknowable? Maybe. Definitely. She'd been seeing him for more than a year now and she didn't feel she *got* him yet; there were chambers that went back and back that she kept discovering. He had his own little boutique immigration law firm catering to Saudi princes, Korean bank executives, Eurotrashistas, people like that. They called him when they got stuck at JFK with visa or passport problems, and he would contact someone in Washington, whisper magic words into the phone, and make the problem disappear. He had two ex-wives he didn't want to discuss. His eighty-seven thousand old girlfriends called him up from time to time, especially if their marriages had just gone bust. She felt the ex-GFs out there, orbiting Paul, monitoring him with their remote sensing devices. He barely noticed, though. In the evenings he listened to baseball games on the radio while reading the business pages. He used reading glasses. Mr. Paul was a little bit older, which she liked. But too much older? She wasn't sure. She was happy in bed with him. He knew what to do, yup. She was calm afterward, actually slept better. He never asked about her old boyfriends, which sort of irritated her because she was *totally* interested in his old girlfriends. On his dresser sat a sealed transparent box and inside it lay tiny shards of glass, chips of stained wood, and some curly black bits she couldn't identify. When she asked him about it, he said the pieces came from a Brooklyn dock fire in 1968. She hadn't understood and he hadn't elaborated. Why did he keep them? She didn't dare ask. He owned a house in Brooklyn. Nothing special, he'd said. But Rachel had never seen it. He'd run the mile in four minutes and seventeen seconds while in college. He was still in pretty good shape. She had completed the New York marathon three years back and could still go ninety minutes on the treadmill or do the hardest hot-yoga classes, but she doubted he appreciated this, how much work it took to look this good, how hard it was when you were directly supervising ninety-six human mammals at work, many of them kids who didn't even know who Obama was, not *really*. On the other hand, maybe Paul *did* appreciate it, knew how the meetings and calls and unending crap wore a person down, drove you to resist the corporate mind-cramp. He was personally a bit of a slob, but his map collection was immaculate. He was obsessive about *that*. The man didn't remember to get his shoes resoled and yet spent thousands on old pieces of paper. She'd been surprised to learn his collection of maps was considered one of the top private ones in the country and that he consulted with experts at the New York Public Library. He had separate pictures of his mother and father on his dresser, but none of them taken together. She believed he carried a certain sadness he wouldn't discuss. He didn't floss *ever*. He forgot to put the seat down. He sometimes wore dirty shirts to work when there wasn't a clean one in the box from the laundry. He had frozen hot dogs and bags of mixed vegetables in the freezer. Supermarket brand, not organic. He did one hundred push-ups each morning. He didn't text much. She had tried to discuss religion with him. "I like churches and cathedrals and temples," he'd said. "But not religion." But what *is* your religion? she'd pressed. Don't you believe in something?

"Maps," he'd answered.

Yet the pieces of him didn't quite add up. Most men wanted a coherent and flattering picture of themselves presented back to them by their women. He didn't. He didn't seem to want *anything* from her.

That worried her. Maybe he was afraid of wanting something from someone. Those two ex-wives he wouldn't discuss, maybe they had chewed him up. She suspected he would be a good father, however, for he liked children, had even admitted regret that he had none. Oh, had she loved him in that moment; it was sweet and damned sexy, too. She'd wanted to cry, *I will have your baby!*

But at the end of the day—*and, Rachel, that is coming sooner than you realize!*—he might need to be pushed into it, cornered even, forced. *Tricked.* Not so terrible a thing to do, as far as she was concerned. When she was in her triumphant and righteous twenties she'd have been oh so judgmental of a woman who became pregnant in order to trick a man into marrying her. Now? Now she *understood*, okay? OMG, what was the BFD? (She had to stop sending *herself* mental texts.) The pretty Chinese girls in New York City were grabbing all the nerdy professional Jewish guys. The little guys with soft stomachs who had studied math at Princeton or MIT and had sex only three times in college, twice by accident, and then they get swooped down upon by these killer-sexy Asian girls. Scooping them up by the dozen. Swooping, scooping, it was a battle out there! Meanwhile the online dating scene was weird and desperate, an infinite array of freaks and losers and smiling perverts and deadbeats and players. Okay, maybe a few decent guys. A lot of her single girlfriends trolled through the listings obsessively, every day, with the same alert yet fickle attention they felt when shopping for shoes. *No, no, no, maybe, he's lying about his height—you can just tell, no way, he's kinda hot, no, you have to be kidding!*

So maybe you *had* to get knocked up. Many marriages began that way, even very successful marriages. Right? And tonight could make it happen. First, the ridiculous charity event. He'd bought tickets as a favor to his across-the-hall neighbors in his building, the very success-ful young executive and his hotsy-totsy American wife. There was a little *something* between Paul and the wife, even though he was old enough to be her father. It bothered Rachel, let's admit it! Maybe it was in her imagination, though definitely not. The girl was very attractive, in that Ohio cornfield kind of way. Ohio, Texas, Nebraska, California. But there was no character in her face, no *intelligence*. Not like Rachel, who was shorter and busty and had mucho curves. But, nope, no Brazilian! And she also had a bit of a Jewish nose, which only made sense, considering she was one. She was attractive in a very New Yorky manner, that was her thing, her personal *brand*. A lot of her friends had given up on men, gone on "man-baticals" in order to "he-tox." She had studied her cohorts very carefully, the algorithmic progression of despair. Getting a cat. Twitter-stalking. Closely reading the customer reviews of vibrators on Amazon. Facebook-lurking. Pathetic!

But not her! Tonight was the perfect night. She was ovulating and was at the peak, the egg crying out, *Get me, drench me with your alpha sperm!* She was going to get good old Mr. Paul, her charming and distracted, sort-of-actually-official boyfriend, to impregnate her tonight. Why *not* do it this way? He'd step up and get married, she was sure of it. She had seen the photos of him as a beautiful teenage boy in Brooklyn running cross-country. Maybe their son would look like that! They would make a child together, and deep down, beneath all the bitterness and internal wisecracking, she was desperate, desperate, *desperate* for that, it was all she wanted, but if she told him, he might be scared off, might see how crazed, how hormonal and lunatic, how totally *whack* she was for this. But would she get pregnant? Her sister Susanna with the three perfect children had gotten pregnant so easily they joked that it was dangerous for her husband to walk by in his underwear. Ha-ha, very funny, and screw you, sis. But that was years ago, and Susanna had always carried a little more fat on her body, hadn't driven herself at work, was just *juicier* in a fertile, baby-making sort of way.

Now she called Susanna. "So, okay, I'm going to do it."

"You're ovulating?"

"Yes. It's *perfect*."

"Does he have any idea?" she asked.

"He's thinking about his maps."

"Enough with the maps!"

"Afterward keep my knees up?"

"That's what I did with Benjamin. Try not to get up from the bed for half an hour."

"I hope his sperm is, like, *active*."

"He's in good shape, it'll be okay," her sister said.

"You saw that piece in the *Times* about older men's sperm, the higher chance of autism?"

"The *slightly* higher chance."

"But—"

"Rachel, don't do this to yourself."

"I feel ridiculous. Except I don't."

"Good luck."

She sighed, pulled herself together, then called Paul. "So I'm meeting you there?"

"Yes," he said. "I'll be the man eating shrimp."

She checked her lipstick in the mirror. "Come on, it'll be *fun.* Then back to my place? I got lots of good stuff for breakfast. Muffins, bagels, berries, fresh orange juice."

"You do think of everything."

Was this good? She wondered if his previous wives had been women who thought of everything. She knew the first one, the Jewish one, might have gone crazy. But that's all she knew. And his childhood was a mystery. He'd once mentioned his father had been a schoolteacher; Paul had majored in history and economics at Columbia, magna cum laude, which she learned from his law firm's website, not him. She'd poked and prowled around his apartment searching for clues while he looked at his maps with those ridiculous magnifying eyeglasses, like he was about to do brain surgery with them. And found nothing. No letters, no photos of the ex-wives, nothing. All his personal papers were in disarray, too. Except for the maps; every one of those was scanned, researched, its computer file annotated with historical sources, citations, cross-references, purchase history, you name it. And yet the guy could barely find his checkbook.

"Okay, Paul, so wear your tuxedo, okay? You look good in it. I'll find you there?"

He grunted something.

"What'd you say?"

"I'll be the man eating shrimp."

4 William Senior watched her pull the F-250 around back, noting how slowly she drove now. Probably shouldn't even be letting her. She stopped in front of the garage, and the truck's door opened and she let herself down carefully, using both canes.

"Don't trust myself no more."

"All right," he called through the dusk. "Leave it running."

His wife took herself slowly into the house. He stepped up into the truck's cab, feeling the AC blast him, backed, made the turn into the garage, and killed the engine. She'd forgotten to take the mail inside with her, even though that was why she'd gone down the road, so he gathered it up off the passenger seat. A few bills. Nothing from William Junior. Not that he would write. He could pack up his truck, throw his army duffel in the back, take all his goddamn money out of the bank, take his goddamn Ranger boots and ten-inch Ranger knife and all his other hotshot Ranger bullshit and put that in the truck, too. And ask them to feed his dogs, then pointedly leave his cell phone on the kitchen table. He could do all that but not tell them when he was getting back or when they would hear from him again or even what goddamn foolishness he was getting himself into up in New York City.

5 WALDORF ASTORIA HOTEL,
301 PARK AVENUE, MANHATTAN

The moths had chewed the crotch out of his tuxedo pants. Shredded it. This is what happened to men living alone; they forgot about the moths. But he'd said he would attend the evening, Rachel was all excited about it, so he found a pair of black suit pants and pulled those on. The color didn't quite match. Didn't matter. After a few drinks no one would notice. He tied his tuxedo tie while standing before an 1855 hydrographic survey of the waters around Manhattan, wishing that he could, if only for an instant, travel back to the city it inscribed. Here was Blackwell's Island, later bluntly called Welfare Island, now named Roosevelt Island, running along the east side of Manhattan, a slender pilot fish to the great whale itself; he could see the workhouse, the hospital for incurables, the lunatic asylum, the women's almshouse, the smallpox hospital. His eyes dropped down to the southern tip of Manhattan, the part of the city that had changed most over time. How he wished to stand at the end of the stone walkway that led over the water out to the battery of cannons that protected the city's harbor and watch the wooden vessels creak past, knowing what was coming, how the water between the Battery and Manhattan would be filled in and built upon, the whole jagged blade tip of the island smoothed and rounded by thousands of antmen laboring over the decades. He had dreamed of descending downward from the never-taken satellite images

of the nineteenth-century city, the street grid smudged by the parallel plumes of smoke from thousands of chimneys and stacks, down, down, down until he could see the clippers, schooners, catboats, and brigs chaotically busy in the harbor, then closer until the narrow streets became perceptible, muddy and horse-clogged, with the many black dots moving to and fro on the sidewalks being the dusty bowlers of the men and dodgy boys going about their dodgy business, the larger and fewer multicolored shapes being of course the ladies dressed in hats and fine dresses—
—oh, tonight's idiocy.

The elevator carried him to the Waldorf's ballroom. The charity event was mobbed, and he felt a keen self-disgust as he was enveloped by the smell of perfume and the parrot-shrieks of conversation, the glint of too many diamonds about the fingers and necks. The room was loaded with lovely women and wifeys and chicks and MILFs and the usual high-gloss rich young things who all knew one another from private schools and name-brand colleges, there with their dates or husbands, not a few of them hedge-fund zombies waiting for someone to die and relieve them of the necessity to appear employed; meanwhile, the older women, ranging from fifty to eighty, represented in their collective totality the *most* current techniques of lifts, tucks, peels, plumpings, de-wattlings, injecto-smoothilations, eyeball whitening, crow's-feet crack-and-crevice repair, earlobe sculpting, neo-pubescent lip re-inflation, and virgin breast rebirth. Many of them gazed vacantly into an unknowable middle distance, such botoxified serenity suggesting the furtive gobbling of pharmaceuticals beforehand. Oh, he was a judgmental bastard. But how could he not be? He *hated* this. Then there were the men, the smug teeth-whitened moguls addicted to the dark arts of testosterone and HGH supplementation, neck-to-pate hair follicle migration, and surgical belly contouring. They and their moguls-in-waiting were all no doubt aware that the sling blade of capitalism routinely took out one or another of them every year (the hedge-fund *bombero*, the partner *defraudissimo*, the divorce *no-prenuptero*, and so on), and yet the party vibrated with a frantic, implausible gaiety. The frozen foreheads, the real-time decryptions of the codes of money, the eyes pinwheeling in mania. Yes, he despised these self-important rituals and always would, not just because the charitable cause was usually dubious, but because—as Rachel kindly understood—a man like him needed an *enthusiastic* wife or GF to do these things with any consistent success. He'd long attended them out of necessity, a form of flattery to certain clients. He never bought the most expensive ticket, but never the cheapest one, either, because these things were actually noticed and tallied in some grand, invisible machinery of social calculation, and he despised himself for even caring about that, too.

But there was Jennifer at the far end of the room, standing in a little black dress and high heels meant to kill men from afar. They had not spoken since she'd left him at Christie's with her soldier.

"You made it!" she said, leaning forward to kiss him on the cheek, which he knew was meant to swear him to secrecy. "How are you?"

"Me? I'm the same."

Her blue eyes were uncertain.

"But are you the same?" he asked.

Jennifer twisted her watch around her wrist, then looked up at him. "I'm guessing you figured out some things."

"Life is relentlessly complicated."

"Please don't tell Ahmed."

"Not to worry."

She mouthed a silent *Thank you*. He glanced around, saw Ahmed searching for her. "You need to work the room, lady."

"I know."

As indeed she did, and he watched from afar as she was guided into and out of one conversation after another, shaking the hands of the assembled personages with real grace. There were other wives and girlfriends there, or, as the case may be, husbands and boyfriends, and the entire ritual was a form of a pecuniary mating dance, certain individuals representing enormous sums of money that, if all went well, would copulate with other sums and create even more money. After a few more minutes, the honorary chairman of thus or such stood up, and, speaking from a wireless mike, made a couple of good jokes that Paul knew had been written for him—they always were—and went on to recognize and thank the assorted piles of money in the room, then introduced Ahmed and asked him to speak.

"Thank you," said Ahmed easily, taking the mike and turning to the assembled. "You know, just yesterday I sailed into New York's harbor on a large ship, and as I saw all the skyscrapers loom up in front of me, I was thinking about the *magnificence* of this city, how there are so many talented and *brilliant* people—people like you—who want to do good things . . . for others, for their city, for people in need, and, you know, when opportunities come along for the private sector to help the nonprofit sector, the good people of New York City really do have an *unparalleled* generosity that—" He was so immediately authoritative and affably confident that the room pressed in toward him. The money wanted to get *a little closer.* The man had a political future if he wanted one, you could just see that. He looked damn sharp in his tuxedo, too— tall, narrow-waisted—and Paul wondered why Jennifer might in any way find him deficient. "So I'm grateful to you all for the opportunity to be part of this wonderful undertaking, and I am confident that with your continued support we will be able to say that what we did here tonight represents the capstone to a remarkable, indeed historic, success."

They clapped for him happily and gulped their drinks again, and Paul saw Jennifer's eyes fix on Ahmed as he shook hands with several men who had come forward. He gathered her into his circle, and Paul wondered why Ahmed had married her; she was lovely to behold, charming and foxy, yes, but Ahmed could have married any number of women. Jennifer brought nothing much more than her natural attributes to the marriage. She was not well educated; she was not a shrewd co-strategist in Ahmed's career. She was not, as the saying goes, well-bred, and as one ascends the corporate hierarchy, that mattered more and more. No, he reflected, Jennifer had to have something that was rarer; it had to fix or fill something in Ahmed, had to appeal to the long-range planner that he was, the innate and uninhibited schemer. Now they were talking to a couple named the Restons; the mister, who was a grand potentate at Citicorp, senior vice-poohbah of corporate implausibility or some such, glanced from Ahmed to Jennifer to his own wife, then back again to Jennifer, then to Ahmed, then to Jennifer quite rapidly, back and forth, occasionally looking at Mrs. Vice-Poohbah. Another couple approached and they made room for them; Mr. Reston knew the man and introductions were made, with polite nodding and hearty handshakes all around. The new fellow, whom Paul recognized as Mr. Ralph Somebody from Grand Swindle Hedge Fund, or whatever it was, which managed a large portion of Saudi Arabia's sovereign wealth, watched Mrs. Vice-Poohbah (vacant, glassy smile), then Ahmed (respectful frown), then Mrs. Grand Swindle (zero interest), then Jennifer (hair-eyes-mouth-cleavage-fleeting guilty smile), then back to his wife Mrs. Grand Swindle (you didn't catch me ogling those young breasts), then Mr. Vice-Poohbah (too bad about all your government regulation), then Ahmed, then Jennifer (I could look at *you* all evening), then Ahmed, and so on. Then Ahmed said something and Mssrs. Vice-Poohbah and Grand Swindle listened in carefully, having heard the clink of money. And so on, with Jennifer now chatting politely to Mrs. Grand Swindle as Mrs. Vice-Poohbah looked away, suddenly worried about the loose skin under her neck. Jennifer saw this and said something sweet that brought Mrs. Vice-Poohbah back into the circle, who smiled in relief, and all was again well. Then Ahmed graciously made another note, and the husbands and wives were brought back together with an easy laugh. Ha-ha . . . ha-*ha!* Thus did Jennifer improve Ahmed's social value and vice versa; they looked good together. And she was so American that an unspoken logic prevailed, Paul realized. It was true that, genetically, Ahmed was from someplace where Arab sand-paddlers had lived for thousands of years, but she—a lovely American woman—had found him acceptable. If she was with him, then he had been ever so subtly Americanized. She *translated* him to others. It didn't matter that he had gone to Harvard and spoke the best English that could be spoken. Or that she might merely have taken a lousy night course or two at Penn State. People were smarter than that; they could see in his jet-black hair, in the density of his beard, even, that he was *other*. Not one of *us*, even at this very late multiracial date. But Jennifer's American-ness, her whiteness, was similarly dense, her nose and eyes by way of a dozen intermingling generations of Germans and Irish and Polish and

Scandinavians and English and Scots scattered across the Pennsylvania countryside, her eyes perfectly spaced and balanced, her brow strong enough, her cheeks bold, her teeth perfect, her chin a delight; she fused with and defused and denatured and renatured Ahmed, she was—altogether now—Grace Kelly, Barbara Eden, Elizabeth Montgomery, Bo Derek, Farrah Fawcett, Cheryl Tiegs, Sharon Stone and Cheryl Ladd, Charlize Theron and Gwyneth Paltrow, Uma Thurman, Daryl Hannah and Cameron Diaz, Jessica Simpson, Kate Hudson, Brooklyn Decker, Blake Lively, and a hundred others in decades past and decades to come. She was not just white and lovely but she carried with her an entire cultural aura, a shimmering multiplicity of millions upon millions of impressions that had been ingested by those who saw her. Mimetic. Iconic. She was not merely flesh and blood, she was irreducibly virtual. She was a Certain Kind of Perfect American Girl. Now, he would grant you that America had every kind of girl, and every kind of color and shape and beauty and ugliness, too. And quite rightly so. But not all of them were archetypes who created a controlling psychic space around others. And it occurred to him that if you were someone like Ahmed, operating in America, then the very best thing you could do to reassure your American colleagues might seem to be to marry someone like Jennifer. She tempered certain problematic impressions—*associations* having to do with Muslims and terrorism and war—that he might helplessly trigger. Every week there was a new Islamic face on the news, a young man with a long beard and unpronounceable name who had killed four marines or beheaded a journalist or shot up a nightclub. Jennifer solved that—she inoculated Ahmed, completed him. She made him safe for others and she probably made him feel safe *with* others, too. Ahmed was a very smart man. He could see the effect his lovely white blond wife had on people around him and he knew that if he was going to rise in corporate America, and perhaps become a governor or senator, then he needed her.

An hour heaved by. Paul drank three gin and tonics. Unfortunately, to his great regret, he knew some people there, including a German man who wished to discuss the immigration status of several executives his bank was bringing over. "If the bank hires you to assist us," he asked, "who is the client? The bank or the people we are bringing to New York?" The bank, Paul obliged. "So if there is a visa issue with an individual, do you *first* tell that to the individual or to the bank?" The bank. Next was an elderly woman who wanted to describe her late husband's tennis game. Then a tiny man in a bow tie introduced himself as an expert on "machine vision." What was that? "I teach robots to see," the man exclaimed. "This is the future, I *assure* you." And then, finally, Rachel, smiling and shoulder-touching her way through the crowd in a fabulous patterned dress, her hair swept back. He liked her confident way with people.

"I found you," she said, kissing him. Then she glanced down. "Those pants—?"

"Don't match?"

She bent down just to be sure. "So you *know*?"

"I know."

"And you *knew* walking out of your apartment?"

"I did."

"What happened?"

"Moths."

Rachel nodded analytically. This meant something, clearly. But she kept it to herself. And then she *had* to introduce him to some women friends, all her age, about ten years younger than he was, and they were scoping him out, he could see, wondering whether he could still give Rachel a good jolting in bed, was he secretly a drunk, how much money did he have, was his hair real, was he harboring any incandescent perversities, was he kind to animals, was he up to date on his colonoscopies, etc., and he announced he was going to go get some more shrimp, and made a clever little half-drunken side-step exit and scurried away, away, away, more or less in the direction of the table of shrimp, which was watched over by three white-jacketed waiters with actors' haircuts.

But mere feet from the glistening orange-pink mountain, he felt someone catch him by the arm, and he turned and it was Jennifer, again, this time with great alarm in her ever-blue eyes.

"I need your help," she said. "I have a really big problem."

"Tell me."

"I have a friend outside. Bill. The man you saw? He's drunk."

"I myself am a bit drunk."

"Not like he is."

"He's out on the street?"

She sighed anxiously. "He's followed me here somehow and is outside asking for me. I told him I'd see him but that he had to go away *now*. I'm afraid he's going to get arrested or something." She turned around, checking for Ahmed. "He needs a place to stay, he is sleep-deprived and drunk and—"

"Talking too much, saying things?"

"Yes, it's a big problem for me, Paul, I can explain later, but I need to get him out of *here*, someplace he can sleep it off."

He studied her. "My apartment?"

"No, no, no, the doormen would—" She stopped that thought. "I mean here in the city, close enough but, you know, sort of hidden." She grabbed a Waldorf Astoria napkin off a side table. "You have a pen?"

He did, and she scribbled something on the napkin, folded it, then handed it and the pen back. "Billy knows who you are, just give him this." Jennifer looked at him, eyes brimming. "Please."

Then she disappeared into the crowd.

He stood there, napkin in hand, mystified, irritated, curious—yet aware that the game had advanced.

Then Rachel found him, walking straight at him with buoyant assurance, carrying what he bet was her third glass of wine. She smiled and leaned forward to give him a skillful little side-kiss, no effect on the lipstick. "How about we get out of here now?"

"It seems I need to do something for Jennifer Mehraz."

"What?"

"She has a friend outside who needs a place to stay."

Rachel frowned at this information. "I don't get it."

"I need to take him to a place to stay."

"Why can't he go himself?"

"He's drunk. No hotel will take him."

Rachel glared at him. "You're saying you are going to leave *me*, leave this stupid dinner *thing*, and take some drunken strange man somewhere?"

"Yes."

"As a favor to that Jennifer woman, who—"

"Who what?"

She didn't finish the thought, forced herself to move on. "You expect to be long?"

"I don't know."

"And why? Because Jennifer Mehraz asked you?"

"That's part of it."

"Well, what is the *other* part?"

"Rachel, he has no place to go."

He knew she was rightly furious. But she followed him downstairs and outside into the cool air in her dress and heels and walked with him to the corner, taxis blowing by continuously. A large, lean man stood heavily against the outer wall of the hotel, just out of the watchful eyes of the doormen.

"You Bill?" called Paul, recognizing him.

The man raised his head, then nodded in a miserable way. He had a small backpack with him.

"Jennifer says you need a place to stay."

Bill nodded again. Paul could smell him. Yes, *that* was drunk.

"I'm going to get us a cab. Think you can sit in a cab and not get sick?"

"Yeah," Bill answered. "Can do, sir." He had a big open face, with a strong nose, eyes widely set.

"All right, I'll be a second." Paul took a step into the uptown traffic, watching for a cab.

"You his wife?" Bill asked Rachel.

"The insignificant other."

"Sorry, ma'am. I bet I'm taking him away from you."

"Yes, in fact, you are."

Paul had a cab now. He opened the door and turned toward Rachel, who was trying not to get more upset, he could see, trying to be a good sport about it. "Can I drop you at your place first?"

"Absolutely not," she said. "He could get sick."

"Take this one, then, we'll get the next one."

"No, I'll get the next one. He needs help." Caught in the stream of moving headlights, Rachel moved closer to Paul, having lost her anger. "I'm sorry," she said. "It's just because . . . Will you come to my place after?" she asked gently, touching his cheek. "Please?"

"Yes," he said.

"You *better.*" She stood on her tiptoes to kiss him forcefully. "I don't care how late it is."

He owned a small brick row house in Brooklyn, which was in fact the home where he'd grown up. After his father died, his mother had lived on in the house, trying to stay busy, but watching increasing amounts of television and talking to her toy poodle. Against his advice, and even though she didn't need the money, she took in boarders to the ground-floor apartment, and after several tenants, she became more casual about checking people out. Her last tenant, a corpulent woman in her late thirties, was discovered to be turning tricks in her apartment, usually two or three men a night, her appointments spaced two hours apart. One of the men drunkenly beat up the poor woman, set fire to her bed, and fled. The mattress smoldered a few minutes then went out. But Paul's mother, who slept ever more fitfully as she aged, smelled smoke and went downstairs to find the unconscious woman on the floor, her face a disturbing pulp. After the police and firemen had come, after Paul's mother had given them her statement, she began to feel ill, and the next day suffered a massive heart attack while carrying home her groceries. In the years after her death, Paul had kept the house, had it repaired, and installed in the living room a bank of architect's cabinets, with long, flat rolling drawers. Here he kept the vast bulk of his maps, including those he had collected as a boy—in all, several thousand that covered Brooklyn, Staten Island, Queens, the Bronx, his lesser and duplicate Manhattan maps, a smattering of Long Island maps, subway maps, railway maps, bridge reports, atlases, various old newspapers that had once interested him, old copies of *Harper's Weekly*, and on and on, stacked and crumbling and beyond his ability to recall each. But the house stayed much the same, a dusty time capsule, where his mother and father's bedroom furniture remained, the dishes, the books, the drawers full of old Christmas cards, his father's tools, all of it. Paul was psychologically frozen by the place, he knew, as if he believed that by holding on to the house, time could someday be reversed and he could see his parents again and tell them all the things he should have told them when he was younger, such as that he loved them and missed them so. On the other hand, the house was quiet and he occasionally took the subway there and spent the night, making sure to inspect the plumbing, furnace, and the small fenced backyard, where enough summer light appeared that his father had successfully grown tomatoes, cucumbers, and squash. Paul paid a handyman a hundred dollars a month to cut the rug of grass and remove the home-repair flyers that accumulated.

This was where he would take Bill. They didn't talk at first, but when they were crossing the East River, Bill rolled down the window to look. "The Brooklyn Bridge?"

"You got it."

"Smaller than I thought."

"Oh, it has a certain grand elegance," argued Paul.

They were up in the air over the water, the lights of the fancy new Brooklyn apartment buildings in front of them and the wind pushing into the cab. "Air is good," said Bill.

"You all right?"

"I'll make it."

"We can stop for coffee."

"Might be a good idea."

Paul leaned toward the front seat. "After your right on Fourth Avenue, there's a deli three doors down and a fire hydrant space where you can park for a second."

The cabbie shrugged, did it, and a few minutes later Paul ran in and out with some coffee and potato salad that was probably a day old.

Bill sipped the coffee, holding the paper cup with both hands. "So you're the guy who was with Jenny at that auction house?"

"Eat some of that potato salad."

"They were selling antiques?"

"Antique maps."

But this was not of interest to him. Bill settled his pack on the seat. "Sorry about taking you away from your girlfriend, mister."

He watched Bill devour the food. "Don't worry about it."

"Not sure what all that girl told you about me."

"I figured you were an old friend."

"We go back, yeah."

"But she's got a pretty possessive husband, you know?"

Bill stared ahead, the lights sliding down his lean face.

Get him talking, Paul thought. "You have a Texan accent, I think."

"That's right, got me there."

Paul had been down to Houston and Dallas over the years to do some legal work involving wealthy South Americans. "I'm one of those New Yorkers who actually likes Texas."

"Why's that?"

"Texans think of themselves the same way New Yorkers do—as the most important people in the world."

"You got that right."

"So, Bill, where in Texas?"

"If you know Texas, I'm from west of San Antonio, eighty miles on Route 90, real close to the hill country."

"I've been there."

"Naw."

"I took a long drive out there maybe fifteen years ago."

"I don't believe it."

"Okay, well, the land is dry and mesquite trees grow everywhere and the ranchers try to get rid of—"

"We use flamethrowers on them," said Bill.

"Yes, and the country roads don't have names, only numbers, and when I was there I saw a huge wild boar lying by the side of the road where it'd been dumped by the rancher who'd shot it."

Bill nodded. "Shot them myself, with my daddy." He paused. "Big black pigs. Seven hundred pounds. Monsters."

The cab lurched along Fourth Avenue. "So," Paul ventured, "how do you know Jennifer?"

"Well, sir, that is a long, *long* story, and basically we're still strangers, so I'm going to take a pass on that one."

Even drunk, Paul thought, he's got self-control. "No problem."

Bill glanced at him. "Appreciate you doing this, man."

"Not a big deal."

"Don't know my first step around New York."

They rode the rest of the way in silence. Paul had the driver make a left on Fourteenth Street, a block of modest three-story row homes, well preserved, but originally built for workingmen and their families in the late 1890s.

He leaned forward to the cabbie. "Wait for me, I'll be a few minutes."

"Got to keep the meter going."

"I know. Keep it rolling. I'll be back."

The house had a fenced alley to the left that ran around the side until it came to a small cement patio. Paul didn't use the front door. He opened the lock on the chain-link fence, and after Bill followed him, he locked it. Then they went around the building to the back. As they turned the corner, floodlights kicked on.

"Motion detector?" Bill said, coffee cup in his hand.

"Yup." Paul unlocked the door. It had been a month since he'd been inside. He was aware of Bill's large angular frame behind him, the smell of boozy sweat.

"So, Bill," he said, flipping on a light in the kitchen, "this house isn't much, but it means a lot to me."

"Understood, sir."

"I got stuff in here I don't want disturbed. It's not like I let people stay here, because I don't, ever."

"Roger that, too."

Inside, he showed Bill around. The living room was given over to the cabinets with their wide rolling drawers. Paul pulled out a few. "These are full of maps. Manhattan maps, Brooklyn maps, subway maps, Civil War newspapers, all kinds of stuff." They climbed the stairs and Paul showed him the two bedrooms, each filled with boxes and map cabinets.

"Why don't you just rent storage space somewhere?" Bill asked. "This is pretty far to go."

"Sure. But I like this old house." He pointed at the bed. "You should sleep in here."

The bedroom was dusty and the air stale. Paul opened a window. In the bathroom, he turned on the sink. The pipes rattled, then shot out some rusty water, which turned clear.

Paul found a spare set of keys and gave them to Bill. "Listen, I'm going to say a couple of things to you and then be going."

"Sure deal."

"You sobered up?"

"Enough."

"Okay, I hope that's true. So, the best part of my map collection is in my apartment in Manhattan. But the bulk of it is here. Something like forty years' worth. It's taken me a lot of time to find these. I could never do it again. The windows are all heavily barred, as you can see."

"Right."

"But I'd like you to be aware of how much has gone into it."

"I won't touch a thing, man."

"Okay, good. You better not. I mean that. Don't touch one thing. Next, I know that you and Jennifer have got some kind of history." Paul quickly put up his hands. "I don't need to know about it, okay? Not my business. But her husband, Ahmed, is not someone you want to mess with, Bill. He's richer than you, he's smarter than you, and he has access to people who will do what he wants. He's the kind of man who won't be happy to find out another man is drilling his wife. You got that?"

"I got that." Bill's eyes were distant and untroubled.

"I don't think you understand," warned Paul. They looked at each other silently.

Bill finally spoke. "Mister, I been a few places. That's all I'll say."

It was hard to know what that meant. Iraq? Afghanistan? Syria? The many places the public never knew about? Paul continued. "I don't doubt that, Bill, don't doubt that for a minute. I guess what I'm trying to get at here is that this city is a lot more complicated than you think. Okay? You can't just parachute in and know what to do. You have to make adjustments, Bill. You go drunkenly hollering around outside the Waldorf Astoria for too long and the cops'll arrest your ass and throw you into Rikers."

"What's that?"

"Rikers Island. One of the prisons here. There's something like ten thousand inmates in there. Not your kind of place."

"Okay."

"And another thing is that New Yorkers can easily make out some-one not from the city."

"Me, you mean."

"Yes, you. There are lots of little clues, like how they cross the street at the light, how they hail a cab, things like this. Right now, you really stick out. People are going to remember you when they see you, Bill. So first, I'd get out of those military clothes. Other parts of the country, people have an uncomplicated response to soldiers. Here, you don't know what you're going to get."

"I know."

"You might know, but you don't *understand* it. I was born here. Listen to me. Buy a hat, maybe a Yankees cap or a Giants or Jets cap. Get into some jeans, running shoes. You got me?"

"Yeah."

"How long you need to stay?" asked Paul.

"Maybe a week or two, depending."

"Depending on what?"

"Oh, you know, see how it goes."

An evasive answer. "How did you get into the city, you don't mind me asking?"

"My truck," Bill said.

"Where is it? There's alternate-side parking around here."

"I got it in long-term parking."

"Nearby?"

"Nope. But I can always get to it."

"You have any money?"

"Don't worry," said Bill. "I'm good."

"You can spend a couple hundred bucks a day doing nothing in this town."

"I got a few thousand on me and some more hidden in the truck."

"Can you give me a phone number?"

Bill winced. "No phone, man, no cell, nothing."

"Why?"

"People can track you."

Paul gave him a slow nod. He pulled out his business card and wrote his direct office number on it. "In case you need to call me. There's no phone here in the house. You're going to have to hunt around for a pay phone. There aren't many left. The check-cashing place on Fourth Avenue might have one. Or a bodega."

"Bodega?"

"A little Latino grocery store, like a deli."

He was forgetting something. Then he remembered. "Jennifer told me to give this to you." He pulled the folded napkin from his pocket and gave it to him.

Bill read it, then looked up. "How do I get to Grand Central Terminal from here?"

So the note was about how they would meet again. "It's easy. Take the subway from Brooklyn up the east side of Manhattan. It's at Forty-second Street."

"Where's the subway?"

"From here? Just a few blocks down on Fourth Avenue, near the check-cashing place. Take it to Atlantic, then switch trains. Maps, my friend, maps. Subway system is full of—" He stopped, drifted over to a drawer, pulled it out, looked, closed it, pulled out two more. "Here, okay, this one is fifty years old, but it will give you the idea."

Bill sipped his coffee. "Can I use this?"

"No, just *look* at it, *go* to the subway and get a *new* map. They're free, right? Okay, I got that cab waiting outside."

"How do I get the keys back to you?"

"Just give them to Jennifer."

He shook his head. "Might be tricky."

Paul had a drawer in the kitchen table where he kept pens and so on. They went downstairs and he pulled out an old envelope, addressed it to himself, and found a roll of out-of-date stamps. He stuck a couple dollars' worth on the envelope. "Just send them to me."

Bill inspected the address. "You're in the same building as Jenny."

"Yes. I live across the hall on the same floor."

"So you *do* know her husband."

Paul smiled patiently. "That's what I've been trying to tell you, guy."

"We go back a long way, me and Jenny."

Paul studied the big raw-boned young man, whose certainty seemed naïve. Now the cabbie outside was honking with impatience. He forced himself to shake Bill's hand, noting its size and strength, clapped him on the shoulder, then let himself out. The cab was moving before he'd even pulled his car door shut.

He arrived at Rachel's apartment shortly after midnight. She greeted him at her door in a wicked black silk nightgown that accentuated her shoulders and breasts and hips. "I'm sorry you stayed up," he said.

"Well," she announced, staring him in the eye, "the *deal* is that I will forgive you your horrible and emotionally abusive treatment of me earlier this evening if you provide me some excellent *attention*. You up for that?"

"You're a tough negotiator."

She put her arms around his neck. "Not really."

"Just a woman taking cruel advantage?"

"That is correct," she whispered happily.

Later, afterward, he returned from the bathroom and found Rachel with her knees up under the covers. He remembered his first wife doing that.

"I have two things to say that I forgot before," Rachel announced in the darkness, her voice relaxed.

"What?"

"The first is, why did you *really* not wear your tuxedo pants?"

"I told you. Moths ate the crotch. All the holes looked like a shotgun blast."

She giggled. "And you didn't care?"

"Not really." He got under the covers. Rachel lowered her legs and fitted herself against him. He loved the lotiony smoothness of her skin. "What was the other thing?"

"Oh, it's weird. I just had this feeling that when you got in the uptown cab with that young guy, Bill whoever, that another car pulled out and followed you guys."

"You saw this?"

He felt her nod against his chest. "As I was waiting for the next cab. They followed you up Park Avenue and made the same right turn, close behind you, pretty sure."

"Seems unlikely."

"Well, if they were following your car, would they be following you or that guy Bill?"

He pondered the question. "It'd be Bill," he said aloud a few moments later, but by then Rachel was asleep. He lay in the darkness and for no apparent reason remembered Ahmed and Jennifer standing next to each other, socializing with the group of couples, and how Ahmed had put his hand behind Jennifer's elbow. She had gently moved her arm away from his grasp. But he had slowly pulled her arm back, and kept his fingers around her, his forefinger stroking the soft inside of her elbow while he looked intently into the eyes of the moneymen.

6

His pills were waiting for him, thirteen in all, seven for his heart and blood pressure, the rest vitamins, and he drank the orange juice first, swallowed the pills, ate the breakfast when it was brought to him, then walked out to the pool to do the watering. He could hold the green hose with one hand while keeping the other on the cane, braced against his hip. The gardener came twice a week, but he liked to do some of it, just to keep his body moving, to remember the old stone house in Tehran forty years back. The family was so dispersed now, some of his cousins and their wives and children still in Iran, the grandchildren of his cousins drinking too much in the secret clubs, he'd heard, caught inside the corrupt theocratic regime. And his own family, spreading inexorably, thinning out. His brother dead, leaving him as the oldest male. What was called Iran had gone by many names and had taken many shapes over the centuries, but there had always been a village and a tribe. Even these were lost now. Now it was just the family.

He turned off the hose and went to sit in the shade near the bougainvillea, the palms high in the sky over the pool, the house bone-white in the sun, mountains rising in the distance. Most beautiful place on earth, so far as he was concerned. Rosie had put out the papers for him. He didn't want to read, though. He despised all of them: the so-called leaders of Iran, the so-called leaders of Iraq, the so-called leaders of Israel, the

conniving, triple-faced Saudis protected by America, the extremist terrorists, the factions, the militias, the illiterate thugs in Toyota trucks
with machine guns. Sunni, Shiite. Muslims slaughtering Muslims for
territory or religion. Americans bombing Muslims. Jews and Palestin-
ians murdering each other. Syrians killing Syrians, Iraqis killing Iraqis.
Egyptians killing Egyptians. Iranians killing Iraqis. Russians bombing
Muslims. Saudis killing Yemenis. Turks killing Kurds. Kurds killing
Iraqis and Turks and Syrians. First al-Qaeda, now ISIS. Monsters, but
smart monsters. Meanwhile the fat Chinese businessmen lurked in the
shadows, taking a percentage on all sides. The problems of the Middle
East were economic, not religious. But no one was interested in the opinions of an old man with droopy balls sitting next to a pool in California.

He heard the phone in the house, with old-fashioned ringing. He
didn't like cell phones, which were hard for him to use.

"You," Rosie called from the sliding door.

He hobbled in, took it from her. "Yes?"

"Good morning, Uncle Hassan."

Amir, calling from New York. Three hours ahead there, ten a.m.

"We're working on our little problem."

Hassan disliked the triumphant tone. "What does that mean?"

"It means we've found the man who insulted Ahmed."

His heart sank. He'd hoped this false drama would go away, be forgotten.

"He was sloppy and our guys followed him to Brooklyn last night.
We know exactly where he is. We talked to the taxi driver who took
him there. He is from Texas. He killed big black pigs there. He looks
like a soldier."

"This is not a good thing."

"We're going to have a talk with him."

If his nephew Ahmed were poor no one would care about this. "No,
that is not a good idea, Amir. You say talk, but I know what that is. This
kind of conversation turns into violence. You may offer him money to
go away, if you like. I will pay."

"What about honor—?"

"Honor is a hat!"

"Uncle Hassan, I do not understand."

"It can be put on and knocked off and put on again! But you are too young to understand that!"

"Yes."

"No force, no violence! This is a private situation!" He remembered his heart and told himself to calm down. "Ahmed is an American corporate executive. At his level there is no tolerance for any kind of personal problem. There has been too much family involvement already, too much risk."

"As you wish."

Hassan hung up, worried he would be ignored. There hadn't been enough argument. His nephews were young and confused. They suffered the fallacy of perception: They thought because they perceived something, such as "family honor," that it actually existed. They were inflamed by the constant news of war and terror in the Middle East, yet they lived in America and enjoyed its freedoms, the protection of its military, and the rule of law. Their Westernization was so complete they did not feel it. They paid for everything with American dollars, ate American food, drove German-branded cars built in America. They screwed American pussy, they drank American water, their *shit* was American. They followed the NFL. They played war games on their phones, pretending to be badass mercenaries. They ate Mexican food. And yet all the talk was about when the theocratic regime would fall so they could go home to a place they had never been: Tehran in the seventies, glitzy and cosmopolitan, casinos and theaters and hotels busy with oil money, an international, sophisticated city filled with Europeans and Americans smoking and drinking in the cafés, business and pleasure and espionage being conducted everywhere. The Shah had believed in education, women's rights, the march of science. But he was also politically repressive, and his family controlled the banks and construction companies, the hotels and the mining companies, the food companies, everything. And when the revolution came, when Ayatollah Khomeini called for general strikes, when the statues of the Shah were being toppled and the CIA men disappeared, when the slitting of throats began, all the families that had been supported by the Shah, such as the Mehraz family, had to flee. Now a million Iranians in Los Angeles sat waiting, like the rich Cubans in Miami, waiting for the restoration that would never come. History moved on, left you at the station holding a heavy suitcase and a worthless ticket. A few of the Mehraz cousins ran illegal import/export businesses inside Iran. But all they really needed to do was tend to small questions—an apartment building, a commercial lease—because there was no war here for them to fight. They were soft and knew it and wanted to prove themselves worthy, as had the previous generation when Iran was stolen from the people who had stolen it originally. And although the cousins had said they would keep Ahmed's involvement minimal, Hassan assumed that they would pester and prod him, to receive his approval. Ahmed was the one the family turned to now, the future leader of the family. Time would show whether the clan stayed together. Hassan doubted it could. His generation, the one that had arrived in the seventies and eighties, was dead or dying. What was left of the family was mostly scattered in Westwood, Brentwood, Beverly Hills. He himself couldn't keep the grandchildren straight. They would be the first true Americans, the ones who were ten or eleven now. It took two generations to become Americans, through and through. And what was wrong with America? His family had no idea how lucky they were.

The phone rang next to him again. He waited until Rosie answered in the hall. He heard her call him and picked up.

"Yes?"

It was Amir calling back. "Uncle Hassan, Ahmed says *he* would like to talk to this man. We're going to get him tonight, then have a meeting."

"Ahmed said this?"

"Yes, we just talked, a minute ago."

"Does his wife know?"

"I don't think so."

"Will his wife be at the meeting?"

"Ahmed did not say anything about that."

"Where is the meeting?"

"We haven't decided. Somewhere private, maybe tonight, maybe tomorrow."

"What if this man doesn't want to go to this meeting?"

"We have some big security guys helping us. He won't have a choice."

"Stupid! Terrible! Ahmed is an American corporate *executive*. This is not how things are done on his—"

"But Ahmed *wants* to do this, okay?"

"It should not be in a public place."

"It won't be."

"Please, you will tell Ahmed that my strongest personal advice is that this is a very bad idea. This is why the world invented lawyers and marriage counselors. To slow down these emotional situations. You guys are just trying to get Ahmed's attention, do him stupid favors."

In the delayed response that followed, Hassan waited to be acknowledged—and then to be obeyed.

"I will personally tell him everything you have just said," came Amir's voice, without enthusiasm.

They hung up. Hassan felt bitterness rise in his sagging old chest. Ahmed's father, his brother, had been the smartest of the family, had mastered differential calculus at age twelve. And before he had died too young of prostate cancer he had made Hassan promise to look after Ahmed, the special one, the hope of the family. Maybe Ahmed was listening to his cousins too much now. Or maybe he was too busy at work to think the thing through. Ahmed's cousins in their thirties and forties did not yet *understand* America, he was certain, no matter whether they followed the NFL and ate Mexican food. They had not driven across it, as he had, many years ago. They had not seen all the little towns and the enormous farms of the Midwest. They had not seen the Grand Canyon. They had not appreciated how big Texas was, the place this soldier came from. It was impossible to understand America without understanding Texas—even for Americans. This, Hassan knew. Town after town: high school football games on Friday nights, hundreds of pickup trucks, men who had been shooting guns since they had been children . . .

He stood and walked outside into the electric-bright sun, troubled. Here he was, looking at the mountains and the palm trees and the pool. Forty years to move an ancient, proud family halfway around the earth. And yet the phone calls this morning meant he had failed in some way. It was not over. His nephews thought that threatening an American soldier because he *may* have had sex with their cousin's wife was a demonstration of family loyalty. This was a barbaric idea. And it showed their naïve underestimation, their righteous assumption that their family identity shielded them from doubt or danger or poor judgment. Did the young men of his family not realize, wondered Hassan, that when a dark-skinned Arab threatened a white American soldier on his own soil for being with a white American girl, this set into motion any number of actions, some obvious, some delicate and unseen, a response that might not be immediate, but when it arrived was no less potent? Did the indulged, soft-chested, pseudo-Iranian young men of his family not realize that white Americans were a savage people?

7

A rich blonde. A rich *bitch*. Probably looking for a purse or cashmere sweater or cell phone. Vivianna watched her enter the office. She saw one of these women every day or two, a *nice* young wife who'd forgotten an item on the commuter train to one of the *nice* suburbs. The women five or ten years older were usually looking for a kid's book bag or a baseball cap.

"Can I help you?" asked Vivianna.

"Yes," said the woman. "I'm looking for kind of a strange item."

"We got a bit of everything here." Vivianna made an obligatory wave at the row of bins and boxes labeled HATS, BAGS, GLOVES, NECK-TIES, PHONES, UMBRELLAS, EYEGLASSES, WALLETS, PURSES, PRECIOUS JEWELRY, COSTUME JEWELRY, KEYS, LAPTOPS, PHONE CHARGERS, LADIES' COATS, MEN'S COATS, SHOES, SCARVES, BOOKS, LOOSE DOCU-MENTS, SPORTS EQUIPMENT, MISCELLANEOUS.

"I'm looking for an army jacket, a man's green army jacket."

"That would be in men's coats."

"Can I look?"

"No, you have to describe the jacket to me carefully."

"Well, a man's green army jacket, kind of beaten and worn—"

"Size?"

"Extra-large. He's a pretty big guy."

"Would it have a name on it?"

"I can't remember if it has a name stenciled on there. If it does it would be Wilkerson."

Vivianna went through the bin. Many items came in on Saturdays and Sundays, after the trains had been cleaned. The riders were tired, drunk, distracted, and left belongings behind.

"What day was it lost?"

"This morning, on the inbound New Haven Line."

She found it, a large army jacket. The name Wilkerson was indeed stenciled on the breast pocket. She felt something inside the pocket, perhaps a folded-up piece of paper.

"I need to see some ID."

The woman fished in her bag for a driver's license.

Vivianna inspected it. The photo showed the woman as a teenager. "This is an expired Pennsylvania license."

The woman shrugged. "It's all I've got."

That was an obvious lie, but Vivianna put the license in the copier, then tore off the ID tag from the jacket, which recorded any name on the item as well as the contents of the pockets, and stapled the copy of the license to it, then filed the two documents.

"Lot of paperwork."

"We do two thousand items a month, know what I'm saying?" She handed the jacket to this Jennifer Hayes and the woman immediately felt for the piece of paper and opened it.

Then she left with the jacket. A moment later a large man poked his shaved head into the office.

"Did that lady pick up anything?"

"That's Transportation Authority business, sir."

He slid two hundred-dollar bills out onto the counter, keeping his fingers pressed down on them. "It could be your business."

Indeed. She leaned forward and spoke quietly. "Man's army jacket, size extra-large, with the name Wilkerson on the breast pocket.

There was some kind of piece of paper in there, as to what, I do not know."

The man's fingers lifted off the two bills and gave them a dismissive flick toward her. He turned to hurry after the lady in question, not bothering to say thank you.

8

"We got him now. His name is William Wilkerson Jr., and he was recently honorably discharged from the U.S. Army Rangers. We were unable to locate any precise records, but his unit saw action in Afghanistan. Then more recently they were in Somalia, probably for covert action. Lots of U.S. bases in Africa doing stuff no one knows about. He's from a small town west of San Antonio, Texas."

Tarek, a Libyan security company operative, looked up from his notes. He was dressed in a loose shirt, a big man going soft from desk work. The four of them—Tarek, Ahmed, Amir, and a muscular bald guy, another Libyan whose name Ahmed didn't quite catch—were sitting in a rotten little office in a third-rate building on the West Side, not far from the Port Authority Bus Terminal, where Eighth Avenue's obsolete, half-empty office buildings harbored block after block of cheap shoe stores, porno DVD shops, bad pizza joints, and any other walk-in business so marginal it could not survive in areas where rents were higher. Hurrying in from the early-afternoon rain, Ahmed had immediately felt nervous inside the building, with its agonizingly slow elevator and scuffed hallways, the walls painted over many times, the doors closed and labeled with suspiciously vague corporate names: TekWing Electronics, 5!5!5! Import Co., M Bro. Enterprises. But the guard downstairs, an old guy with bloodshot eyes, seemed comatose and didn't require anyone to sign in, and there were few if any security cameras.

"Go on," said Ahmed, wondering if the bald Libyan guy had been staring at Ahmed's watch.

"Okay," said Tarek, "so his parents own land, acreage. He played in the minor leagues of baseball for two years after high school. You can look up his statistics online. He never went to college. After baseball he went into the army. His family belongs to the West Oaks Baptist Church. They are people of modest means. He is staying on Fourteenth Street in Brooklyn. Between Fourth and Fifth Avenues. The property is owned by your neighbor Paul Reeves." Tarek glanced up from his notes. "He drives a red, six-year-old Ford F-250 pickup truck. We watched him get into it. We have the plate number."

The three men looked at Ahmed, their respectful silence acknowledging the humiliation he was feeling. And the anger, the deep wish to attack, even to kill. Finally, trying to keep his voice even, Ahmed said, "How often is he seeing my wife?"

"Now and then, not so much. We have been following your wife, with only some success. We followed her to a variety of stores on Broadway, Columbus Circle, down Sixth Avenue, to the grocery around the corner from where you live, to the gym where she exercises, and about eleven this morning to the lost-and-found in Grand Central."

"Then what?"

"She retrieved an army jacket after successfully describing it to the clerk. That's how we got his last name, just a few hours ago."

Ahmed felt fury at the idea she was touching his clothing. The intimacy of it. Her lovely fingernails gently brushing the collar and shoulders. He knew she would lift the jacket to her face and smell it reverently. "Go on."

"She is not communicating with him electronically. She has eluded us several times, going into a store quickly and then out again to hail a cab. She knows the subway system better than our guys and has been able to make some switches they could not follow."

"Meaning she got away from them."

Tarek met Ahmed's eyes. "Yes, unfortunately."

She and the soldier hiding somewhere so that they could fuck. The intensity heightened by the danger of it. "How long did they lose her?"

"Usually for a couple of hours. Our guys would reestablish surveillance when she returned to the apartment building or the gym."

They could be meeting in a cheap hotel somewhere. The city was full of them, in Chinatown, or near the West Side Highway, places where you paid in cash and stayed a few hours, screwed like crazy, tore up the sheets, and no one was the wiser.

"Anything else on my neighbor?" Ahmed didn't like Paul Reeves, mostly because he knew Jennifer did. The man presented himself as a rumpled, distracted fifty-year-old, but that didn't fool Ahmed. Reeves was smart, but kept it hidden. As a high-end immigration attorney, he was used to threading complexities and dealing with the federal government.

"This man named Reeves goes to and from his apartment to his office near Rockefeller Center," said Tarek. "He has a girlfriend he was with last night."

"Go back to him letting this Bill guy stay in his house. That means he knows what's going on."

"I can't confirm that."

"So, okay," Ahmed said, looking at the big, bald Libyan now, "maybe Amir told you guys I want to talk to this Bill guy."

"Do you speak Arabic?" the man asked in Arabic.

"No," said Ahmed.

"Okay, I will say in English best I can. Yes, so we get him tonight," the Libyan said. "It is not difficult thing. We get him in this house where he sleeps and bring him to the place to meet."

"Where?" asked Ahmed. "Not here. Not anywhere there are other people or cameras. No one can see this meeting."

"Of course," said the Libyan. "This is thing we already think about. We are going to get this William Wilkerson to take him to a place so you can come there, too." He pulled a manila envelope from his pocket and unfolded a large piece of paper with lines and writing on it. He checked to see that Ahmed was paying attention, then turned the paper around in front of him, his thick index finger pointing out each place.

"I draw this for you. Manhattan here, Brooklyn here, the expressway here, right? Pretty good, right? I can work for Google, yes? This is Belt Parkway, okay, yes? You get off, go over the bridge. This is old military base called Fort Tilden in the Rockaways in Queens. It is public park that opens early in the morning and closes when night. No cameras nowhere. You take Barrett Road here to big parking lot and we are parked with van at the back." He pushed the piece of paper forward. "Here, look."

Ahmed pulled the hand-drawn map in front of him. It had a detailed diagram of the fort, Barrett Road, and the parking lot, with arrows. The Libyan had carefully written the English street names in capital letters and made some other notations in sloppy Arabic that Ahmed could not read.

"What's this say?" he asked, touching the handwriting on the page.

The Libyan crooked his neck to read. "That is information of this man, name, you know, this is how old he is, things like that. This is your number, this is identification of our car, this is Tarek's number. I want all informations in one place."

Ahmed glanced up at him. "You have to get rid of this paper."

"Yes, yes, I promise I will burn this when I do not need it no more."

Ahmed retraced the overall route with his finger, concentrating on it. From Manhattan you took the Brooklyn Bridge, around the belly of Brooklyn to the Belt Parkway to Queens, then south on the Marine Parkway bridge to the Rockaways, bear right, then a quick left into Fort Tilden, Barrett Street, parking lot in back. He didn't know Brooklyn or Queens very well, so he studied the document carefully, knowing he could never do an Internet search for the place.

"In the parking place in back, no one can see. Very empty place. You can park car and walk to our van."

"I got it," Ahmed said, handing the map back to the Libyan.

"You want to keep?"

"No, no, it's fine," Ahmed said. "I've got it."

The Libyan folded up the paper. "Okay, so Tarek and me, we are in very messed-up old blue van that has no marking. We will have this William in van. The fort opens at six o'clock a.m. People run on beach, all that stuff. Meet us tomorrow morning, six thirty. No phone call. If you are not show up by six forty-five we take him to beach and leave him there. He will be drugged and not wake up for some times, you know? But he will not be hurt. Then we drive to Long Island to garage where van is painted red."

"When will you get him?" asked Ahmed.

"Tonight, maybe sometime around ten o'clock. Just me and Tarek. I call Amir when we have this man. We tell how he is doing, every information, very up-to-date. We hold him in van overnight, then meet you. Give him water, candy bars. You do not worry about nothing. We are very good at this thing. Tarek and me, we did this many times already before, in many cities everywhere in world places, you know? Paris, London, like, okay, Brussels, some places like that. Istanbul, Madrid, we do all these things. This Bill Wilkerson is very ready to talk tomorrow morning."

"You going to hurt him?"

The Libyan shrugged, as if he had no say in the matter. "If he fights us, we need to, like, you know, hurt him. But not so bad. Nobody will get killed, okay? If you tell us to hurt him in van later, then, yes, we hurt him for you."

"Why keep him so long?"

"We get him at night, that is easier, but meeting in this place is only possible in light. Also your cousin says you go in Central Park about this time. I think you can get there in half an hour, talk to him for half an hour, something like that, then take one hour to get back with traffic."

"Two hours in all."

"This is too long?"

"No. Sometimes I go out for my run, then have breakfast out," said Ahmed. Now he addressed Tarek. "So you two have worked together a lot?"

"My friend has done many years in the Libyan security forces. Excellent professional training." Tarek smiled. "He is very good, okay? Totally number one guy. Nobody is worried. We know how to do this."

"Anything else you need?" Ahmed said.

"What kind of car you drive?"

"It will be a black Lincoln Town Car, the kind that all the car services use," said Amir, eager to finally take part. "There will be mud on the plates, hiding the number. I am driving it into Manhattan from New Jersey tonight, will only go in the cash lanes for the toll on Staten Island, parking it nearby, then, okay, then I will meet my cousin by six a.m., get out of the car, and he will get in and drive alone to where you guys will be."

The Libyan unfolded his map and wrote in Arabic on it. "Black Town Car. Give me your number. I call from pay phone."

Amir took the map and wrote a phone number next to the Arabic notation. "Call this number tonight at eleven. Don't put this number in your cell phone."

"No, no. Of course. Just pay phone." The Libyan shifted his eyes to Ahmed. "Remember, take Brooklyn Bridge both ways not Battery Tunnel, that is E-Z Pass. Your car, it has no E-Z Pass transponder."

"Why?"

"Because of course it is easily tracked," explained Tarek, who'd been watching with detached interest. "That's why Amir will take the cash lane from New Jersey. And so then, Amir, you'll pick up the car when your cousin gets back to Manhattan?"

"Yes."

The Libyan nodded at Tarek.

"Okay, I think that is everything." Tarek looked at Ahmed. "Do you know what you want to say to this Bill Wilkerson?"

Ahmed nodded. It was a confrontation that he craved. "I have a pretty good idea," he said.

9 CORNER OF EAST SIXTY-EIGHTH STREET AND
MADISON AVENUE, MANHATTAN

"You *do* seem a little shaky," her doctor agreed.

Jennifer bobbed her head apologetically, trying not to cry. "I've just been under some *stress* lately, my husband is working very hard and traveling, and an old friend of mine has kind of . . . I'm just feeling this very high level of—of *anxiety*, generalized anxiety. The usual dosage isn't really doing it, you know? I keep just feeling like bad things are happening that I don't know about . . ."

They were in the doctor's office after the checkup. She'd been weighed and prodded, had her heart and lungs listened to. Dr. Ripley was a no-nonsense woman with gray hair pulled back in a ponytail. She wore no makeup, her posture was perfect, and Jennifer would've been glad to have her as an older and much calmer sister who'd given her the advice she could have used along the way. Years ago. But that hadn't happened.

"Your blood pressure is usually excellent, but now it's up," said the doctor. "You've lost a little weight and I don't like to see that in young women like you, okay? It can easily go too far. Now then—" The doctor lifted her eyes from her notes. "You have generally been pretty stable the last two years. And now you are not. So that means something unusual is going on. But I agree, you don't seem depressed, just anxious, and so what we want to do is to bring down the anxiety and let you cope with whatever is causing it, okay? Let you get things together a little bit. It's really important you maintain your sleep. What I'm going to do is double the Xanax and prescribe two other medications. The first is a mood stabilizer, Lamictal. I'm starting at a low dose, fifty milligrams a day, going up twenty-five milligrams every two weeks, trying to get to one fifty, okay? If you get a rash, stop taking it and call me immediately. That's an allergic reaction we don't want. It's very rare, though. Then, also, I'm starting you on Klonopin each morning for anxiety. It sort of keeps things smooth and steady. I want you to take this each day with breakfast. You should tolerate it fine. Then, as I said, I am doubling the Xanax for sleep. You can and should still take them for panic attacks. But I want you to get your sleep. I could give you a sleeping pill like Ambien but we are seeing a lot of problems with it. Sleeping pills are *so* physically addictive and we'd like to keep you off of them. So one of the higher Xanax each night for sleep. Got that?"

Jennifer nodded.

"Now, I want you to eat and exercise, okay? And practice good sleep hygiene. Turn off all the screens, stop the e-mail and texting and everything. Maybe a little deep breathing, too. I know who your husband is and how crazy busy and stressed out he is. I read about him in the newspaper the other day, in fact. But you need to tell him about what is going on with you so that he can be supportive—"

Oh, sure, thought Jennifer, *supportive.*

"—because we want this to be just a bump not a crash, okay?" The doctor waited for Jennifer to affirm this goal. "The last thing is this, Mrs. Mehraz. I don't think I need to tell you, please, don't drink alcohol with the Xanax or Klonopin. If you do that, you might pass out or trip and fall. Especially with the higher dose of the Xanax. Please do not drive or do anything physically difficult requiring coordination or make any kind of important decision. The best thing is to take the Xanax half an hour before sleep and just kind of let it take you into a deep sleep."

"Okay," Jennifer said, feeling relief that she had her pills now. "I promise."

She walked back from the doctor's office, sensing in the cool air and the wet leaves the relentless approach of fall. She wondered if Ahmed knew about Bill. It was possible.

That night, with the prescriptions filled, she ate some chicken and rice in the kitchen, then waited for Ahmed. He would be home around eleven. She took the Klonopin to get it started. Then she changed into her nightgown, weighed herself, took off her nightgown, weighed herself again, then put on her nightgown. She opened a bottle of red wine and drank a glass or two—it wouldn't hurt, no matter what the doctor said—as she watched TV, then took one Xanax to help with the sleep, as prescribed. The pill was twice as big as the one she had been taking. A few minutes later, for some reason she wasn't sure if she'd actually taken the Xanax. Maybe I just *thought* about taking it, she wondered. I can't feel anything. I could count all the pills. But that was a bother, so she took one. How bad could it be if this was the second one? Especially compared with the stuff she'd taken in high school? *That* was bad.

She was in bed trying to read when he came home. It was almost midnight.

"In here," she called, listening to her own voice in case it sounded odd—and it did, she thought. "How was the day?"

"We got some good decisions made," Ahmed answered from the hall. He walked into the bedroom and pulled off his tie. "You look a little funny."

"Just relaxed. Drank a little wine."

Ahmed stared at her lying in the sheets. He had a look she had not seen for some time. She liked it. "Take off your nightgown," he told her.

He turned the lights out in the bedroom and headed toward the bathroom.

When he came back to the bed, she said something to him.

"You're not making any sense," he said, "but that's okay."

She felt him getting into bed with her, both close and far. She could sense her breathing slowing, getting deeper. It felt good.

Ahmed straddled her and ran his finger slowly from her forehead, down her nose, lips, into her mouth, then out, chin, neck, between her clavicles, breasts, down her belly until it stopped between her legs, then gently pushed one thigh wider than the other.

He slipped himself into her and she was surprised how wet she was, because she had not been thinking of it. He was much stronger than she was, of course, and held her down with his arms and pressed into her as far as he could go.

"Listen to me," he breathed aloud. "You listening?"

"Mmm-hmm."

"I want you to understand some things, okay? That you are mine. You belong to *me*." He thrust hard. "Say it."

"I belong to you."

"Again."

As she tried to say it, he pushed so fast she couldn't make words. He went at her for a while. Then his mouth was at her ear.

"Now, you know who takes care of you, right?"

"Yes, yes," she murmured.

"I give you *everything* you need."

"Yes, Ahmed."

"Say it. Say I give you everything."

"You do, you give it."

"And you know you are mine to fuck when I please, right?"

Before she could answer he thrust into her ten or fifteen times or more and she could barely breathe. She cried out something but didn't know what it was.

"You need to tell me anything?" he asked.

"No," she whispered. *I will not tell you anything. I washed the sheets and pillowcases right afterward and vacuumed the bedroom, too, and even threw out the half-full vacuum cleaner bag. Nobody knows.*

"You love me and only me?"

Before she could answer he went at her hard for a few minutes, maybe longer it seemed, proud of his stamina, sweat coming off his chest, making her lose her breath. Which excited him, of course. He was being a little rough with her, knowing she was on the edge of consciousness, trying to keep her there, in the narrow margin between compliant response and surrendered oblivion. She was excited but somehow distant, interested in her own vulnerable dilation, her complete lack of strength. She was not quite sure where the edges of her body were. It thrilled her but was so peaceful. Now he was speaking again to her . . . "You are mine and no one else's. You look at no other man, Jennifer. You think only of *me*, Jennifer. You must think of having sex with me every day. But we will only have sex when I want to, you hear?"

"Yes," she thought she said. *I will agree with you even if I don't agree with you.* The paradox was pleasant to her, had a kind of perfect harmony that only she understood.

"You are mine. You belong to *me*."

She murmured something she hoped sounded agreeable, but felt a lower floor of her consciousness drop downward and knew she was barely there, that the man on top of her who was saying things wanted her to respond but she couldn't. She did not mind that he was pounding away at her, because it made her feel wanted, which was not so far away from feeling loved, but she could not say anything to him, that man, she could not say what he wanted her to say anymore, just as she could not tell Billy that she didn't want to go back to Texas with him, could not tell any of the people who hated her for what she had done that she was sorry and confused by it still, years and years afterward, and she did not know what else to do except cleave to the man who had married her and whom she loved in a certain way but who did not know her, not like Billy did, *still*. But she could not tell Billy that she had seen too much of the world now, the *high* end, the *rich* end, to ever go back to his world, his level. She went to excellent doctors who didn't take insurance, she had a walk-in closet full of new shoes, she was shopping for a larger apartment. She was in *another world*. She was just a good-looking girl from Reading, Pennsylvania, and she did not ever plan on going back—there or anywhere else like it. She would go farther away but not back. Now the man on top of her was almost done, she could tell, hurrying and rising to the end, and she tried to make some sounds that he would like even as he was saying words she had never heard, praying or cursing or grunting something in some other language thousands of years old that she had never known was inside of him. I like these bigger pills, she thought. They are good for me.

Then he was done with her and rolled away.

She sensed light moving in the room and opened her eyes. He was standing up, checking his messages, a blue glow shining in his face from the little screen. He's not nearly as tall as Billy, she thought. Now he was rapidly punching in a call.

"Jennifer?" he asked as the numerals chimed electronically.

She might have made a sound in response or maybe she dreamed it.

"Fucking babbling," he muttered.

Babbling.

Then a small voice answered in the phone.

"Amir, what do you mean? You *said*—" An irritated pause. "No *wait*, listen to me, *you* said those guys were *professional*, were going to be careful. I was supposed to talk to—" Another pause. "So you don't know where— They never checked back?"

She did not know what that meant, but it didn't sound good. She turned from her back onto her stomach, and it was momentous, like a giant barrel roll in the sky, dizzy, eyes in the back of her head, and then she dropped into a deep, drugged abyss where no one could get her.

10

The lies of luxury. Unlike most people, he didn't worship the fabled old apartment buildings on Park Avenue, the huge inlaid marble lobbies, the spectacular floral displays, the hushed and gorgeous mahogany woodwork—all meant to symbolize the inherent superiority of the buildings' inhabitants, the impregnability of their wealth, and the utter irrelevance of the little people, the service people, the poor people, indeed anyone who not only couldn't afford to live in such a building but more important could not possibly pass the righteous inquisitions of the membership board. In these buildings, the elevators were full of chatty people in lovely cashmere sweaters who you preferred not to meet, talking of museums and sailboats and the granddaughter at Yale. The men had clean pockets and the women all went to the very best doctors.

Gibbs was waiting for Paul in the lobby. They had met a few times over the years.

"Mr. Reeves." They shook hands, without conviction, then headed to the elevator. Neither man spoke until the doors opened at the fourteenth floor. Then Gibbs said, "Stassen is one of those guys who is so old that people don't think he's ever going to die. I believe he is ninety-four. But he is in fact failing now."

"You trying to sell the map before he dies?"

"I expected you to get to that question, and you did. Yes, it's very simple. His will says that any maps in his estate *at the time of death* will be donated to the New York Public Library. The estate would then take a deduction. However, his family would like to monetize the asset *before* he dies so that its proceeds may be distributed swiftly across the family."

Probably selling off as many high-dollar antiques as possible, reducing the estate. "Seems like they waited a long time to make this decision."

"No, Mr. Stassen changed his will three or four months ago to allow for this and it is only in the recent anticipation of his death that the family studied the new will."

That sounded unlikely. "Have they declared him incompetent?"

"Yes."

"You are his attorney?"

"Yes."

"*Is* he incompetent?"

Gibbs paused, ever so subtly, and Paul knew that Gibbs was in on any arrangement that had been made with the family of the dying man. "In fact, he is incompetent now, and I am directed by the will to hew to the instructions of his children in such an instance."

"Has a court declared him incompetent?" asked Paul. "Because I don't want to buy this map and then find out that I have to fight for it in court or against some other unhappy heir."

"We have the court certification," said Gibbs, "which we received last Thursday."

"I was at the auction Friday when your messenger came. You're moving quickly."

Gibbs blinked, a subtle affirmation. "Let's go in."

He knocked gently at the door and a uniformed maid opened it immediately. Paul could see that she recognized Gibbs, with a warm smile. Expected to be taken care of after the old man died, yep. She took their coats, then quietly led them through a large living room, down a hallway covered with framed letters and photographs. Governors, presidents, grip-and-grin ceremonies in Washington, D.C. Nelson

Rockefeller, Ronald Reagan before the fog rolled through his brain, Bush the Elder. Another hallway showed many beautiful children in athletic uniforms, on beaches, at graduation ceremonies. Dozens of framed photographs documenting the destruction of the passing decades. They came to the door of what could only be Stassen's bedroom.

"Is he asleep?" asked Gibbs.

"Oh, yes," she answered. "Most of the time now."

The three of them stepped inside an enormous room, thirty feet on a side, with three arched windows on one wall. An antique bed stood against the opposite wall, and it took Paul a moment to realize that the bed's corrugation of blankets and pillows contained a human being: Mr. James McKinley Stassen, appointee to the Nixon and Reagan administrations in his prime, member of a dozen corporate boards into his seventies, once a fine golfer, long admired for his thick head of hair and stately posture, outlived three wives, sired several batches of children, traced his family history back to Virginia tobacco farmers already rich before the American Revolution. The nurse stood to the side, watching the two men approach.

"We'll be just a few minutes," said Gibbs.

"I can step outside if you like."

Gibbs appeared to consider this, then thought better of it. "Thanks, but that's not necessary."

She retreated to the far corner of the room, sat at a desk, and addressed herself to some paperwork.

Paul was alert now, more awake than he had been in months, it seemed, his blood pressure up and in his cheeks. The two men stepped closer. "There it is."

Indeed. Right there, the grand item itself, hung over Stassen's bed. He took a nervous, incomplete breath. He was looking at a map of the city of New York that had been commissioned by the British Admiralty in the reign of King George III as tensions between the American colonies and Britain rose. Based on landscape measurements done in 1766 and 1767 by Bernard Ratzer, a royal surveyor, the map was first printed by hand in 1770 and presented to King George. There were two known versions of that map, one in the British Library and the other in the collection of the New-York Historical Society. The map, suddenly militarily useful, was then reissued in more or less identical form in 1776, in the early days of the American Revolution, and there were five known existing examples of this version, two belonging to the New-York Historical Society, one belonging to the Museum of the City of New York, a large, torn fragment belonging to the New York Public Library, and the fifth and very last one, the one before him, owned by Stassen. The large map showed, in stunning detail, the charming young city of New York set amid farm fields, swamps, ponds, streams, and woods, complete with harbor soundings in fathoms. Only months later, in September of that year, much of the southern tip of the city would be consumed in a ghastly fire that broke out in a bordello frequented by British sailors, the first of four great fires in New York City. Some 483 houses burned and many women and children perished. The map also depicted the quaint little village of Brooklyn, spelled "Brookland," and nearby, the marshy waters of Wallabout Bay, where twelve thousand American prisoners later died in prison ships anchored there. The map's lines were crisp, the detail so magnificent that actual wisps of smoke from individual houses were depicted. Such beauty and precision and provenance made the map fantastically important. But *this* copy had been in the personal possession of Washington's aide-de-camp at the time, Richard Cary Stassen, a brigade major in the Continental Army appointed to Washington's side in June 1776, who served with him until December of that fateful year and survived the war, unlike some of Washington's other aides-de-camp. Why had Major Stassen carried the map? Because it was especially valuable for its detailed elevations and contours of the terrain—essential for hiding armies. Rolled in waxed cowhide and cinched by a purple ribbon, the map had been carried on horseback by Stassen during the Battle of Long Island, fought on August 27, 1776, the first major engagement of the Revolutionary War, when, after a series of murderous skirmishes across what was present-day Brooklyn, thirty-two thousand British troops surprised and overwhelmed the Americans and forced them to a panicked retreat. Threatened with the annihilation of his army of nineteen thousand men, Washington and his officers consulted *this actual map in front of me*, thought Paul, and Washington then gave his orders for a regiment of 270 Maryland troops to attack a stone house where the British cannons were well positioned and blocking the Revolutionary forces. The attack would slow the British advance, but it was a suicide mission, known to all who undertook it. The British soon turned their cannons on the Maryland companies, slicing them to ribbons. Washington watched from a nearby hill with a spyglass and was reported to utter with melancholic finality, "Good God, what brave fellows I must this day lose." Some 256 men were killed and the bloody sacrifice of the Maryland troops ultimately allowed Washington to stealthily evacuate the rest of his army by water to Manhattan and live to fight and win another day.

Paul released his breath, his eyes wet. He touched his fingers to the glass tentatively, with reverence and wonder. This was the culmination of his forty-year obsession, this was the pinnacle. The map bore the elegant signature of Richard Cary Stassen and was marked with the troop movements in Brooklyn of August 25 to August 30, 1776. In the far lower-right corner, Stassen had written in a flowing hand, *This map consulted during the Battle of Long Island, August 1776 Geo. Washington, Commander.*

The map had stayed in the family of Richard Cary Stassen, who after the war became a judge in Virginia and began to expand the family fortune that now afforded his great-great-great-great-grandson the money to die in peace in a fourteenth-floor apartment on the East Side in the twenty-first century. Because Stassen had never loaned the map for display, because it had never been sold at auction, and because Stassen was generally secretive, the map was not widely known.

It made Paul's most recent purchase, the Valentine map, seem in comparison like a crumpled napkin from McDonald's. *You will never have this opportunity again*, he told himself. He withdrew his surgical glasses so as to be able to check the printing at the bottom corner of the map. To do so, he leaned over the dying man, whose eyes were nearly closed and whose mouth gaped upward, dry and shriveled lips flecked with white gunk in the corners. Paul bent close and switched on the pin light of the glasses and examined the foxing at the margins of the large map. There was indeed a lot of it and the damage would require the services of an expert preservationist. Although somewhat unsightly, the cloudy brown stains did not affect the structural integrity of the paper. Some said foxing was caused by fungal growth; others claimed it was caused by oxidation of iron or copper in the rag content of the fibers. In any case, it was impossible to fake, because it was an organic process that took decades to develop.

Despite his condition, Stassen seemed to sense Paul's intrusive presence and moaned softly, exhaling upward into Paul's face a breath so putrid that he barely stopped himself from gagging and leaned back sharply. It was as if the dying man had made a great effort to protest the removal of his map from his bedside.

The nurse, who undoubtedly had attended to many dozens of dying people, stood and moved protectively toward the bed.

"Do you need to see anything more?" asked Gibbs.

The chances that the map was a fake were infinitesimal, but none-theless Paul produced his cell phone and took half a dozen shots. "What's on the reverse?" he asked.

"We don't know. No one has seen the reverse in more than thirty years," said Gibbs. "The map is wired into the alarm system, and we need the security company to disarm it."

Paul bent forward and shined his pin light on the edge of the antique burled maple frame. As he expected, the wall paint behind the framed map was fresher, its edge matching the map's frame perfectly. At this, old man Stassen issued a plaintive groan, and his hands appeared at his chest, clutching and pulling at his blanket. He turned his head from side to side, revealing some very long and old teeth, their crevices jammed with decayed food matter. He lifted his head an inch and one of his venous blue eyes opened halfway, to see who the intruder was. It rotated until it fixed on Paul. Then, as if exhausted by the effort, the eye gently shut and the old man's head sank back into the pillow. The nurse hurried close.

Gibbs and Paul stepped away and headed for the door.

"Shall we discuss a fair price?"

"The family is looking for—" Gibbs wrote a number on a slip of paper and showed it to Paul. A monstrous sum. Yet an exact sum nonetheless, a defined amount, for something that was invaluable, to those who knew what they were looking at. The two men retraced their way down the hallway toward the front door. "They know they can easily get that on the open market."

"How do they know that?" asked Paul.

"Certain discreet inquiries have been made."

"Then why offer it to me?"

"If they sell the map publicly at auction or through a dealer then the NYPL may find out."

"I thought there was no legal problem."

"There is no *legal* problem. But one of the children is a major patron of the library, and she feels it would be most embarrassing for her if—"

"Not too loyal, is she?"

"I have no comment on that. She wants to sell the map quickly, quietly, and with no fuss. The family has a list of potential buyers, seven in all, and you are first. The price is quite firm, Mr. Reeves. You have only two and a half business days to tell me if you want to buy the map. To be clear, that's this coming Friday afternoon, we'll say four p.m. If I do not hear from you by then, I will assume you are not a buyer and move on. But if I do hear from you, then you have exactly one business day after that to complete the paperwork and settle the transaction by wire transfer, which would be next Monday afternoon. My office will be in touch about the details. Any questions?"

"Friday four p.m., no later, I call you and say yes, Monday I sign papers and money gets wired to your bank."

Gibbs nodded severely. They stepped into the elevator. Paul checked his phone. There was a voice mail from the old woman who lived across the street from his house in Brooklyn. He hadn't heard from her in at least five years.

"Let me know Friday," Gibbs warned him again as they left the lobby.

"Yes," answered Paul. He waited until Gibbs had gone ahead, then called the neighbor.

"Is that Mary Reeves's son?" came an elderly voice.

"Mrs. Girardi? Yes, Paul Reeves here."

"Paul, oh yes, I called, see, because I noticed that the side fence of your house was *open*. It wasn't open yesterday afternoon when I came back with the groceries. Well, I went around the side of the house, past where your father used to grow his radishes, and it looked to me like the back door was broken into. We've had some crime around here and I thought I'd better give you a call."

"Any other damage that you know of?"

"No. I had one cataract done and now I have to do the other one."

"Meaning you see pretty well?"

"Just okay. But I'm sure about this."

"You notice anything else?"

"No, I didn't, but you have to remember I don't hear so well these days."

He thanked her and called his office to say he'd be late.

Forty-five minutes later he was looking into Mrs. Girardi's eyes. One was indeed cloudy and the other not.

"The gate didn't seem right," she explained again. "I tied it shut with some knitting yarn so maybe people wouldn't notice. I hope I haven't bothered you over nothing."

"Not to worry."

He crossed the street, knowing that Mrs. Girardi was watching him from her window and that she drew great satisfaction from having been vigilant. She had never liked his mother but had gone out of her way for his father, often bringing him tomatoes from her garden in the late summer.

Now he pushed the gate open slowly and closed it behind him. The lock had not been broken; it had been cut. There were two tools that could do this; either a saw of some sort, which left a smooth or subtly striated slice through the metal at more or less a constant angle, or a large pair of bolt cutters, which cut the metal by crimping it until it broke. A hacksaw took a few minutes. A gas or electric saw took five or six seconds and made some noise. Bolt cutters were fast and quiet but depended upon the brute strength of the one who wielded them, not to mention the blade sharpness and the strength of the steel being crimped. This lock had been crimped, which suggested that whoever had done it knew he was strong enough to use the tool and wanted to be sure no one heard him doing so.

Paul continued along the alley next to the house, noting nothing unusual except a rake that had fallen over. The back door, however, was open. He stepped inside and switched on the lights.

The kitchen and living room seemed fine.

"Bill?" he called.

Nothing. He inspected the downstairs bathroom. All looked normal.

"Bill?" he called up the stairs. Again, no response. He pulled out five or six of the long drawers holding his maps. They appeared to be undisturbed, so he retreated to the kitchen. He saw that some of the pots had been used and washed. He looked in the trash and saw a frozen-dinner container. He opened the refrigerator. Mexican beer, bread, milk, juice. So Bill had shopped a bit.

If thieves had broken into the house, they appeared to have picked the back-door lock—not hard considering it was a cheap one from the hardware store—and hadn't stolen anything. I should check upstairs, he thought. But his eye was drawn to a small stain on the white wall paint near the molding. He bent down on his knees and tried to examine it, but that was not close enough. He pulled his surgical glasses from his pocket and lay down on the floor a few inches away from the wall. That was pretty good, enough to see that the stain was a brownish red and tear shaped, the liquid hitting the wall with force and at an oblique angle. Blood? He really wasn't sure. He looked for other marks but saw none.

Paul checked his watch. As the boss, he had some control over his schedule, but nonetheless really needed to get back to his office in Manhattan, back to the phone calls and e-mails and document filings that consumed his life. So he took one last look around and closed the back door as best he could, then checked the basement door. Untouched. He slipped off the padlock and returned along the side of the house, closed the gate, and locked it with the second lock. This meant Bill would not be able to get inside without breaking the second lock. Too bad, Paul thought, I can't have my house broken into again.

When he turned, Mrs. Girardi was indeed peering out her window at him from across the street. He nodded, pointed to the replacement lock, then crossed the street. Her door opened.

"All fixed now," he called heartily.

"Did they steal anything?"

"Maybe some garden tools," he lied, to satisfy her.

She nodded in keen appreciation of the habits of miscreants. "They'll take *anything*, of course."

"I was lucky, I think."

"You going to call the police?"

He pretended to consider it. "I don't think so."

She stepped out to the stoop, happy to discuss matters of importance. "Yes, I called them when my garbage cans were stolen and it made no difference."

"Thank you for contacting me, Mrs. Girardi. Always nice to get out to the old neighborhood."

He was twenty steps down the sidewalk when he heard a sound from beneath a stoop.

"Hey, yo, *bud*."

A barefoot man of about thirty emerged from a ground-level apartment. The light bothered his eyes and he blinked in confusion. He sported a not-so-recently shaven head and a collection of lightning bolts tattooed on his forearms and biceps. "You own that place, right, where you just went in?"

"Yes."

He turned his head inside his house, heard a woman's husky voice. "I'm coming, give me a freaking minute!" He turned back. "My girlfriend's very needy, like. I mean, she, like, *she needs it*, you know what I'm saying?" His lips adopted a lurid smile. "Anyways, I was saying that, like, there was a hell of a lot of badass *noise* over there last night. You got that place rented or something?"

"I had a friend staying there."

A sound came from inside the house. The man looked at the doorway then turned back, unconsciously cupping and lifting his genitals through his pants as he spoke. "She's a hound, a freaking *hound*. I'm a young guy, you know what I'm saying, and she's running me ragged here."

"You guys use coke?" asked Paul.

The man laughed, revealing teeth that needed dental intervention. "She does. That's part of the problem."

"Sounds like you guys like to party."

He shrugged. "Sometimes a little of this, a little of that? She got this settlement from the car accident and we kinda been celebrating for a while. I feel sorry for her, you know? She lost her foot, like, in the accident, and she needs comforting. She still feels her foot even though it's, like, not there, and that messes her up. She needs special comforting. I mean, really good stuff is hard to find sometimes, so I kinda go with the flow."

"Last night?"

"She had her container of party pills. I never went to bed, I think."

The man had been awake, jacked-up, hyperalert.

"I don't think it was the drugs talking to me." He reconsidered. "'Course, it mighta been."

"Just tell me what you remember. I understand your memory might be a little foggy."

He was happy to report it. "Yeah, all right, like, so me and my woman are having a fine old time and she's the one who understands what these drugs *do*, know what I'm saying, I mean, I ain't exactly some innocent, but it's like she's the one who *appreciates* them, okay, so anyways, I was taking a little break and standing outside to get some freaking *air* and I heard a lot of noise and shit—" His eyebrows shot up in synaptic replay. "Some yelling, but it lasted like two minutes maybe, no more, and then it was quiet. And I'm wondering what's going on, you know, like, am I *hearing* this or is it just, you know, *the drugs*, and then maybe like an hour later or maybe it was like forty-five minutes or two hours, I don't know, there's a red pickup truck outside your house and I see some big dude getting in it. All the house lights was off, and the lights of the truck was off, too. Then I see he takes the brakes off, because the brake lights go off and he just kinda coasts along the block, real smooth like, without his freaking headlights, and goes down the block and that's *it*. I mean, it was *smooth*, man, and that's basically it. Did you check the place out?"

"I did. Somebody broke a lock and stole some garden tools."

"That's all? Man, I thought it was like *The Terminator* in there or something."

"I was surprised, too." Paul turned to go. "Listen, I appreciate the info."

The man smiled and pushed his hand over his unwashed head. "I was uh, like, hoping maybe you would actually, like, show your appreciation for my, like, *reconnaissance*, man."

"I see." Paul pulled out some cash and peeled off three twenties. "Are we good?"

The man took the bills, seeming to calculate their pharmaceutical equivalent. "Very good." He had a half-smile frozen on his face. "Wait, I just realized something."

"What?" said Paul.

"You know who that big guy *is*, don't you? You didn't ask what he looked like or was wearing or nothing."

Paul examined the young man's face; he had a kind of feverish intelligence, distorted and perverse, but capable of perceptive, accusatory leaps. He also had a fat mouth, Paul realized.

"Should I call the police and tell them?"

This took the man aback. "Um, dang, I don't know."

"Well," said Paul, "I guess I'd *have* to send them over to you to question you about what you saw, and what was going on that night, get the complete statement."

The man appeared to worriedly contemplate that possibility, the notion of NYPD cops standing in his apartment and poking around. "Maybe we could kinda avoid that?"

"You sure?"

"If'n you don't mind, like."

"You tell me," said Paul. "Does it seem like this event rises to the level where we should have Brooklyn detectives here talking to you and your girlfriend?"

"No, no, no way, man, we got to avoid that."

"You sure?"

"Please, dude. I'm not sure what I saw last night, anyway. I was totally blown out, you know? Like mentally *eradicated*. So who knows what the freak I saw?"

11

Rats! Ferris knew them, he needed them, he loved them. Yes, he loved them for two reasons. The first was because he identified with them. They were the lowest of the low, and in New York City that was saying a lot, boss. Lower than the dirty pigeons pecking for food at people's feet. Lower than cockroaches. Ask anybody, would you rather have rats or cockroaches in your apartment? They would say cockroaches every time. Why? Because cockroaches, my friend, can be killed easily. Just put out the boric acid or fipronil and the cockroaches eat the poison like it was a buffet dinner. Humans were smarter than cockroaches. But they were not smarter than rats. And people knew that; it's why they feared them. Go to any hardware store, the rat poison and traps fly off the shelves. He knew all the ways to kill rats. The poison, the mechanical traps, the glue traps, the fumigants, the high-frequency noisemakers. None of them worked well. The best was a mix of anticoagulants, such as warfarin, which caused internal bleeding, and calciferols, which mineralized the internal organs. But that worked only sometimes. Sorry, boss. The latest form of chemical attack was bait traps filled with sugary-tasting 4-vinylcyclohexene diepoxide, which cut down on litter size and made male rats infertile. Worked sometimes, but house cats catching and eating those rats got sick. The only surefire way you controlled rats was by controlling humans, and humans were *uncontrollable*. Explain that they need to keep garbage in tight cans until Sanitation picks it up. Simple. A five-year-old gets it. But not adult humans. All over the city, people let their garbage spill out, they threw garbage on the street, they didn't clean up after their dogs, which meant the rats ate the dog shit. *Eagerly.* And if humans shat in the subways, which they did, the rats ate *that*, too. Sorry. The truth *hurts*, boss. Civilians didn't ever really think it through. They avoided knowing. They avoided even knowing what they didn't know. But if they only knew! Knew about the rats in the hospitals and school lunchrooms and restaurants. In the beauty salons (they ate fingernails and human hair and tissues with human skin cells on them) and the fancy dog kennels. Not just the subways, not just the streets. Rats ate soap, leather, chicken bones, candy, snails, frozen food, live baby birds, earthworms, and each other. They consumed one-third of their body weight every day, the equivalent of a grown man eating three huge turkeys every twenty-four hours! The city of New York spent something like $50 million a year to control rats. That was a drop in the bucket compared with what private industry and individuals paid. But the rats were still here!

Like him. He was still here, too. He wasn't going nowhere, either. He, a trained and licensed city vermin-control officer, was pretty much the lowest of the low. But he would have a job as a rat inspector forever. That was the second reason he liked rats. They put food in *his* mouth. Civilians put food in the rats' mouths and they put food into his. It was a virtuous circle, a beautiful thing. They were never leaving, too. Hurricane Sandy in 2012 had drowned thousands of rats, but according to the city's chief rodentologist, the rat population had been entirely restored. So what are you going to do? Osama bin Laden couldn't kill the rats, hurricanes couldn't kill them.

He had been in the department for so long that he didn't do the regular street duty inspecting residential cases. Those were rarely serious. People got motivated for a little while and started being better about their garbage, and the rat problem temporarily improved. Wasn't solved, maybe shifted a block or two. The department put newbies on those jobs, soft-voiced Caribbean girls with the nice clean uniform and a clipboard who were patient with the residents complaining about getting summonses and fines. He didn't do that. He did the jobs no one else wanted. The big jobs. The *infestations.* Tunnels of rats squealing and squeaking to one another in their high-pitched, demonic rat talk. Send Ferris. Abandoned cars filled with rats, living inside the seats. Rats in dumpsters filled with warm slop, rats by the dozens chewing through cement walls to get at a meat locker that lost its power over a long holiday and nobody noticed. Send Ferris. Rats in the funeral parlor basement, he had seen *that*, yes, eating the body on the mortician's table. And rats in the giant water tunnels being constructed a thousand feet underground, living off the lunch litter of the sandhogs. How did they get down there? They took the sandhogs' elevator, of course, way underground. Rats in the fish store, running over the pretty cuts of salmon and swordfish, tearing away the cellophane and eating the raw fish, their whiskers touching the glistening wet pink flesh. *Ferris will do that one.* He had seen the famous department training video of rats pouring out of a heating vent in the laundry room of a big Manhattan luxury hotel, dropping by the squealing hungry dozens, running in a complex 163-foot pattern, lit only by red fire-exit lights, through a series of turns and hallways to get to the hotel's restaurant supply room, where they poked and chewed and gnashed at dry foodstuffs, bags of cookies, pasta, tubs of cooking lard, anything. The hotel couldn't figure it out. So the department set up infrared motion sensor cameras. The rats preferred scuttling along the sides of walls. They would remember as many as three hundred turns, corners, steps, and holes. The best way to track rats was after a new-fallen snow. They went in and out of their tunnels in the snow, leaving little trails darkened by their greasy, low-hanging bellies. Send Ferris, they said, and his answer was Yes, boss, send me. Give me your fucking rats. And today's adventure was a report of a new rat infestation near the old docks of Sunset Park. Called in by Sanitation, which meant it was pretty unusual, since garbagemen saw rats every day.

So he pulled his blue city vehicle over a block from the water and started checking for burrow holes or droppings. Earlier he had examined the city's photos of the sector, checked the database they shared with the fire department and the department of buildings. The weedy lot had plenty of things that did not attract rats: old tires, a discarded baby stroller, the axle of a truck, bottles, rusted cans. But as he moved through the grass he saw the source of the rat activity: two dark shapes dumped against a fence in a tangle of high weeds. They'd probably been there a day or two, long enough to get ripe in the day's heat. Didn't take long, an hour at most. Flies by day, rats by night. He approached, knew he was right about what he saw, then took out his box of Jujubes candies. A red one stuffed up each nostril, half a dozen mixed flavors in his mouth, to chew on. Couldn't smell a thing. Artificial cherry flavor, artificial licorice. He drew closer. The flies lifted up. Two men, maybe in their thirties. Facedown. One was bald. The other had dark hair. Both had dark skin. Latino? Didn't quite look it. Something else. Big men. Fleshy but muscular. They had not died there. Been dumped, definitely. The rats had chewed into one man's pants. Up and down the leg. Anus, the softest place. Ferris circled the two corpses. One had a watch on his left wrist, a gold bracelet on his right. The flesh was swollen. He found a stick and lifted up the coat jacket. A wallet. Nice and fat. He slipped on his rubber gloves—regulation, required in any "close inspection"—and closely inspected the wallet. It held a bunch of weird-looking bills from another country in one compartment and in another about $1,900. He took $1,700, being sure he was so far down in the weeds no one could see him. Then he slipped the wallet back in the pocket and pushed the coat down. Checked to see if he'd left footprints. None, boss.

He stood up and backed away, then took photographs. He took another step back. The men, he realized, were well dressed. Good shoes, though the rats had chewed through the toe of one. He took too many more photographs, because they would all be turned over to the police, then walked back to the car and called it in on his radio. Procedure was to stay and wait for the cops, provide a statement. But first he shut his car door, retrieved the $1,700, folded the bills, took off his left shoe, and slipped the wad into his sock, under his arch, then replaced the shoe. Nothing to do now but listen to the Mets on the radio until the cops arrived. Maybe he'd blow the cash at one of the Atlantic City casinos on the Jersey Shore. Steak dinner, get a balloon-titted hooker to come up to his hotel room for an hour, give him the professional girlfriend experience, and *still* have cash left over.

Rats. *Loved them.*

12

Jennifer liked to look at him naked. She crept out of the sheets and pulled back the curtain just enough that the afternoon daylight fell across his shoulders and back and legs. Her fingers had sensed the scars, but she hadn't seen them. And now she did. They started at the back of his right thigh and sprayed upward, spattering all the way up to his left shoulder. She counted three long, nearly parallel gouges across his buttocks and lower back, plus a knot the size of a half-dollar where one of the pieces of metal had plowed inward, just stopping short of his spine, thank god. She had fallen in love with a boy years ago, but here she was looking at the body of a man. The injury was nothing, he'd said, really. Three weeks in the American military hospital in Germany and then back. Best doctors in the world. No significant nerve damage, no deep muscle damage. Nothing compared with the things he'd seen—the men on stumps, the men with jellied brains—nothing compared with what he'd *done*. Which he didn't talk about, ever. Except once. Something about secretly hunting terrorists house-to-house in Somalia. Carefully choreographed bad-guy missions. Calling in drone strikes. People have no idea where our military really is, he'd told her, maybe a dozen countries no one knows about. She hadn't asked anything else. She didn't really care, frankly. Of course that reflected badly on her. But many things did. She bent and kissed one of the scars. Oh, Billy. What happened to you? What happened to *me*?

Anxious suddenly, she checked the time; she had fifty-one minutes to get back to the midtown Equinox health club, where she'd left her bag in a locker, bringing only the key, phone, his army jacket, and some cash to pay for the room. One of the gym attendants had showed her how to slip through the rear of the gym. Ahmed's guys hadn't figured it out yet. They stood out front, looking at their watches, knowing it would be a while. She'd taken a quick cab ride down to Chinatown, to a "hotel" where you could rent rooms by the hour. Next to a fish store with live octopuses in tanks of filmy seawater. Billy had been there, waiting for her, looking impatient, scanning the street. You pressed a button next to the door and they buzzed you up a narrow flight of stairs. She'd never go into such a place without Billy. But she was safe with him, she knew, safe anywhere. The clerk didn't ask for identification, just cash. You paid and they handed you a numbered key and you walked along a dingy hallway that smelled faintly of insecticide until you found the door with the same number. She loved the unadorned cheapness of the place; no one was pretending that this wasn't just a place where people went to have sex privately, and that, itself, was erotic. The sheets had been folded into a pile on the mattress. She'd held them to her nose; they'd been bleached clean.

Billy sighed and rolled onto his back. Now, *there* was a beautiful man. His shoulders and chest, his tight belly and hips, the big thighs. That amazing penis, with the fat vein running up it. She could not resist lying down on top of him, and he wrapped his long arms around her instinctively, still asleep. She listened to his breathing and kissed his unshaven cheek. He hadn't taken a shower recently and she didn't care. She drifted in an easy half sleep—it wasn't the Xanax, either—and then awoke with a start, worried about the time.

"Use your phone?" he asked, reaching for his wallet in his pants.

"Who do you want to call?"

Billy found a business card. "That guy who let me stay at his house."

"Paul?"

"He gave me his office number, said I could call him."

She wondered what Ahmed might make of this, assuming he monitored her calls. "Okay, I guess. I mean, I've called him there a few times."

"I think I left the back door unlocked. I want to tell him."

She retrieved her phone. Then she went to the bathroom and checked in the mirror to see if anyone could tell what she'd been doing just by looking at her. Her mascara was smudged, so she fixed it. She heard Billy talking.

"Get him?" she asked when she came back in.

Billy handed her the phone. "Left a message." He reached out his hand. She let herself be pulled onto him. "Don't go," he whispered, his voice gravel.

"Have to."

She bent and kissed his chest and neck and chin. Then he was crying softly, shaking, arms crushing her close. Ahmed has *never* cried over me, she thought, wouldn't actually know how.

"There's not enough *time*," he said.

"I know." She hushed him and he became calmer, though his cheeks were wet.

"Two days from now?" he asked.

Not communicating with phones made things difficult, and they'd decided to abandon their lost-and-found trick at Grand Central. Too risky, too subject to failure. And maybe she had been followed there already.

"I think so."

That morning, Billy had rented a little private mailbox at a place in the Village. One box, two keys, perfect for her to leave him a message. She could be in and out in twenty seconds.

"Can you get there without them following?"

"I got here." But she wondered how long she could evade Ahmed's men.

He studied her. "You been thinking?"

She held his fingers. "About what to do?"

"You know, it takes me almost two hours to get here." He'd said he thought Ahmed had people looking for him so he'd moved from Paul's house and camped on a planted-over mountain of garbage near JFK International.

"Billy, I think you could be in a cheap hotel just as easily."

"It's not bad. I lie there and watch the planes come in low. Plus it's close enough to check on the truck. I can see everyone coming."

"Couldn't you put your truck in a garage in Manhattan?"

He laughed. "Baby, you haven't seen how big this truck is. Crew cab. Extended bed."

"You can't stay there forever."

"No, but I can stay there as long as it takes."

She didn't know how to respond.

He sensed her hesitation. "You want me to stay? Wait for you?"

"Yes," she said, wondering if she should hate herself. "For now." That was the best she could do.

She gently extracted herself from his arms. He curled onto his side in misery and watched her, the sun from the window lighting his blue eyes. She didn't want to stay longer and she didn't want to go yet. She gave him one last hurried kiss and left quickly, not looking back, feeling the door click behind her.

He lay there a long time. He smelled his hands, hoping to catch her scent, any of her smells. He rubbed his right hand over his pubic hair and penis, then smelled it again. Yes, there. His chest heaved and he gave in to it, knowing he was exhausted and strung out.

He'd been in much more difficult places, however, and in time he breathed evenly, feeling calmer, and sat up to pull his clothes on. Boxers, pants, socks, boots, T-shirt, jacket. Knife. The blade was clean now.

13

Like a hunched giant sitting with his back turned, history
was indifferent to the fates of countries, and just how catastrophic
America's failed war in Afghanistan was wouldn't be known for a very
long time. But despite the continuing chaos there, one could begin to
map the future, which was also to say how money could be made. Ahmed
checked his watch and ordered another drink. From a corporate resource-
extraction point of view, America's military campaign had been a huge
success, for its doomed involvement had allowed boots-on-the-ground
exploration for oil and natural-gas companies, as well as updated map-
ping of the Pamir Mountains near the Chinese border. Some $11 trillion
worth of confirmed resources rested underground in the country, or a
pie-in-the-sky $35 trillion, according to the Department of Defense,
and Ahmed's group had applied two weeks of game theory, using a retired CIA consultant, to see how the fight over those resources would
play out in the next thirty years. They'd assumed that the tormented
U.S. military involvement would dwindle year by year; that the inter-
tangled networks of Taliban, al-Qaeda, Pashtun clans, ISIS operatives,
and straight-up gangsters that controlled various parts of the country would in time follow the Chinese model and establish pseudo-
corporate entities for themselves, perhaps employing actual trained
executives, and that the Afghanistan government would never cease to

be a hall of mirrors, corruption reflected as due diligence, malfeasance flashing outwardly as goodwill. Opium, the glue that held the economy together—and always exchangeable for cash, arms, disposable phones, plastic explosives, mountain ponies, vehicles, prostitutes of every nationality, diesel fuel, protection, medicine, gold, and basic consumables—would continue to be cultivated with impunity. What the game theory exercise showed was that the tribal and insurgent groups, despite being sophisticated in the logistics of war and terror, would understand that they needed to engage with multinational entities that had the deep technological expertise necessary to gain access to the massive amounts of global capital required to take advantage of the country's natural resources. There were, for example, barely any railroads in Afghanistan even as the surrounding countries used three different track widths, with Pakistan depending on the Indian gauge, China and Iran both using the standard gauge, and the Central Asian republics relying on the Russian gauge. Building a copper mine with dozens of 300-ton trucks that stood thirty feet tall—a commonplace in open-pit mines in Arizona, say, or Australia—was beyond the logistical might of the tribal associations or the battle-weary Taliban generals. Ahmed's group would provide financing for a sizable piece of the action, which in the case of mineral extraction could last decades, even generations.

His new drink came and he took a long pull, to soften his ticking anxiety. His group had decided to establish an office in Kabul and another in Kandahar, where tribal leaders could be entertained and paid off. There were multiple difficulties, however. The Afghan banking system depended on large international banks to clear their currency transactions, and many of these banks were under scrutiny from American and European bank regulators watching for drug-profit laundering. Some had decided that business in Afghanistan wasn't worth it. But if you wanted to invest in Afghanistan, you had to play ball with an international bank that might be looking the other way. That made people nervous. You also had to work with banks that the Afghans trusted, and they didn't trust anyone. And even worse, the Afghan government wanted to see substantial foreign deposits in Afghan banks if business was to be done there by foreigners. Yet only fools and the U.S. government had ever kept money in Afghan banks. The problem would require some deft negotiation. So, in fact, he needed to fly to Europe soon, to Geneva, where the Afghan warlords felt comfortable, especially because they stacked their gold Krugerrands—real ones, not the excellent fake ones made in China—in Swiss bank accounts.

But first—okay, *deal* with it!—there was the terrible question of William Wilkerson Jr. What was Ahmed supposed to *do*? Wilkerson was a vexation he hadn't asked for, hadn't created! Right? Well, that wasn't strictly true. Ahmed had listened to the security men's boastful assurances, had confidently set them in motion to collect Wilkerson for the meeting with Ahmed so that they could *talk*, and it had gone bad from there. Wilkerson had probably resisted, and a fight had started. What had they stupidly said to Wilkerson, trained as an Army Ranger? Enough that he had killed them. That was Ahmed's nervous supposition anyway, the only one that fit the facts. The two bodies had been found near the Brooklyn waterfront, according to the news. They had died of knife wounds, and soon had been identified as "former employees" of Palm Enterprises, a Middle Eastern company that provided private security. Self-important goons, intimidators, perhaps, and no more. The balding, muscular man had been wanted in Paris for allegedly beating a hotel clerk. The other, Tarek, the one who spoke better English, had been trained in the private security force of Colonel Muammar Gaddafi before he was overthrown in Libya's civil war. Fellows with an international pedigree. Not your usual Brooklyn drug-trade victims. The fact that each dead man trailed a long string of underground connections and criminal involvements was not good. It meant someone in the FBI or even the CIA would be interested.

But he, Ahmed, *hadn't* killed those men! Yet this fact seemed no consolation. Their violent deaths adhered to him; their heavy dead arms hung around his neck. He assumed the NYPD would soon link the two men to the overseas security firm Amir had recently contacted. That might then easily lead to Amir himself. But Amir was now on his way to Hong Kong with ferocious instructions from Uncle Hassan and Ahmed to have no interaction with *anyone* for six months. Zero: no phones or e-mail or snail mail. No computer, no Internet, no bank account. Everything was to be done in Hong Kong dollars, a wad of which was to be handed to Amir every week by a friend of Uncle Hassan's. So long as Amir was silent, the money would keep coming; but if they heard from him or about him, the money would stop. It was easy to disappear in HK; if you had an American passport and showed the border control a return airplane ticket then you didn't need a visa to get in, unlike the rest of China. You could board the high-speed train from the airport, walk from Central Station down to the Star Ferry dock and take the boat over to the Kowloon side, and there you could hike back from the harbor, away from the Peninsula and the other plush hotels, and disappear into 1970s Hong Kong, the huge decrepit apartment buildings encrusted with air conditioners and laundry lines. Tens of thousands of illegal East Asians and Middle Easterners scraped by in Hong Kong, living tiny, lost lives, and Amir would have to pretend he was one of them, no doubt drinking too much and making use of the hookers lurking outside the night market . . .

I'm thinking too much, Ahmed told himself, but that's all I can do. He glanced to the door, hoping to see his uncle. Nothing. Just Manhattan businesspeople telling each other the usual lies. He saw a middle-aged woman checking him out. They made eye contact and she smiled warmly. He turned away and went back to the problem. The other link to the two dead men was, of course, Wilkerson himself. Yet what would make the NYPD connect the men to him? That was a good question. That was *the* question. Wilkerson wouldn't have known about them until they were upon him; they'd encountered one another only once. The men had gone to the house in Brooklyn for Wilkerson but their bodies had been found many blocks away near the Sunset Park waterfront. Maybe someone had seen Wilkerson fighting the two men. Maybe there was physical evidence at the scene, blood, hair, skin cells. All members of the U.S. military had DNA profiles stored by the Defense Department to aid the identification of remains. *Maybe anything, Ahmed, maybe anything.*

He had to assume that the NYPD would get to Wilkerson quickly, within a week or two, even. The city had tens of thousands of security cameras. The police used intelligence tools they didn't tell people about: facial recognition software linked to their optical surveillance systems, a geostationary satellite right above Manhattan. And once the detectives had Wilkerson, they would make him talk, especially if he claimed self-defense, and then they would get to either Paul Reeves, who probably knew too much, or to Jennifer, and a minute later they would have Ahmed. The news outlets would have a lot of fun with the story, and within a few days Ahmed's career—his life!—would be over. An American soldier attacked by two Libyan goons working for a preening and too-rich-for-anyone's-good Iranian corporate executive jealous over his blond wife's affair. It would look like Ahmed had hired the men to attack Wilkerson and he had heroically fended them off. And *Iranian*, in the cultural equation, meant *Islamic*, not that most Americans really understood what that was, and for them *Islamic* meant, when you stripped it all away, *suspect*, linked by language and custom and appearance to the impossible-to-distinguish terrorists cutting people's heads off around the world. ISIS, al-Qaeda, all the rag-head bad guys. Delicious! Page one, *New York Post*, maybe showing one of the society benefit photos of Ahmed and Jennifer usually taken at these things. Jennifer radiant, a hot piece of ass. Page one, *Daily News*. Second page of the Metro section, *The New York Times*. First page of the New York section, *The Wall Street Journal*. And those outlets would be slow compared with the real-time conflagration of the Internet. Ahmed would instantly become a flaming scrap in the air, then cinders, and the world would whirl on. He wasn't guilty of the murders of the two men, but he had definitely been *connected* to them—there was no way around that. His employment contract had a "moral turpitude" clause; he'd be fired within hours.

But take Wilkerson out of the picture and what do you have? It was a chilling question that made him more nervous, sickened that he was even thinking this way. But, okay, *if* Wilkerson were not around, his connection to the two dead guys might be much harder to demonstrate, right? Ahmed knew Jennifer wasn't using her cell phone to communicate with Wilkerson, and ironically enough, that fact potentially *protected* Ahmed if Wilkerson were to disappear. Time would pass, blur the details. Ahmed wouldn't be interrogated. He checked his hand device. It showed that he was scheduled almost completely for the next nine weeks, with the trip to Geneva, then Paris, Berlin, then a week later to Riyadh, the capital of Saudi Arabia. He had no time for this problem. Yet he couldn't wait around and do nothing.

Finally, Uncle Hassan appeared at the door, entered quietly, using his cane. Circles under his eyes, posture stooped. Ahmed kissed him, held his meager arms, and helped him sit uneasily on the barstool.

"How was the flight?"

"I took a pill."

His uncle looked unwell. His suit was out of date. "Does your back hurt?"

"Old age, nothing more." His uncle ordered a drink. "So you have a real problem, I think."

"Yes."

"You did not cause the problem, but you made it much worse."

"Can't argue with that."

"Amir is also responsible," noted his uncle, yet his tone suggested that parsing out blame was wasted effort. "But we are done with him. He has never had good judgment. Has this Wilkerson threatened you personally?"

Ahmed said no.

"Or Jennifer? Threatened her?"

"Not that I know of."

The drink came. "What does he want?"

"I'm guessing he wants my darling wife to leave me for him."

Uncle Hassan grunted. "Oh, come on, Ahmed. She won't."

"How do you know?"

A crinkle of old mirth appeared in his uncle's tired eyes. "I know about wives. I'd just let him play himself out."

"You're not the one whose wife is sneaking around and maybe fucking him," Ahmed said with bitterness, realizing that it might have been a decade or more since his uncle had been with a woman.

His uncle waved his hand slowly, as if pushing away an invisible fly. "Let him exhaust himself, run out of money. These things run a course and blow out."

"Sure, but judging from his actions, he seems pretty intent."

His uncle blinked in consideration. "What does Jennifer say?"

"I haven't exactly brought it up with her."

"Why not?"

"Because . . ." Because Ahmed wouldn't be able to control himself, his fury. "Once we have that conversation—"

"By not talking, you keep her worried about what you know and you don't know. You keep your dignity, too."

"Yes, exactly. Okay, I admit that I'd like to just *erase him* and then see her face when she learns this. She'd be shocked."

Uncle Hassan shook his head in blunt disagreement. "That is *emotional*. You do not want to be emotional about this."

"That's why I haven't talked to her. I want control."

His uncle tasted his drink. "Everyone wants control and no one gets it. I thought you knew that. That's one of the lessons of life, okay?"

Ahmed glanced down the bar. He'd taken Jennifer here once, he realized. His uncle gazed at him, eyes ringed with age and sickness, his expression showing his awareness that the situation was dire, that Ahmed did not yet have the patience one learned with age, and that the problem, left untended, would get worse on its own.

"You are too talented, too smart for this *kossher.*" This bullshit. "You've worked very hard, but it rests on what the previous generation did for you."

"I know," Ahmed said. "I am grateful."

"Always a *khar* for the *cos eh lash!*" An idiot for the loose pussy.

Ahmed nodded miserably. The obligatory tongue-lashing was starting. "In any case, this is no longer about the happiness of my marriage," he replied, leaning in. "Right now this is about the fact that those two dead guys'll be connected to *me* if the police find Wilkerson. That's my problem. *He* is my problem."

His uncle took a swallow of his drink. Then he put down his glass. "I still know people here. In fact, the other reason I'm in New York is to talk to someone about your cousin Tala."

Ahmed had dozens of cousins and second cousins. "The one who finished college about a year ago?"

"She's living in an unacceptable situation in Staten Island."

"What is it?"

"Some kind of cult."

"Maybe it's just a bunch of kids living together in a house."

His uncle munched his mouth, which was his way of eating his words and not saying them; it was not just kids living together in a house.

"So what are you going to do?" asked Ahmed.

His uncle gripped his cane, tapping it against the floor, as if deriving resolve from its support. "We have people who have been recommended and I will make the right inquiries. You forget that I lived under the Shah in the 1970s, and for a while under the Ayatollah."

"I didn't forget that. You bugged your own house."

"Yes, sadly."

"You should bug my apartment. And my neighbor's apartment, too, on the same floor."

"Why?"

"Because Jennifer likes to talk to him. She called him at work this afternoon. All her cell data bounces to me. She could easily be communicating with Wilkerson through the neighbor! That's probably it, that's why we have no record of her calls to Wilkerson directly."

His uncle sipped his drink, enjoying it now. "Getting into a building, getting access, is not always easy."

"The super in our building is very accommodating," responded Ahmed. "We have an arrangement. He likes to be paid in casino chips from the Foxwoods Resort up in Connecticut. Won't take actual cash."

"Why?"

"Casinos wash their chips very diligently. No fingerprints."

"What about this Bitcoin, this electronic money that I do not understand?"

"Nope. Chips only."

His uncle exhaled, seemingly tired of yet another petty gambit involving greed and deception. "Let me say some things that you do not want to hear, Ahmed, then I'm leaving and going to my hotel."

"Okay."

"I do *not* think it is necessary, but I will ask if listening and video devices can be put in your apartment. This is not illegal, since you requested it. But that's all. Not your neighbor's. I want to keep the total risk as low as possible. Because you are not thinking straight, Ahmed. You made a terrible, stupid mistake in wanting to have a confrontation with this Wilkerson. That was just anger and pride. You are an international businessman who knows important people around the world, not some hothead off the street. Right? I knew a lot of men like this once and they are all dead, you understand? You *must* do a better job of controlling your—"

"I know, yes."

"—your emotions. So this is what I want you to do. Just go about your work. Be nice to your wife. Do *not* confront her. Make love to her. Take her out to dinner. Be *good* to her. Do not make her think you are watching. Go to all of your meetings, go on all of your business trips, everything."

"Okay."

"That leaves a difficult question, Ahmed. If this man disappears, your wife will soon know it. What will she think? What will she *do*?"

Ahmed pondered this. He'd noticed that Jennifer had new prescriptions for Xanax and Klonopin and something else. Plus she liked to drink wine, to excess. There were no hours of the day when she didn't have something in her system, taking the edge off. "Well, I think she will privately freak out and get totally weird and take more pills, because she won't be able to tell anyone that she can't get in touch with him. I think it will destabilize her, at least for a while. I don't like saying that, but it's honestly what I think will happen."

His uncle listened closely. "All the more reason to treat her well."

They sat there quietly a minute, lost in their own thoughts. *This is not just about my marriage*, Ahmed told himself again, *this is also about protecting my career*. "But how'll you find him?" he asked.

"By following Jennifer and by looking for his vehicle."

"He has a red pickup truck."

"I know." His uncle stared at him without blinking, and for a moment Ahmed wondered what it must have been like in Tehran after the Shah fell, what his uncle and his father had needed to do to survive.

People had disappeared from the streets, cash and gold had been moved secretly, informers injected with battery acid while tied down in cellars.

"How do you know about his truck?" Ahmed asked.

"You and I don't need to discuss anything further."

Ahmed suddenly felt very young, or rather felt his uncle's great age, the long shadows of his experience. "Understood."

"Can we trust each other to say nothing?"

"Sure," said Ahmed.

"If the time comes for me to tell you something, I will. It could be years from now, it could be never, and never is not so far away. My health is not too good. Perhaps my heart can go on for two or three years." He coughed lightly. "When I die, I will take many secrets with me. Most of them do not matter anymore. Do not be surprised if we never discuss this again."

"Got it. Thank you."

"I am doing this for you and for the family and for your father, his memory. I will be here a few days. Don't call me. We understand? People will be talking to me, *not* to you." His uncle stood, his back clearly bothering him. "I'm leaving now, alone."

"I'll get the check."

"Pay in cash." His uncle smiled vacantly, his mind already at work, and then he was gone, a bent-over old man in a raincoat leaning on a cane, a figure who appeared spent and harmless, which was exactly as he preferred it.

14

Three clients, many problems. The first that morning was a married Korean bank executive who had accidentally sired a child with a French-Cuban woman who lived in Copenhagen. Paul did not ask about the circumstances of the extramarital impregnation, for the Korean man—balding, dressed in a tailored three-piece suit—was so nervous and ashamed that he spoke in a near-whisper, forcing Paul to lean forward during the conversation. The woman had successfully proven paternity, and the client, Mr. Cho, who was not yet an American citizen, wanted to know how successful the mother's claim for support would be if he remained a citizen of South Korea or, as he hoped, became a naturalized U.S. citizen. The answer was not straightforward, because Mr. Cho was not sure of the woman's nationality: Was she French? Danish? Even somehow Cuban? And where had the child been born? If in France, that would be very different than in, say, Denmark. I do not know where this baby was born, said Mr. Cho, she will not tell me. She is the kind of woman who would know which country was best to have the baby. As Paul laid out the complexities of the questions and what was involved in trying to answer them, Mr. Cho shrank into his expensive suit, sensing, quite correctly, that it would be years before this situation was resolved. The second client was the general counsel for a minor league hockey team in Buffalo, New York, that wanted to sign up a talented defenseman they had discovered in Scandinavia, where there were indeed many talented hockey players to be found. His nationality was not in any way European but, amazingly enough, Brazilian. And yet, having grown up in Norway, the player did not have a Brazilian passport and had traveled through the EU countries with a Norwegian passport whose supporting documentation included a fraudulent birth certificate. They needed a legitimate U.S. work visa. The third client was a tall, fortyish woman from Philadelphia who had met a Turkish woman in a bar in Cozumel, Mexico, and now wanted to bring her to America more or less permanently as an alternative sexual partner. Her husband, an aggressive and flamboyantly successful personal injury lawyer, was well known in Philadelphia legal circles, so she had taken the train up to Manhattan to use a New York City attorney. As she spoke she unconsciously fondled the heavy gold bracelets on each wrist as if they were handcuffs that had been cut apart but which would not come off.

By noon Paul was done with all three of them. His executive assistant, Elauriana Jackson, came into his office and set down a résumé and cover letter. A Haitian woman in her fifties, Elauriana was sending two grandchildren through college, and was thoroughly unimpressed by more or less everyone, including Paul, which greatly commended her to him.

"I need to call that guy Gibbs this afternoon, three p.m."

She noted this on her pad of paper. "Gibbs? He a client?"

"I gave you his card. It's a map thing."

"I'll get him. Also, did you see the message from a Bill Wilkerson? He called yesterday afternoon. He wants to meet you at nine a.m. in a long-term parking lot at JFK. Tomorrow."

"Jesus, it can be an hour drive out there, even on a Saturday."

"He didn't leave a number."

Paul sighed. Of course not.

"Who is he?" asked Elauriana.

He just shook his head.

"You want me to order a car for eight a.m. tomorrow?"

"It'll have to wait then bring me back."

Elauriana made a note on her pad, then pointed to the letter and résumé. "Also, you remember you have lunch today with that young associate from Gracken and Rothstein?"

The boutique law firm that was his chief competition for high-end clients with immigration problems. "I said I'd do that?"

She shrugged. "You did, at the end of the summer. He's been waiting."

"I really agreed to that?"

"It would appear."

Paul glanced at the résumé. The young lawyer's name was James Marone. He'd been at Gracken less than two years.

"Should I cancel it?" Elauriana asked.

"Twenty minutes before lunch?"

"Right," she said. "Even you are not that horrible."

In the restaurant a few blocks away, he shook hands with Marone, a tall, thickset Italian kid who had grown up in Brooklyn and gotten into St. John's law school. As soon as Paul heard Marone was from Brooklyn, he understood the situation.

"Let me make an educated guess," he said as the waiter brought their entrées. "Gracken Rothstein is a snooty place. Very high-tone clients. You're a little intimidated, maybe getting tripped up somehow."

Marone hung his head, sighed. "That's pretty good, Mr. Reeves."

"Also, some of the partners over there are super impressed with themselves, right? A lot of talk about the Larchmont Yacht Club and what private school tuition costs, stuff like that?"

Marone nodded morosely. "I brought my fiancée to the office party and some of the wives just kind of chopped her to bits. She said she's never going to one of those things again."

"How are your billable hours?"

"I'm working long-enough hours, but the partner is cutting them down."

"When's your next review?"

"About three months."

"Dreading it?"

"Basically."

"If you were going to self-diagnose your difficulties, as objectively as possible, what would you say?"

Marone thought. "Too eager to please. Agree too quickly. Talk before I analyze. Also, I made a few citation errors early on and the judge reading the pleading caught the mistake and reamed out the partner, who of course had no idea it was wrong."

"You've stepped on some land mines, lost a couple of toes."

"Yup."

"Where did you go to high school?"

"Xaverian, in Brooklyn?"

"Catholic school. Pretty good football team."

Marone smiled. "Absolutely."

"You played?"

"Noseguard."

"You start?"

"Senior year. Guy ahead of me played at Rutgers. I was forty pounds heavier then."

"Is it true all these high school kids are taking steroids?"

"We took everything, man. Protein. Creatine. T-boosters."

"Did you get a football scholarship?"

"No, I broke both my fibula and tibia in the last game, senior year. Guy got me from the side. They put in screws and plates. That was the end."

Paul saw an earnest young man who needed seasoning, who now could do a lot of mop-up work while learning the business. If Marone was a noseguard by personality, he could take all sorts of abuse. Paul believed in hiring lawyers by analyzing what positions they'd played in sports. Each position elicited and reinforced a certain kind of personality. By the time an athlete finished college he or she had spent more time inhabiting that role than doing anything else. One of his very best attorneys was a woman who had played ice hockey for the University of Wisconsin, and he'd hired her on that basis alone. If noseguard Marone bought a better-fitting suit, aged a little, and relaxed a lot, he'd be valuable in a few years.

"Okay," Paul said. "I think you could use a new start. But I don't know if and when I might need you. I suggest you keep working your ass off, and when people ask you your legal opinion that you look them in the eye and nod, like you are *actually* considering the question. Give it a few beats. It'll improve your thinking. When the client comes in, stop worrying about whether he likes you. Start worrying about what *he's* worrying about. He's looking to you for reassurance. It's showbiz, guy."

"Got it."

Marone, he saw, was just starting to understand what law firms really were. The unwashed public tended to imagine them as stable, monolithic entities, but this was hardly the case, a fantasy encouraged by the firms themselves, which, large or small, could not help but achieve a self-parodying identity: hushed inner sanctums of mahogany and burled walnut; bookcases stuffed with identically jacketed case-law volumes, expensively worthless art on the walls, the primly lettered stationery listing columns of partners and satellite offices in Chicago or Miami or Shanghai, as if controlling a vast global ganglia of immense legal power. In fact, firms were unstable, churning caldrons of hatred, fury, jealous greed, revolution, florid egomania, sexual intrigue, Shakespearean betrayal, alcoholism, cardiac blackjack, drug use, thievery, and even grandiose fraud—and were most instructively seen as high-risk mountaineering parties in which some climbers were guaranteed to die. Firms broke apart, collapsed into civil war, snapped together, grew, shrank, spawned new parts that ate the old parts. They metastasized, abscessed, and necrotized. They raided one another for talent and suffered mass defections; they were in every way frenzied rat-fucks of the highest order.

"I'm assuming you want to keep our lunch confidential?" asked Paul as they stood to go.

Marone searched his face. "Appreciate it."

They shook hands, and Paul gave the kid a gentle pat on the back. "Don't worry," he said. "It's going to be fine."

Just after two p.m., Rachel called him. "I was hoping I could get another legal consultation this evening."

"Depends on the situation."

"The situation is that I *need* a legal consultation."

"Alas, miss, I may not have the expertise that you are so urgently seeking."

"Oh, but you *do*," she said.

Okay, he thought, I'm smiling. "How do you know?"

"Because your recent *consultations* have been so successful."

"And you feel you were well served?"

"Yes, I certainly do. Multiple times, in fact."

"Excellent legal advice can go on for a prolonged period, you know. Expertise and judgment are important."

"Yes, but I feel these are skills that you do indeed possess."

"I did hear a disgruntled report that I had not worn the correct *pants* to a recent formal affair."

"That was, in fact, a serious style violation, but it shall be overlooked for the time being." Rachel let out a sigh, the banter done. "Okay, I have to go into a meeting, sweetie. And I have a work dinner, even though it's Friday. Just get here by ten tonight, okay?"

"You got it." Paul hung up. He buzzed Elauriana. "Please call Gibbs right now. And please have that car pick me up at Rachel's place tomorrow morning instead."

"She's keeping you *busy*, Mr. Reeves."

"Tough to argue against that."

"She's a lot younger than you." Elauriana laughed. "If you know what I mean."

"What *do* you actually mean?"

"She gonna run you ragged. That's what them young ones *do*. She too young for an *old* man like you," she cackled. He saw one of the other phone lines blinking. "Hang on." He waited on hold. "Okay, I have Mr. Gibbs now."

The main event of the day! He lifted his phone and stood up to gaze out the window toward the south, a view that showed the Empire State Building seventeen blocks away, the curve of the East River along

Manhattan, the Manhattan and Brooklyn Bridges—all built long after the Stassen-Ratzer map was printed.

"Mr. Reeves, what can I do for you today?"

That sounded a little strange. "I'm ready to go forward on the Stassen map. I have the money ready."

"That's what I thought you were going to say, and unfortunately it's no longer for sale."

"What? Why? Did you sell it to someone else?"

"Yes."

Paul sat down heavily in his chair. "What? I am getting back to you an hour before the deadline!"

"I am sorry, Mr. Reeves, I truly am. We had another buyer come forward and contact us the very same day I saw you. This buyer made an offer superior to the price we were asking and made it on three conditions, namely that we not shop the offer, that we not reveal the name, and that we decide within one hour. So we decided. We took the offer. The map left Mr. Stassen's apartment yesterday, in fact, and is already being cleaned and restored."

Paul couldn't believe he was hearing this. "But you came to *me*!"

"We had a verbal understanding, but we did not have a contract."

Lawyers, he hated them all. "We had a firm *oral* agreement. We had a price and a time frame consistent with industry practices. This sounds like misrepresentation."

"Mr. Reeves, please."

"You can't tell me who?"

"I cannot."

"Can you at least tell me whether it was bought by a dealer?"

"Yes. It was not."

"Was it bought by an institution such as the Smithsonian or the New York Public Library? That would make me feel better, at least."

"It was not."

"So a private collector."

"A private *buyer*."

Not a collector, whatever that meant. "How did he find out?"

"It appears the buyer heard about the map from another source."

Could Gibbs be more evasive? It was infuriating. "Sounds to me like you told the eventual buyer of *my* interest and made that buyer hurry up, no? Right? For fuck's sake, you told the buyer how I had visited and seen the map and was due to get back to you, that you were sure I would buy it. I'm feeling played here, counselor!"

Gibbs's voice became low and defensive. "No one got played."

"Right, no one got played, but somebody got fucked!" Paul told himself to calm down. "All right, all right, I lost the best goddamn map I ever saw."

"I am sorry. I *personally* would have preferred it go to you."

"Then would you be willing to *personally* convey a message to the buyer?"

"It depends," said Gibbs.

"Two things. I can tell from your tone that the buyer is not a collector. That map has a serious foxing issue. It's solvable but needs very careful attention. You said the map is already being cleaned. But the best person in the city is Sally Watanabe. She has a restoration studio down in the Village."

"Thank you for this information. The other thing?"

"Please tell the buyer I would like to discuss purchasing the map from him at a premium to what he paid you."

"I cannot do that," answered Gibbs quickly. "It might indicate that I had spoken to you about the price, which I have not, and the buyer would be most displeased by that very fact."

"Surely he knew I would find out the map had been sold?"

"Yes. But that is different from me discussing it with you."

"So your advice would be . . . ?"

"You're out of cards, Mr. Reeves."

"You might have done me the courtesy of calling me to let me know where things stood." Paul felt his anger surge again. "But it seems you were incapable of some minuscule, face-saving courtesy."

"Now, wait a minute—"

"I played by your rules, Gibbs, but you changed them without telling me! Being a lawyer myself, I might have expected as much. Call it the professional *dis*courtesy." He could feel the blood rise in him. "And you know, a lot of people in the collecting community will find the news of the sale interesting. Surely you were aware that word would get out. A rare map? The American Revolution? General George Washington? You didn't make me sign a nondisclosure agreement. Right? Right! Why? Let me tell you what you were thinking, Gibbs! Since you have already forgotten! You assumed, correctly, that I would be a *gentleman* about the whole thing, right? I *wouldn't* mention the problem with the New York Public Library and a man's valuable belongings being sold out from beneath him as he dies. And then you *fuck* me over? Is this the way you win friends and influence people, Gibbs?"

"Aah, well, I can say . . . aah," came the tormented response, "that the seller's family, ah, knew the buyer in, ah, in a preexisting context and there was a friendship involved that, ah, *superseded* the previous understanding."

"Well, that's pretty mysterious."

"I would be unable to disagree."

"Is Stassen still alive?"

"He's on a respirator."

"Would there be any relationship between the fact that he is being *kept* alive with a mechanical respirator and the urgency with which his apartment full of priceless antiques and rare collectibles is being sold off?"

"Paul, I'd heard you had a temper. Look, I'm sorry. This is just one of those things that happen. Please accept my apology on behalf of the buyer. And, oh, yes, the restorer you mentioned, she would be considered knowledgeable in this instance."

That was a crumb of info. Interesting. Gibbs seemed to know about the restorer Sally Watanabe. Paul hung up. *I was right*, he thought. Over the years he had learned to trust his gut instinct with maps; the lightning-swift calculation when he first saw a map was rarely wrong, and he maintained a list of maps that he had neglected to pursue or had dithered about while someone else came along. A few times the same or similar maps had reappeared later and he had gladly pounced on them. Had he misplayed the opportunity this time? Perhaps. Yes, perhaps he should have agreed to Gibbs's terms right away and then just executed the buy. But it had taken a couple of days to get the money moved around. And the buyer knew the seller ahead of time and had bought the map just after Paul had seen it! How could he have competed with that?

He stood up and dolefully went to his window, staring at the north–south sprawl of Manhattan, that land slab of ambition. Yellow taxis nosed along the avenue, toy cars in a vast toy world. He had no heart to do any more work that day. When a man reaches a certain age, his banged-up fifties, he knows whether it's been a good day or not, whether he spooned enough coal out of the mine. Today was a very not-good day. Although he was seemingly successful in what he did, the founding owner of a small law firm, it was a rather thin accomplishment, very weak gruel, yes sir, more the product of working *diligently* (such a pathetic and uninspiring word), a mule on the beaten track, and having the luck to be in a field that many more talented lawyers had no interest in pursuing. The greatest legal talents of his generation had pursued politics or large-corporate work, mergers, constitutional law, even, while *he* had plodded forward with the filing of certain forms with certain government agencies, facilitating the arrival of minor German banking executives or, as with that day, Brazilian ice hockey players. In the grand scheme of things, there was not much money in it, because the work didn't scale up; the firm made only a certain amount, sometimes less and occasionally more, on each immigration case. A little like weaving carpets by hand and selling them one by one. He had survived because he'd chosen good young people to work for him, people like James Marone, given them a chance, and hung on to them as long as possible. He'd leased the office space during the most recent downturn and had never expanded. In the years that the profits had been slender, he'd generally taken less himself so as to retain his most talented younger lawyers.

But had it been worth it? At some point in his mid-forties Paul had realized that he'd already amounted to all that he would ever become. He was never to teach jurisprudence, never to win a great case. Like many professionals his age, he'd come to that inflection point where he knew that things were very likely to go along as they had been, with little to intrude on or unbalance the equation of his life. This was not exactly boring, but neither was it utterly unwelcome. Meanwhile, after two wrecked marriages, his consolation had become maps. Where would such single-mindedness lead? Nowhere, of course. His maps took him no further from death nor any closer to heaven, a place many true believers had attempted to map, in fact. And now he'd lost the best one he'd ever seen.

But a good lawyer, he reminded himself, keeps working the phone. So he called Sally Watanabe, who answered in such a quiet voice that it was as if she were far away in time, as well as space.

"What's up, Paul?"

"I'm trying to contact the new owner of a big New York map called the Stassen-Ratzer. It was printed in 1776, an example of the rare Ratzer, and it has a—"

"Serious foxing problem."

"Yes! Ignored for decades, I think."

"Will need a lot of delicate work."

"Yes, do you have it?"

She sighed. "I'm too busy and so asked just to consult. I have a feeling Mulberry Street is doing the work."

Another high-end restoration shop. "Who is the map's owner?"

"All I know is she is some super-rich lady with red fingernails who wanted it for her big new apartment, something like that."

"You're kidding."

"No."

"Makes me *sick*."

"Sorry, Paul. I heard you got that big Valentine, the one that mentions Lincoln and Charles Dickens?"

"Yes."

"Any work needed?"

The answer was no, not really. The map could be left as is for another fifty years and little would happen to it. But he said, "You know, I was thinking I should send it to you, maybe take a look at a couple of thin spots, margins may need some support."

"Great. Happy to do it."

"And, Sally, please, if you happen to just accidentally and surprisingly and totally unexpectedly learn the name of the buyer of the Stassen, please do let me know, okay?"

He hung up and returned to the window facing south. Maybe Sally would tell him. Not today, not tomorrow, but sooner or later. He'd been so close! His mood shifted from melancholy to anger. I need that map, Paul snarled silently, standing at the window still, watching the city pulse beneath him. His head hurt and he felt odd, feverish. In his mind's eye, the Stassen-Ratzer map rotated to the same north–south orientation of his view, expanded, and dropped down perfectly atop the street grid he gazed upon. The delicate lines drawn by a British surveyor in 1766. The irregular lettering set in type. The attention to inlets where ships could be hidden, the heights where cannons could be placed. The implicit message, given the enormous care and detail of the map, a loyal warning to the King of England: this rich, fabulous island of Manhattan will be fought over, this New York City will be where destiny turns. My city, Paul thought. This is my city, where my life is, and this is my map. Somehow, he would find out who had it. And when he did, he would do whatever was necessary to get it for himself.

15

Godless, but in a house of God. The cathedral was an echoing, overawing cavern where tourists gawked even as Catholic services were performed. Hassan watched the priest, a short fat man with a solemn face, give instructions as to which hymn would be next. He'd seen the same self-important expression on the imams in the mosque in Tehran when he was a boy. And now men, and it was never women, who called themselves the truest Muslims were preaching holy war, craving apocalypse, making al-Qaeda look like, well, choirboys. Hassan was tired of all religions, all the pompous men in their robes and their beards. You get old and see that just because someone else is also aged doesn't make him wise. What had Shakespeare said? "The wise man doth know himself to be a fool." Hassan believed in the blood of family. Only families outlived regimes and holy wars and empires. He looked up from his pew to see a tall Egyptian man in a soccer shirt slide in next to him. He was young, with strong slender limbs.

"You noticed me come in?" asked Hassan.

"I saw an old Muslim, yes."

Hassan lifted the hymnal and found the correct page. "Your name is Omar?"

"For you it is Omar."

"Let us discuss our two questions," said Hassan, keeping his voice low, despite the singing churchgoers. "The first is important. I have a granddaughter, Tala, living in what the young people call a commune."

"A commune?"

"Yes, a big house with many people unmarried, living together, following one leader, taking drugs, living a filthy life."

"She was kidnapped?"

"No, no, not that. She has *chosen* this. She is young and foolish. She went to an American college here called Sarah Lawrence. For smart, rich American girls. She will not answer her mother's phone calls, she will not speak to her father." Hassan followed Omar's comprehension. "The family is most upset. The house, the commune, is on Staten Island. They are trying to live without technology, no cell phones, no Internet, nothing. Why Staten Island, I do not know."

"Where all the Italians are?"

"Many, but my family tells me it is changing. More African, Chinese, Spanish, everything. All mixed up. The kids are in an old house on a place called Van Pelt Avenue." Hassan handed Omar a folder. "This has the address. The landlord is not happy with the group and the neighbors don't like them, either. I want you to get her out of there and into a car driven by my associate Shalib. All the contact information is in this folder. Once she is in Shalib's car, then that is not your problem anymore. Shalib will pay you the cash for this job right away, as soon as it is done."

"How do I *know* she is there?"

"She is there."

They looked at a photo of Tala for a moment. She was a lovely dark-haired girl with big, trusting eyes that seemed to yearn for something.

"I have two daughters," Omar said. "I think I understand."

"Good."

"And then there is this American man who has killed two of my Arab brothers?"

"We know where he is."

"Tell me."

"I will, once you have extracted this spoiled little girl who doesn't know any better."

"This one interests me personally. Tell me *now*."

Hassan shook his head slowly, firm in his decision. "Once I tell you, then you will think of nothing else." He saw Omar was angered by this answer. That was good. "Bring this girl to Shalib, then I will tell you where you can find this man."

"What is your proposed payment?" asked Omar.

"For the two jobs we pay three for little job, twenty-five for big job."

"You will pay me five and forty."

Hassan looked up to the soaring rafters of the cathedral. A pigeon swooped from one side to the other, a momentary blur through light and shadow. My life is nearly over, he thought. "Three and thirty."

Omar frowned unhappily.

"Four and thirty-two," said Hassan. "You finish with thirty-six."

Omar shrugged his agreement.

"But how do we confirm you did the second job?"

"I bring you no proof. Too dangerous."

"Then what is the confirmation?"

"It is that you look for him and he never appears."

Hassan considered this. "No one can find him?"

"Yes, no one can ever find him."

Hassan nodded. "When it is done and no one can find him, you will contact me at this number"—he handed him a slip of paper—"and I will have someone bring you the cash. You discuss this with no one else."

Now Omar also lifted his eyes to the rafters of the cathedral. So beautiful. "No one needs to know," he agreed.

Three hours later, as the afternoon softened toward dusk, Omar was parked in Staten Island on Van Pelt Avenue. The clapboard house was large and in poor condition. He watched two young women in long skirts push shopping carts full of food up the driveway. They exchanged words with someone and a gate opened for a moment. Then they were inside. Crazy American kids, hated their country, their parents, themselves, something. He didn't blame them. Maybe it was not a good time to be an American anymore. But he liked living in America. So much better than Cairo, where he had grown up. And his daughters would have good lives, he knew, much better than if they were growing up in a conservative Islamic country. They loved school, and got good grades. It made him proud to pay his property taxes.

The sky darkened. Shalib's car sat a block away. Omar got out of his car and decided to walk around to the back of the house. He trespassed through a neighbor's yard littered with bicycles and sporting equipment. Baseball gloves and lacrosse sticks. He waited to see if any motion detector lights went on but they didn't. He cut around the back fence of the commune and from there had an excellent view of the house. He could hear voices and see a big room filled with people. He pulled a pair of miniature German binoculars from his pocket and set one of the scopes between the slats of the fence. Twenty or thirty people were eating a communal meal. They seemed unwashed. Some were white people with dreadlocks. The men looked young and soft, full of empty slogans. No Justice, No Peace. And Shut Down the Entire System. The room was lit with candles. He examined the fence and found a loose slat and gently pried it back, giving him a better view. There were more women than men. He saw the girl Tala at the table, spooning something from a big bowl onto plates. She looked relaxed and happy. Why must he do this thing? What was so wrong with how she was living? But that was a question he could not answer. Maybe he should have turned down this job. But doing it meant he could have the other job, the valuable one.

As Omar watched, someone else came through the gated driveway, again let in, he could see, by a young man sitting on a chair. The boy looked fat and bored. Were these girls having sex with these lazy and fat boys? Of course they were.

Maybe there was another way into the house. He tramped around the far side of the property without success and then went back to the street. He gazed down the block and could see Shalib waiting for his signal. He walked quietly toward the front of the house, then edged up to the gate. From his pocket he pulled out several twenty-dollar bills. He knew the sentry was right behind the fence.

"Hello?" came a voice.

Omar reached over the fence and dropped the money. "I want to make a political donation," he called.

"What?" The boy scrambled to attention and was picking up bills. "Hey, thanks!"

Omar kicked in the gate. It cracked open easily. Inside, the boy was on the ground, rubbing his head. Omar leaned over and punched him in the temple. He retrieved his money, rolled the boy onto his stomach, and tightly zip-tied his arms and feet. He bent over and punched the kid again. Then one more time. Then a kick in the gut, making sure to point the toe of his boot. He pulled out his cell phone and dialed Shalib. Just one ring. Shalib would bring the car up quietly. He slipped inside the door to an old-fashioned mudroom off the kitchen. Inside several people noticed him. He walked over to Tala, who was holding a wooden spoon over a bowl filled with tabbouleh salad, and grabbed her wrist.

"Hey!"

He clamped a handcuff on her, clamped the other end on himself.

"You are under arrest," he said. "Come with me."

He pulled Tala, who weighed nothing, toward the door. A large young black man with broad shoulders and a long beard blocked their way.

"What the fuck is going on here?" he said. "You can't just—"

Omar forearmed the young man in the face, pulled his fist back to his front pocket, then had his knife out in an instant, the blade tip touching the kid's neck. "Die or live?" he inquired softly.

The young man's eyes rolled crazily. "*Live*," he breathed before stepping aside.

Omar turned back to the room of terrified kids. "This is a family matter, little boys and little girls. If you call the police, then she will suffer. And then I will bring my friends back here and make you all suffer, too."

He dragged Tala out the side door and through the open fence, where the sentry was groaning. Shalib had pulled up close. Tala seemed dazed and was not resistant. Shalib had the car door open. Omar took off his cuff with a key, cuffed Tala's other hand so tightly she cried out, and handed Shalib the key. "Hey!" she cried.

Shalib pushed the girl into the seat and ran a chain through her cuffs and locked the chain to a ringbolt in the floor.

"Payment," Omar demanded.

Shalib fished in his coat pocket and pulled out an envelope.

Counting the $4,000, Omar looked up and watched the car roll away.

He drove his car around Staten Island for a few minutes. What a horrible place to live, he thought. Like Brooklyn had been sexually mounted by urban New Jersey and this was the offspring. He wondered if the commune kids would summon the police. It seemed unlikely.

Now he called Hassan.

"Done," he said. But the old man already knew that because Shalib had called him. "You must tell me where the American is."

"His truck is parked in the JFK long-term lot number nine at Lefferts Boulevard. Near the south fence. A red Ford F-250. He comes to it every day or two, between the hours of one and three in the afternoon."

"How did you find it?"

"We have friends in the airport parking company. We ask them sometimes to keep an eye out for cars there, you see, because we sometimes use that place ourselves."

"Thank you."

"You must understand that no one knows what you are going to do. No one has ordered any action. You could do nothing or you could do something. It is not my affair. None of my family members knows about this, you understand. If you are arrested, then we will say we had no idea that you were going to do something. Do you understand this?"

"Of course."

"It is important that you do not go to the truck or actually touch it. Our friends say that the security cameras cover every vehicle in the lot."

"I will watch from at least a hundred meters and follow him when he leaves this place."

"Excellent. Anything else?"

"Nothing. The next call you get from me will be for payment."

Omar hung up. He would need food and water and a bottle to relieve himself in. He would have to watch the truck for a day or two. Not so long. He would take extra contact lenses, he would turn off his cell phone, he would get in close at the right moment.

When he arrived home to New Jersey, his wife came running out to the car, waving her hands like they were burning. "It's an emergency! Where have you been?"

"Working." He couldn't tell if she was furious or just upset.

"I texted you!"

He'd left his phone off, in order to be unreachable.

"Mrs. Doyle can't drive the girls! Her gallbladder burst and she is having surgery tonight and all the girls need a driver! Her husband is flying back from Dallas to be with her! The tournament starts tomorrow morning in Virginia! They should have left hours ago! The team meeting in the motel is tonight! We can use the Doyles' minivan! I called and they will switch her reservation to your name! The tournament takes three days!"

The front door flew open and Omar's two girls ran out, wearing their matching blue soccer uniforms. Mia, the younger one, twelve, had more talent, but Lia, the older one, fourteen, was more determined.

"Daddy! Daddy! You have to take us! We have to leave! There are three other girls who need a ride, too!" They collapsed against him, sobbing and hugging him and beseeching him, their dark beautiful eyes large and anxious and yet hopeful that he would save the day. "You have to! Please?"

This is Allah giving me a choice, Omar thought. This is a moment when you have to choose. Am I a killer? Yes. Do I love my two girls with all my heart? Yes. Love must be greater than hate. That is in the Qur'an. I do not want my daughters living in a cult someday. He pictured himself buying pizzas for the whole soccer team, using some of the fat wad of cash in his pocket.

"Okay, okay, *okay*," he said, which spurred another round of tearful hugs and thank-yous and kisses. "Ten minutes we leave."

"I packed a bag for you," his wife said.

And in those ten minutes he did not call Hassan back to tell him he could not be stalking and killing Bill Wilkerson over the next few days. There was no time for that long and uncomfortable conversation. Besides, he still wanted to get paid his $32,000 and keep a good part of it. Instead, he called an acquaintance named Lorenzo who worked in a garage along Roosevelt Avenue in Queens and said he had a job that needed to be well done, no bullshit, I need a stone-cold professional on this one, someone as good as me. Ten thousand dollars in all. Three thousand up front.

"Hang on a minute," came the response, and the phone was filled with the sound of traffic and whirring speed wrenches and some indistinct voices. You could get anything on Roosevelt Avenue. There were vans with prostitutes in them available curbside, toy stores that sold every kind of generic drug, all the pills coming from Indian pharmaceutical companies, shops where you could get fake Social Security cards, green cards, driver's licenses, even bogus New York City plumbing licenses.

"Yo, *man*, I got the perfect guy!" exclaimed Lorenzo, as if he had found a rare engine part needed to make a repair. "Mexican dude. Nasty, too. I think he once worked for El Chapo. The drug lord, right? Pretty sure he's free. I'll deal with him directly."

Omar watched his wife pile two large mesh bags of red-and-white soccer balls and matching team duffels into their car. The girls flitted around the car happily. Why were they in their uniforms if the games didn't start until tomorrow? Why? Because the uniforms were new and the girls were *so excited*. Then he repeated in a low, slow voice the information he'd been given about Wilkerson from the little card he'd written. He had to go over it a few times. The name, the appearance, the truck's location at JFK. Don't get near the truck, don't *touch* it. That the body had to disappear, not be found. Did you get that? Read it back to me. Good. Now, about the upfront three Gs? It was tricky because he was about to drive south. But money was money and they worked out a rendezvous at a New Jersey Turnpike rest area in about an hour. It was named after someone named Alexander Hamilton. He'd still be up a thousand dollars on the day. Omar said goodbye and tore the card into confetti and dropped it in the trash that would get picked up the next morning. The girls jumped in the car and his wife came out and bent down and kissed him on the lips and said breathlessly, "You are *such* a good father."

16

She'd never seen him so upset, about *anything*.

"I need to find out who has my map." Paul showed her the photos he'd taken on his phone. "I saw it, I stood before it, I studied it, I was told to my face that I could buy that map, and now it is *gone*."

"You never mentioned this," Rachel said, unable to hide the hurt in her voice. It was another example of how little she really knew about Paul. He'd come over to her apartment that evening as planned, and she'd seen right away that something was bothering him. "You said the buyer knew Stassen, the seller?"

"Stassen's lawyer said that. My friend the restorer says the buyer was a woman who wanted the map for her new apartment. They probably took it to a shop called Mulberry Street Restoration."

"Maybe they will tell you?"

"Doubt it."

"Sounds like the buyer knew someone in the family?"

"Maybe. Stassen himself has been on his deathbed for weeks. Now he's on life support."

Rachel took out her phone and logged in to her company's database. Then a series of passwords. "You know, we have this new research software that figures out the connectivity between particular individuals. It's totally ridiculously invasive of their privacy. What's his name again? James Stassen?" She typed that in, then the Park Avenue address. "It's a combination of the standard consumer info, the more specialized proprietary databases used by the political parties in presidential campaigns, and customized Venn diagram analytics that we think some CIA genius sold privately to Israel and then got stolen. The woman's got a new expensive apartment? And given the price of the map, I'm thinking second wife, playing with a lot of new money, and is between the ages of thirty-five and forty-six, forty-seven, depending on how old the new husband is." She looked at her screen. "It's loading."

"I'm sort of surprised you haven't used that on *me*."

"How do you know I haven't?" She looked at her screen. "Okay, James Stassen, age ninety-four, lives on Park Avenue, has no presence online. *Zero*. Wait, there are *New York Times* articles from the 1980s. The Reagan administration. And his name is on some old public records, but that's it? He apparently doesn't know anybody." She laughed in amazed disgust. "Our zillion-dollar software just *failed*."

"He's been out of circulation for twenty years, anyway. Also, he protected his privacy."

The screen popped up some info. "But he has four children living in that apartment building!"

"I did see a lot of old family pictures."

"This is an ancient rich guy who kept buying apartments for his kids."

"Four other apartments there?"

"Yes, looks like four *daughters*. Four women, ages sixty-two, sixty, fifty, and forty-eight."

"Two batches," guessed Paul. "Different marriages. One of the daughters bought the map?"

"No, I bet one of the daughters sold it. But that's just a guess."

"So, have you?" Paul asked a moment later.

Rachel looked up. "Have I what?"

"Used this freakishly smart software on me, checked me out with it?"

She rolled her eyes in mock-but-real shyness. "Yes."

"What'd you find out?"

"Very little I didn't know before."

"Well, of course you had special access already."

"Are you *mad* at me?"

"Nah. Vaguely flattered that you'd go to the trouble."

"There was a lot of bar association stuff."

Paul nodded. "Boring even to me."

"I couldn't find out who your ex-wives were, though."

He stared at her silently. *Why do I keep bringing this up?* Rachel thought. *It does no good. He doesn't want to tell me the story.* But she got up, went into his bedroom, and returned with the little glass box that he kept on his dresser, the one with the pieces of glass and burnt-up stuff.

"And I also couldn't find out what *this* means."

Paul's eyes glanced away, softened. "No, I would suppose not." He took the box from her and gently set it on a side table.

"And I couldn't find out what you really, *actually* think of me."

"I really, actually think you are a hell of a babe."

Rachel tilted her head. "Now you are just trying to get me to go to bed with you."

Paul stood up. "That's true."

"And you think you'll be successful? Just sort of toss off a line that I might like and I'll jump straight in bed with you?"

He looked right at her. "That is exactly what I think."

She wasn't sure if she was mad at him. Maybe. No. How could she be, especially if she wanted him to get her pregnant? "And you think that on the basis of what?"

He came over to her, bent at the waist, and gave her a soft kiss on the lips. "*My* proprietary database," he whispered. "*My* customized analytics." Then he headed toward the bedroom.

She got up and followed him.

They had been going at it for minutes piled on discarded minutes, having found the perfect cadence in and out such that known time had stopped but for the moist stroke after stroke, in and out—Rachel was impossibly, fantastically wet—and the soft sound of the stroke deep then out, rhythmic and instinctive and on and on and yet on, the sweat gathering in the hollow of his back, trailing down his ribs, on and on and on, like running long-distance when he'd been young, impossibly, in and out again, again, deep again, her wetness flowing between both of them, her splayed fingers grasping his backside, then dropping to his hamstrings, pulling him to her, hastening the rhythm, urging him as he loomed above her, his chin on her forehead, her lips pressed against the hollow of his neck and whispering in her private language of exhalations, this all the sound he wanted, for he was nowhere else, and in strobelike moments of lost consciousness not even there, either, the pulling out and plunging in slower or faster, then slower now or faster *again*, their breathing shifting with it, maybe then much faster, unsustainably but not yet unsustained, her breathing quickened and surprised as he maintained the stroke, and though he had looked at her and into her eyes any number of times in the many minutes past, now in affection he looked again and saw that she had turned to one side such that her eyes were half open and glazed, not seeing, blinded by the relentless cadenced pleasure, eyes not moving, not blinking, neither closed nor open, all the vision turned inward, the animal woman living only in the temporal . . . lost in the pure wet rhythm, in the stroke that did not yet stop, could not yet stop, all language lost, her consciousness consumed by pleasure, breath ragged, starting to pant, lips slack as she gave over to it, eyes rolling upward as she let him do what she needed him to do.

Later, in the darkness, she pressed her face into Paul's armpit and snuffed deeply. His smell. Something about it drove her a bit crazy, dizzy almost. She breathed in. It was manly. It was a smell that only comes from a big, clean, healthy *man*. A good smell, maybe the best smell *possible*. She couldn't explain it, even to herself, and didn't need to, just so long as she could have it. The smell just went in her nose, then *through* her. *Oh, Paul.* She could almost not get enough of it and she found herself gently nibbling at the skin where his biceps met his shoulder muscle, nibbling and maybe actually sucking a little, all the while her nose filled with his smell. She felt so safe doing this, so female, a little embarrassed and amused by herself, but not caring anyway. His hand came around the back of her head gently, stroking her hair, finding her jaw, caressing her neck. Her sucking increased. *Please,* she found herself thinking, the thoughts under the thoughts, *pleasepleaseplease* . . . His hand moved softly from her neck to her shoulders and to her neck again, making her breathing deepen, her lips go slack, barely moving against his skin. Then his hand came around to her throat and cupped it. She moaned plaintively. His hand trailed down to the soft space between her collarbones and then down to her left breast and rubbed her nipple, making it harden again, and then slowly finding its way to the other breast, touching that nipple, too. She wanted him again but could tell from the movements of his hands that he was thinking of something far away.

"What?" she whispered in the dark.

Paul cleared his throat. "So, Rachel, I'll tell you about my first wife or what the burnt pieces in the glass box are. You pick. I'll tell you about *one* of them and then I have to sleep. My car is coming here at eight."

"But I want to hear about your second wife, *too.*"

"That's not on the psychobiographical menu tonight."

"Oh, okay," she whispered into his armpit. She took his hand and clutched it with both of hers. "I want to hear about . . . ? About the *first* wife."

He didn't answer.

"Okay?" she prompted.

He cleared his throat. "I'm going to tell you and then you must let me sleep. You can stay up half the night thinking about it, sweetie, but I have to sleep. I'm an old, old, *old* man."

"You really will tell me?"

"Yes, if you go pour me a big Sambuca and bring it here and then get back into bed."

This she was happy to do, and a moment later he was propped up on the pillows, sipping his drink. She lay on his chest and then couldn't help sliding over, her nose in his armpit again.

"I'm going to do this in one long blast, Rachel, and if you have questions, ask them all *afterward*, okay?"

"I'll *try*."

She felt him pausing to think about how to begin. And then he did.

"My first wife, Rebecca Stein, was, basically, an empire builder. She decided—"

"Wait, wait, what did she look like?"

"Aha, that's the first interruption."

"No more. I just need to *picture* her."

"Curly dark brown hair, blue eyes, very physically healthy, tremendous energy."

"Did she have nice breasts?"

"Yes, I'd say so."

"Like nice shape? Or size?"

"Oh, you know, just nice."

"Wait, did she actually have a totally killer rack?"

"She was just fine."

"That's a yes, right? Was she very, like, superorgasmic?"

"Oh, Jesus."

"I want to know *that*, too."

"No you don't."

"I *do*. I *have* to know this."

"I said please ask questions later."

"Just this one."

"I can't really remember."

"Yes you can!" The less he wants to tell me, the worse it is, she thought. "Come on! A girl is curious about these things!"

She felt Paul inhale, and instantly she regretted asking the question.

"Well?" she pressed.

He sipped his Sambuca. "I'm not going there. I haven't asked you fifty-two questions about your illustrious past lovers, not that I'm not curious, but because I know better. I'm here with you and you are here with me and that's what matters."

"I *hate* her."

He sighed.

What's wrong with me, she thought. *Why am I doing this?* "Oh, just go on," she said miserably.

"Why don't you listen to what *happened* and then decide if you hate her?"

"Okay, but now you are all, like, fundamentally irritated with me for my response, right?"

Paul said nothing.

"Right? You *are.*"

She could hear him being patient with her, not saying what he was thinking.

"Rachel, did we just have sex?"

"Yes."

"Sexual congress? Intercourse?"

"Yes." He was just being playful.

"So you enjoyed it, this mating and sexual congress stuff?"

She clutched his hand tighter. "Yes."

"Was it of sufficient duration and quality, in your well-informed experience?"

"*Yes.*"

"And, switching to the third person, your appointed lover was reasonably adept and energetic?"

"Um, *yes.*"

"He did things to you and you did things to him?"

"Yes, totally. All the things, yes."

"Did he enjoy it?"

"You, I mean he, seemed to, yes."

"Did he *seem* in any way reserved or noncommittal or abstracted or disinterested or—"

"No, no, not at all."

"Did he yawn or burp distractedly?"

"No, I guess."

"Did he check his messages during the festivities? Did he comment on geopolitics?"

"No. He seemed—"

"Did he add up large numbers in his head?"

"I don't think so."

"He seemed quite pleased to be there, no?"

"Yes."

"Switching back to the first-person plural, are we here in the bed?"

"Yes."

"And you like being here?"

"*Yes.*"

"And I have my arms around you and—"

"Well, I—"

"What happened to all those yes answers of a second ago?"

"Oh, I don't know," she said contentedly.

"And we are here together now and seem happy with each other and you need to ask silly questions about someone I have not seen in twenty years?"

"*Yes.*"

"You *do* need to ask the questions?"

"Okay, wait! I understand what you are saying!" she protested. "Thank you! You are being very caring, and I *do* appreciate it. I *do*! But please *please* just tell me now, anyway, about her and you and everything. You said she was an empire builder, right? That's kind of a weird thing to say."

"So," Paul began again, "yes, Rebecca basically decided that I would scramble up the ladder at a law firm while she created a family and—"

"And had all those or-*gasms.*"

"Good grief."

But he could tell, she knew, that she wasn't *really* seriously upset about it because, after all, *she* had plenty of orgasms, too, herself, *actually*; had just had six or seven or eight, *anyway*; there was a lot going on in those moments, all of it OMG very good, he turned her into an orgasm *doll*, and she hadn't exactly been counting, not that she could have if she'd *wanted*—and, now, like he was reading her mind, he just rolled her around in his arms and continued as if he hadn't been interrupted. "That was the plan, Rebecca's plan. She told me that she wanted four children, and if she could have four children, then she didn't want much else. She'd thought about a career but wanted kids. She'd been pre-med at Columbia, she'd worked a few years, knew she wanted children. This disappointed her parents because she'd been a bio and chemistry major. She was like that, very determined. Early in our relationship, she presented me with a list of questions that I had to answer if she was going to be serious about me."

"Really? Like what?"

"Like, do you know how to throw a baseball? Does anyone in your family have Tay-Sachs, that hereditary brain disease that runs in some Jewish families, even though I'm not Jewish. Have you ever had any homosexual experiences? Things like that."

"Have you?" asked Rachel, suddenly curious.

"Nope."

"What were the other questions?"

"Ah, one was had I thought deeply about the Jewish experience in America? Answer: no. Then I had to tell her my SAT scores, LSAT score, and so on."

"She was doing a genetic evaluation of your fitness."

"So we got married and I worked all the time. We kept expecting her to get pregnant. And she didn't. She insisted I get tested. They evaluated my sperm just to—"

"How was it?" she asked quickly, unable to stop herself.

"Fine, fine. Her doctor said relax, it can take a year. She would pull her legs up to her chest after sex, thinking it would help."

"Oh."

"Like you did the other night, miss." But before she could respond, he continued. "So a year goes by and she starts having tests and she was informed by her gynecologist and then the fertility specialist that she was incapable—"

"Oh, God."

"—of having children. Not unlikely to conceive, but *incapable*. The uterus was completely screwed up, deformed. No egg could stick to it. Donated eggs, shots, none of that would work. At the time, working long hours, I didn't fully appreciate the enormity of what this meant. I said we could adopt. I said all the right things, you know? I didn't really understand them, but I said them."

"But . . . ?"

Paul tipped back his Sambuca. He'd gone through it pretty quickly.

"What I *should* have done was pay more attention to the sad expression on the face of Rebecca's father."

"Why?"

"*He* knew what it meant. He had seen his little girl become a young woman. He'd had problems with depression and he confessed to me that he'd always feared it would surface in her and it did. It really did, all right."

"What happened?" Rachel felt sad for the first wife, but oddly thrilled, too, for somehow if the first wife hadn't been able to become pregnant, didn't that—okay, this *was* superstitious and illogical—kind of *protect* Rachel from having the same problem?

"She lost weight, she drifted through our apartment at night, unable to sleep. Doctors were consulted . . . medications prescribed. So, I mean we tried everything. All the therapies. They didn't work. She became disinterested in sex, and if we tried, you know, she ended up weeping in the midst of it. There I am doing my thing and she starts sobbing, convulsing with tears. Not too erotic."

He stopped talking. She didn't dare comment. She herself had some-times suddenly started weeping during sex in years past and knew first-hand how it could freak out a guy. Suddenly he becomes a stranger in a bus station checking the departure schedule. She resolved she would never do that with Paul.

"But I guess I understood," he continued. "Because it was inseparable from the fact she couldn't have children. Eventually she would scream and start hitting me. One time we were having sex and I was being gentle and careful, I thought, and she reached out to the side table next to the bed and grabbed this Chinese bronze figurine and smashed me in the head."

"Were you hurt?"

"I was, yes. Dazed, at the least. I just sort of fell over and lay there. She hit me *again* and I had to take it away from her. That was the end of the sex. I was so young, I didn't really get what was going on. A few days later she cut off all her hair with scissors. Just tufts left, sort of spiky and uneven. She put all the cutoff hair in a bag and burned the bag in the sink. I came home and the super pulled me aside in the lobby and said the smoke detector had gone off and the firemen had come while I was at work."

"Women can be so-o-o crazy," she said, unable to suppress a nervous laugh.

"Men are just as bad."

"Yeah, okay, maybe, but you have to keep telling it."

"So then she started doing various weird things. She had some kind of Arabic inscription tattooed on her wrist. Wouldn't tell me what it was. Then something in Greek, then Aramaic, then Old French. I said, will you please stop having mysterious messages tattooed on your wrist, and she just looked at me like I was an idiot. All these hipsters would stop her on the subway and tell her how cool it was. I was worried I'd come home and she'd have tattoos on her *face*. But the arm thing kept going. Eventually it was like this snake circling her forearm. So that went on awhile, then her parents got very involved. Too involved, maybe. But they meant well. I wasn't sure what to do, what the boundaries were. I was only twenty-seven, and now this strikes me as very, very young . . ."

She could hear something in his voice, a sadness. "Then what?" she prompted.

"So, one day Rebecca comes home, her eyes bright, even manic. What? I said. *What?* I know what I'm going to do, she said, I am going to Africa to care for sick babies. It is the *only* thing worth doing and I'm going to do it the rest of my life. Here we are in an apartment on West Seventy-first Street near the Hudson. Trump hadn't built all those high-rises along Riverside Boulevard yet. I'm just a young guy going to work in a law firm every day. I don't know anything, not really. But I'm trying to be the responsible party, you know? I called Rebecca's parents. Yes, yes, Africa, the babies, we know all about it, they said. So I met her father in a bar over at about Sixty-eighth and Lexington, O'Malley's. Still there. I've been by this place since then and absolutely can't bring myself to go in. It's radioactive for me, I get . . . a sick feeling. So anyway, I go in there and he's slouched in the back booth, trying to be interested in his whiskey, and he says he'd always feared for his daughter's stability and that he had no answer. He said he'd learned a long time ago that things happen and there isn't a good explanation for them. And sometimes the things that we think are rotten and awful turn out to be good things. He was more torn up than I was, probably because I thought it was all just a bad dream that would go away with the right kind of pill or something. But he had *raised* this woman. He had held her as a baby, and he just kind of lifted his eyes, totally red, he'd been crying, knowing that I loved his daughter and would do *anything* for her, that I had lost my own father years before and needed a father's advice. And he said something like 'Paul, this is something you have no control over. You realize that you are the husband who could not get her pregnant, right? Of course, it's *she* who can't get pregnant. But *you* are the man who *manifested* that truth. In a sense, Paul, she hates you.' He was a wise guy, very smart about people. This was hard for him to say. But he had to tell me. Then he said something like 'I think she has gone around the bend, but there's a logic to it, undeniably.' He added that we—he and his wife and I—could have Rebecca involuntarily committed to a mental hospital but that seemed, well, cruel and deeply wrong. Going to Africa was making her happy. She had actually started to eat, her energy was back. Maybe it was a wild mania but he preferred that to the opposite. I was beginning to understand that I was losing my wife, that the idea of marriage was just that, an *idea* that could be dissolved by another *idea*. I'd thought I was married forever. If we couldn't have children, then okay, we'd adopt, I guess, we'd figure it out. But that was gone, blown up. He said, 'We don't blame you in any way. It is important you understand this. You're still young, with great prospects, and so on. We see this as a tragedy not just for Rebecca and us but also for you. We have given this a great deal of thought, my wife and I. We feel that it would be best if you let her go.'"

Paul lay back and talked to the dark ceiling. "Then he says, 'The divorce paperwork can be fairly simple. There's no need to divide the marital estate since your assets are minimal. I'm just telling you where we stand as her parents. We are a generation older than you, we've seen some things.' I looked into his face a long, long time. He was a good guy. A real guy. Realistic about things. Not a zealot. Thoughtful. This was killing him. He would have spent his last dime on therapists and shrinks and whatever else. But he had his skepticism. There was a philosophical issue. Maybe she *wasn't* crazy, maybe she just had decided in a grand bold stroke that was itself sort of *magnificent*. I mean, you had to consider that was at least a *possibility*. And if you loved her, as he did, and as I did, then you had to maybe say, okay, we have to *consider* this. I pictured Rebecca in a white gown holding little African newborns. She'd be good at it. Who could honestly say that it was *not* what she should do with her life? So I told her father that if she wanted to go to Africa I was willing to wait awhile, see if she was going to stay."

"Then what?"

"He shook his head. He said, 'Don't wait. Don't *ever* wait. It goes by too quickly. Find another girl, the city is full of great girls, just let it go . . .'"

Rachel waited for him to resume.

"So I let her go, agreed to a divorce, which was completely handled by the parents. They even paid for it."

"What happened when you said goodbye to her?" she asked.

He was silent.

"Paul?"

"Well, actually I never got to say goodbye."

"What?"

"She was living at her parents' apartment by then. She told me to come to JFK at whatever time it was, and I left work and took the taxi to the terminal and she wasn't there."

"Not there?"

"She'd left the day before and not told me. Didn't want to see me."

"Did the parents explain it to you?"

"They knew. They apologized. They had argued with her, but in the end let her do it."

"Did you ever see her again?"

"Nope."

Rachel sat up in the bed. "You have literally *never* seen her?"

"Not once."

"You were married to her, you were going to have children and the whole thing, and you've never seen her since?"

"Sometimes I wonder if I'd even recognize her."

"Where is she?"

"I don't know."

"Could you find out?"

"I suppose. Her parents died about ten years ago. Maybe she came home for the funeral. No one contacted me until much later."

"You were never curious where she was, how she was?"

"I was very curious for years. But I didn't want to find out. I made myself not ever find out, because whatever had happened would have just been sad, one way or the other. Eventually I hoped she'd found happiness, love, whatever . . ." He stirred. "I've got to take a piss."

Paul stood up and headed to the bathroom. Rachel took his glass and sipped the last drop of Sambuca.

"You all right?" she asked when he came back to the bed.

"Yes." He dropped into the sheets.

"That's a sad story, Paul."

"But it was a long time ago." He pulled the covers up. "Over and out, baby."

She leaned over him. "Thank you for telling me," she whispered, kissing him. "Thank you, thank you, *thank you*."

"Mmm. Yup."

In the dark, curled against him, she listened to him breathe, trying to hear the exact moment when he fell asleep. Why had he agreed to tell her about his first wife? Was he finally opening up? Or had she just worn him down? She had no idea. But what a sad story! People had them, of course, stones in their pockets. She had a few herself. She'd learned that men revealed their personalities quickly but their histories slowly. They did not necessarily *want* to share it all. Paul was the kind of man who got quieter as he aged. All those years alone. Women coming and going from time to time, she figured. Was she destined to be yet another? *I'm going to find that stupid old map*, she thought in a flash of insight. *If I find that map, he will want me.*

Awake, he dreamed. The car carried him toward the far edge of the city, and he followed its movement in his mind's eye across the rag-paper expanse of the Ratzer map, which showed just farm lanes and solitary buildings in Queens in the 1760s, the city not yet more than a large town of church steeples and wooden houses linked by muddy lanes to villages, with no macadamized roadbeds, no railroads, no highways, no small regional airport called Idlewild, later the sprawling and dysfunctional monstrosity named after John F. Kennedy. The early-morning sun was hitting the left side of Paul's face, which meant the car was headed south, toward the entrance to New York Harbor and the Atlantic Ocean. The light pulsated red through his closed eyelids as he saw the shallow saltwater channel off the coast that had guided ships right to the island of Manhattan for four hundred years. Galleons, clippers, frigates, schooners, men-of-war, ironclads, sloops, and catboats. Bootleggers had floated offshore in the shallow water there during Prohibition, hulls stuffed with gin and rum from Canada, as small craft off-loaded their treasure; later Nazi U-boats lurked along the sandy bottom, the officers using their periscopes dazzled by the wheeling lights of Coney Island.

"This is it, guy." The driver pulled over at the entrance to a long-term parking lot within a tangle of roads and ramps and fences. Above them a jet lifted away. "You really want me to drop you here?"

"Sure," said Paul, leaving his suit jacket and briefcase in the car, "just circle back in half an hour."

Then he saw Bill sitting on the roof of a red truck thirty yards off and headed in that direction.

"So," he called when he was a few steps away, "why am I here?"

Bill jumped down from the truck, tall and loose-limbed in blue jeans and an army coat, and offered Paul a handshake. "Got some things I want to talk about. I know the back door of your house was broken."

"How about we sit inside your truck?"

"Sir, how about we don't?"

"It'd be more comfortable, no?"

"Can't do it." Bill dropped the tailgate and they sat on that. "Truck's a private place for me."

"Right, okay." Paul remembered his conversation with the drugged-out neighbor in Brooklyn. "So, what I hear is somebody broke into my house on Tuesday night and attacked you. There was a fight. It was loud, then it was quiet. Later you pulled your truck up to the house."

"Something like that."

"What's that mean?"

Bill looked away. "Means I wasn't expecting them."

"Them?" Paul looked at Bill's hands for any wounds or cuts from a fight. None. And no signs on his face. "Who were they?"

"Don't know."

"You have no idea?"

"They didn't introduce themselves." Bill pushed away from the tailgate and stood in a ready stance, on the toes of his boots, as if about to fight again.

"What did they want?"

Bill was bent at the knees, slowly moving his arms in rhythmic martial art sequences. "They wanted me to go with them to meet someone."

"They say who?"

"Nope." Bill shook his head in defiance and then he rotated on the balls of his feet as his hands moved into a defensive posture. "I told them I wasn't going anywhere and that was that."

"Then there was the fight?"

One hand struck in slow motion as the other parried. "Yes, sir, then there was the fight."

"You didn't get hurt?"

The other hand struck, chopped, struck again. "I look hurt?"

Paul noted the defiance in Bill's voice. "No," he said carefully. "You look just fine. But what happened to them?"

"They went away," Bill said, dropping his hands and standing straight. "They'd had enough."

Paul felt the vagueness of this answer. Young men who won fights usually didn't mind people knowing that. "You call the police?"

"Nope."

"Why?"

"We had our little disagreement and then they left."

"But maybe they are coming *back*, Bill."

"Maybe, but I'm not too worried."

"What did they look like?"

"Just two guys. Nothing special."

This was all bullshit, Paul knew. "I think we were followed in the cab when we went out there Monday night."

"Figured it was something like that. I'll keep away from there. They won't find me now." Bill pulled Paul's house keys out of his breast pocket and handed them to him. "Sorry I caused you trouble. I tried to clean—"

"Here's the thing," Paul interrupted, irritated by the conversation. "I did you a favor and ended up having my house broken into, right? Someone went to a lot of trouble. They cut the lock. I looked at it. They used a bolt cutter. They planned ahead. People don't just walk around with those. You had some kind of a fight and you won't tell me what happened?"

Bill stood motionless—too still, thought Paul. He's controlling his response.

"You don't know anybody in New York except for Jennifer, right?"

"That's right, sir."

"So who knows about you seeing her, other than the two of you and me?" Paul waited for an answer, but Bill just shook his head again. "I think her husband, Ahmed, might. There's no other way to explain it. I don't know him well, but he's a pretty aggressive guy, wound tight, lot of pressure on him, lot of visibility. He's very possessive. My feeling is that this is a screwed-up situation and it's just going to get worse, for somebody, sooner or later."

"Suppose you think I'm some dumb-ass, chasing after this rich girl."

"You *really* care what I think?"

Bill examined his knuckles. "Not really, no."

"Listen to me, guy, you're in a situation you don't understand. Somebody is following you. You should get in your truck and hit the road."

"She's got to make up her mind, that's all there is to it."

"And you're going to sit here until she does?"

"I got a lot of time, dude. And I got my reasons. I done my tours in the army and that went okay, but now I'm going home. I can get there sooner and I can get there later. There's no rush. I was missing Jenny almost the whole time. She wrote me, too."

"She did?"

"Sure." He pulled some letters from his coat pocket and held them out. Paul could see that the envelopes had no return address.

"No e-mail?"

"I like this more. Also, she thought it was more secure."

"You going to miss the army? Some people do."

"Parts of it, parts not."

"What parts not?"

"I'd rather not go into it."

Paul looked at his watch. Even though it was early Saturday morning, the traffic would still build up as people went out shopping at the malls or out to Long Island. He decided to ask one of the questions he used with his clients. "Looking at the big picture, what do you want to happen?"

"Buddy of mine been laying foundations for houses all over west Texas, says he's got more work than he can handle. My parents got a little three-hundred-acre ranch that's going to be mine and I got a whole, complete life that can just start up, and I want to take her back with me."

"She's gotten used to a certain kind of lifestyle here."

"That don't mean nothing, not really."

"Maybe not to you, but it means a lot to her."

"We'll see."

"She has a very accomplished husband."

Bill lifted his eyes to a jet taking off. "Sir, I saw all kinds of big-deal men in the military and my thinking about it is that a man is just a man. I seen big old boys get the shit knocked out of them and I seen mean little men, skinny and not much there, ribs sticking out, and seen them go all day and outlast the big old boys everyone thought was better."

"Which are you?"

He laughed. "Little of both."

"What if Jennifer doesn't want to go?"

"Then she better start acting like that soon." He turned toward Paul, his blue eyes intent, and not friendly. "She ain't happy with him, that's plain to see. She can have a whole life with me, she knows that. We got a— There are things we got in common and we can just work it out from there."

"She's married, does that matter?"

"Not to me." Bill shrugged. "They don't have kids, so it's no big deal, really. Get the divorce, keep going. We're in our twenties. All that goes behind you pretty fast."

Paul couldn't tell if the young man was a dangerously romantic fool or in fact the possessor of a beautiful, not-quite-impossible dream that could come true if all the cards fell right. So often it was hard to tell the difference. "So how did a guy from Texas meet a girl from Pennsylvania?"

Bill smiled. The story was in his eyes, but he wasn't sure he wanted to tell it. "I played a lot of baseball, see. I was on a dang good seventeen-and-under team and we played out of Uvalde County, Texas, and I was a right fielder, played a little first base, too. And we had a hell of a summer and we got to where we won a big tournament up there in Georgia and then from there we got invited to a tournament in Reading, Pennsylvania, where they got a minor league team and a ballpark. We took the plane to Philadelphia and then we got on a bus to Reading, and we were in a motel there. We won a couple of games, and then at the place we were eating dinner, a Denny's or someplace like that, I see this girl and we start talking and she said you all one of them out-of-state teams and I said yes, I'm from Texas, and she said I could show you around here, show you the countryside."

"That was Jennifer," said Paul in wonder. "Just a girl."

"Yes, sir, and she had a car and we went out to these green cornfields and drove around and pretty soon we were doing the things, you know, like teenagers always do, and then she drove me back and I was in love and she was in love and she said she would come see me at the game the next day. And I knew her first name, see, but never really caught her last name because I was sure I was going to see her the next day. But then the time for the game came and we played it and I think I struck out twice, looking on three pitches, I was so distracted, and then they had the bus waiting for us with our bags right there at the park. We never went back to the motel, nothing. I was all tore up about it, mister, this was the most beautiful girl in the world as far as I was concerned, and then I got on that bus pretty confused and then we were on the plane back to San Antonio and that was that."

Bill stopped. It was an ancient fable to him, repeated uncountable times. "And I missed that girl something awful, but I didn't know her last name and I had no way to get back there on my own, and pretty soon school started. There I was in my senior year of high school and I had no idea where she was and I missed her and hoped I was going to see her again, and then, you know, time started going by. I figured she could easily look up the name of my team in the schedule and get in touch with me. She knew my name, she knew I played outfield, and it would have been kinda easy for her, I figured. But she never called or wrote. One day I actually found the restaurant on the highway where we was and called them up, but nobody ever heard of her so that was no good, too. Then I got drafted right out of high school and played on my first rookie league team, in Virginia. And I had a little time off and I went driving up to Reading from there, just a couple of hours, and asked around for her and told people I was looking for this beautiful girl named Jenny, and what do you know, I found her and it was like we had never been away from each other, and after that we were in touch all the time, the real deal." Bill stopped, rubbed a patch of rust on the tailgate. "Then a year later, in Single-A, I broke my thumb sliding into home and the doc said you also tore all the ligaments and this kind of injury takes two years to heal if it really does heal, so that was going to be the end of baseball for a while. Couldn't even swing a bat. And meanwhile all these other young guys are coming up, trying to take your position away from you. That's how the system works. Minor league baseball pays terrible anyway, maybe a thousand bucks a month during the season if you were a low draft pick." He lifted a pant leg to reveal a sizable knife strapped to his shin. He pulled out the knife, which looked long and very sharp. He inspected the blade, carved the air once or twice, then slipped the knife back into its sheath. "So after the cast came off my hand I went into the army and saw Jenny as often as I could, but then I started getting these long deployments. I'd see her every time I came back, even if just for a few days. Things got kind of estranged between us, even though we wrote letters, and pretty soon I hadn't seen her in something like six months, and I don't really know what the hell was going on anymore. I figured she found another guy, and to be perfectly honest there were a lot of women around in the army who were looking for love or sex or whatever. So nobody was ever lonely. But the thing with Jenny wasn't finished, like, it wasn't *done*. I called her but she wouldn't take the calls and then I heard she had left home and gone to New York City. That was like six years ago. I didn't really know what to think. And then a month or two ago I decided it was time for me and Jenny to get back together."

"What made you suddenly decide that?"

"Sir, that's a private thing, but I gone over it backwards and forwards and got it figured out once and for all." Bill looked straight into Paul's eyes. "So what I'm saying is, I know I seem like some crazy motherfucker cowboy who don't know his ass from a hole in the ground, but it's a lot more complicated than that, mister."

Paul eased down off the tailgate of the truck to stretch his legs. His driver had returned, and flashed his headlights to be noticed. Paul gave him a wave. Then he turned back to Bill. "I think that's a nice story, I really do. Very romantic. But—" He stopped, troubled by what he saw in Bill's eyes. "But I hope you wise up and get out of New York City anyway."

They shook hands, but neither man enjoyed it.

Later, floating uptown in the car as the weather report on the radio talked about a possible hurricane off the coast of Florida, Paul remembered the moment when Jennifer had seen Bill in the auction room at Christie's. Her sudden gasp, her instant desire to rush toward him. He was amazed, and not for the first time, how little he really knew about anybody.

18

FITNESS ULTIMATUM, QUEENS BOULEVARD,
QUEENS, NEW YORK

The history of shopping malls on Long Island is a pattern
of paradigm formation and decay. The first ten-acre pull-ins, built on
the edge of New York City and just beyond as the suburbs burgeoned,
were profitable for a relatively brief twenty years, then were replaced by
the fifty-acre, three-thousand-parking-space behemoths, with anchor
tenants such as Sears, JCPenney, or Kmart, and augmented by banks,
specialty clothes stores, and "family-style" restaurants. These were
then supplanted in the 1980s by the "shopping experience destination"
mall: a huge single structure with three or even four floors, a central
atrium, a chain bookstore, upscale specialty shops, and a movie theater. With huge fixed costs, these megastructures reached annual profit-
ability each year sometime between Thanksgiving and Christmas,
which was the occasion for shop windows decorated with spray-can
snow, cherry-cheeked cardboard Santas printed in China, and other
ephemera symbolizing a happy American time that never was. These
iterations of the suburban shopping experience were soon undercut by
their relentless proliferation across the landscape and a corresponding
propensity to attract increasingly obese, tattooed, and pierced teenagers
at all hours of the day; the unemployed; budget-conscious seniors tired
of watching television; small-time local drug dealers; and various subpopulations needing safe, cost-free activities that could be supervised

by poorly trained and underpaid counselors, such groups including developmentally disabled adults, mentally ill teenagers, addiction halfway house residents, and last, the demented elderly, often heavily medicated and pushed in convoys of wheelchairs. Thus did these malls no longer offer an entertaining flight from reality but instead a grim intensification of it. In time, the malls became lifeless beached whales as a new paradigm was hatched, the big-box trend: enormous stand-alone stores that offered every possible iteration of products in specific categories: hardware, home remodeling items, sporting goods, household appliances, electronics, car parts, etc. But these, in turn, were soon endangered by manic overbuilding, not to mention all that was available on the Internet, and would also be obsolete, proving yet again that capitalism never stopped consuming its own tail.

The relentless sequence of marketing revolutions left uncountable small, outmoded malls to fend for themselves in the shopping landscape, and forced them to drop their rents and house marginal pizza parlors, nail salons, discount clothing stores, head shops, discount car parts stores, Chinese restaurants with food cooked by Mexicans, specialty shops for tall and ever fatter men, tattoo parlors, massage parlors employing semi-enslaved Filipino women, and hard-core weight-lifting gyms, such as Fitness Ultimatum on Queens Boulevard.

Here the clientele was highly specialized and did not include the following: married women; educated women; divorced women; older women; single professional women; teenage girls who didn't like to have their makeup run; any female between the age of fourteen and sixty who was in any way reasonably attractive; any human primarily interested in any of the many esoteric permutations of yoga, Pilates, cross-fit training, cycling classes, aerobics, or Zumba; openly gay men; men older than about fifty; educated Asian men; men with physical disabilities; men with high incomes from legitimate sources; men interested in finding attractive available women in a health club; men who were not interested in any sports; men who did not understand football; men who did not own work boots; and men sickened by the smell of gasoline. Those many deletions left a subpopulation that itself was composed of many subpopulations: current high school football and baseball players working out in the off-season; *former* high school football and baseball players working out by virtue of habit and self-identification; former convicts, not a few of them black, who had gotten huge in prison and who, now back in the world, found it occupationally advantageous to remain jacked; blue-collar workers and deliverymen who exercised after getting off work, actually lifting weights in their striped FedEx or brown UPS uniforms; men in hard-core motorcycle gangs, often working out in T-shirts bearing the insignia of their clubs or chapters, featuring a leering skull with wings sprouting from the temples. Another population was the Mexican males who had clawed their way from the bottom of the ladder and now felt sufficiently comfortable with the master culture that they could pursue a more purely American physique: swelling deltoids, jacked chest, wide lats, squats-thickened glutes and thighs, calves popped out by donkey raises, and hands and wrists wrapped with tape, wristbands, and black leather lifting gloves. They stayed to themselves and spoke Spanish to one another. The last group of lifters were the monsters: hard-core bodybuilders and muscle freaks who either revealed their fifty-eight-inch chest and twenty-two-inch biceps in tight wifebeater T-shirts, all the better to display the ornate tiger or dragon tattoo wrapping around one side or, more mysteriously, wore sweat-sopped hoodies that did not mask truly, disturbingly giant chests and backs but did hide the faces atop those torsos. Like a strange cult of medieval executioners or Goth video-game villains, these men said little to anyone not similarly garbed or muscular. That many of them used such steroids as stanozolol, norbolethone, or tetrahydrogestrinone was an inescapable conclusion and perhaps another reason they remained cloaked and uncommunicative to others outside their tribe.

The layout of the gym, random to an uneducated observer, was in fact highly organized. Once past the desk, where energy fluids, useless protein drinks, and bottled water were for sale, the room opened out first to a field of exercise bikes, running machines, and elliptical motion machines. Then came perhaps a hundred weight machines, the kind in which the user sits and places a key into a stack of weights. These machines were poorly maintained, chipped, rusty, and often bore the stenciled logo of the more upscale health club that had disposed of them in the used-machine market when upgrading to new equipment.

Beyond these machines were the ones requiring the placement of loose steel plates varying from five to seventy-five pounds, and this was where the larger men clustered. Beyond them, on the far wall, were the pure free weights: long racks of barbells and dumbbells, and it was here that the monsters reigned, men weighing 250 pounds or more, even 325, talking, showing off, jacking up huge numbers, dropping the bars with a heavy clatter to the floor, and in all ways enjoying their status as the strongest men in the place. Here the acne-pocked latissimi dorsi wrapped beneath the men's arms like body armor and the veins snaked pencil-thick through the deltoids and biceps, with the chest muscles spider-veined from the clavicle to the nipple, pulsing with blood. One of the biggest men, known in the gym as Jesus Spook, or J-Spook for short, and who wore an oddly medieval-looking beard in the shape of a shovel blade, went through elaborate preparation rituals with long black elastic wraps, winding them around his knees while muttering about praising God. His calves were decorated with tattooed Irish and Chinese inscriptions whose meanings were debatable. Then he got beneath a long barbell set shoulder-high on a rack; the barbell was so ridiculously heavy with huge plates that he needed two spotters, who performed their duties with cold-eyed solemnity. This was big weight and even a very large man could get hurt, cracking a vertebra or blowing out the gut or tearing the tendons that stabilize the knees. J-Spook huffed and hyperventilated into a state of ferocious red-faced intensity and then screamed out "Praise God!" and lifted the immense weight onto his meaty shoulders, stepped back, did a deep-knee bend until his rear end was lower than his knees, and repeated it four times. This was a squat, one of the trinity of pure lifts that comprise power lifting. Then J-Spook was done and hung the barbell back on the rack with a loud clattering of the plates; the others fist- or forearm-bumped affirmatively with him; he was weird and huge and probably mentally ill in some way and no one wanted to be on his wrong side.

The place was always too warm and at night the fire door in the back was jammed open with a ten-pound plate to let some cooler air in and to release the smell of mildew and sweat and hammy flatulence. Just outside the doorway lay the ill-defined backside of the little mall, where a pitted service road ran around the whole place. It was thus reachable by vehicle, and a quiet zone of undocumented commerce could be found there, the lifters controlling who had access to the space through the gym, and then stepping outside if they wished for air, or convivial conversation, or a quiet purchase of the most potent muscle-juicing potions not sold on the Internet or in vitamin stores. That a security camera was "trained" on the outside of this area was both well-known and disregarded; the camera did not record sound, was aimed too high, and so ancient that its swimmy black-and-white images were nearly undiscoverable. Moreover, the video feed led back to the front desk, where the monitor was perpetually disregarded by the clerks behind the desk who, when not checking in patrons, had three cable channels to watch instead, including a soft-core porn channel whose screen was hidden from the patrons' view.

Thus was the patch of cracked asphalt behind Fitness Ultimatum an excellent place to momentarily meet someone driving around the back of the mall. And this was what Hector Ruiz did, carrying his phone and keys and protein sauce with him as he stepped out into the cool air, feeling a sweet chill hit his sweaty skin. He took three steps into the darkness to the driver's side of a vintage, half-restored 1978 Corvette, engine rumbling under its sharkish hood.

"Yo, Hector," came a voice at the window. Lorenzo, in a Yankees cap. A fist bump followed.

"What you got, mi hermano?"

"This is the dude." Lorenzo lifted a piece of paper that said:

Billy Wilkerson. Six ft. 3 in. plus. Blond hiar. 210 Pound. 25–30 yrs. 2011 Ford-F250 (red, Texas plates) parked in space 88, Lot 9 Long Term Parking, JFK airport, comes to truck every day or two in afternoon, DO NOT TOUCH TRUCK STAY AWAY FROM AIRPORT CAMRAS OBSERVE FROM DISTANSE. Carries a knife. Make sure corps disappear completely.

Hector took the piece of paper. Eight thousand dólares for a few days of work. "How soon they need this?"

"Right away."

"I'll get on it, pero I got to sit there and wait for el hombre."

"Maybe you will get lucky."

"Maybe you are a fucking pendejo with a beer can in tu culo."

"Here." Lorenzo held out a paper bag. "Two thousand, up front. The rest when it's done, my nigger."

"How come Mexicanos be calling each other mi nigger?"

"'Cause we cool now."

"No me gusta, you shithead."

Shadowed in the car, Lorenzo shrugged. "I'm telling the guy it'll be a week."

"Sí, pero I'm starting now."

Hector headed back to the gym, sipping his protein sauce. After a minute the car rolled out, then was gone.

Hector went back to the bench press. He'd be away from the weights for at least a few days, so why not get a few more sets in. He got a spotter, lay down on the padded bench, set his feet wide and flat, placed his hands on the bar, felt the textured steel in his fingers, took five quick deep breaths, then grunted "Okay" to the spotter as he pushed up the bar, then reeled off twelve reps of 320 pounds, the last one a grinder.

"Not bad, man," said one of the huge guys with a shaved head and shoulder tattoos. He was six-three, perhaps 290 pounds, had played in the Canadian Football League before blowing out his ACL.

"Especially for a fucking *little* Mexican guy," grunted J-Spook, who was standing next to the other man.

Hector got up, gathered his keys, phone, bottle, and the slip of paper. He didn't bother to look up.

"Yo," said J-Spook, "I was just joking, dude. Seriously, that's some impressive shit."

Hector looked at J-Spook and smiled broadly, lots of teeth, crinkly dark eyes. I'd kill you, *too*, he thought, pero no one me pago eight thousand dólares to do it.

19

Preoccupied by desire for what he did not have, Paul studied the walls of his map gallery, where the Stassen-Ratzer would fit perfectly, be the centerpiece of the whole room. He decided he'd call Gibbs back and make a blind offer to the new owner for the map, bumping up the price by twenty-five percent, see what happened. In fact, why not call now, have a message waiting for Gibbs on Monday morning? He found the work number in his e-mail and dialed.

"Hello? Hello?"

"Gibbs?"

"Who is this?" came a voice.

"Paul Reeves. I know it's the weekend. I figured I'd leave a—"

"No, oh, no, it's fine . . . the office-line calls are being forwarded to me in case, well, in case Stassen dies tonight."

"I thought I'd make a Hail Mary pass here, throw a blind offer at the new owner of the map."

"I see." Gibbs sounded wary.

"So I'd like to make an offer that is twenty-five percent higher than what we agreed on."

"I'm afraid that won't do it, I suspect."

Paul drifted toward the window. The days were shorter, and dusk had fallen. "What? Won't do it?"

"I suppose I could convey the offer since some time has gone by, but that really won't be close."

Paul turned to look at the open space on his wall where the Stassen-Ratzer would, and should, be hung. "One hundred and *fifty* percent? I'm going up by *half* here."

"No, that won't do it. Good night, Mr. Reeves."

Misery. More misery, in fact, because he had failed a second time. He stood in thought at his slatted windows, yet noticed lights had just gone on in Ahmed and Jennifer's apartment. Another visit from Bill? He pulled a slat down with his finger. Across the way he could see two men in suits moving about the bedroom, inspecting it. One waved a handheld device at the light fixtures. He checked something on his device, unscrewed the switch plate, inserted something, then replaced the plate. He repeated this in Jennifer and Ahmed's grand living room— Paul followed to the next window—then checked the device in his hand. Their apartment was decorated in a plush decorator's style that featured pastel tableaus the eye could linger over, finding expensive knickknacks and subtle proofs of travel and culture; it was all too perfect for him, too professional looking, and besides, there were no maps. But why would anyone bug Ahmed and Jennifer's apartment, unless Ahmed knew about Bill's visit?

The man drew toward the window and produced a high-powered flashlight, throwing a sharp beam against Paul's window. He dropped the slat and eased back, watching the striated beam play back and forth across his maps until the beam passed away and reappeared in his kitchen, the next room over. They could see into that easily enough, but all the beam would reveal was a typical Manhattan apartment kitchen with high-end steel appliances and some pots hanging above the oven. The light faded from there, too.

A moment later he heard footsteps outside his apartment door. He eased close by. A hand tried the doorknob. Locked. Pulled on it. The voices conferred. They were low and male. He could barely hear them, but it seemed they were not speaking English.

Paul quickly unlocked the door and yanked it open. "What do you want?"

Two younger men in suits, carrying briefcases. "Oh, mistake, we apologize."

"Why did you just try to open my door?"

They just stood there, saying nothing.

"You went to the wrong apartment, you mean?"

"Yes, yes, that it is."

"There are only two apartments on this floor."

"Yes, wrong apartment."

One of the men's phones rang. He answered, in whatever language he was speaking. An indistinct pause followed. The man grunted to his partner, then went to summon the elevator.

"But you were in the other apartment already."

"No, no. We came to wrong door."

The man turned to go.

"Hey!" Paul said. "You *were* in the other apartment. I just saw you there."

"No, no, you are mistaken."

"Get the fuck out of here!" Paul said. "Go on, get out of here before I call the cops." He pulled out his phone and opened the camera. "You guys willing to smile—?"

The man slapped Paul's hand, sending the phone across the floor.

"Hey!"

The elevator doors opened and the men hurried inside. Paul felt a sense of relief. He wondered if he should call the desk downstairs. But maybe that wasn't a good idea. If Ahmed found out, he would think, correctly, that Paul knew he was up to something. Better, perhaps, not to tip him off.

He was standing in his own doorway, wondering what to do, when the other set of elevator doors binged open and Jennifer stepped out, just like that. Blond hair up in a perky ponytail, bangle bracelets and rings, green dress above the knees, low heels. She smiled immediately. "Well, hello! Were you faithfully waiting for me?" She was carrying a thick bundle of mail and two big bright shopping bags in each hand.

"Come with me," Paul told her firmly. "Straight to my apartment."

Mystified, she nonetheless followed him through the door, dropping her mail and packages on his kitchen table. "What?" she said. "Paul?"

He closed and locked the door.

"Sit."

She did. "Now you're scaring me."

"I think two guys bugged your apartment just now."

"What?"

He explained all that he had just seen. Jennifer took it in. "I'm getting a little freaked out by what's going on. I'm being followed, you know."

"I saw Bill this morning."

She nodded brusquely. "I know. He said you told him to leave town."

"And he wants you to leave Ahmed and go with him."

Jennifer didn't answer. But her expression told him that it had all come to this moment, a woman choosing, or forced to choose, between two men.

"I think he got in some kind of fight."

Jennifer looked up, frowning. "When?"

"Tuesday night, in my house."

"He seems fine, not like he got into a fight."

Paul studied Jennifer, irritated on his own behalf, and maybe Bill's, too. "Hey, let me see if I got this right, okay? You go to the Christie's auction with me. Ahmed is on an ocean liner in the middle of the Atlantic. Bill shows up, surprises you. You come back here with him and jump in bed."

"You saw us?" Jennifer cried.

"I did."

"You watched?"

"Just for a moment."

Her expression was cold. "That's kind of weird and upsetting, Paul."

"And also completely unexpected by me. Let me continue, okay?"

But she had cast her expression away from him, in fury.

"I didn't seek this out, Jennifer."

She exhaled. "I know."

"Anyway, so then Ahmed comes home, may or may not suspect something, but then, mysteriously, the next night, Monday, my cab gets followed when I take Bill to my house because he is drunk. Which you asked me to do. Then Wednesday morning my neighbors call me up and tell me a vicious fight just took place inside my house! Apparently Bill got the better of his assailant but won't discuss it, not with me, anyway. Now he is hanging around somewhere, living out of his truck parked at JFK, waiting for you to leave Ahmed, except I don't think you really are going to do that."

I have to remember how much younger she is, Paul reminded himself, there are things she doesn't know yet. But Jennifer said nothing, instead running her hand along his kitchen counter absentmindedly.

"Bill and you go way back . . . he told me the whole romantic story. Then there are men in your apartment who look like they are bugging the place, or something. You see what's going on?"

"Of course I do!" she snapped. "Ahmed's *playing* with me! He's pretending not to know, but letting me know he does!"

Paul let her calm down. Then he said, "Why don't you just tell Bill it was all a big mistake and let him go?"

"Because it's not exactly all a big fucking mistake, okay?" Jennifer searched his eyes, angry and on the edge of tears. "Okay, I'm sorry."

Paul shrugged, then smiled, and she seemed to relax.

"You have any wine?"

"Of course." He maintained a modest wine rack, and found a bottle of merlot.

"Where's Ahmed?"

"He has some golf thing in New Jersey and won't be back until, I don't know, whenever."

"I'm going to order some food for us."

"Now I feel weird about going back to my apartment."

He put down the bottle and two glasses. "Understandable."

"Is Rachel coming over tonight?" Jennifer asked.

"She's entertaining clients who are in town."

"Are you sad not to be invited?"

"I'm ecstatic not to be invited—but she knows that."

"You guys have a good thing." But it was more a question than a statement.

"Yes," he agreed, to keep things simple.

"You do know she's *totally* in love with you."

He didn't know that, or what it really meant even if she were. But this was all deflection by Jennifer. He suggested she go sit in his living room, then ordered some Indian food from a place that delivered quickly. "So Bill was telling me how the two of you met."

"That was a long time ago." She fell back into the sofa, her eyes far away. "I knew him as a girl, back when I was in Reading . . . I don't know if I can really talk about this, Paul. There's a lot of stuff from that time, you know, that I don't like to remember much."

They sat quietly. A siren ran away on a far avenue, the soft under-hum of the city out there in the night. Jennifer topped off her glass of wine. "You have to understand what kind of childhood I had, okay?" She searched his face. "My mother was, like, a *really* good-looking girl. I've told you that before. She got pregnant and had me. She and my father were married and he did these long contracts working on oil rigs in the Gulf of Mexico. He was gone for three months at a time. It was the best way to make money. They had a small house, just a little two-bedroom, nothing special. There was a backyard and a swing set. I grew up there. When I was four, my mother got a phone call from the plat-form subcontracting company saying there had been an accident . . . What had happened was that a load of pipes had broken loose and fallen onto one of the lower platforms and killed my father. Each pipe weighed eight hundred pounds. They sent his body back. So that was my daddy. I sort of remember a funeral, but I'm not sure if it's because people told me about it later. I guess I still— I don't really know what it means. I was so young." She looked at her wine, then drank. "My mother got this job at a bar waiting tables, then one day her dentist said he was trying to start promoting himself and had an idea. So in the summers at the Reading Phillies games, she would do a seventh-inning promo-tion for the dentist. She would dress up in this white fairy costume— cut really short, you know—and take this big five-foot-long toothbrush and go out and scrub the bases with the brush, like they were big teeth.

At first she was self-conscious about it, but then she liked it, everybody knew her, and she kind of started to vamp it up. Bend over a little, stuff like that. Then they put me in the same little matching outfit and I would go with her with my little matching toothbrush and people totally loved that."

She paused, remembering it, and Paul realized that Jennifer was still young enough that her childhood was available to her in ways he had now lost, that she could easily conjure the feeling of being a little girl.

"We'd have the radio on in our kitchen broadcasting the game and in the second inning we would get dressed and then drive over to the park, which was just a few minutes away. We would go in the press door and go down around through the tunnels and then come out the home team dugout when the music started in the seventh-inning stretch. People liked us and cheered and the lights were on us and it was the happiest I was with my mother. The happiest time, *ever*. She was young and beautiful and I was with her with my hair brushed and with combs in it and it was just kind of this magical four minutes."

"Sounds fun." Jennifer now seemed a little drunk to him.

"It *was*. She would go out first and start scrubbing first base and kind of bend over in a provocative way—you know, wiggle her butt as they started to play the ad for the dentist over the loudspeaker system— and then as soon as she was done with first and starting to move to second, I would run out and give first a few extra scrubs with the brush. Then I would almost catch up to her by second base, and I would catch up to her by third base, and then we would go down the third-base line holding hands and scrub home plate together. It was a big show. There was cheering and we'd always wave to everybody, then prance off just the way we had come. We were supposed to go through the home dugout as fast as possible. Then we'd go to the press office, and the stadium manager had hot dogs and Cokes for us, and then we'd drive home. She washed the costumes out every few games and left them on the line to dry. Mine next to hers, exactly the same, except smaller."

"That's a sweet story."

Jennifer smiled, but her eyes were distant. "We did that for every home game for three summers in a row. They paid her two hundred dollars a week during the season. It helped business at the bar because men noticed her at the park and they wanted to see her. Also the ball-players who were in town for the summer would see her and get her number. She was older than a lot of them, they were nineteen or twenty and she was already twenty-eight, but it didn't matter. She was *hot*. I know that's weird for a daughter to say, but it's true! Every summer there was one new guy, usually. I learned a lot about baseball, let me tell you. In high school I was the manager on the boys' team and scored the games."

"You ever see a Yankees or Mets game with Ahmed?"

"He doesn't really like baseball. He goes to games when it's a work thing, but otherwise, no."

"Does he know you like it?"

"He does, yeah. But it reminds him of where I came from and he doesn't like that."

Their food arrived and they sat eating. "So you were a teenager when you met Bill?" he asked.

"We met once earlier, when I was like sixteen, then got together a year later. It was the summer before my senior year in high school. He was a year older. He was playing for a team down in Virginia that summer. My mother wasn't really paying much attention to me anymore. She started working at the bar and when I was twelve she got pregnant with this guy who was some kind of mortgage broker in town and he took her out a lot. They had the baby and it was a little girl, and my mom was really involved with her when I was growing up. Her name is Stephanie, she's really sweet. I miss her. But my mom really liked working at the bar and kept on doing it, which probably wasn't great for her relationship, and eventually the thing with the mortgage guy didn't work out and there were all kinds of custody problems and stuff, and she basically drank too much, partly at the bar, and things got, like, *rough*. The mortgage guy got married to another woman and wanted custody of Stephanie. I don't like to think about all this, okay? It's not much fun. I was just kind of going to school, and then that summer here comes Bill Wilkerson from Texas and I was praying he wouldn't be sent to another team during the summer. The rookie league schedule is pretty short. Anyway, that's how I had this thing with Bill. He was an outfielder and could run and swing the bat. He had a great arm from right field."

"You stayed in contact when he went overseas later?"

"Not really at first."

The chronology seemed jumbled up to Paul, but he didn't press her. "Then how did he know where—"

"My mother told him," she interrupted. "She called to tell me he was coming to the city to talk. I didn't want to see him again. But I guess he looked me up, got the apartment address, and then followed me without me knowing. I walked to your office that day, you know, just because it was so nice."

He caught a tone in her voice, the sense that she was listening to her own words a little too carefully to see how they sounded. Jennifer seemed to have forgotten that Paul had been sitting next to her at Christie's and seen her sudden reaction to the sight of Bill. It wasn't one of measured reserve or wariness. She'd gone straight to him, left, and headed to her apartment. Her story somehow wrapped the real sequence in a blurring, warping narrative in case anyone, that being Ahmed, inquired.

"When did you come to New York?"

"I was nineteen, almost twenty."

He realized he hadn't fully considered what it took for a young girl to come to New York City and to make her way in the world. Even given Jennifer's beauty, this would not have been enough, not necessarily, to deliver her to a greater degree of safety.

"I didn't know anything." Jennifer lay back on the sofa and looked toward the lights outside the window. "I mean, there were lots of people my age, but I didn't know how to, you know, operate."

Upon her arrival, she said, she found a room in a cheap tourist hotel in Chinatown and went looking for a job. "I had exactly six hundred and twelve dollars. I remember that. I didn't even understand how little money that was." She applied to be a typist with a temporary agency and lied on her résumé, what there was of it, anyway, and claimed she had two years of college at Penn State, majoring in event planning. But a pretty girl is a pretty girl. The interviewer, who no doubt had seen and heard every possible prevarication involving employment and had nonetheless learned to make placements with the stream of variegated humanity that presented itself, assigned Jennifer a job with a catering company that needed servers. She would wear a white blouse, black pants, and black sneakers. And tie her hair up. The interviewer took Jennifer's basic information and told her to report the next evening to an address on Central Park West.

Over the next few weeks, Jennifer said, she made enough money to eat, do her laundry, and pay her room rate in the hotel. She discovered the used-clothing stores in the Village and in Brooklyn, and with careful bargaining began to amass a bit of a wardrobe, including a fetching cocktail dress that she knew she could wear when the weather got warm. When some of the other servers were putting together a group house in Williamsburg, they asked if she was interested. Yes, she said. Within a year she had worked as a waitress, a food server, and then as a "personal assistant" to one of the many faded movie stars who lived in Manhattan. She told Paul the man's name but it meant nothing to him. "He was in his sixties, super skinny, kind of half-dead. My job was to call the same number every morning and have his heroin delivered. Nice, right? A guy showed up with a paper bag that had a baggie and a needle. It was a regular service. Then I got this guy his lunch at a deli, which was always a Philadelphia cheesesteak and potato salad, then came back to his apartment and woke him up. Then he lay around and shot up. It was kind of scary, I thought he was going to die. One time he called me into his bedroom, which smelled terrible, and made me help him shoot up by injecting into his penis. Because he couldn't find other good veins. He needed me to hold the needle because his hands were shaking. It was totally disgusting. That weirded me out and I quit the same day."

"Sounds like a prudent decision."

Jennifer laughed. "Then I got this job as a 'product hostess' at rock concerts handing out sample products from the sponsors. Totally stupid job."

But at one of the events, she said, an older British man approached her and asked her name. She ended up back at his apartment and was aghast at the dazzling, panoramic view from his bedroom window. "I don't know if I was having sex with him or with his apartment," she said. "It was ridiculous, the sixty-eighth floor or something. You got dizzy looking down."

Within a few weeks, the man had rented her a small apartment in Morningside Heights. He was married, with a family in London. They had three children, the youngest a boy who was autistic. His wife was clinically depressed. The bank the man worked for insisted he stay in New York, and he was, he admitted, long on cash and short on companionship. He could not let Jennifer move into his Manhattan apartment because his family visited him every month or two, and moreover, there were people in the building who would notice her coming and going. But he wanted to make an arrangement, which was that he would spend several nights a week with her, when he wanted, and that she not sleep with anyone else. He would be the first to admit that he was not physically prepossessing in any way, but he would try to make up for it by taking her to the best restaurants and entertainments.

"You must have liked him at least a little," Paul said.

"Actually, I really did. He was *nice*, you know? Sweet. Totally kind to me. He took me to Broadway shows and good restaurants and to some museums. I felt sorry for him, and I wasn't really seeing anyone else," Jennifer remembered aloud. "So I just sort of did it. I asked him how he was going to handle the money. It was four thousand dollars a month. I remember that. Because my rent was thirteen hundred dollars and I had about six hundred a week for everything else. It was basically enough.

"His name was Philip. He was so decent to me. I have to say that. You could tell me it was totally immoral and all that stuff, but I chose to do it. He was lonely and didn't want to get into a real relationship. Of course, we started to *have* a relationship. I cooked for him in my apartment. He bought me clothes, too. He was pretty out of shape, and he smoked too much. But he was witty and he didn't take himself too seriously. Loved watching the European soccer games on cable. He liked to read me stories out of the newspaper, which I liked, too. It was kind of a daddy thing, I admit. One time his wife called him and I could hear the kids screaming in the background, their high British children's voices going, 'Oh, Mummy,' like that. Here he was trying to support them by living in another country." She shrugged, recollecting it. "He was unhappy and I just made him a little happier."

"New York is full of arrangements like this."

"I guess." She looked at Paul. "You ever do anything like that?"

"Not exactly."

"Tell me!"

"When I was between wives, I had various girlfriends. Sometimes they asked me for help financially . . . I didn't mind. This is a hard city. How did it end with Philip?"

"Oh, I didn't tell you that." Jennifer froze a moment, the memory coming to her. "The little boy, the one who had autism, drank something that was under the sink, something to clean pipes, and he was rushed to a London hospital and Philip met me the next day and said that he was very, very sorry but he had to go back to England, probably for good. His wife was in terrible shape. I think he felt guilty about being with me and that somehow it was his fault that the little boy did that. It was the end of summer, when the city just empties out in August, and we went for this long walk through Central Park, and he took me to some Italian place on Amsterdam Avenue, and then we walked back to his apartment. He had taken out some pictures of his wife and children. He'd been looking at them. I'd never seen them before. His wife was absolutely beautiful, and so were the children. I was pretty moved by it, you know? Here was this man with these children and this wife and yet he was lonely enough to be with me."

"Well, you are, shall we say, an attractive woman."

"Thank you for noticing, Paul. I thought I left you cold."

She gave him a flirty little smile, and he did not know what it meant, if anything. At some level, Jennifer still needed the constant approval of men. That she was married to Ahmed seemed to be a rigid truth in some moments and an insubstantial technicality in others. He could understand why the memory of her, the future possibility of her, would have driven Bill to do the things he had done.

"Finish the story about Philip."

"Right. So I just walked through his apartment with him. The windows were open and it was hot, like it gets in August. He said he was flying out the next day and had put in for a transfer back to London. His company didn't want to do it but would. His career was probably damaged a bit. We sat on his little balcony. I had very conflicted feelings. I liked him. Being in bed with him was okay, you know, good enough. But he was my means of income and I hadn't saved any money. So I was panicking about that. But I couldn't say anything really because here he was upset about his family. So we sort of sat there. He was going to miss me emotionally more than I was going to miss him. He told me not to think about our relationship, just live life forward. He said he knew I needed money and he was leaving me in the lurch, as he put it. I said, don't worry about me. I had something like seven hundred dollars to my name, and the rent was due. He said he had been trying to figure out how to help me. He took his watch off. 'This is a Patek Philippe watch,' he said. 'It's one year old and sells new for thirty-eight thousand dollars. I bought it for myself when I got this job. It is what I have looked at every time I was waiting to see you. I look at the minute and hour hands and I think of you. When I will see you next. So if I take this watch home with me, I will just think of New York and you. That will not help me. In fact, it will only make me sad. So I contacted the local dealer. Today. I told him I wanted to sell it back, and he said he would give me seventeen thousand for it and they would be able to resell it for twenty-five maybe. I said fine. But I told him that I was going to give it to you and that he should pay you the money. It will be a check made out to you.'"

"Clever," noted Paul. "No record."

"I was surprised, of course. I'd never heard of such a thing. Then he gave me the dealer's card and told me to be there at two p.m. the next day. So I took the watch and put it in my bag. We sort of sat there, the night going on. Then I told him I wanted to go to bed one more time. And we did. It was sad. He had problems doing it. Afterward he cried and everything was just awful. His life was crashing down on him, I guess. I told him it was best if we never contacted each other again and he agreed. So I left that night, took a cab. It was lonely. The next day I went to the dealer and he said there had been a misunderstanding and the most he could offer was nine thousand dollars."

"He was ripping you off."

"Total rip-off, but I took it."

With that money, she said, she could exist for a couple of months, if she was careful, and her first order of business was to find a job.

"It was scary, but kind of exciting. No one from my past knew where I was. I could do anything, be anywhere. I should have called home more."

"How did you meet Ahmed?"

"That's a long story. Will you open another bottle?"

He retreated to the kitchen, found a bottle, and returned. Jennifer held up her glass. She was, he saw, enjoying the reprieve from her current situation, and indeed, it appeared she had forgotten about Bill entirely.

"Thanks, Paul. I guess I'm a little drunk, but it's okay. So, okay, so I was like twenty-one then, totally alone, and I knew I needed to find some kind of work before my money ran out. I didn't know what to *do*, but my lease was up and I found this cheap apartment on 106th and Amsterdam. It was a share and this girl named Allison was my roommate. She was always on her phone to her mother crying and fighting. It was pretty bad. She had some kind of eating disorder where she would buy these expensive chocolate candies with creamy fillings and chew them, then spit them out into the trash. She would eat ten, one by one, spitting them out. Weird. There was drug dealing on the block. But I still didn't know the city very well. So I just walked up Broadway and saw the Columbia campus. I had heard of Columbia, of course, but I had never been on an Ivy League campus and I was sort of amazed that I could just walk in. Nobody stopped me, nobody told me I didn't belong. All these genius people around me. You could *see* the girls were smart, just by the way they talked and carried themselves and looked."

"Oh, there are many kinds of smart."

"I know. But it was attractive to me. I started hanging out there and then got asked out. The guys didn't really care I wasn't a student there.

They were mean about the Barnard College girls, called them 'barnyard,' stuff like that."

"Same as when I was there," Paul said.

"Oh, I didn't know you went there."

"I was a punk. Keep telling the story."

At Columbia, she said, she met young men whose parents were doctors and lawyers and executives and lived in places like the Back Bay of Boston and Chevy Chase, Maryland, and Hyde Park, Chicago. She was acutely attuned to the signifiers and habits of wealth, knowing she had started to make her way in a crowd of people who would soon inhabit this world. She bought better dresses and skirts and sweaters and shoes, and through cultural mimicry and genuine self-enlightenment positioned herself for whatever might come next, so long as it was a step upward. She made herself peruse *The New York Times*, she tried reading literary novels, and watched the ladies shopping at Bergdorf Goodman.

"You ever see your family?" Paul asked. "Did you go home?"

"Not really. At Thanksgiving. But it was hard. I sort of didn't know them anymore."

Again, he sensed a hesitation in her voice, the same halting articulation that some of his clients suffered when the topic of their backgrounds came up. Everyone had a private journey, though, and no one was ever completely known by anyone.

"But then some good stuff happened," said Jennifer brightly, perhaps trying to distract him from his perception of her. "Totally unexpected." One of her friends explained how much she was making in a real estate office, and that to be a junior agent all you had to do was take a twelve-hour course and pass an easy test. The days were long but you made real money. A late-afternoon, ten-minute interview was soon arranged, just a hi-nice-to-meet-you. The head agent, a flinty blonde who had ridden not just a few real estate cycles but back in her better days the fleshy haunches of various clients, welcomed her into a mammoth, glass-walled office, and ten minutes became an hour, the agent probably recognizing in Jennifer the right proportions of beauty, hunger, psychic desperation, illusion, stamina, and emergent greed. Yes, the first inklings of Manhattan greed, the wish for more and then more again and then triple that. Her name was Ms. Kate Riven. "I *loved* her," Jennifer said, excited to talk about someone other than herself. "She was so *so* wicked and honest and smart. She dressed perfectly, she drank too much, she had great legs, she was such a creature!"

Ms. Kate Riven took her out for a drink, continued Jennifer, and told her that she needed to understand that the real estate market in New York City was presenting yet *another* once-in-a-lifetime opportunity. Cash was everywhere, pouring out of windows, being blown into the gutters by taxis, spinning in the revolving doors of Rockefeller Center, falling out of people's mouths. Her own plan, said Ms. Riven, was to make as much as possible as quickly as possible, because it was all going to crash sooner or later. She'd gotten her tits done, in anticipation of the cresting market. "I hope they stay up as long as the market does!" she shrieked agreeably. But, meanwhile, she needed help, because she was one person with "only three phones, two hands, and one twat." And she, Ms. Riven, had identified Jennifer as the person who was going to help her and make money herself. Jennifer was to listen to Ms. Riven, do as she said, be available constantly, and be loyal. "I just totally worshipped her, okay? She was brassy and cool and fearless and *mean*. She used to gossip about all the other agents—who was getting a divorce, who was drinking too much. I knew I would learn *everything* from her."

Finally, Jennifer realized, she was meeting New York City head-on, confronting raw opportunity, the city overtly challenging her in the way it was so fabled to do. "If you are loyal to me," Ms. Kate Riven told her, "you will be fine. If you are not, I will cut you *out*, do you understand me? I expect groveling and fear. *Really*. I can be nasty, okay? Just ask around. Now then, I am going to tell you all of my secrets, but one at a time. You are a beautiful girl, but we are going to make you *more* beautiful. We are going to put you on a six-thousand-dollar-a-month draw for now. You will make more eventually. All you have to do is make a few deals happen this year and you will have paid for yourself. I know that you don't have any education. You make spelling errors sometimes and more important you make diction errors. We are going to fix all that, okay? You sound like you come from someplace, not New Jersey exactly, but somewhere . . . Pennsylvania? Yes, that nasalness, you hear it in Philadelphia sometimes. It's *ugly*. People here will judge you for it, okay? Also, no visible tattoos or piercings! You want to stick a pin in your navel, no problem. But I don't want to *see* it. If I see it, you're fired. Most of the people you are going to be dealing with are fancy women. The *wives*. Get it? Wives *pick* the apartments. Listen to me, in real estate everything is a family relationship. What do I mean by that? I mean that the client, the buyer, has to be able to put you in a family role. I know that is confusing, but I want you to listen to me, okay? For middle-aged women, you are a *daughter*. You are dutiful and respectful and you don't ask them questions that are too personal. Never bring up the husband, unless they do. Don't be *interested* in the husbands in any way! Now, for the younger women, maybe they have a hot husband or boy-friend, something, you are the *confidante*, okay? The girlfriend. That's easy. For older men, older than sixty—you won't see too many of them because they are either dead or rich or can't be bothered—you are the *granddaughter*. Now, for the tricky part, the younger men. For the men around fifty, you are either the super-young trophy wife or the *mistress*. I'm not saying you have to sleep with these schmuckos, and lemme tell you, a lot of them are pure barf-o-rama, just to *think* about it—I was with one guy when his toupee came off at just the wrong moment, right? Don't get me started—but you are standing there in that apartment and they have to have this big revelation, that *this* is the kind of hot girl who likes apartments like this one! You are sort of dressing the place up, okay? You got that? See, everybody has a different role! For me, it's different. For the sixty-year-old men, I'm like the second wife, maybe the third. They know nasty *bee-atches* like me want the ring, the cash, the house upstate. For women around forty, forty-five, I'm the *sister*, right? I make suggestions, I listen, I know what they are going through. All the problems. For the younger women, I'm like the older sister, maybe a little more worldly, like a younger aunt even. Someone who *knows*, okay? I'm wise to the world. They like that. For the younger men, I always try to make them feel attractive. I try to make them feel that I wish I was younger so that they would want me. Now, sometimes in this business—

are you listening?—you come across the killer. What do I mean about that? I mean the guy who is the pure stud. He's a corporate guy, he's got his own business, he's a hotshot doctor, probably a surgeon. You want to be sure you get the deal done with *him*. Because he has the knack of identifying good people. He didn't get there by himself, baby. He knows where the money is. He moves fast when he likes what he sees. You want to be on *his* list. Try to get the seller to come down, especially for that guy. With him . . ." Kate Riven paused. "You *do* what you *need* to do, okay? Now, the last thing we've got to talk about is a very touchy subject. You probably don't know much about it, but I'm going to discuss it anyway. It's one of my professional secrets, okay? If a woman is over maybe forty-three, more or less, you have to figure out one thing. You have to figure out if she's premenopausal! You *have* to know, because it will affect your business. Do you *actually* understand what happens during menopause? No? Don't lie, I can tell you don't know! Most girls don't. You're too young! It's like this terrible secret no one talks about! Your hormones crash. These women are in *crisis*. They might look good, but their hormones are going wild on them. They are getting weird hot flashes and sweating all the night. Their breasts hurt because they are getting their periods like five weeks straight. They are angry for no reason, I mean wild freaking *bee-atches*, they are tearful, they can't sleep, they are exhausted. Not much fun for hubby, either. You can't imagine it, honey! For you it's all juicy and tight and fun. These ladies are having a lot of trouble in the sex department. Things are kinda unhappy down there. Things are *dry*, okay? There are weird new pains they never had before. They don't have any desire. And their husbands don't like it. Their husbands are being patient but starting to understand that it's only going to get worse! Okay? So, guess what, there's a real estate transaction happening! Why? Maybe the couple is looking for a new nest, to be happy again! Probably the husband agreed to it because she's driving him up the wall. Could be a lot of things. These women will be very, very unpredictable! Very emotional. Excited one day, suicidal the next. I'm not kidding! They go up and down and they can be very, very bitchy. They will tell you that you wasted their time, that you don't understand what they are looking for, that your properties are all dogs. They will be nasty and rude and change their minds a million times. They will call you a *cunt*—I have actually had that happen! When a woman calls *another* woman a cunt it's a totally different thing, right? Your job is very hard here, do you know why? Because they *hate* you! They know that you are still young like they were. You are young, they are *old*. You have healthy eggs, they have . . . I don't know *what*, but nobody wants to know. They think you don't understand their problems, and guess what? You don't! You can't take it personally! Young women always take everything so, so personally! I was like that, too. Then you learn, okay? Do your job with them, get the paperwork back and just keep it moving. These women also have kids in school driving them nuts, teenagers drinking, doing things they shouldn't do, husbands who are fed up with everything, okay? Maybe tomorrow I will talk to you about the foreign buyers, the Chinese women, the Russian women, they can be nasty like you don't know what. And gay men, that's a whole other situation! But we will get to that. That's enough for now, okay? You're with me, Jenny—no, it's always *Jennifer*, sounds like a perfume, classier, Jenny is a sixteen-year-old cheerleader, okay?—you are going to work that nice little fanny off for me and make me some money and make some money for yourself. I want you here in the office by eight thirty every morning. I don't care if you were drinking Manhattans until four or the boy was actually nice to you. I don't care if you had a fight or your roommate is suicidal or you have a temperature or a migraine or a yeast infection. I want you in the office, looking totally *great*. Mascara, mascara, mascara. Sexy stuff, mascara, right? Lip gloss, perfume, a little necklace, maybe modest pearl earrings. You can pick up a nice pair for nine hundred dollars at Tiffany's. And you will be at work until you are *done*. Don't schedule anything, dinner, whatever, until eight p.m. We have money to make, okay?"

And six months later, that was how she met Ahmed, Jennifer said, while trying to make money. He was buying an apartment and Ms. Kate Riven, sensing a fabulous prospect, had set up a series of showings for him and could not make the last one, due to a bad Botox reaction, and so Jennifer took the contact card and met him at the building, an old one in the East Seventies. He was twenty minutes late, and when he came through the door she introduced herself, suddenly made nervous by him. Tall, elegant in a great suit, very confident of himself. "He wasn't expecting someone so young and asked me about my qualifications, and I had to lie, basically, and he didn't seem interested at all in the apartment. But he said he was taking me to dinner that night. And I think we went out to dinner the next four nights. Then he had a business trip to London, where I'd never been, and he flew me over, I had to get my passport in, like, one *day*, and then I had to explain to Kate Riven and she was pretty understanding actually, and then basically he took me over." She giggled, her head flush with wine. "It wasn't a *hostile* takeover, but it was definitely a takeover."

"How soon did you get married?"

"That's sort of the crazy part, it was after just three months. I hadn't even turned twenty-three."

"Wow."

"Yes. Crazy. It had to be between business trips. His family didn't like me, I could tell. They thought I was just a floozy gold digger he'd found. His mother said, when we met for the first time, and I quote, 'Oh God, not again.' "

"What was that supposed to mean?"

"I don't know. Whatever. I mean, Ahmed was so certain and so aggressive and so totally everything that I just thought this man really wants me and I'm kind of lost in my life and I'll never have this opportunity again. I know that sounds crass or something, but *it's true*." Jennifer glanced at her phone. "He's going to be home soon."

She started thumbing through her texts in the mindless, automatic way her generation did now. Three months, not long enough to get to know someone. She'd basically sold herself to Ahmed. Not that anyone had admitted it. His company's funds, Paul knew, had no less than $259 billion to invest, an amount so huge that it had to be broken down into many lesser amounts in order to be properly invested. The horizon of the fund's management was literally limitless; there was nowhere on earth that it could not go, if it so chose. They managed hundreds of investments, all affected by political realities on the ground, regulation, the volatility of commodities, management ability (and error), technology changes, and the intersection and overlapping of markets and competitors. Ahmed kept as much of this in his head as could perhaps be expected, reading reports and updates at night, and heading off to morning meetings before eight nearly every day. Paul wondered what Ahmed's marriage to Jennifer might actually mean to him under these circumstances. While it was apparent that Ahmed had more than enough to challenge him, it was also clear that Jennifer had little that she was required to do. Of course, she could amuse herself with new exercise regimes, beauty treatments, shopping experiences, travel, reading, movies, music lessons, and so on and so on. Yet the moment she'd seen Bill Wilkerson in the Christie's auction room, her internal structures of passivity and compliance had reversed their polarities and become unified into pure, defiant passion. She had been in a public space where people might well know her husband, and yet she had given herself over to the sight and presence of Wilkerson. It made Paul wonder if instead of individuals having one central identity, fused and consistent throughout, they had a basket of identities that, while not necessarily in conflict with one another, were nonetheless distinct and surprisingly independent of the others. Had the arrival of Bill Wilkerson caused the temporary abandonment of Jennifer's identity as Ahmed's wife and corporate helpmeet? And illuminated another of her selves, an older one, perhaps, but also a more essential self, one kept dormant? That no transition from one to the other was required was notable, but not shocking. But perhaps everyone was like this, Paul thought. It seemed so. Now he saw Jennifer's head bent in concentration as she sat texting, her blond hair a luminous veil hiding her eyes from him. She was beautiful, every minute of every day, without trying, and for a moment he again understood why Bill had launched himself after her.

Jennifer looked up now, perhaps sensing his scrutiny. "Oh, Paul, I'd better go before he gets home." She stood up unsteadily and he helped her to the door and made sure she got into her apartment.

"Good night," he said.

At the doorway, she turned back and gave him a friendly but absolutely affectionate kiss, hugging him tightly enough that he could feel her breasts against his chest. "Thank you so much, Paul, thank you for listening to me," she said, the wine in her breath. "You know me just so well."

I doubt that, he told himself as he closed his own apartment door, I doubt that very much. He noticed then that Jennifer had left not only her bags of packages, which could wait until tomorrow, but also the fat bundle of mail she'd picked up downstairs. Out of curiosity he inspected it. Bills, flyers, catalogs from high-end retailers and vacation spots, bank statements, the usual junk that floods the mailboxes of the wealthy. Morgan Stanley, American Express, Louis Vuitton, Cunard cruises, Mercedes-Benz. He flipped through piece by piece. Under a bright catalog for a Swiss spa lay a thick manila envelope addressed to Ahmed from a small-town attorney in Ocean City, Maryland. Fat with documents, so fat the flap had been taped shut as a precaution. Paul had seen thousands of envelopes with legal documents, and this one had a portentous heft to it. Why would a high-powered corporate executive in New York have dealings with an obscure Maryland lawyer? Why would that same man hire men to bug his own apartment who then tried to gain entry to Paul's apartment? Why? He didn't know, except that it suggested that Ahmed was interested in secrets, either learning others', such as Jennifer's, of course, or perhaps keeping his own hidden. Paul again felt the weight of the envelope. There were dozens of pages in there, he knew. It's not my business, he thought. Only Ahmed's, strictly confidential dealings between an attorney and his client. Sacrosanct. Opening the envelope would violate federal law. And be professionally unethical. Really not a good idea. And yet, maybe not a bad one, either.

He was about to brazenly slit it open—but then had a better idea.

20

Prostitution was legal in Hong Kong, so long as each working girl conducted her business alone and not in a brothel, and this fact came as a joyful revelation to Amir, but less so than the more amazing datum that there were entire decrepit apartment buildings filled with working girls, hundreds of them advertising on the Internet and in the daily newspaper, and to say that he had indulged himself, taken advantage of his newfound opportunity, would be a gross understatement. The plan had been to use his unexpected tenure in Hong Kong to earnestly research new business opportunities, to finally go to the gym and lose fifty pounds, and to read serious books on serious topics. He had never been particularly successful with women, perhaps because he had always been somewhat fat, with thick adipose tissue concentrating itself around his nipples in a most unfortunate conical way, but whatever male anxieties he'd suffered about that and certain other measurable deficiencies had become more or less irrelevant in Hong Kong, so long as money continued to arrive from his uncle Hassan. By his count he'd had sex with five working girls, all of them Chinese, in the first three days after his arrival, and been introduced not only to their cooing sounds of transcendent pleasure as he mounted them but to certain of their more obscure yet memorable practices, one of which involved a string of jade stones placed most privately and pulled out with ecstatic timing.

Thus had the sting of his sudden dislocation from the United States been lessened, though when he was not out drinking or consorting with his chosen working girl, his mind returned to the troubling sequence of events that had gone bad so quickly. There were, Amir felt, several facts that he wished *clarified*, several points he needed to remember. This effort, however, was increasingly difficult to pursue once he had smoked opium, upon the teasing suggestion of one of his consorts, who may well have noticed that he never negotiated for her services, instead forking over the cash mindlessly, as if it had no real value to him, as if he knew there was an unlimited supply of it. That she worked for a Chinese triad was a foregone conclusion; despite its former legendary ubiquity, true opium that had not been converted to heroin was very difficult to procure, and came out of China only at great risk. But if you had the money, honey, people would do things for you. Once Amir had smoked the opium, his interest in sexual intercourse disappeared entirely. Sex with skinny, kiss-kiss Chinese hookers with gumdrop nipples was not peaceful; opium was *peaceful*. His habit started at three pipes a day but was soon ten. The apartment house on Temple Road contained, he learned, an apartment set aside for pilgrims such as he, and there, all the windows darkened, he met Russians, Americans, Brits, Germans, South Americans, Aussies, and Pakistanis. They said little to one another, barely registering other travelers on the road to nirvana. Amir's mind now wandered to the most delightful and pleasing of places, and he understood as never before how blighted and tense, how vapid and joyless, his former life had been—a deeply satisfying revelation. Yet in moments just after he awoke, he glimpsed memories recently forgotten. One such occurred as he waited for the girl to bring him the loaded pipe. He remembered that the Libyan operative had written down Ahmed's name in Arabic and his cell number on the hand-drawn map when planning William Wilkerson's abduction. The paper had been passed back and forth a bit. Amir could read Arabic but Ahmed could not. That beefy Libyan, alas, had of course turned up stabbed to death in a weedy lot near the old docks of Brooklyn. But what, Amir wondered, as the pipe was set gently before him, had become of that piece of paper? There were many other things written on it, particular elements of the plan. Ahmed had even said it should be burned, hadn't he? Was Amir remembering that correctly? It seemed quite likely the Libyan had kept the paper with him on that evening in question, since he'd have wanted to refer to it. But where was that paper now? Did the police have it? The hand-drawn map was potentially important, wasn't it? Important for Ahmed. I must remember this, Amir promised himself as he took his first puff of the pipe, and he quickly found a pen and endeavored to write himself a reminder on a folded bar flyer he found in his pocket.

But when he discovered that flyer in his pocket a day later as he stood at the rail of the green-and-white Star Ferry that churned between Hong Kong Island and Kowloon, he did not remember what had caused him to make such an indecipherable scrawl upon it. So he crumpled the piece of paper and flipped it into the turbulent emerald waters with no further thought.

21

Very few people understood the history of tape. That it was first made with tree sap, animal parts, and especially boiled fish bones, all natural adhesives slathered onto strips of eel skin, fabric, and rag-content paper. The invention of cellophane tape—cellulose plastic coated with pressure-sensitive, polymeric adhesive—in the 1930s changed everything, was an instant success. Since then, people had always loved cellophane tape; they bought it and stuck it on things and forgot it immediately. Although designed to mend, cellophane tape was also highly destructive, and once placed onto an historical document—such as a map—it was nearly impossible to physically remove without damaging the underlying fibers of the document, to say nothing of lifting away ink that had adhered to the tape's sticky surface. If you tore a piece of tape off the paper to which it was affixed, one could almost always tell. To make matters worse for the conservator of maps, dozens of different chemical compounds had been used in the creation of cellophane tape.

Yes, few people understood cellophane tape, but Paul knew one who did, Rollie Martin. He worked in a loft in the Williamsburg section of Brooklyn, in a high-ceilinged space painted white. Rollie himself wore a white jumpsuit every day, and he received calls or visitors for only one hour late each afternoon. This was when collectors of old letters, deeds, maps, and random documents made their way to him, beseeching him to somehow remove the crisscross of yellowed tape from their prized piece of paper without destroying the document itself. He was tall, skinny, bald, and altogether strange looking, which was probably good for business. It was said Rollie had a backload of three years of work. But Paul had been a good customer for much longer than that and Rollie always let him jump the line. Each day, even on Sunday, as George Winston played from his speakers, Rollie selected the documents to be worked on, inspected the paper, the tape, and the ink or inks on the document, and then tested them with liquid reagents in a marginal area to be sure that he'd identified the chemical structure of each. The goal, as he had explained to Paul in a bored monotone, was to apply the right chemical to the right compound—though it was rarely that easy. In a perfect world, he would quickly bathe the document in a customized solution in a broad shallow pan beneath a fume-exhaust hood specially made for him. Wearing heavy rubber gloves, he would draw the document across the pan, submerge it, and then watch closely. Sometimes the tape would instantly be liquefied, other times float in pieces above the document, or most likely be softened such that after Rollie lifted out the document, quickly blotted and flattened it, he was then able to remove the pieces using a magnifying glass and tweezers. It was painstaking work for which he needed absolute concentration and no interruption. Other documents were more complex. What if the document was crumpled, brittle, *and* taped together? Answer: Hydrate the document first so that it may be unfolded, flatten it, de-acidify it, and then remove the tape. What if the removal of the tape meant the document would be left in many pieces? Answer: Take a cheap document of similar type and age, cut unlinked strips, wet them, pound them into paste, and then connect the pieces of the original document with the paste, filling the gaps between them. Rollie could do that, too. He was a wizard.

But that was *restoration*. Paper conservators also could be helpful with *subterfuge*. Ha! Paul stood before Rollie with the envelope that Ahmed had received from the attorney in Maryland.

"You didn't want to just steam it open, I guess," Rollie joked.

"I didn't trust myself. Also, that can pucker the envelope flap. And can you even remove the tape that way?"

"You can, but it's a mess. And the envelope flap's polymeric adhesive will be pretty useless when it comes time for resealing." Rollie tried a fingernail under the flap edge, noted the tight seal. "Yep, they didn't want this opening accidentally." Then he measured the tape length and width with a ruler and made a notation. "But you knew that. And this, presumably, is very important to you."

"Yes." Well, maybe. He had no idea what was in the envelope.

Rollie consulted a spindle that had fifty-odd different kinds of clear cellophane tape, selected one, made sure it matched the one on the envelope, and noted, "We are breaking the law here."

"Yes," said Paul.

Rollie put on a new pair of latex gloves. "And you, my attorney friend, could be disbarred."

"Only if caught, Rollie. I'm sure this isn't the first time for you."

"Oh, please." He smiled a great crease of amusement. "You'd be *amazed* at the unhappy husbands and wives who come in here. Letters from lovers, credit card bills, doctors' bills, phone bills, wills." He took the envelope, held it up against an extremely bright light, inserted a long needle-thin device in the tiny opening that existed between the flap and the body of the envelope on the right-hand corner, and threaded it gently through the envelope such that it traveled between the back of the envelope and the document inside it. The light served as a kind of X-ray of the layers of paper. Then he penetrated the tiny orifice at the left-hand corner of the envelope so that it was effectively skewered.

Now Rollie depressed the plunger end of the needle device, and the thin metal rod bowed outward in two pieces, separating the interior documents from the envelope by a good inch. Then he took a small bottle of smelly solution, dunked a flat brush into it, and painted the tape and sealing areas of the envelope. "Count to thirty," he instructed. "And put on those gloves." He pointed to a spare pair. "Be careful that your skin does not touch the paper in any way."

On twenty-eight, the tape fell off wetly and the flap curled a bit at the edge and dropped open. Rollie pinched out the documents inside and handed them to Paul. "Cover letter facing the back of the envelope, with signature down at the bottom."

"Now what?"

"Take off the paper clip carefully and put it back in the same place. Do not read any of the documents. You have forty-five seconds. Otherwise I have to reglue the flap, and that is riskier."

Paul took three steps to Rollie's photocopier and put the stack into it, not reading the cover letter. The copies shot out with a satisfying rapidity. He made sure they were legible, then returned the originals to Rollie, who checked his watch and was waiting. "Cover letter was facing the back, with the signature toward the bottom," he repeated. He slipped the papers into the envelope, pressed the flap closed even as he contracted the interior metal bow, and put the envelope beneath a vacuum hood to extract any remnant odors of the solvent. Then he inserted the envelope in a large hydraulic press and brought it down with soft force. He lifted the press, inspected the sealed envelope, then cut off a measured piece of matching tape, bent down to get the placement of one end correct, smoothed it with a thumb swipe across the flap, did it again in the other direction, and held it up for inspection.

Paul nodded. "Amazing."

Rollie slipped the envelope into a larger translucent envelope. "Remember," he warned, "*drop* the envelope out of this one, don't pull it with your fingers."

"My fingerprints are already all over it."

"Oh well, then you'll need some explanation, though chances are the envelope will just get thrown away."

Paul paid Rollie his fee—five hundred dollars, in cash—and a minute later was downstairs. Manhattan yellow cabs were not always easy to find in the side streets of Williamsburg, so he took a Hasidic car service, and while the car lurched toward the Manhattan Bridge, he read the copy of the cover letter from the Law Offices of Burdett & Rush:

PERSONAL AND CONFIDENTIAL

Dear Mr. Mehraz,

Greetings. It's been many years since we have been in contact, but I have noted with satisfaction the progression of your remarkable professional career.

I am writing you today because from time to time we review our client files to see what reductions in file space can be made. Although as a matter of firm policy we inform clients that we may choose to destroy all paper files ten years after the time that they are closed, we do not always do so, especially when clients are still working and may need legal services in the future. Upon recent review, and in anticipation of my probable retirement in a few years, I noticed that we still had your paper files from your case of some twelve years ago last August. Instead of destroying the documents I am sending them to you for you to dispose of or to retain as you see fit. I have retained a complete copy, and if you would like me to send this copy to Mr. Roger Metcalfe in Manhattan, I will do so. (According to our records, he does *not* have a complete copy.) Please call or e-mail my office in the next month to confirm you would like this done; otherwise I will destroy my copy and consider the matter closed.

It was a pleasure to be of service to you all those years ago and I remain pleased that we were able to achieve a satisfactory result. I wish you continued success in your remarkable career and I remain,

Very truly yours,

Edward M. Burdett III

A perfunctory letter by a small-town lawyer, with a bit of flattery, the package sent to the home address and not to the office, which suggested that the enclosed pages were better left un-date-stamped and unfiled in Ahmed's corporate offices. And uninspected by a curious secretary. Why? Roger Metcalfe was an older, highly respected immigration attorney who'd handled naturalization cases at one of the full-service firms but might have left in one of the purges, no doubt taking his clients with him. Paul wasn't sure where he worked these days. He went on to peruse the file, which was arranged in chronological order and seemingly complete, including copies of court forms, official letters, billing notices, and letters from the Los Angeles offices of one Hassan Mehraz, who apparently was Ahmed's relative. On initial inspection, the documents suggested that an unfortunate personal incident had resulted in legal consequences requiring the massaging action of a well-connected and local law office. Hassan Mehraz, it was clear, had been paying the legal fees.

Then Paul found the essential documents in the stack and read them carefully. In the summer that Ahmed was twenty, he had been enjoying the beaches and summer sights of Ocean City, Maryland, and one night followed a young woman referred to as "Miss Colleen Jacobs" from the beach to a local restaurant to a bar called the Sand Pit. The nature of their interaction was not detailed, but it resulted in a harassment charge from Colleen Jacobs detailing "lewd, repetitive, and grossly suggestive comments" that the young woman did not find irresistibly charming. But there was more than that. Upon trying to enter the Sand Pit, Ahmed was carded by the bar's personnel and presented a false California ID that said he was twenty-three years old. An undercover policeman standing next to the bar's entrance confronted Ahmed in order to write him a misdemeanor ticket, but then also, perhaps irritated by Ahmed's good looks or entitled manner or, who knows, even his expensive clothes, cited him for public intoxication, the making of a false statement, and interference with police procedure. A scuffle ensued, which technically constituted assault of a police officer, a serious charge. Ahmed was arrested and put in the Ocean City jail for the night, released the next day after signing a variety of forms, and sent on his way. His relative Hassan, identified as Ahmed's uncle, whom he no doubt immediately called, swiftly retained Edward M. Burdett III, and the resulting paperwork indicated that the uncle had insisted the law firm make every effort possible to ensure that no permanent record of these events survived. After lengthy negotiation by Burdett with the court, Ahmed agreed to pay a fine of $10,000 and perform two hundred hours of public service, more than five times the typical amount for comparable charges. Burdett attributed this high number to the arresting officer's insistence that Ahmed had berated him and addressed the attending officers as "cracker rent-a-cops."

As for the charges by Miss Colleen Jacobs, they were dropped after Hassan Mehraz agreed to donate no less than $150,000 in the name of the Jacobs family to a charitable organization of their choosing, to have Ahmed undergo three months of monitored psychological counseling, and to formally apologize by a notarized letter. The Jacobs family was a locally prominent family in Cedar Rapids, Iowa, and they chose a Cedar Rapids Catholic church as their charity. A review of the billing detail showed extensive conversations between Edward Burdett III and Conrad Jacobs, presumably the father of the young woman, who felt his daughter had been publicly disgraced by a drunk Harvard student with a strange last name. In a letter from Jacobs to Burdett, the father wrote, "Upon my insistence, my daughter repeated word for word some of the vile things this overprivileged young man said to her, in public, statements involving his genitals and her orifices. The recollection of these statements brought her to tears and we have been forced to engage a therapist to deal with the trauma of this experience. Her grades and social confidence have suffered greatly, and we are fearful as to what the long-term consequences will be."

I bet minimal, Paul thought. Sounded to him like a hot college girl was trying to escape her overprotective Midwestern parents and may have given rich young Ahmed at least a hi-guy smile early on in the night in question, before Ahmed then became, yes, a complete jerk.

When Paul arrived home, he locked the file in his safe, and did a quick Internet search for Colleen Jacobs of Cedar Rapids, Iowa. He found that she had married a heart surgeon at University Hospital in nearby Iowa City a few years after the incident in Ocean City, Maryland, and that they had made their way to Chicago, where both their names appeared on various charity circuit items. The marriage-announcement photo, taken professionally and published in the Cedar Rapids *Gazette*, showed a beautiful blond woman with clear eyes and perfect features. She was, he saw, a certain type—*that* certain type, a woman who had much more than just a passing resemblance to Jennifer. An uncanny resemblance, in fact. Though maybe taller. But similarly striking. These beautiful blondes have always driven Ahmed mad, he thought.

The next morning, on his way to work, Paul rang Jennifer's doorbell. It was long after Ahmed usually left for his office. She came to the door looking sleepy, a little dazed, her hair unbrushed.

"You forgot all this mail the other night." He handed her the pile of magazines and bills that included the envelope from the Ocean City law firm.

"Oh, thanks," she said. "We get so much stupid junk." She threw the mail into a basket on a side table and stepped out into the hallway and closed the door behind her. "Can we talk?"

"Sure."

Jennifer lowered her voice to a whisper. "I think I'm going to leave Ahmed."

"Really?"

"I've been thinking about it."

He didn't quite believe her.

"Just wanted to tell you." She opened the door, and before she closed it, looked back. "Will you help me?" she asked softly.

"Of course, but how?"

"You know, the lawyers and stuff."

"You're sure?"

She didn't answer, instead staring at him until her beautiful blue eyes filled, then she shook her head *no* and disappeared behind the door.

22

She would have known by now, right? "You said you felt it within like two days," Rachel said to her sister on the phone. "I don't feel anything."

"Okay, so maybe it didn't happen this time."

"You don't *understand*. It's not like we are living together and having sex every night." Her sister just wasn't *authentically* sympathetic. Then Rachel remembered Paul's comment about how his first wife had lifted her knees up after sex. "Do you think he might think I'm trying to do this?" Her cab was crawling along, looking for an address. She didn't know this part of Brooklyn and doubted many did.

"I have no idea, Rachel. Men are totally weird. They can get some stuff and be totally unconscious about other stuff. Maybe it's an emotional thing for you. Maybe you are sort of not wanting it to happen?"

"What?"

"There are some doctors who say that if the woman isn't *open* to getting pregnant, like, *emotionally*, that it's less likely to happen."

This was why she hated her sister sometimes. "That's fucking nuts. I *want* to get pregnant!"

"This is not an argument!"

"Actually it is. Bye."

The taxi dropped her off next to a row of beaten-down structures that had been remodeled and re-sided so many times that it was hard to say what their original purpose had been. Outside a metal doorway stood perhaps a dozen people, most dressed in black, a few girls in short dresses. Rachel checked the address. She knew instantly she was dressed incorrectly for whatever was inside. She smiled at the people outside the door, one of them a lanky hipster with a man bun and skinny jeans that ended three inches above his ankles.

"Show's inside?" she asked.

"Yep," he said, his unspoken message being: *And people as uncool as you shouldn't be allowed to see it.*

Being a genuine hipster gentleman, he didn't bother to open the heavy door for her, so she yanked it open herself to reveal an industrial steel staircase and music throbbing from the floor above. She tramped up to the next landing and confronted a darkened cave of at least two hundred milling men and women, most in their twenties, many smoking and phone-obsessing and drinking and otherwise checking out the scene. The coolness factor was mega, through the roof. OMG, I am really old, Rachel mentally texted herself, but she pressed onward. Ten minutes of exploration and pushing past people revealed that there were two huge exhibit spaces with every inch of the walls crammed with art. The second floor also had a darkened DJ area with sunken chairs in which sat a number of girls, who, it was clear, were not there for the art but for the party later, which loomed as the real attraction for the crowd. The girls sat with their knees together in their short skirts, dancing in their seats or looking around or talking excitedly while smoking. Half of these chicks are going to have sex tonight, Rachel thought, and none of them knows yet with whom. Well, she had done that herself, back in the day. She had done all the things with all the people, and somehow survived her own stupidity. But she'd gotten quite an education in who men were, had survived long enough to actually be very clear about what she wanted in a man, and Paul, she knew, was it. He was just right. He had no idea how *perfect* he was, which made him all the more perfect still.

The third floor had a similar display space plus a stage area where a band was setting up, and then beyond it was an illegalish bar, where two young men in fedoras and white T-shirts slung drinks.

She was looking for a piece of art by Enid Silvera, thanks to the proprietary software her firm used. She'd typed in "Mulberry Street Restoration," and within seconds she knew all too much about several dozen people associated with it, including its office manager, Enid Silvera. The expensive software, she realized, worked best on young people, who uncaringly left fat trails of digital exhaust in their wakes. So where were Enid Silvera's paintings? The exhibition rooms had hundreds of pieces of art hung in them, floor to ceiling, with no organizing principle that Rachel could see. Most of it was pretty *bad*— art student stuff, collages of magazine images . . . political words on canvases . . . pseudo-bondage drawings of girls . . . paintings of women's shoes . . . photos someone had taken with his cell phone and then added effects. A few pieces showed real artistic ability, however, including a lovely but unsigned painting of a piece of an oriental rug, in which the artist had lushly re-created every stitch of the handmade piece, somehow capturing the rippling surface of the rug, the worn areas, the very texture of woven wool. Price $900. Wow, Rachel thought, that would sell for $10,000 in a gallery downtown.

But the pieces of art were hung so close together, two or three inches away from each other, that the total effect was overwhelming, especially as the crowd pulsed and chattered behind her. How was she going to find Enid Silvera? It seemed no one was in charge. Rachel moved slowly along the wall reading the printed card that described each painting until she had worked her way completely around the room. The whole noisy situation was a bit depressing and she knew she would smell of cigarette smoke when she left later.

But she persevered and finally, on the second floor, found two small paintings by "E. Silvera," both of them of cats looking out a window at a fire escape. Colorful, but *so* bad. Rachel bent close to read the card. Each painting was $325, a ridiculously hopeful sum. She lingered and studied the others inspecting the walls of work.

"Do you know the artist?" she asked a young man.

"Nope," he said. "Do you?"

She asked a few other young people until one said, "I think Enid is over there."

The woman pointed at a tall, rather plain girl wearing heavy boots that somehow accentuated her mannish torso. Rachel wove her way over to her.

"Hi, are you Enid?"

The girl looked suspicious. "Yes."

"I was just looking at your paintings and admiring them."

"Oh, wow, thank you."

Reel her in carefully, thought Rachel. "Yes, they jumped out at me."

"Oh, wow, thanks, I kind of just finished one."

"I was wondering if I could maybe buy the one with the orange cat?"

"Oh, sure."

"Maybe we could sit down?"

They found a spot in the corner of the illegal bar.

"What do you do?" asked Rachel.

"Well, I got out of Cooper Union a few years ago," Enid answered.

"A great art school."

"Yeah, I guess."

"Then what?"

"I just kind of have been working on my stuff."

A waiter in fedora and T-shirt came over. "Sorry, but this table is for people who buy drinks."

"Then we will buy drinks," said Rachel heartily, "my treat."

A few minutes later they were both drinking vodka and orange juice.

Rachel waited to see Enid relax. "So how can I buy the cat painting?"

"Um, well, you just give me the money and you are allowed to take it off the wall."

"Really? That's so great. So, Enid, I'd like to buy that painting but I also need a little bit of information."

The girl seemed confused. "Like what?"

"Well, you are the office manager at Mulberry Street Restoration?"

"Yeah?"

"I need to know about a big map that came in recently."

"For foxing issues?"

"Yes, a big old map of New York City."

Enid stared at her. "You want to know about that?"

"I would like to know who owns it."

Enid was aghast. "That's, like, kind of totally private information."

Rachel nodded. "Oh, of course." She paused a moment. "I'm trying to contact the owner."

Enid sipped her drink enthusiastically. "I can ask my boss, I guess."

"I'd rather you not do that."

"And you want to buy my painting?"

"Yes. Tonight. Now." Rachel opened up her bag in search of her purse. "I even have the cash."

"Oh, wow, great."

"But I want the name of the owner of the extremely rare 1776 Ratzer map of Manhattan that came into your shop last week, maybe on Wednesday."

"Or—?"

"Or I'm afraid I can't buy your painting."

"Really?"

Rachel smiled. "Yup."

"I'll be right back," said Enid, getting up suddenly, lurching a bit.

Five minutes passed, then ten, and Rachel finished her vodka and ordered two more to hold the table, but was worried that Enid wasn't coming back.

But she did, dragging a young man behind her.

"I ordered us another round," Rachel said in a friendly way.

Enid glanced at the young man, who was carrying a small wrapped package. "I brought it," she said. "This is my boyfriend, Paco."

"Hey," Rachel said, shaking his hand.

Paco pulled up a chair. "Enid says you want her painting?"

"And some information."

Paco looked hard at her. "I think there's a serious problem."

"What?"

"You are paying for a painting, not a name."

Rachel inhaled. "Well—"

"And I, and *we*, think you should pay for the name *separately*."

"Oh, how much?"

"We were thinking like fifty extra bucks."

Rachel looked from one to the other. "Sounds fair," she said. "Yes, let's do that."

"I have it in my work e-mail," Enid said. "Right here."

Rachel counted out $375 and handed the bills to Paco.

"Okay," she said, taking the package from him.

Enid was flipping through her e-mail. "Here's the work order." She enlarged it on her screen.

Rachel took out her phone and took a few photos. "You're sure?"

"Read it."

She did. The description was correct. The estimate for the restoration to be done was $8,500, and the owner's name was Mrs. Hillary Larabee Morton, with an address on East Seventy-fourth Street.

"Thanks," Rachel said. She rose to go. "I think you are very talented," she told Enid, who smiled and looked shyly at Paco. "And so, now this old lady is going to leave here before all the fun begins."

"We understand," said Paco obligingly.

You understand, thought Rachel in the cab back to Manhattan. Well, so do I. Feeling a touch drunk, she pondered how to approach Mrs. Hillary Larabee Morton on East Seventy-fourth Street. The car reached her apartment building and she paid the driver, then quite purposefully left the wrapped painting in the backseat of the cab as she stepped out, rather pleased with herself.

23

You have to leave now. Couldn't she just say that? *Billy, you have to leave or everything will just get worse. I'm really not very strong right now.* Or maybe she should just say that she wanted to stay with Ahmed. But that wasn't true. *Billy, please just go. Leave me and forget about me. I had my chance a long time ago before everything got screwed up, before—*

"Jenny?"

The High Line was weird, she thought, just some old elevated freight-train tracks turned into a narrow park above the streets. She didn't understand what all the excitement was about, the foreign tourists, the people every five feet taking photos with their phones. Billy had bought a postcard that made it look better than it was. But, okay, she enjoyed walking there. Of course, Ahmed's man was probably behind them somewhere, though she wasn't sure because she had jumped in a cab.

"I'm supposed to leave with him for five days." To Geneva, then Ahmed would go on to Paris, and she would return.

"Leaving before the hurricane gets here tomorrow night."

"I guess. Won't you get all wet?"

"Actually I'm kind of looking forward to it."

Nothing could be more unappealing to her. While Billy shivered in the deluge, she would be in Geneva. The hotel would be beautiful, the huge white enamel claw-foot bathtub so big she could lie down completely in it, the tiny bar of Swiss milk chocolate placed on the pillow each night by the maid. Orchids in the window. At breakfast, your choice of French, German, Italian, English, Spanish, Japanese, and Chinese newspapers. The city's architecture, the harbor, the shopping along the Rue du Rhône. Leather Italian handbags. Shoes. Ahmed had also arranged for a dinner at a traditional restaurant she quite liked. "And if I suddenly don't go at the last minute, he'll be totally suspicious."

Billy's sharp face was troubled, his eyes drilling into hers. "So what? If you're going to come with me, it won't matter."

"I know," she said.

His expression softened. "I'm trying to do the right thing here, girl. I've had a lot of time to think about it."

"I'm supposed to go *tomorrow*."

He held her shoulders. "I can wait."

Billy seemed so sure of his feelings. "Show me the picture again?" Jennifer said distractedly.

He pulled out his wallet. "Take it," he said.

She studied the photo, but feared having it. She handed the photo back. "I was so young."

"There's still time to start everything up."

She pulled at the idea of leaving Ahmed, trying to feel how large it was. But such a thing didn't seem real, or even ever *possible*. He was so possessive. *Did* he possess her? Her name was on the apartment deed, she had accounts at the best stores, she had closets of beautiful clothes. Did these things matter? Yes. No. *Yes.* She remembered years ago her mother taking home the leftover french fries after a trip to McDonald's and saving them in the freezer for later. The money had been that tight. Mom, she thought, I should have taken care of you better, not left you by yourself.

"Hey," said Billy sharply.

"What?"

"You have that look."

She said nothing.

"The look you get when you think about your mother."

"I've got to go," she said.

He caught her hand in his, quick, holding it. She found herself looking at his forearm and how thick his wrist was.

"But when you come back," Billy said, firmness in his voice, "I want an answer, the final answer."

"That's fair," Jennifer said. "That's very reasonable."

He kept her hand. She knew better than to pull against it. "What I want to *know* is that you're coming with me," he said in a low, aggressive voice, his eyes locked on hers. "All you have to do, Jenny, is just get in my truck and we can start driving. A suitcase and your wallet is all you need. No law says you got to stay married to somebody. Anything he got, I can get you, girl. I got almost ninety thousand dollars saved in the bank, my truck is paid off, and I'm going to inherit the ranch someday." He released her hand. "It's a little better than break-even, but we got oil rights and offers to buy the acreage, and someday maybe I will sell."

Jennifer looked at him and was confused by love and pity and sadness. What could the ranch be worth, at most? A million dollars? Two? That didn't sound like much to her anymore. She stood to go.

"You'll be back in five days?" An edge to his voice, fear.

"Yes."

"Then let's meet right here in one week, exactly. Right at the corner. Same time as now." He pointed down at the street. "Where that taxi is. I'll have my truck parked right down there and we can hop and go. I mean it. Gassed up, coffee ready, sleeping bag in the backseat. It's three days on the road. Let's leave this place behind." He believed it really would happen, and his eyes brightened, the same deep-set blue eyes that had seen the things men do in war, seen what he had done, too. "You have no idea how beautiful the Texas hill country is."

She nodded forcefully, trying not to cry. The idea was ridiculous but appealing. Cut loose. Free. Free of Ahmed. She'd be Jenny again. Long hours in the pickup cab, country-and-western music on the radio, nights at highway motels, breakfast at the truck stops with all the heavy men eating eggs and sausage. She would pack her jewelry just in case.

"Okay," she said. But did she mean it? She wasn't sure.

"So you *definitely* want me to wait for you?" Billy asked. "I'm making sure here, baby. I'm looking you in the eye. This is the moment."

She needed to take a Xanax to calm down. She had them in her purse. She leaned over and kissed his cheek. "Yes, yes, yes, I swear to you I do, I want you to wait for me," she whispered in his ear, knowing it made him weak, a little crazy. She kissed his forehead, watched him close his eyes in the private pleasure of her touch. Then she kissed him ferociously, thrusting her tongue into his mouth, deeply penetrating him in the way that possessed him, that reminded him that he belonged to her, only to her.

"Bye, Billy," Jennifer said. Then she left him.

24

Mi madre would not recognize me, thought Hector Ruiz, straddling his 1982 Harley-Davidson FXB Sturgis. But she was dead, like a lot of people he once knew. He watched from the roadway a hundred yards off as the body opened the door to his red pickup truck and stepped inside. Hector counted jets taking off. About one every thirty seconds. Five minutes passed, then the truck door opened and the body stepped out. He locked the truck and headed off, strides long and practiced. That man has walked some long distances, Hector thought. The body followed the off-ramp to the parkway and Hector started up his bike. Between the road and the water rose a landscaped mountain of garbage that the city had capped with topsoil and new trees. The body hurried along the steel mesh fence and disappeared. Hector marked the place in his mind. He would have to go around and come back the other way on the road, which would mean the body would be farther away. Couldn't be helped. He drove west four hundred yards, jumped off at the exit, turned around, and came back along the eastbound side, looking for the spot where the body had disappeared. Then saw it. A big flap had been cut in the eight-foot fence. Hector got off the bike, well aware of the traffic zooming past in both directions. He bent back the flap of fencing and wheeled the immense black bike through as quickly as he could. Once inside the vegetation he looked back at the road and didn't see that anyone had stopped. A rough foot-path led through the brush, and although the FXB Sturgis was a giant beast of a machine, one of the nastiest production road hogs ever made, it was no dirt bike. Also, he didn't want the body to hear the sound of the bike starting, in case he was still close. So he rolled it deeper into the brush and set it gently against a tree. He was in his motorcycle leathers, difficult to move around in. He stripped down to his jeans and T-shirt, then removed his crossbow from its fitted case, assembled it, and took four bolts with him. Each carbon-shaft arrow was twenty inches long and tipped with a 125-grain broad-head tip designed to open upon im-pact and cause a deep razor cut two inches wide.

A minute later he was hiking the trail, which broke through the brush and up the man-made mountain. There were places one could lie low and hide. He followed the path another hundred yards as it climbed, and he wasn't expecting to spy the body so soon, but he did—there the body was, sitting on a cinder block eating from a bowl. Hector pulled back. There was no easy way to approach. He squatted down and de-cided to wait.

When he stood up three hours later, the cloud-dulled sun had fallen to the edge of the horizon. To the northwest, like a crystal mirage, rose the spires of Manhattan. Hector was stiff but shook out his legs. A faint chemical whiff tingled in his nostrils, the concentrated perfume of tons of garbage venting out of the hill—methane, ammonia. He crouched and started to move, eyes watching the body's camp, and circled through the low grass, moving incrementally closer. He fitted a bolt in the crossbow, checked the scope for accuracy. He needed to get within thirty yards if at all possible. Ten steps more and the body was within range. There was virtually no wind yet, though that would change. The body was moving around his camp. He came out of a small tent and stood and changed his shirt. The body was in excellent shape, naturally muscular, especially in the shoulders and back. Hector had an idea and moved uphill so that his line of sight was on the tent itself. The aerodynamic, finely balanced bolt moving three hundred feet per second would easily pierce the tight nylon tent material. He drew his bolt to be ready when the body went back in the tent. Then he scuttled forward another ten yards and got set, bolt in its nock, pulled back ready for release.

The body went into the tent and Hector raised the crossbow, sighted through the scope at the shape in the tent, and released. The bolt hit the tent about six inches lower than he had aimed but penetrated it easily. He heard a wretched groan and could see thrashing against the side of the tent. Hector immediately drew another bolt and hurried downhill to get a bead on the opening of the tent. There was no sound. Unless the arrow had hit the chest or head, the body would still be alive, for a while. Hector had seen white-tailed deer have bolts pass completely through their lungs and run forty yards before collapsing. He had also seen men run with bolts sunk a foot deep in their groin. Hurts to watch that, my nigger.

The tent rippled and the body leaped out of it, rolling as he hit the ground. Hector didn't have a clear shot, but he saw blood all over the body's pants; the arrow had pierced the right hamstring and passed through the leg. The body was crawling rapidly along the ground and Hector ran closer. He drew again, but before he could release, the body rolled into the brush.

Hector took two steps closer and knelt quietly. The body suddenly crawled forward, and in surprise Hector let the bolt go, knowing it had missed as soon as he released it, hissing into the brush somewhere.

Now the body crawled up the hill behind the tent and Hector had to guess at his intentions. Seemed the body had no gun or he would have tried to use it. Hector moved within fifteen yards, then ten. The body was behind the tent.

"Come on, you fucking peckerhead! Come on and get me."

Okay, thought Hector, I will. He stood with his arrow drawn.

The body had his rucksack lifted before him like a shield and peeked over it.

"Come on and get closer, fuckhead! Then we can have a good old time."

Brave words from a bleeding man. Hector didn't answer. Instead he steadied himself on one knee and aimed for the top of the pack, waiting for the body to show his face. But nothing happened. The pack moved and Hector let the arrow go; it sank perfectly into the pack, driving six inches deep, but hitting something hard inside it. Oh shit, he thought, I have only one arrow left. He ran up the slope to see that the body had somehow stood and was hobbling with awkward bravery down the hill toward the highway. Hector ran after him, easily gaining ground, and came at an angle to force him away from the fence opening. The body stopped, standing on one leg and bent over.

Hector set his last arrow in the crossbow, pulled it back all the way and sighted, aiming low. He released. The carbon-shaft bolt rose as it flew—the body had turned and dived as soon as he saw it. The bolt missed! But had it? Hector heard a groan and drew closer. A moment later, he understood. The bolt had run through the body's neck from the back, catching just an inch of flesh to the side. But that was the carotid artery. The body was on his hands and knees trying to stand, his head hanging down. "Oh God, oh fuck," he cried. "Oh, fucking God, oh please."

He rolled to his side, blood hosing upward from his neck.

And your mother would not recognize you, either, thought Hector.

"Oh, oh. Jenny!" came the voice, gruff yet despairing at the same time, weakening. "Oh."

Hector had shot thirty-eight deer, nine wild boars, two horses being ridden by informants trying to escape their destinies, and one black bear. And who knew how many wild dogs for practice, certainly a hundred. He understood that animals died slowly sometimes. There was no hurry. He checked his watch. He sat on his haunches. The body tried to crawl, coughed a lot, then lay down. It wouldn't go on much longer.

Hector inspected the body's camp, sleeping bag, water bottles, dry meals, tiny butane stove, looking for anything that might incriminate him, such as the bolt in the tent. He picked that up and put it in his quiver. He found the bolt that had missed, so that made four. The tent's interior was smeared with blood. He rolled it up, gathered any other personal articles, and put them into the fire pit. He noticed a photograph, some kid, and threw that in, too. There was a green army jacket with a wallet and a set of truck keys. He threw the wallet unopened into the fire pit and slipped the keys into his pocket, because they would not burn. He lit the items in the pit and they burned briskly, toxic black smoke lifting. The fire was small, unlikely to be spotted in the dusk.

Meanwhile, there was a lot to do. Hector hurried to the bike to retrieve his gear bag, then returned to the body. It had only the two wounds, the one in the leg and the mortal one in the neck. He tore open some large adhesive bandages, cleaned the wounds, wiped them dry, and bandaged them tightly. The body's liquids would continue to settle, but at least they would not leak out. So important to get the body in position before it stiffened up. He opened the gear bag. The first thing was to get the body into racing leathers. He pulled off the bloody pants. They went into the fire, along with the bandage wrappers and gauze pads. There was an excellent hunting knife on a leather sheath strapped around the body's shin, and this he removed and put on himself. He sliced off the body's boxer shorts, exposing a sizable penis and the testicles. Using a small knife he kept in his breast pocket, Hector quickly sliced open the scrotum and removed the testicles. They went into a small stainless-steel canister. He used a piece of tape to repair the incision to the scrotum. Then he pulled the large leather pants he'd bought for this very purpose over the body's feet, hoisted them up the shins and thighs to the waist, and zipped the fly. The knees of the pants were heavily padded. The body was wearing a wool work shirt soaked with blood, more trouble than it was worth to remove. Hector got the matching top half of the racing leathers around the body's arms, being sure that the collar covered the bandage on the neck wound. Next came large black leather boots for the body, bought at a motorcycle club yard sale, and black riding gloves. The body now looked like a dead motorcycle rider. Which would soon be an accurate description. Hector rolled the body onto its back, grabbed both arms, made the corpse sit up, then bent down and let it flop over his left shoulder. The absolute amount of weight was not difficult—after all, he could squat 475 pounds—but there was an awkward moment getting his legs set beneath him before he had the body up on his shoulder and off the ground. He carried it down to the bike and set it on the ground faceup. Then he unrolled a harness vest from the saddlebag and zipped it onto the body. The harness had specially sewn nylon channels that housed removable, semi-rigid fiberglass rods. He slipped the curved rods into the back, running from the shoulders down to the waist. He ran more rods along the arms, which straightened them, like those of a zombie sleepwalker. He pulled the vest tight around the chest and snapped it closed. Next he got out the cervical collar, which was important. He'd experimented with various medical supply-house versions and this one was perfect, except that it was white. He'd spray-painted it black to match. It went around the body's neck to keep the head propped up at all times. The helmet followed, a matte black full-face style with a smoked visor that matched Hector's own. He snapped the padded strap under the jaw, feeling the cold, stubbled chin.

On the ground lay a fully geared biker ready for road touring, his legs loose, his torso oddly rigid, his arms straight out in front of him.

Hector pulled the FXB Sturgis up out of the ravine and set it on its kickstand, which wasn't easy on the uneven ground. Then he stood over the body's head, bent down, and hoisted it up by the jacket, sliding his hands under the armpits, lifting it to its feet, and dragging it to the rear of the bike. The Sturgis had a huge king-and-queen double seat with a raised backrest; he'd seen some gigantic-assed women sitting in the backseat at biker rallies out west, some of them naked except for boots, drugged out and waving their arms in the air. One time he'd even seen a man fucking a woman on a Sturgis from behind *while she drove*. Anyway, back to business, back to the eight thousand dólares, muchacho. He lifted one leg of the body over the king-and-queen, then leaned the torso against the backrest. It sprawled awkwardly, but the head stayed up. He adjusted each leg on its respective side, snapped down the bike's buddy pegs, and slipped each peg through a fabric stirrup cleverly sewn into the bottom of both boots. More or less undetectable to the casual observer. Both of the body's legs were bent perfectly at the knee in riding position.

Almost done. He remembered the small steel canister with the bloody testicles in it and slid it into a grooved slot on top of the exhaust manifold. Next he retrieved his own leathers, which matched the body's, and put them on, followed by the gloves and his own helmet. He climbed onto the bike, jolted it forward so that the kickstand snapped up, and kept it upright with his legs. He took the body's gloved left hand and connected it by Velcro to a loop sewn into the front of his jacket. He did the same with the right hand. In the early days he had simply connected the hands together, but if the link somehow slipped apart, both hands fell back at once, and the body would lurch to the side or even collapse backward on the bike, which could cause a wipeout. This way, even if one hand connector failed, the other could not and the body would stay upright.

Hector turned the key and the panel lit up. In his forward compartment was a squirt bottle of high-caffeine energy drink and protein bars. The bike had a GPS, but Hector had disabled it for the trip. He knew the way.

The light was failing, just as planned. The engine rumbled smoothly. He bumped slowly over the uneven ground until he came to the hole in the fence. He nudged the bike back through, being careful that the sliced fencing didn't scratch his exhaust pipe or fender. Then he got up on the margin, waited for a break in the traffic, took it, and finally switched on his headlight. He knew this road. He also knew how to get out of the city. Sixteen minutes later Hector buzzed across the Whitestone Bridge, headed north. He had a New York State E-Z Pass that billed to a drop box in Miami, and legit Florida plates registered to his cousin Tino, who lived in his mother's house, connected to an oxygen bottle. If they ever traced the plates back, they would find the bike in Tino's garage. It was a dead 1989 Honda 350, a piece of junk, transmission frozen, tires flat.

The Harley-Davidson FXB Sturgis, by contrast, was the most totally badass road bike ever built. Eight monstrous feet long. Made for only three years in the eighties. A cult favorite. Engineered when gas was cheap and steel was king. A big bike for a big country, brother. Dual primary and secondary belts and thick-spoked wheels. Weight, 609 pounds. Low-slung, black, with gold wheels. Eighty-cubic-inch shovelhead engine strung out big. Imposing, grand, 64-inch wheelbase, 31.4

degrees of rake, five inches of trail. Would hit 94 mph in a quarter mile. Top speed, 112 mph. A man hawg, with no apologies. Go big or go home.

He raced north, not stopping for gas or rest or food. The bike was so powerful it barely felt the extra two hundred pounds, but nonetheless he was careful to never go past sixty, especially since the body didn't know how to lean into and out of curves. He kept out of the passing lane, too, in case some asshole state troopers were lurking. At some point he pulled the set of truck keys out of his pocket and flung them into the dark high grass next to the highway. North of Albany, New York, he ran into a traffic jam and had to slow to a crawl. A tractor-trailer pulled up to his right and the driver rolled down the window.

"Nice ride, dude!"

Hector gave him the thumbs-up.

Later a Toyota minivan filled with shrieking young girls pulled alongside him and, thrilled at the sight of badass bikers in full black leather—one who didn't seem to be noticing them—they took turns lifting up their shirts and pressing their breasts and lips to the windows. *Hey, boys!* Hector nodded appreciatively, but he didn't like this situation, because the body couldn't turn its head and react. So he hit the throttle and left them behind like they were standing still.

Just south of Rouses Point, New York, three hundred miles north of New York City, he pulled off 87 and found his destination, an abandoned industrial site with hundreds of empty drum barrels piled in a marshy area next to Lake Champlain. He bumped over the pitted earth, watching for pieces of metal or concrete in the grass, stopped, unhooked the body's arms, slipped the boots from the buddy pegs, and let the body topple off the bike. Hector removed the boots, the leather pants, the helmet, neck brace, gloves, and jacket, being careful to avoid getting blood on himself. All these went into an open barrel. Using a pre-filled plastic bottle, he poured gas into the barrel and lit it. The flames leaped up inside but did not reach the top. A few feet away, the body lay on its side, eyes open, as if quietly studying its predicament. From his kit bag, Hector pulled a bottle of bleach and poured it over the places on the body he had touched, and over the face itself. The liquid would burn off any DNA of Hector's it encountered. Next he pulled a contractor's garbage bag over either end of the bloody body, ran a piece of duct tape around the middle, and lifted it up like a man carrying his bride over the threshold. He took the stiffened package to another drum, half-filled with fetid water. The trick was to drop the ass into the barrel first. The body jackknifed at the waist and the head fell forward with the arms. Last to go in were the feet and legs, which bent at the knees. It was in. He hammered the drum lid on, knocked the whole cylinder over, rolled it twenty feet away, and stacked a few empties on it. The drum could be there for ten years before anyone found it, maybe more, and by that time the flesh would have rotted away forever.

He checked the fire, threw in the empty plastic bleach bottle, and stirred around the last pieces of clothing so that they would burn completely. He hated to lose a good helmet, but what could you do? At last he hurried back to the bike, just as a light rain began to fall. Only now would he allow himself the delicacy he had been anticipating. Only *now*. He removed the canister from its fitted slot on the exhaust manifold, which was still quite warm, and twisted off the cap. The two roasted testicles were in there, and he removed one with his leather-gloved fingers and ate it, chewing thoughtfully, washed it down with the energy drink, then ate the other. There was no other taste like that. Gamy, with the consistency of fried scallops. It had meaning.

The rain got heavier, storm coming up from the south. Riding a motorcycle on a wet roadbed was always dangerous. But tonight it couldn't be avoided. He had a poncho with him and snapped it on. He drove at low speed on the highway without any lights for a few miles. Not many cars out. The wet poncho flapped like evil bat wings in the wind. Finally he flicked on the headlight, gave it a little gas, and roared away, the big engine between his legs thrumming. No one knows me, Hector thought. Nobody except the body. Only it knows who I am.

25

"It's so *sweet* of you to meet with me," said Rachel as she and Mrs. Hillary Larabee Morton sat down to tea. They had both come in out of the lashing rain, which was forecast to continue for two days. "I know it was an unexpected call."

Mrs. Morton, secure in her superior societal position, smiled patiently. She was about sixty, and had undergone the usual facial procedures, giving her soft, unlined visage a look of continuous surprise. "You were very mysterious on the phone."

"Oh? I'm sorry. I just wanted to talk in person." Keep it moving along, thought Rachel. "So I was downtown at Mulberry Street Restoration checking on a piece and I noticed a big beautiful map of New York City."

"Did they tell you I was the owner?"

"No, *no*," cried Rachel. "I just happened to look at it and there was a tag with your name on it."

"They shouldn't have let you see that."

"It was *absolutely* all my fault, I promise!" Rachel smiled. "But I have to tell you, it is the most beautiful and spectacular thing I have ever seen!"

"Thank you." Mrs. Morton preened happily. "It was in a rather prominent New York family for generations and I was very lucky to be able to acquire it."

"Did you know the family?"

"Yes, yes, I went to school with Mimi, one of the daughters."

"Of course."

On an instinct, Rachel told the waiter she would rather have a glass of white wine, given that it was late in the afternoon, and Mrs. Morton obliged her by ordering one herself.

"So you saw the map and just had to have it?" Rachel prompted.

"We just had our barn in Bridgehampton redone, you know, and we were looking for something, you know, special, something that makes a *statement*, to fill up one of the walls."

To fill up one of the walls of a *barn*. Paul would weep and gnash his teeth. "Yes, beautiful. Do you have any photos?"

From there it was twenty minutes of iPad shots showing the Bridgehampton estate, the barn with the vintage beams, the cerulean pool, the mahogany decking so tidy that it appeared every unauthorized leaf had been tweezered away, the gardens with exactly eighty-one different varieties of daylilies, the restored main house, the garage with four antique cars, the young grandchildren playing sports, the *so wonderful* old quilt she found at the antiques place in Maine, the sailboat, her husband Bernie's watch collection, Bernie's antique men's shoe collection, and then on to discuss—yes, I'll have another glass, thank you—Bernie's art photos of young boys, some of which reminded people of Mapplethorpe's "classic" work, Bernie's amazing career as a fashion photographer, the guesthouse on the property where Bernie's young male assistant lived, the parties they had there, the police were called three times over the summer, the wild things all the boys were doing and how the pool was a shocking mess in the morning, the, um, *items* they left around the pool, she knew it was all a little irregular, but what was she to *do* at her age, don't you know, her husband was just expressing himself. And then in response to Rachel's intimate look, her large, soulful eyes and the caring hand touching her lightly perfumed wrist, not to mention the third or fourth glass of wine, Mrs. Morton went on to say that when she'd told Bernie what she had paid for the map, he went completely apeshit—not the word she used—and told her she had paid way more than what it was worth and she was *an idiot who should have known better*, and that he would see her later, like in a week, as he and the male assistant, whose name was Shaquelle Jones, would be gone on an overseas work trip, maybe Morocco, details to be announced later. Which left Mrs. Morton feeling a bit unappreciated, because she just knew the map was so wonderful—it was very *historical*, you know— and she had gone to so much trouble to acquire it.

"I have a friend who collects maps," Rachel said offhandedly. "I mean, just on the chance, if you ever might think of selling it."

Mrs. Morton's eyes brightened. "I suppose it's become a point of conflict with Bernie . . . I hadn't thought . . . But I'd just need to get what I paid for it, plus the restoration costs, of course. And the shipping."

"Of course," purred Rachel. "May I give you my card?"

"The restoration should be finished soon," said Mrs. Morton. "I think it would all add up to about—"

Rachel leaned forward, ready for the sum Mrs. Morton was calculating.

"—a million dollars."

Whereupon Rachel lurched back in her chair and finished her wine.

I can't tell Paul, Rachel thought later that night while sitting in his apartment, but I have to.

"So, mister, I have some news that you can use."

Holding his absurd surgical loupe, he was inspecting the D. T. Valentine map of Manhattan that he'd bought at Christie's. The map lay on a dead-flat draftsman's table, each corner held down by a weighted felt bag. "This is a very good piece," he said, not looking up. "Under other circumstances, I might actually be happy I have it."

"Right." Outside, the rain was battering the windows as the seasonal hurricane churned north toward the city, massive flooding predicted in its path, the exact point of landfall not yet known. She liked all the rain; it was cozy. She poured him some Sambuca. "Here. I want you to tell me about your second wife."

"Oh geez, not this."

She took his hand playfully. "Come on!"

"I told you about the first one. That was enough pain and suffering."

"I want to know about her!"

"How about we discuss it after the next presidential election?"

"Paul!"

"It's boring. It's stupid people named Paul Reeves making mistakes."

"I want to know. Because it's about *you*."

He didn't respond.

"Okay," Rachel warned, "you are forcing me to play total hardball."

"Fire it at me, miss."

"I happen . . . to know . . . who has the Ratzer map."

"What?" He blinked to attention. "Who?"

"Sorry, buddy." She snapped her fingers playfully. "We need some quid pro quo here."

Paul stared at her, plainly irritated. She felt a zing of satisfaction.

"Hell's bells." He glared at her. "You're going to get the executive summary, though."

"But I want the emotional complexity!"

"I can't *do* emotional complexity right now."

"Just *do* your best."

Paul exhaled, stood up, and carried his drink to his reading chair. "Her name was Gretchen Scarborough. To say that she was ambitious would be to miscategorize her. Gretchen worked harder than a person ever should. She was the vice president for marketing and operations at a big insurance company by age thirty-nine. She was the smartest one in her company. It wasn't even close. The CEO was totally scared of her. The chairman wanted to season her for five more years, then hand her the company. She was totally—"

"What attracted you to her?"

"Frankly, I don't remember."

"Come on!"

"She had a big smile and nice hair. She was athletic. She seemed self-sufficient."

"I'm self-sufficient, right?" asked Rachel.

Paul nodded obligatorily. "You are, indeed, sufficiently self-sufficient."

Rachel watched him closely. "Are you being mean?"

"No. You want the rest?"

"Yes."

"So she was always busy with overseas travel. She didn't want children. I did, then. Children would be the end of her career, she said. But the window is closing, I said. Doesn't matter, she told me, not to *me*. I was going even deeper into the maps and she really didn't like that. She thought it was morbid and depressing. She used to say it's all about the past. That really bugged her. We got into an argument over something, and she said how about if I just tear up a map right now?"

"Amazing."

"Yeah, you can get mad at *me*, Rachel . . . but don't get mad at my maps."

"I get it, believe me."

They both sat there, a little on edge.

"So what happened?" she asked.

"She tore the map into about fifty pieces."

"What?"

"I just watched her. Let them flutter out the window, gone."

"Was it valuable?"

"No." Paul grinned wickedly. "But she didn't know that."

"Then what?"

"While she was on a work trip to London, I met a sociology professor at an idiotic NYU party. She was divorced with two young children. She needed a father figure for her kids and another income. I really liked those kids. Total angels. She was very friendly. But my heart wasn't in it . . ."

"Though another part of you was."

Paul grunted and cleaned his loupe on his shirt.

"How long did *that* last?" Rachel asked. "You never told me about her."

"There was nothing much to tell."

"What was her name?"

"I'm sticking to just telling you about Gretchen."

Rachel sighed. He didn't understand how *interesting* all this was.

"So, the sociology professor decided everything was too messy and got back together with her ex-husband. I said okay, no problem. He made a point of calling up Gretchen to give her a little information. So I suppose I got what was coming. When the end of that came, she informed me that although she believed in no-fault divorce and the basic principle of dividing marital property, she had zero intention of splitting the assets equitably because she had earned far more than I had during our time together."

"Really?"

"Even more to the point, she was due to have an enormous number of stock options vest, and the potential value of these was more or less life-changing. Millions. I guess it made all the years of work and sacrifice worth it."

"Wow."

"Moreover, as her attorneys told mine, any attempt to divide the marital property equitably would trigger a series of events that would damage my professional reputation. The attorneys could find ways to mess with my little firm's reputation, and so on. Real hardball. Nasty and illegal. I frankly didn't care, so long as they didn't touch my map collection or my firm. I rented an apartment in Washington Heights, took a few suitcases of clothes, and never went back. She got everything in the apartment except my maps, every spoon and dish."

Rachel was always interested in women such as this. They were scary but inspiring, too. "What happened to her, to Gretchen?"

"She rose several more rungs up the corporate ladder, and then about the time they really should have made her the CEO, the financial crisis of 2008 blew apart the company. Her entire division, which she was running, was sold to a Japanese investment bank, which stripped it of its best international clients and transferred them to their own company, and then the gutted entity was sold back for one-tenth the price to what had been left of the original company, which I think relocated near Princeton, that highway where all the corporate campuses are located. I'm pretty sure that she'd left by then. Last thing I knew she had built some kind of fabulous Buddhist retreat–slash–yoga thing–slash–vineyard out in Northern California. I'm on the mailing list."

"I've seen those flyers *here!*"

"I need to get off the list. It's pathetic. I'm a goddamned name on Gretchen's mailing list."

"That wasn't *quite* as good as the first-wife story," Rachel thought aloud in a distracted voice. "But it's interesting. Especially about the sociology professor. I kind of want to *meet* her."

"What you kind of want to do is tell me about the Ratzer map."

"Oh, right." She explained her underhanded reconnaissance at the art show and Enid Silvera. And then her luncheon. "And Mrs. Hillary Larabee Morton said she paid a million dollars for it!"

"It's worth six hundred thousand," Paul said bluntly.

"You were going to pay that?"

He wasn't going to tell her about his latest attempt to buy the map at a much higher price. "My final number was more. But a million is more than I expected."

"Now we know why the family sold it to her so quickly without talking to you."

"Because they were actually robbing her."

"Right."

"Larabee is her middle name?" asked Paul.

"Yes. From the mining fortune, the guy in the early twentieth century."

He shook his head. "She literally has so much money she doesn't know what to do with it."

This wasn't going the way Rachel had hoped. "I guess. She's married to that guy Bernie Gunston, a pretty famous photographer who I think has parties and a boyfriend or something."

Paul had never heard of the man. "So the incredible one-of-a-kind map that really should be in the Smithsonian, or *here*, ends up in a barn in the Hamptons where some geezer is cavorting with all his young—"

"But, Paul, it was in a bedroom before. I'm sure a few things happened there, too."

"Yes, but Stassen *revered* that map. He appreciated it. He knew what it meant."

"Maybe I shouldn't have told you all this?"

He was silent, then picked up his loupe and returned his attention to the Valentine.

You could at least have said thank you, Rachel thought darkly, it wouldn't have been a lot to ask.

Paul looked up. "But thank you," he said. "I appreciate it."

"I have her contact info."

The rainy wind rattled the windows. "Good."

"You never know, you know."

They looked at each other, listening to the storm arrive, wondering whether they would stay together. "Sometimes," Paul said, "you do know."

She was feeling good about the Red Delicious. Those were just right. The McIntosh were also in the barn, ready for the trucks, and that left the Gala, which were close, maybe two days off. She'd had the men out picking until the rain and wind made it impossible. They'd been cold and unhappy, but hey, too bad. She was paying and they needed the work. She pulled on her plain wool jacket and headed out down the hill. The mist was coming up from the lake but would burn off.

"Miss Robinson?"

Jimmy came around the side of the storage shed. She didn't bother to hide what was left of her nose from him. He'd been looking at what wasn't there for ten years. Had never said anything about it.

"Reds are going out at nine," he told her. "Macs at eleven."

"Road's muddy?"

"I'm putting gravel out now."

"Good. I'll come back to sign as they finish the Reds."

Jimmy limped away. Growing apples was hard on people. You fell off of ladders, or got skin cancer, like she had.

She continued on, feeling the damp chill in her hip. No matter. In the pasture stood three gnarled Seckel pear trees that her father had planted in his late years, his favorite, and according to him, Thomas

Jefferson's favorite, too. She stopped and pulled four of the small crimson pears off the tree and slipped them into her coat pocket to eat during the day. They'd be buttery and sweet. A woman couldn't live on apples alone.

She'd been walking down to the lake for all of her sixty-nine years and had seen what the heavy current and rains could bring. Pieces of docks, trash, canoes and plastic kayaks, baseball bats, tennis balls, broken Adirondack chairs, drowned deer, dogs, cats, raccoons, possums, dead fish, even a soggy suitcase or two. But this? As she dropped into the mist, she started counting metal barrels. Most on their sides, a few standing up. Dented, rusty. Twelve, thirteen . . . There were a lot. They'd floated down from the old dump site a half mile away, she was sure. With New York State highway department stenciled markings. Well, that was exactly who she would call. She stopped counting barrels at thirty-eight and headed back up toward the house. It was the state's problem. Her men would be busy picking apples. She'd have to put on the sunglasses with the plastic noseguard, out of courtesy for the people who hadn't ever seen her. She always did this when going into town, especially for the children, who scared easily.

27

Hours of seconds, days of minutes. Time was dismantling her sanity. She'd flown home from Switzerland while Ahmed went on to do business in Paris. So many days had passed since she'd seen Billy! He and his truck hadn't been at the High Line, as they'd agreed. And she'd gone to the cheap hotel in Chinatown at the hour they used to set, and checked the rented mailbox in the Village, too. But nothing. A strange silence. Had Billy just decided it was over and left? That didn't make sense . . . He'd been begging her to go with him. Should she have gone? She was starting to wonder. Switzerland had been *nice*, but she'd thought about Billy all the time. Now Ahmed was calling home every day, but the time zone was so different; she was just waking up while he was at work and he was going to sleep seven hours before her. She sensed distance in his voice. He wasn't asking nosy questions so much. Maybe he was just preoccupied by work, so typical of him. She thought about calling up Billy's parents in Texas, but figured they didn't want to hear from her. That would be too awkward, would lead to other conversations she didn't want to have with them. One more day, she kept telling herself. And then another. She needed to eat more, she knew, but she had no appetite. The only thing she *wanted* was her pills, and in an abundance of self-weirdness, she took them all out of their plastic containers and lined them up on the kitchen table, one after another.

Klonopin, Xanax, Lamictal. So she could see them there, ready, protecting her.

She wrote a message on a card: *I can't find Billy. He seems to be gone. Have you heard from him?* She put on a coat and slipped the card under Paul's apartment door. That made her feel a little better, maybe. Then she forced herself to get into the elevator, where it seemed everyone was still talking excitedly about the hurricane, how it had just missed New York City to the west, then gone like a hooking bowling ball careering straight upstate, dropping epic levels of rain all the way up to Canada. She was surprised by the branches that had been blown to the ground, the weather suddenly cooler. She walked east along Fifty-ninth Street, noticing two trees had been knocked down in the park, and marched straight into the Plaza Hotel and ordered a big piece of German chocolate cake. With mint-chocolate-chip ice cream on the side. She ate both with a spoon, going back and forth between them. So delicious, so perfect. The sugar gave her a wild lift and she told herself that Ahmed was coming home soon and she had to pull it together before then. Yes. It had all been a sick fantasy, and now Billy had left—had *abandoned*— her. Well, okay. Fine. Fine! Truly. It was better this way. She was suddenly glad. She loved Ahmed, she really, really did.

28

To great friends, yes! Ahmed put down his drink. His host, Christophe, a high officer at France's largest bank asked, "And when will you finance?" He smiled at the two other men, acknowledging the directness of his question. But you were allowed to be direct when you represented the fourth-largest bank in the world and the three larger ones were Chinese. Christophe wanted in on the deal, of course, and this was the point Ahmed had been waiting for. The evening had been a long, gentle seduction, the setting an immense apartment in a massive nineteenth-century building, a showplace of draperies, period paint, beautiful inlaid parquet floors, and, it was explained, a bedroom where President Valéry Giscard d'Estaing had once bedded his mistresses. Ahmed had discussed how the assets found in the Pamir Mountains had yielded better core samples than expected. Demand for rare earths was cyclical, as everyone knew, and it would be three years before they had any substantial production, but they expected that once China's economy stabilized, global demand would resume its inexorable rise upward. "We plan to have the financing in place by February," Ahmed answered. "I think we should have no trouble."

"I could see us in for perhaps four hundred million euros," said Christophe. "We like this kind of project."

Because France can't compete globally anymore, Ahmed thought. Just deploys capital in other countries. "That would be excellent," he answered. "We can start some preliminary paperwork soon?"

"Yes, of course. It would be our absolute pleasure."

"We will send the first packet Monday."

They clinked glasses. The evening had been consummated, and Ahmed was eager to get back to his hotel.

"I did arrange for some companionship," announced Christophe with a wicked grin. "Strictly optional, of course. And my employer specifically prohibits such activities."

"Which is why they are so desirable," noted one of the other men.

Ahmed nodded noncommittally. Stalling, he checked his messages. In his encrypted e-mail was this message from his private detective: W [for "your wife"] *traveled to small hotel/Chinatown, waited outside one hour. Did not meet anyone. Appearance: flustered, concerned, crying. No other meetings. Usual shopping, health club, etc. Today: Went to Plaza Hotel and ate dessert.*

Excellent! This meant William Wilkerson was not . . . around? Uncle Hassan had been as good as his word.

He rejoined the other men. In the large second parlor sat four young women, each in a different chair.

"Please," said the host, gesturing. "These are very lovely ladies who would like to meet each of you. Ahmed?"

He stepped forward. Any ambivalence he'd felt had vanished. The blonde. Tall, perhaps Russian. Perfect, almost as perfect as Jennifer. She met his eyes with confidence and smiled, not demurely. He felt the hot focus coming to him, the furious need.

"You are all alone on your business trip, monsieur?" she asked, her voice rising at the end of the sentence. Not a native French speaker.

"I am," he said with a quick nod. He had not looked at the other women, but each was talking with one of the other men.

"Would you like to tell me about it?" She rose and took his hand in a friendly, matter-of-fact way. He smelled her perfume. "You are an extremely handsome man."

Ahmed smiled. That's what they all said, of course.

"No, no, I mean it!" she protested. Now she rested her other hand on his forearm, and was close enough he could see the exact line of her lipstick. "You are what *every* woman wants."

29

MILE MARKER 6.2, COUNTY ROAD 330, UVALDE COUNTY, TEXAS

Spitting was a bad habit. But seemed like he needed to do it now all the time. He did it right into his hand, to look. Nasty, red and yellow, thick. He wiped his hand on his jeans and kept looking for the bicycle. The phone rang, in the house and right there also, in the old garage. A mechanical clatter, same for the last thirty, forty years. He didn't pick it up. She would, he knew. He waited. There, she got it on the third ring. Maybe it was William Junior. They'd just gotten his postcard from New York City. He'd been brief: *I'm fine up here in this big crazy city and hope to have more to report shortly. Please feed the dogs on time and make sure they run. Love to everyone. Billy*

He had a pint can of John Deere green paint he used to touch up the tractor's rust spots and it would be perfect for William's old bicycle, which they still had, hanging up somewhere in the garage. Probably need new tires, no big deal. Little bit of steel wool on the chrome, it'd be just right.

If the call was anything, she'd holler out the back door to him. But her voice was weak now, he remembered. Plus, he was curious, so he put down the can of paint and picked up the old black phone receiver. The caller identified himself as a Department of Defense official. There had been hurricane flooding in upstate New York, he said, pushing around a lot of old highway barrels onto Lake Champlain, making some float into a nearby apple orchard. They had been opened, in order to empty the water out. A male body had been discovered and the identified victim had been an Army Ranger who—

". . . I'm so sorry, ma'am."

He heard her breathing on her end. Then she hung up.

"Hello, hello?" came a voice. "Is anyone there?"

He said nothing and wandered out into the driveway. It'll take her five seconds to get to the back door, he thought. He waited, and as he did, the endless Texas scrubland around him, full of mesquite and live oak and herds of longhorn cattle, fell crooked, up and down instead of across under the big cloudy sky. Then he heard her calling his name, her voice just exactly as he'd always worried it would sound. Their only child, his only boy. *William. William.*

30

Time to get paid. A man works, does the job, then he needs what was promised him. After his workout, Hector waited for the vintage Corvette to pull up. If Lorenzo is on time, he's nervous, Hector thought, feeling the pump in his shoulders, peeling off his sweaty lifting gloves. The car pulled up, engine rumbling.

"Yo," came the voice from within.

Hector tapped the roof with his fist. "Job es completo."

"You got proof?"

"I got proof for the man que me paga. That you?"

"I got to make a call."

"I can call him directly, yo."

"But I don't know if he wants to hear from you."

"This is how it is," said Hector. "You are my friend. No, you are exactly not my friend. You are just some pendejo I know, comprendes? I did the job. I need to be paid. You *can't* pay me. If we wasn't both Mexicano, then I'd have to do something, hombre. But I think the better thing is you just digame the name, digame el número. Also digame what the real amount of money was, like how much you were fucking cutting out for yourself." Hector noticed Lorenzo still had his right hand on the seven-gear shifter in the Corvette's floor. "Put your car in park. Take your foot off the brake."

"Why?"

"Just do it." Hector waited until it was done. "Necesito una cosa más."

Lorenzo looked increasingly concerned. "What?"

"I'm being *nice*, sí?"

"Right, right. So, yeah, okay, just let me call him and—"

Hector's hand snaked out, clutched Lorenzo's neck. He leaned in closely. "Yo no voy a esperar, motherfuck. Give me his name right now."

"Hey, I got this job for you," Lorenzo croaked.

"I'm not waiting."

"Hey, yo, man—"

Hector took his own leather lifting gloves from his pocket and stuffed them into Lorenzo's mouth. "I can't stand to hear you talk no more. ¿Entiendes? I will collect the money and then give you lo que creo you deserve." He had his left hand pressing the gloves into Lorenzo's mouth and his right hand cradling the back of his head, pushing forward, hard. "I am the one who did the nasty *business* while you fucked your fat puerca in her ass. I could hear her miles away, se quejó, 'It's too pequeño, Papi, can't you go in más, Papi.' I could hear her the whole time I was killing that dude. We understand everything?"

He released his grip, and pulled out the gloves. Lorenzo slumped over, coughing. He made a waving motion with his hand.

"Qué? Digame!"

Lorenzo lifted his hand up weakly, pawed at the sun visor. A piece of paper fell down into his lap. Hector grabbed it.

"Este New Jersey cell number! The guy's nombre es Omar? Some Arabic Muslim motherfuck?"

Lorenzo nodded in defeat.

"You ever meet him?"

"Once," Lorenzo coughed. "He does HVAC work in Jersey."

"HVAC?"

"Heat, ventilation, air-conditioning."

"Get the fuck out of here," Hector said.

Lorenzo jerked the car forward, tires pealing. Both men knew they would never see the other again.

No Internet name searches. Nothing traceable. He bought a burner phone and called the HVAC Muslim.

"Hello? Who is this?"

"Yes, buenos días, hello, I am looking for heating repairs."

"Who is this?"

"My name is Alexander . . ." He almost said Rodriguez, after the former Yankees star. ". . . Montoya, and we is looking for someone who can fix my aunt's deli heating in Hoboken."

"Who gave you this number?"

"My friend, here in Queens—" He had the name ready. "Johnny, says you are good HVAC guy, but very good price."

"Johnny who?"

"I think it is Johnny Carbone. You know, Italian guy."

"Don't know nobody like that."

"Oh, sorry. He said you do a good job for his friend or something."

A thoughtful pause. The barbed hook going into the flesh painlessly. "Tell me the problem."

Here Hector had done his homework. He described a ten-year-old oil-fired unit used to heat a deli.

"I can look at it."

"Good, good. Jefferson and Seventh Street, just past the Dunkin' Donuts."

"Tomorrow, ten a.m.?"

"I'll be standing outside, man. You will recognize me, I'm like forty-eight years old, six feet, kinda overweight, I admit it, and will wear a blue baseball cap and, okay, I'll be right there."

This is fucked up, Hector thought after he hung up. I'm working too hard. He didn't like it. What am I missing? he thought. What's my other play?

Late that night, what looked like a fat old man in a long coat, wearing gloves, a hat, and sunglasses, waddled out of the darkness and into the JFK long-term parking lot. Moving slowly, he found his irregular way to a red Ford F-250 pickup truck, right where he remembered it would be. He unlatched the tailgate and slipped a ratchet wrench from his coat. A few quick turns and the eight-millimeter bolts holding the left rear taillight housing popped out. All you did was slip the tracker (the size of a pack of cards, available at any electronics store, especially ones in Queens) behind the brake light, pull the bulb out of its socket, slip it into the matching orifice connected to the tracker, and slip the tracker's bulb-shaped plug into the original socket. A tiny blue pin light indicated the tracker was operational. Then you put the taillight housing back on and no one was the wiser. Unlike many such devices, the tracker had its own lithium battery, good for three months, and would not draw down and thus disable the truck's own battery. *You got to think things through, you fucking chulo motherfucker.* As soon as the engine was started, the brake lights would be engaged, sending a tiny charge to the device, which would send continuous location data to a programmed cell phone number. He glanced into the truck's cab using a tiny flashlight. *Lot of weird shit in there, but yo no tengo los llaves.* He'd thrown them into the grass next to the highway upstate, and breaking into the truck now seemed like a bad idea. Like there were ghosts in there or something. The old man hobbled away, somehow walking more quickly than before.

31

Coffee did magic things to his brain. Sitting in his office, perusing the latest edition of *New York Lawyer*, he'd just realized that Roger Metcalfe, the immigration attorney mentioned in the letter from the Ocean City attorney to Ahmed, worked at Gracken and Rothstein. This was the same firm that employed James Marone, the young attorney he'd recently met for lunch. It was a logical coincidence, though, because there were only so many boutique firms where seasoned immigration lawyers could—

"Paul, it's Mrs. Girardi on the phone," came Elauriana through the intercom, "and she *insists* on talking with you."

He picked up the phone.

"I'm terribly sorry to bother you again, Paul, but there's a gentleman with a truck parked outside your house who'd like to speak to you."

"What's his name?"

"It's uh—tell me your name?" A pause. "William Wilkerson. He's from Texas."

The handwritten card from Jennifer that she had slipped under his door was still on his kitchen counter. "Tell him I will be there in one hour. Do not let him leave."

The subway was the fastest way to go, but even then it seemed to crawl along. Finally he was there, turning the corner and looking down the block. Expecting to see Bill. Instead he saw an older man standing outside a white pickup truck in jeans, boots, and work jacket. Tall, bony, and angular, the father of the son.

"You Mr. Reeves?"

"That's me."

Paul came up to him and offered a hand. "William Wilkerson?"

He nodded slowly, not interested in a show of heartiness. "You know my son?"

"I've met him, but I haven't seen him in a couple of weeks, maybe."

"They found him."

Something in the still flatness of the man's voice stopped Paul from asking what he meant.

"They found him, yes sir. What was left of him." His mouth was tight, his eyes suspicious. Then he coughed, a mean, hacking, irresolvable cough, and when it had settled down he brought a handkerchief to his mouth. "They found him in a barrel in a flooded orchard way up in upstate New York."

"Jesus."

"So you didn't know?"

Paul shook his head, leaned hard against the white truck. He felt sick.

"They say he got stabbed to death and got stuffed in that barrel. I'm headed up there to identify the body."

"I just saw him!" Paul cried. "What was he doing up there, does anyone know?"

The father considered Paul, probing for some connection to his son's death. "Can't answer that. They're looking for his truck up there. Wasn't no wallet on him, nothing. They tried to hide the body." He squinted with hatefulness. "But what them killers don't know is that our U.S. government is pretty smart. When you are on elite counterterrorism combat duty they ask you if you want a little plastic identification chip in the skin inside your upper arm, in case of if'n you get blown up and there are no dog tags left. Most people, they don't know about this. Otherwise they got to run a DNA search, which can take a while. Billy said yes, and so the county coroner up in that small town saw his old shrapnel scars and figured he might have been a soldier and found that chip in ten seconds and contacted the military and they called us. I been driving straight for three days." The grief was rock hard in the man, an irreducible element that could not burn or crack or erode. Fury and grief and incomprehension, all mixed through and through him, in his blood and bones and lungs, in the eyes he saw through. "My boy fought for years for his country and he never complained about nothing and almost got killed half a dozen times, and then he travels home and come up here to this city"—he spat out the word *city* like it was a piece of indigestible and rancid meat—"and gets into some trouble, all because of that girl Jenny Hayes."

Paul was trying to make the connection. "Wait, how'd you get my name, sir?"

The older man nodded at the logic of the question. "I been trying to find Jenny Hayes, but I ain't got her *married* name now, just her address, from her mother. I told the police up there in upstate New York and maybe they can find her. Then I remember Billy said he was staying in a house in Brooklyn that belonged to her neighbor in her apartment building. So I got the police in my hometown, guys I know all my life, see, to get all the names of folks who lived in her apartment address, which was only about sixty names, and there weren't no Jenny Hayes on that list, and then I crossed those with the public record names of homeowners in Brooklyn, 'cause I figured, how many of those people also own a house in Brooklyn, couldn't be too many. So that was how I came up with this address, and then I drove here and started asking folks."

"Well, you found me."

"I'm just trying to locate somebody who can give me some answers." He looked at Paul accusingly. "You probably didn't know my son well."

"I met him a few times." That didn't seem to be enough. "I liked him right away."

"He got mixed up in something up here, didn't he?"

Paul could only nod. "I think he did."

"Tell me it wasn't drugs or nothing like that."

"No, nothing like that, I don't think."

"Way I look at it is, he messed with the wrong people. Could have been all kinds of people. Jenny Hayes was a married woman, I got that part. My son had a temper, I admit it. Maybe something happened on account of that."

Paul didn't want to say anything more. He glanced around, saw Mrs. Girardi watching them from inside her house.

"Since the body was found up there," continued Mr. Wilkerson, "they're investigating up there. Could be a long time before they make any progress. I tried to tell them the trouble probably started in New York City, but they don't know about that." The older Wilkerson shrugged at the incomprehensibility of it all. "I tried to call up the NYPD and say my son's body got found in upstate New York, but they don't want to hear about that, they say they got to be contacted by the New York State Police before they open a file, especially since my son was not a resident of New York City. Just some kid from Texas. So I'm kind of at my wits' end, mister. I'm done my crying. My boy is gone, but I got another kind of problem."

Paul was absorbing all of this as fast as he could. "You want to go sit somewhere?"

"I'll stand. I don't mind standing here."

Standing. Like a sun-battered fence post, as if when you weren't upright you were by definition lazy or loafing or, in this case, brought low by grief. Finally, he began. "See, my son and this Jenny Hayes, she got pregnant almost seven years ago, when he was on leave and visited her, but he didn't know it at the time, and she didn't tell him. That's a hell of a mean thing for a woman to do to a man, if you ask me. I know they weren't married, but it don't make much difference about what the woman says to the father. Not when the man is a quality individual and brought up right, like my boy." He drew a breath and let it out, not in a hurry, because there was no need to be in a hurry ever again. "So Jenny, she gave birth when Billy was in the service, overseas, and then right away, maybe two, three days is the way I heard it, she left her hometown in Pennsylvania and that baby boy was never given up for adoption, see, he was claimed straightaway by her mother, who named him Henry, which was her father's name. And then later, when she became addicted to the painkillers and the social services took the boy—"

"The mother?" interrupted Paul. "Addicted to painkillers?"

"I heard she nearly died, yes sir. They found little Henry alone in the apartment, with no food, diaper soiled, the woman passed out and near death. Neighbors broke down the door. Some kind of overdose of these painkillers everybody is addicted to. I didn't know she had a problem. The terrible thing of it is that she *was* devoted to Henry, though, we're sure about that, she worshipped him and cared for him and poured all kinds of love into him. I'm saying that even though she *was* unfit. Some people are like that. They love the child but they are unfit to raise the child because they do not love themselves. But we have raised him proper and good. He's a fine young fellow, good in school, good at sports, nice manners, and you would never really know he has never known his real mama. Now I got to tell you, sir, my wife, she got cancer of the ovaries and she's not going to make it. My son, I don't know if he quite absolutely understood that. Although maybe he did and that was why he ran off on this mission. I can't really say. My wife, she's got just a little time left. And me, I have my own troubles that I'm not going to go into."

Mr. Wilkerson looked at his watch. "All right, this here is what else I got to say. Listen up, sir, because this is the only time I'm going to say it up here. My boy is dead, my wife is dying on me, and I ain't good much longer. There's spots on my lungs. They did the needle biopsy and there's no doubt. Stage three already. That's hard, but it's the Lord's way. I come up here to send Jenny Hayes a message. I can't find her. She's too smart for me. But you live in the same apartment building, you know the young lady. You tell her something for me, hear? You say it comes from her son's grandfather. Where we come from down in Texas we believe in family and love and doing the right thing. This boy Henry is raised up good, but now he's missing his mama, who he never knew, *and* his daddy. Henry don't know about his daddy, but he seen my wife crying her eyes out and he's going to figure it out. It's going to hit him pretty hard. He loves my wife like she's his mother, and when she dies, it's going to be a hell of a thing, sir. He's a little boy, just six years old. Can't even quite ride a bike yet. We's going to have to give him to my brother's son and his family pretty soon now. Problem is, I believe in direct blood. I believe in family and I don't like to see family broken up. It's the damnedest thing. I seen it happen over and over. You can practically kill a man ten different ways, but if he's got the love of his family, he's going to be all right. I want that boy to know who his mother is and I want that mother to know who her son is." He paused, his frustration and passion collapsing into grief, and he wiped his eyes and coughed hard again until he had cleared his throat. Then, in a quieter, distraught voice, he said, "Henry's a fine boy. He's a hell of a good boy, but he needs somebody to step up now. He needs his blood. I'm saying that with charity in my heart. I believe in Jesus our Lord and I believe we must try to do what is right in His name. I try to find the goodness in things. Now, I ain't gonna lie to you, 'cause quite honestly people down where I come from generally think a woman who abandons her child and then goes and lives the high life in New York City is the lowest skunk of them all. I don't know what kind of real woman does that. But my wife says that Jenny was just a mixed-up, hurt young girl at the time and we can't say if she's bad. We don't know what hurt her so bad that she would run away like that." He looked mystified by sadness. "We sit down there and talk about it, mister. My wife says we have to give that gal another chance. This is her boy, her son, and we owe it to them."

Mr. Wilkerson started to cough again, then coughed badly, and Paul put his hand on the man's back, patted him a little. "I'm all right. It just starts up." He pulled a pack of cigarettes from his breast pocket and lit one. "This is a hell of a place, mister. I had a hell of a time getting in here." He pointed at his white pickup truck. "I'm give you two things, mister. The first is these." He pulled some car keys out of his pocket. "These here go to my son's truck. He had a couple spare sets 'cause we used the truck, too. I don't know where it is now, here or upstate, but if you find it, let me know, please. And if you need to drive it somewhere until I can come get it, use the keys." He opened the door of his own truck, pulled out an index card with some writing on it, and gave it to Paul. "That's our phone number and address. I'll be back in Texas in about five, six days. If Jenny wants to see her boy, she can call that number. My wife is the one who wants to get this done the right way. We got the original birth certificate with the name Jennifer Hayes on it. Nobody is ever going to say she ain't the mother. 'Course, with DNA now you can prove it one hundred percent. We are trying to do the right thing here, son. Part of me thinks that my boy is dead because of Jenny Hayes and part of me thinks that my boy would want me to do this anyway. Like I said, we believe in Jesus and the Good Lord. We turn the other cheek and we seek the sweetness in our brief life on earth. But if my wife don't hear nothing in the next couple of weeks, then we got to start the adoption papers quick. If Jenny Hayes wants to know who her boy is, then she better do it soon."

He slipped on some sunglasses and a cowboy hat, started the truck, gave Paul a solemn nod, and pulled out down the street. And that was when Paul found that he had sunk to his knees, his palms on the bluestone slabs of the sidewalk, placed there in the 1890s, when the neighborhood had been built. He'd grown up in this very place. He discovered that he was pounding the stone now, hating something, someone. Maybe Jennifer. But Ahmed, for sure. *Ahmed.*

32

I was on time, Omar thought, so where is this guy? He waited outside the deli for ten minutes and then went inside. An older Korean lady was behind the counter. She eyed him warily, like he might steal a pack of gum or a phone charger.

"Excuse me, I'm looking for a guy named Alexander Montoya?"

"Don't know that man, very sorry."

"He said to meet me here, that you got heating, air-conditioning problems?"

"Very sorry, we got no problems like that."

"Alexander Montoya?"

"I do not know this person."

Omar stared at the energy drinks in the cooler and bought two for his daughters. "Is there a manager here?"

"Just my son."

He paid for the drinks and stood outside, looked around. Plenty of people and cars. But no fat middle-aged Latin guy. Strange. Not good.

Two hours later, at the soccer game in the park, Omar watched his older daughter's team dominate a Staten Island team. It was 3–0 within ten minutes and he knew she would get playing time in the second half. The team parents standing on the synthetic green turf chatted with one another and cheered one another's children, as was the protocol, and at halftime Omar made sure his daughter had water and the energy drink and then went to use the portable toilet set up at the field's edge. Inside the fetid green plastic box he pissed into the dank hole of shit, remembering the same smell from the Manshiyat Naser, Garbage City, a sprawling Cairo slum. His father had taken him there as a boy, and as they watched the ragpickers standing next to a lake of sewage, waiting for the trucks piled high with garbage to arrive from the better neighborhoods, his father had said, "I want to show this to you, so you are grateful when you are successful in America."

When Omar was done and zipped up, he unlocked the plastic door and pushed it open, but a man suddenly knocked him back inside, a small, extremely muscular man.

"Listen good!" He pushed Omar over the hole.

"What the fuck? What?"

"Don't fight me!" the little man ordered.

But Omar was a trained fighter, and he pulled his knife from his ankle and stabbed—but was stopped. The man was that strong.

"Don't fight me!" the man hissed. "Or I will kill you right now."

They struggled in the tight dark space, the man holding Omar's right wrist firmly and punching him methodically with his right hand. Omar head-butted the little man, and he fell backward, just long enough for Omar to get his hand loose and plunge the knife at the man. But he missed and the man spun around on top of him and lifted him up, wrenching both arms behind him, and pressed his face into the dark hole of shit. His nose and mouth filled with the smell of piss and ammonia and excrement. He went limp. He was beaten.

"Listen, motherfuck, listen!" came the hot Latino voice in his ear. "I swear honest to God I do not want to kill you."

Omar tried to answer, but he was talking into the darkness, to a mound of wet shit inches from his face.

The man lifted Omar up a bit.

"No fight?"

"No, no fight."

The man lifted him up a little more.

"I'm throwing your knife in the hole. Goodbye."

There was a splash.

"Listen to me good now."

Omar nodded, trying to catch his breath.

"You called a man named Lorenzo in Queens and told him about a job."

"What job?"

"To kill a big white dude with a red Ford pickup truck."

He remembered. "Yes."

"*I* did it."

So this was the Mexican who Lorenzo had called, the man who'd worked for El Chapo. "Okay, so you did it."

"I want to be paid all of the money."

"I have to call the guy."

"Call him now." The man's breath was rapid and hot.

"Here?"

"Cell phone works here, too."

The man let Omar reach the cell phone in his front pocket. He watched him dial.

"Put it on speakerphone."

Omar complied.

"Yes, yes?" came a female voice.

"This is Omar," he breathed. "I need to speak to Hassan Mehraz."

"Yes, please, one minute."

Then, an older man's voice: "Hello, yes?"

"This is Omar. We need to— The man you ask me to kill is dead. He is killed, and I need the money now."

"Ah, well, yes," came the voice, suddenly guarded, "we discussed how we would—"

Hector grabbed the phone, then pounded Omar twice. His grunts echoed in the darkened plastic box. With his own phone, Hector took a photo of the number, which looked to him like it was in California, and then was about to speak into Omar's cell, before realizing that Omar would overhear everything he'd say.

"Hello? Hello?" came the small voice from the phone. "What is happening there— Hello?"

Hector flung Omar's phone into the shit hole, gave Omar a wicked kick in the ribs, then hammered him on the back of the head. He knelt down and put his mouth next to Omar's ear. "If this man does not pay me I will come back and kill your family," he said.

Then he opened the door of the portable toilet. He heard cheering at the game across the field and headed in the other direction.

A few minutes later, Omar pushed open the door of the toilet, his wet hand clutching something, and staggered out into the sunlight. Never had he felt so happy to be alive.

33

The universe, proclaimed random, was nevertheless marked by chains of causation. Once upon a time, Paul remembered while waiting for his friend Bobby Passaro, New York City detectives arrested a man named Michael Crossette, the corpulent red-haired owner of a failing bar in Hartford, Connecticut, now a tough town fallen on hard times. Crossette had attempted to become a player in the local ecstasy trade and needed capital. His deceased father, a stockbroker who favored red bow ties, had been a minor but proficient map collector when Crossette was younger, and the boy had picked up quite a bit of incidental knowledge about rare maps. His father preferred to have color in his maps, so he trained his son to add or restore pigment to them. The requirements were patience, skill with a ½₂-inch paintbrush, a rainbow selection of inks diluted from full strength, a blotting pad, and yet more patience. Color on maps, even a light wash along the contours of a shoreline, is always preferable, so long as it isn't garish, and dealers often add it and then allow, ambiguously, that the map's color is "contemporary," which may mean that it is recent or was added when the map was printed. Young Crossette, meanwhile, became middle-aged Crossette, and needed to amass money to enter Hartford's drug trade. Being adept at tasks that depended upon subterfuge, dishonesty, and a general disrespect for the sanctity of personal property, Crossette began to pilfer maps from libraries and archives in Connecticut and New York City, often finding folded maps in rare volumes, and expertly slicing them out and secreting them on his person. Then he would go to work on them. It is possible to disguise a stolen map by adding color or damaging the paper carefully. Antique maps don't have serial numbers, after all, and most were made under circumstances that guarantee no one alive could know how many originals ever existed.

Paul's phone rang.

"I know I'm fucking late! I'm looking for a spot."

"Bobby, there's no street parking around here."

"Hey yo, for me, there is *always* parking."

Crossette also knew the dealers who would buy such maps, no questions asked. He took one of his stolen treasures, a 1635 edition of *Nova Belgica et Anglia Nova*, a spectacular example of Dutch cartography, to a rare book dealer in midtown. The Nova Belgica, created to spur interest and investment in the New World, showed Manhattan Island as "New Netherland" and depicted New England as populated with deer, bears, beavers, foxes, otters, egrets, rabbits, and turkeys, all originally inked in splendid greens and browns and reds. The map also showed two Indian villages and several European ships. Crossette reinked all of the animals and other features, then purposefully damaged the map in several places only to repair it, further disguising its identity.

The New York Public Library, Yale University, and the other affected institutions had, by this time, made a coordinated effort to get out information on their stolen maps. The shop owner to whom Crossette took the map, one Janet Doughty, had a sharp eye. She played along, agreeing to purchase the map in question, but only after she went to the bank to secure the required funds. Thief and shop owner affably made an appointment for the next day, Doughty contacted the NYPD, and upon his return Crossette was promptly arrested. Connecticut and New York City detectives working together found nearly $500,000 worth of ecstasy pills in his barn, and it was very clear that he would not be a free man for many years.

But to prosecute Crossette for the map thefts, detectives had to prove that the maps he had in his possession, or had sold to others, had been altered. They turned to several experts, one a dealer, one a restorer, and the third, a private collector with expertise in New York City maps. The collector had been Paul, and that was the way he'd met Detective Bobby Passaro of the NYPD's Major Case Squad, the forty most elite detectives in the city. Paul had examined before-and-after photos of five maps for Passaro and explained what he saw, and then testified as an expert witness in the case. He and Passaro had liked each other, in the way of world-weary middle-aged men, and kept in touch.

Now the detective pushed into the bar, overweight, with a full head of rumpled, graying hair and the shambling gate of a man who had done his time as a beat cop, grinding down his knees and spine while patrolling on foot and sitting too long in stakeout cars drinking bad coffee.

"Bobby, you look like *hell*," Paul said, shaking his hand.

"I know I do," Passaro answered. "But I still have a new girlfriend. She's very serious about everything."

"And?"

He waved dismissively. "Oh, it won't last."

Passaro had a kind of craggy, self-destructed charisma. Women found him irresistible and he lurched amusedly from one to the next. They eventually decided that his charisma had in fact self-destructed already and that he was increasingly resistible.

Paul handed him a menu. "You're sure?"

"Absolutely. I told her. I tell all of them."

"You go on the record, huh?"

"I tell them—I really say this—I say, if you want some good fucking, then don't come to me. I *used* to be good, but I'm all washed up now. Look at this stomach, right? I admit it! But some of these women don't care. Or they *say* they don't care, that all they want is love. What-ev-er. Okay, what's this about some guy got killed upstate? You think he was killed here?"

"Yes," said Paul. "Just seems more likely."

Passaro studied him, not blinking. "And your basis for that statement is what?" he said, his voice deepening into a practiced cadence of questioning.

Paul explained that, while staying in his house, Bill had gotten into some kind of fight, according to the druggy neighbor. And there was a little mark on the wall inside his house that might be blood, just one tiny spatter. "So it'd be more logical that he was killed here."

"And your basis for that statement is what?"

"He was *here*."

"How do you know?"

"I saw him about two weeks ago."

"Maybe he left town."

Paul shook his head. "I told him to leave town, and he wouldn't. He was definitely sticking around."

"And who do you think the murderer is?"

"I have no idea who it is. But Bill was seeing, I guess, my neighbor Jennifer Mehraz, who is married. She was sneaking around with him."

"The victim is an honorably discharged army serviceman who had seen action abroad?"

"Yes."

"Did he drink or use drugs?"

"Well, he did drink, because I saw him drunk."

"How long did you know him?"

"Just a few weeks."

Passaro nodded. "That answer is not reassuring."

"Okay."

"Did he have a known domicile here in New York?"

"Besides my house? Not that I know of."

"Did this woman commit herself to him forever and ever?"

"That I doubt."

"Why would the fancy Manhattan businessman have this fellow killed, in your professional opinion?"

"My opinion is not professional."

"Are you sure?"

"Yes."

"So, in fact, it is an amateur opinion, and might be flawed, in some way."

"Bobby, enough already."

Passaro picked up his menu, scanning the Irish fare. "You do realize that if you are an old, burnt-out fart like me, then the *last thing* you want to do is to *try* to make a case against a smart, rich international businessman who probably knows people who could get me retired."

"You only want the easy cases?"

"Yes, I do, exactly!" Passaro smiled at the obvious logic. "I only want the easy-can't-miss-because-they-are-airtight cases."

Paul groaned. "Give me a break."

They both ordered shepherd's pie. Passaro was silent until the waitress had left. "You haven't told me if this Jennifer is attractive."

"She is very attractive."

Passaro's eyebrows shot up. "Did you fuck her?"

"No."

"Would you if you could?"

"That's a terrible question."

"Why?" Passaro frowned in disgust. "I myself would probably fuck her if I got the chance!"

"Neither one of us is getting the chance."

"Maybe you are secretly in love with her and want to get rid of the husband. Maybe *you* had the army guy killed and are trying to frame the poor rich hubby."

"That's a genius theory. Why would I come to you, then?"

"Because you are trying to get yourself ruled out as a suspect."

"Thanks."

"Are the state police involved?"

"I don't know."

"If they get interested in the case, then they may ask our assistance."

"What if they don't get interested?"

"Then the local cops will have to solve it."

"I don't think there are that many local cops. It's one of those small towns up near the Canadian border."

"Sounds like this soldier was a little unstable. Impulsive."

"Could be."

"Ready?" said Passaro. "Here's my version of events, just as plausible. He goes into a bar in Brooklyn, very trendy and cool, and meets

Kissy-poo the Magnificent sitting there. She has great lipstick and she crosses her legs a lot, see? He misses Miss Jennifer Uptown Girl so much that he has to flirt with Kissy-poo and she gives him a little wet kiss, which is witnessed by Big Dawg, her boyfriend and motorcycle gang member. Big Dawg thinks it will look good on his résumé if he kills your friend, which he does, outside in the parking lot an hour later, after making sure the bartender gives him a couple of free refills on his whiskey. They put the body in Big Dawg's truck and throw a tarp over it. They weigh the tarp down with some old bricks. Kissy-poo, who long ago learned to suspend moral judgment of the men whom she spends time with, is made all the more lubricious—that's a real word, right?—and anyway, Big Dawg and his pals are riding up to Montreal for whatever the hell no-good reason, and when they get close to the border they dump him in a metal barrel near the lake where they hold summer barbecues. These are events up there where several hundred bikers meet and sell drugs and get in fights and generally believe, heh, that they have found the moral center of the universe."

"Sounds a little far-fetched."

Passaro churned his steaming shepherd's pie. "Okay, scenario two, then. Your friend Bill is sitting in Williamsburg in Brooklyn at some teahouse filled with artsy student types who think they are Internet revolutionaries–slash–commerce visionaries–slash–indie movie directors. I mean everything is everything these days, right? He gets to talking to some skinny kid with a beard who wants to be the next Martin Scorsese. He's sensitive and brilliant and ambitious and insecure with chicks. Scorsese the Younger has a brilliant screenplay set in a bar in Brooklyn and wants your pal Bill to play a motorcycle gang member, okay? But his girlfriend Suzy just *decides* that your friend is, *like*, a 'war criminal' because he served in the U.S. military and that a symbolic execution has to take place. They will film it for an experimental documentary she is trying to make. So Suzy dissolves six of these Mexican fentanyl pills made with Chinese precursors into a drink. They have pills now, you don't have to shoot it. Except that she has no idea that six pills of fentanyl would kill one of those huge flying dragons in the *Lord of the Rings* movies. So Bill drinks his drink and in about three minutes is unconscious and foaming at the mouth. He actually dies, which wasn't part of *the plan*, and then Suzy's eminent brain-surgeon father calls her from Vermont and says let's go make maple syrup, honey, so Suzy and Scorsese drive the dead body in her new Volvo station wagon, dump it upstate, which she records on her iPhone, then they go on to Vermont."

"You make maple syrup in the spring, not this time of year."

Passaro put up his hands. "These scenarios are *at least* as probable as what you just told me."

"What should I do?"

"Look, Paul, if the state police or the cops up in that small town get something *real* and want to *consult* me, then fine."

"What are you going to do?"

"Me? I'm going to the Giants game this weekend."

"Are you going to talk to Jennifer Mehraz, or Bill's father? Anybody?"

"For a whack that took place in upstate New York?" Bobby threw his crumpled napkin on the table. "Not going to happen."

How do I tell Jennifer? Paul thought later as he climbed the subway steps near his apartment house, feeling a chill in the air. How do I say they found your lover a couple of hundred miles from here, dead? But who else was going to tell her? Yet when he reached his apartment there was an envelope taped to the door. Her stationery, with her name, JENNIFER MEHRAZ, in classy blue serif type on the back flap. The note said:

Paul,

Hi, I think your cell phone is off? Anyway something terrible has happened. The police in some town way upstate NY just called me and told me they found Billy's body there. He's dead. I can't believe it, I don't know what to do. Somebody killed him. I am very very afraid of Ahmed and I am going to just go away. I took cash with me and will be fine for a while. I wish you were here to talk to me. I am so sorry for everything. This is all my fault. But please do not blame me, I did not know this was going to happen. No one knows where I am going. I think maybe only you understand.

Love, Jenny

The next morning, Paul found he could not go to work, troubled by his memory of Bill's father. *Listen up, sir . . . my boy is dead, my wife is dying on me, and I ain't good much longer.* The son was supposed to bury the father, as Paul had done, not the other way around. And how could Ahmed *not* have anything to do with it? He phoned his office and said he wasn't feeling well. Rachel called but he didn't pick up the phone. Instead of reading the paper, or checking his e-mail, or being in any way productive, he sat in his kitchen mulling. On the wall there hung one of the giant official Metropolitan Transportation Authority neighborhood maps that adorn local subway stations. His, dated March 2001, was from the Chambers Street stop and showed the twin towers before they'd been destroyed.

The phone rang, and he thought it would be Rachel, so he picked it up.

"Mr. Reeves, my name is Emily Kent. I am a village police officer in Rouses Point, New York."

"Up there near the Canadian border?"

"Yes, sir."

"What can I do for you?"

"First I would like to ask you for permission to tape this conversation."

"That's fine."

"You are providing your explicit permission of your own free will to allow this conversation to be captured on a recording device with a police officer, is that right?"

"That's correct."

"Very well, do you know a man named Bill Wilkerson?"

"I did, very briefly. I just met his father, who told me Bill was dead, how they found him up there."

"Not a pleasant piece of information for a father to be told."

"No . . . a terrible thing. What can I do for you?"

"Well, sir, Mr. Wilkerson, the father, said you were one of the two people his son knew in New York City. The other is a woman named Jennifer Hayes, or now her married name, Jennifer Mehraz."

"Yes."

"And you two, you and Mrs. Mehraz, know each other how?"

"She's my neighbor here in our apartment building." Paul looked at the note Jennifer had left him. "You talked to her already, right?"

"Sir, I cannot comment on a police investigation."

"Of course."

"I'm trying to get a handle on what Bill Wilkerson might have been doing up in our neck of the woods."

"I don't think he'd have much reason to go up there. He came to New York City to see Mrs. Mehraz here."

"They knew each other from the past, I see?"

"Seems so."

"I can't seem to get in touch with Mrs. Mehraz."

"She travels some."

"Please, sir, tell me your means of employment?"

"I'm an attorney specializing in immigration law." There was an appraising silence. Now the police officer knew she was talking to a lawyer. "Mrs. Mehraz asked me to find a place for Bill to stay in New York," continued Paul. "He didn't have anywhere else to go. I own a small house in Brooklyn. I told him he could stay there. He seemed to be attacked on the premises and left, according to a neighbor. I wasn't there. I'm not sure exactly what happened. But I saw him soon after that."

"How did he seem?"

"Physically? He seemed fine. He was quite a physical specimen."

"Who would have reason to attack him?"

"You know, I have a friend down here who is a detective first-grade and I just outlined the whole story to him and he basically laughed it off."

"A New York City detective?" He heard the awe in her voice.

"Yes, I told him I thought the attack was somehow arranged by Mrs. Mehraz's husband. But I have no proof."

"I see. Was there a romantic relationship between Jennifer Mehraz and the deceased?"

He'd seen them fucking expertly in her bedroom. That was proof, in a court of law. "There was," Paul said. "But I don't know what Mr. Mehraz knew or didn't know."

"And yet you think he might be responsible? On what basis?"

"I have no proof, I just said that. Just a feeling."

"Did the deceased ever mention this part of the state?"

"I don't think he thought about anyplace besides New York City. Because Mrs. Mehraz was here. He was from Texas, Officer. I doubt he knew much about upstate New York."

"He say how long he planned to stay?"

"I doubt he had a particularly good plan."

"Have you ever been up our way?"

The officer had plenty of questions, it seemed.

"I've taken the train through Plattsburgh on the way to Montreal. Long train trip."

"We're fifty miles south of Montreal."

"Are the state police interested in the case?"

"I can't comment on that," Officer Kent said.

"What do you want me to do?"

"I want you to think of everything you might possibly know about the deceased."

"Did he die up there or down here?"

"Well, that's police business."

"Of course."

"Would you give me this New York City detective's name?"

"Bobby Passaro."

"His number?"

Paul did that.

"You've mentioned the case to him, you say?"

"Just saw him yesterday."

"I'll call him. One last question. Do you know where Mr. Mehraz is?"

"No."

"Thank you. Is there anything else you can tell me?"

"No, Officer."

But of course there was, he thought, after hanging up. I have the keys to Bill's truck, and a pretty good idea of where it might be.

I cannot escape Richard Nixon, thought Hassan as he read a copper plaque explaining that Nixon had dedicated a stand of huge redwood trees in honor of the wife of President Lyndon Johnson in August 1969. That would have been about seven months after Nixon assumed power, Hassan realized. Using Henry Kissinger as a go-between, Nixon had quickly built up Iran's military and thus the Shah's power, which resulted in the Mehrazes getting the contract to build mile-long runways for the hundreds of new American-built fighter jets and bombers Nixon sold to Iran. But that was not why Hassan was there; his daughter and granddaughter wanted him to see the gigantic thousand-year-old trees, and he'd said he would go with them. Little did they realize that the man who'd dedicated the park where they were had been instrumental in creating the wealth that supported them, even now. But this was yet another useless perception of an old man, he realized, watching them walk ahead of him on the trail beneath the colossal trees, pointing upward at their improbable height. His ten-year-old granddaughter suddenly skipped along the path in delight. How perfect and happy and sweet she is, he thought with contentment.

Just then, his phone rang.

"Hello, this is Omar."

"Yes, hello, Omar. I was waiting for you to call me back."

"Hassan, I have a very big problem."

Hassan stared up at a giant redwood. "Yes, I am listening. You said before that the assignment was completed? But then I heard noise on the phone and nothing more."

"I need to explain that I did not finish the big assignment."

Hassan listened, didn't respond.

"I arranged for another man to do it."

"Why? You *wanted* the assignment."

"I was— I needed to do something else. So I called someone I knew and he arranged it with this other man."

"What is this man's name?"

"I do not know. But then he found me . . . and he wants to be paid."

"Then *you* pay him."

"He wants you to pay him, to pay him *more*."

"I am not involved in this, I know nothing of this!"

"He found me and forced me to call you. That was what you heard when I called before. He took my phone and got your number."

Forced. Hassan understood what that meant. He felt the beginnings of an undertow, pulling at him. "He will call me?"

"I think, yes . . . He is *very* dangerous. I am telling you now to be careful of him. I am scared of him."

"How about if I pay you to make him not talk to me? I would pay you for that on top of the first job."

"No," said Omar quickly. "I can't— Maybe with another case, but not for me, no. Not this man."

"I am saying I will pay you what I said I would pay and some *more* so that you deal with him and not me."

"Yes, yes, I understand," answered Omar, sounding increasingly panicked, "but I cannot—he is too dangerous! I am telling you, I am warning you. But you have to pay or he will kill my family!"

So this is where we are, thought Hassan. A man is begging me to protect his family. Only bad things can happen in such a scenario. Do not argue or become mad, he counseled himself. Get information that is useful. "What can you tell me about this man?"

Omar waited to calm down. Then he spoke. "He is short, maybe thirty years old, very muscular, he is the strongest man I have ever fought. Spanish, I mean maybe Mexican or Latin American. Very tricky. He will call you."

"You have given him no money?"

"No," answered Omar. "You have not paid me for the job, either."

"And I am not going to. But you were paid to find the young woman on Staten Island." Hassan felt tension in his chest. "Do you know how to reach this Mexican killer?"

"I knew you would ask this," responded Omar. "I called my friend. We had a big argument. He says he cannot give me the number, or he will maybe be killed by this man, too."

Hassan watched his daughter and granddaughter far up the trail, nearly unreachable, it seemed. Enchanted by the massive trees overhead, they'd forgotten about him, which was just as well. If all went right, they would never really know who he was. All the old secrets would die with him. "So, Omar, I have to wait until I get his call?"

"Yes."

The muscular Mexican man would call him, Hassan realized, and then he, Hassan, would probably have to deliver the money himself. He couldn't trust anyone anymore. But maybe he could deliver something *else*, he thought, something he had not done since the dark days in Tehran. He still had the injector, given to him by a friend who worked in the CIA. "You can't give me any more information?"

"No."

"He has my actual complete name and my actual phone number?"

"Yes, this number that I called right now."

"Did you mention any of my family members?" Meaning Ahmed.

"No. Just you."

"Omar?" said Hassan.

"Yes?"

"*Yixrib beitak,*" he said quietly before hanging up. *May God destroy your house.*

35

Her mother had made *every* possible mistake in life. Bad men, bad marriages, pills, shoplifting arrests, bankruptcy, several probably avoidable abortions, two serious car accidents because of her drinking, addiction hospitalizations, and the loss of custody of Jennifer's half sister. And yet she was a survivor. Somehow she had scammed the government into sending her disability checks that she augmented with an unreported cash salary as a waitress in a local sports bar, one frequented only by white, working-class men. Her mother was, in fact, exactly the kind of person who Ahmed said was ruining America: uneducated, unproductive, uninsured, unhappy, uninterested in the greater good. A malingering, self-pitying parasite. But, Jennifer said, arguing with Ahmed in her mind, you don't know how *beautiful* she once was, how good life had once been, how full of hope she had been, how she had *tried* . . .

Now her mother lived in a garage apartment, her beaten-up Honda out front. Jennifer had taken a taxi from the Reading bus station. The small city looked worse than ever, certain neighborhoods too dangerous to even enter, her mother's not much better, and the houses, many with foreclosure signs in front, stood unpainted, their yards filled with junk cars and broken toys and rusty equipment and children who seemed dazed and somehow malnourished. Her mother was not even fifty years old, but the years had not been good to her, and she had become an "alcorexic," painfully skinny and drinking too much booze. Blurred by pills, eaten away by fear and bitterness.

"Mom?"

"Yes?"

They were sitting in the "front room," one of the two rooms she lived in. "You were saying?"

Her mother considered her and pursed her mouth thoughtfully. "I'm just saying I got to move to a better place, is all. The crime is getting worse around here. The whole neighborhood's different. I don't know who's worse, the blacks or the whites. There have been a lot of overdoses and robberies, things like that. Least the Mexicans actually *work*."

On the table before them was a manicure set her mother was about to use. "You still doing shifts at O'Malley's?"

"He gives me the daytime, the shitty ones. Problem is the good-looking young girls come in and swish around and work for a few months on the best shifts and then they always leave when they meet some guy. But he won't put me on Friday or Saturday night."

Jennifer had only told her mother that she and Ahmed were having problems, nothing about what had happened to Bill. But she feared her mother's weird mind-reading abilities, nonetheless. That and a request for money, which she had already decided to turn down. In her handbag, she had all of her jewelry, all the gold bracelets and pearl earrings and chokers and double-strand necklaces and two sweet little gold watches and everything else Ahmed had given her over the years. Dozens of pieces. How much was it worth? Maybe $250,000? She could of course give her mother some of this, but she knew her mother wouldn't even bother selling it on eBay and would instead just take it to a local cash-for-gold shop and sell it for a fifth of its value. And then what? The money would be gone before she knew it, and might even facilitate another slide into drugs. Besides, it really was Jennifer's wealth; she had earned it; yes, she had.

"You seeing anyone?" asked Jennifer.

"An actual *man*?" Her mother laughed. "I'm tired of men. They're overrated." She looked for a cigarette in her bag. "Seriously, nothing but trouble. They don't understand women, and women *do* understand men. Men actually think that because they have dicks they are superior to women. You do know that, right? That's the whole problem, *we* do understand what assholes *they* are and we *still* want to be with them!" She found her lighter. "I wish somebody had explained it all to me thirty years ago. It's getting late in the day. Late in the *game*. I'd say it's the eighth inning and we are down by seven runs and the home crowd is leaving." She gazed at Jennifer, her eyes softer. "Sweetie, I know you want my advice. But god*damn*, I don't know what to tell you. Men who are rich tend to stay rich. Okay? I *do* know that. They're smart about how the world *really* works. You want to live a rich life, and I hope you do, then you got to ride it out and stay with him."

"What about little Henry?"

Her mother blinked in sudden distress as if slapped. The topic they never discussed. Too painful. The perfect newborn boy whom Jennifer had abandoned, the sweet grandson her mother was forced to give up to the other set of grandparents because she became trapped by Oxy-Contin tablets she'd bought on the street from young men in hoodies and was thus later deemed by the local child services department to be unfit. She shook her head and started to cry. "I *can't*. I just can't do this! That's the *one* thing. It makes me sick. I think of him every single day of my life! Sometimes I think I'm punishing myself and maybe I am. And maybe I *should* be."

Jennifer moved closer to her mother.

"No!" she screamed. "Don't touch me, get the fuck away from me. *You* did this! *You* walked out on that baby and it made me sick and then I did the drugs and it all fell apart! Let me tell you something, you can't have *both*, girlfriend, you can't have your son, your flesh and blood, and have that rich Ahmed guy. It doesn't work that way! You have to *choose*. And you know what? Too bad! Too fucking bad! I want you to get out of here now. You're upsetting me."

Jennifer stood, getting ready to leave and return to the station in downtown Reading. She'd get the next bus back to New York, and keep hiding in a crummy hotel she'd found on Staten Island not far from the ferry. She gathered her bag, remembering her cell phone records could be visible to Ahmed. She didn't want him to know where she was. "I need to call a taxi from your phone."

Her mother was weeping, banging her fists against her meager thighs. "No! No! Just get away from me, get the fuck out of here!"

36

He is *totally* not telling me something! Rachel decided. Paul has been just too quiet, a little distant, maybe. Right? She could feel it. She entered the building and the doorman gave her his customary wave. Paul had instructed the front-desk staff just to send her up every time, not bother with the call upstairs. Yup, that meant official GF status, right? She saw a hand holding the elevator door open for her.

"Thank you!" she called, rushing to get inside. There, wow, standing alone, was Ahmed, in a beautiful gray suit, white shirt, blue tie.

"Hello," he said.

"It's Rachel," she answered, admiring his thick black hair, his dark eyes. "We've met a few times."

"Yes, yes, of course." He smiled softly, then pressed the floor button. "And how is Paul? I heard he was at a map auction recently?"

"Yes," she answered, happy to have something to discuss. "But he just lost a *very* fabulous map that he wanted very badly."

"Another New York City map?"

"Yes! He was going to buy it, but another person got there first."

"A disappointment."

"He is ridiculously obsessed," she admitted. "But do you like maps?"

Ahmed considered her. "We often use them in my work when companies have mineral holdings, including under the ocean. We use this cool stuff called satellite radar altimetry imaging, which gives us computer modeling of sea-floor deposits."

She was both impressed and irritated by his display of knowledge. "Paul would say you should should hang on to those."

"Most are on screens, of course."

"Nothing on paper."

"Alas, no."

The door opened. They nodded a polite goodbye. He *is* totally gorgeous, Rachel thought, but there's something creepy about him.

In his apartment, Ahmed immediately sensed that Jennifer had not returned. Yet. If, in fact, she was *ever* going to return. He smelled air freshener and furniture wax; the housekeeper had been there, and—yes—accepted the food delivery and put all the items away. He dialed Jennifer's cell, waited five rings and got her message. "Jennifer," he said, "hey, come on, tell me where you are."

The only explanation for her disappearance was that she knew Bill Wilkerson was dead and had connected Ahmed to that fact. But how could she know that? Who did she talk to who might know? Her cell phone data showed nothing, except that she had received a phone call from upstate New York two days back that had lasted eight minutes. He'd been tempted to dial it and discover the caller but decided against it. And anyway, didn't the fact that she'd left Ahmed *acknowledge* that she had been involved with Bill? If she hadn't been involved with him, and had received the news of his death, she would not have just vanished. So she had painted herself into a box of sorts, he thought. But maybe she didn't care. He drifted into their bedroom and into the large walk-in closet where she kept her things, wondering if he could determine her behavior by what she had taken with her. He knew the jewelry would be gone, had checked for it right away when he suspected she'd left. And she'd drained the joint checking account of $29,000. Jennifer owned a matching three-piece Tumi luggage set. She'd taken the middle-sized one, which suggested more than an overnight. Didn't want the burden of a large suitcase, needed flexibility. He opened her underwear drawer, suddenly aware of the flowery smell of her clothes, an odor he quite liked. Jennifer had so many underthings and bras and panties and socks that he could not tell which she had taken. Then he thought of Jennifer's passport, usually kept in her desk. He found it, the most recent stamp in it from her return from Switzerland. Okay, still in the country. He remembered the report from his private detective that she had seemed distracted and weepy in those days after her return. Maybe expecting to meet up with William Wilkerson, and then worrying why he hadn't appeared? That made sense. If Jennifer knew Wilkerson was dead, and connected Ahmed, then of course she would flee, perhaps in fear of her life.

It was beginning to dawn on Ahmed that he might somehow be a suspect in a murder case. Yet *he* had not committed a murder. He did not even know who the killer was! Only his uncle knew this. But despite his rational analysis, he was aware of a low hum of worry in his mind. Conspiracy. In the state of New York, all that had to be proven was the *intent* to commit a crime in order to be charged with conspiracy. Had he conspired with his uncle? If he were a prosecutor, the answer would be yes. *Conspire* meant to breathe together. And he had certainly conspired to kidnap Wilkerson. There was no getting around that; but two of the witnesses were dead and the third, Amir, was out of the country. If he recalled correctly from cramming for the state bar exam, there were six different degrees of conspiracy under the New York Penal Code; the most severe, a Class A felony, carried a maximum punishment of life in prison.

I need some advice, Ahmed thought, not legal advice but goddamned life advice. He wished he could speak with his uncle, yet thought it better to avoid contact now. But what would Uncle Hassan have done? Or his father, all those years ago? Growing up, he'd listened to his uncle and his father discuss how in the late 1970s they'd set up foreign accounts for themselves so that money would be available if and when they fled Iran, and this had proved prudent. There had been a point when the Shah began to turn against his loyal supporters, having them dragged from their homes, imprisoned, efficiently tortured—boiling water in the anus, extraction of teeth—and even executed, in order to placate the revolutionaries calling for his head. Ahmed's father and uncle had trusted no one in these panicked days but each other; they carried concealed striking batons and thumb knives in case they were attacked. Ahmed's father had flown to Switzerland carrying three suitcases packed with thin, old American dollars and, in the cargo hold of the plane, fifty crates of wet figs each containing ten one-pound bars of gold. Five hundred pounds at $200 an ounce amounted to $1.6 million. These days, that sum maybe bought a crummy two-bedroom apartment in lesser Manhattan; then, it was a fortune that could save multiple generations of a family. The crates were shipped to a warehouse in Geneva, where Ahmed's father received them and quietly established a bank account. He'd converted the dollars to Swiss francs and housed the gold at the bank. And hung on to it. When Jimmy Carter failed to rescue the American hostages kidnapped from the U.S. Embassy in Iran, the price of oil skyrocketed, lifting gold upward with it. His father had sold quite a bit of gold just then, tripling his money; such a smart man, and Ahmed missed him. Never extravagant, always practical. He'd made a point to dry the figs he used to smuggle the gold and had happily eaten them over the next year.

Now, of course, one could move money instantly, but it could be tracked more easily than ever before. Nonetheless, Ahmed had that morning moved the bulk of his liquid wealth to his Swiss bank account. It was still available, but beyond the reach of American law. Only he knew about the account. Jennifer had no idea of its existence, nor the millions that he had secreted in it over the years. Were he to have to flee the country while his legal trouble was cleared up, he could live a very long time on the money he had stashed away, decades if he existed frugally. Not that he expected this to come to pass. But it was a comfort to know this money was there, waiting for him.

Across the hallway, fifty feet away, Rachel found Paul in his chair brooding. "I've come to cheer you up," she said, rubbing his head. "Okay?"

"Thank you."

Paul looked tired. "What's going on?" she asked.

"Oh, too much," he replied vaguely.

"Work stuff?"

"Just a lot of craziness."

A total nonanswer. She decided to change the topic. "I was wondering if you would tell me about those little burnt scraps and things tonight. In the sealed glass box, from a Brooklyn dock fire, you said?"

Paul sighed. "I don't think I can."

"No, not really in the mood?"

He had been preoccupied with what had happened to Bill, but wasn't ready to discuss it with Rachel. "I confess, Rachel, I'm not very chatty right now."

"But I *want* to know!" She took his hand playfully. "Because I'm interested in you! And you *told* me that you would tell me."

"Right," he answered in a noncommittal voice.

"Come on," she teased. "It's a moment of intimacy."

I need to pay attention here, Paul thought, there's an edge in her voice. "I'm happy to have all kinds of intimacy . . . but I just can't discuss it now."

"Okay, I guess . . . though I'm a little *hurt*."

But the rest of the evening went fine, fine enough, fine-*ish*, and while he cleaned up in the kitchen, protesting that he wanted to do it, she snooped a little in his office, not finding much of interest, just map stuff and work papers. Paul got a lot of mail from antique and rare book dealers, she noticed.

Later, when they were in bed, he was just starting to move inside her, in and out, and she felt an urge, an unstoppable urge. "Wait, wait!" she commanded.

"What?" he said, ceasing all copulatory rhythms. "Are you okay?"

"Will you tell me after? About the little box?"

Here he was, a man with an erection, having sex, being asked to make binding statements about the future. He paused. Answering the question required many psychic transitions that he preferred not to make, many delicate linkages and delinkages. "I, uh, I'm—"

"You're not going to, are you?" Rachel cried, twisting out from beneath him, making sure he was no longer inside her. "You're plenty happy just to *have sex*, and *everything*, but this one little thing, this *intimacy*, which is about love and trust and closeness, you can't do that, can you?" She flew out of the bed with remarkable agility, holding the pillow pressed against her breasts defensively, knowingly denying him the pleasurable sight of them, her voice laced with grief and righteousness in equal measure. "You just want to have *sex* and go to *bed* and not *talk* about things, right?"

"Rachel, I'm—" Resting on his knees and elbows, he hung his head in defeat. His erection was now somewhere far away, speeding on the New Jersey Turnpike, perhaps, headed flat-out for Philadelphia or points south, anywhere it might be wanted.

"What? *What?*"

Paul rolled over. He had, of course, experienced *many* fights in bedrooms over the years, and he had learned that it was best to slow them down, not to escalate. But the fact that this relationship had found its way to a familiar setting of romantic destruction did not bode well. "Well, *first* of all, I'm sorry, let's start there."

"Sorry? Sorry for *what*?" Rachel cried. "Sorry because you don't *want* to tell me, *refuse* to tell me?"

She ran out of the room with her clothes. Then she came back, seemingly having dressed in ten seconds, and the juxtaposition of her being clothed and his being naked seemed to strengthen her fury. "Okay, I'm leaving. I'm walking *out* of here. I'm *upset*, but I know I'm doing the right thing, because I can tell that this—this is a *thing*, this is an important moment where you are holding back! I am giving you *everything*, all of myself, and that isn't enough, you are just rejecting *me*, implicitly and explicitly, and I think that's very bad, Paul, so withholding, just such a *failure* of trust, such—" And here her rage faltered a bit, teetered toward tears, but she pulled her fury back together, tightening her fists, and said, "Goodbye, and *don't* fucking call me!"

He listened to the sound of her storming through the kitchen and out into the foyer, followed by the particular click of the door being unlocked then closed behind her. It would take a minute for the elevator to arrive. You could still go after her, he thought, but you're not going to.

37

This Billy was a legit badass, Passaro thought, reviewing the military file of William Wilkerson Jr., deceased. His Army Ranger unit had performed special ops in many countries, including Syria, Afghanistan, Iraq, and three African countries where the politics were so complicated that Passaro didn't pretend to understand them. But that was not the issue, not now, for he had before him, thanks to a court order and the NYPD real-time crime center, a massive data warehouse filled with genius geeks, a time-and-motion digital map of the cell phones used by the two Libyan men who had been discovered killed in Brooklyn a few weeks back, their bodies located just a five-minute drive from Paul's house. The first one, used by one Tarek al-Badri, showed entry into the city across the Goethals Bridge from New Jersey to Fourteenth Street in Brooklyn, Paul Reeves's house, to be exact. The movement over the map, represented by a series of red dots indicating cell phone tower pings, was a progression of vectors and turns that corresponded perfectly with avenues and streets, which meant that Tarek was in a car. After the phone arrived at Paul's house in Brooklyn, it stayed there less than an hour, then moved around the neighborhood somewhat haphazardly—turns, short blocks, doubling back on itself as if its holder had changed his mind—until it arrived at Fourth Avenue and Sixth Street, where there was a taxi garage. From there the phone-location map showed red dots returning to Manhattan, where it made a series of uptown and downtown transits. Thanks to the car-tracking technologies mandated by the city's Taxi and Limousine Commission, Passaro was able to perfectly correlate the phone's movement with that of the transceiver of taxi medallion number 5X55, driven at that time by a Pakistani immigrant who clearly did not know the phone had been duct-taped to the underside of his bumper during a shift change until it had been removed by detectives that very morning.

Now Passaro keyed in the cell phone number of the second Libyan, Abdul Jalloud, and watched its track of cell tower pings. On the day in question, it met up with the first phone in New Jersey and then moved in perfect unison with the first phone for almost sixteen hours, which meant that the two men were in a car together. Then, just as with the first phone, the pattern altered on Fourteenth Street in Park Slope at the same time the first one had and zagged through the streets until it reached a city-subsidized apartment building that housed elderly residents. From there the phone's path went in methodical movements to a series of similar apartment buildings in South Brooklyn, then made a straight line to a city-funded community center in Coney Island. The next day it began another series of visits to apartment buildings in South Brooklyn, at one point arriving onto the previous day's path and then perfectly overlapping it, the time of overlap within half an hour at each stop.

So, thought Passaro, the confrontation took place near or inside Paul Reeves's house, as Paul had told him, based not only on the little splatter that might be dried blood but primarily on what the druggy neighbor had said. The killer of the men, probably Bill Wilkerson, very carefully attached the two cell phones to vehicles that would obviously move around the city a good bit, a taxi in the first instance and what appeared to be some kind of social service or meals-on-wheels vehicle in the second. The idea looked smart, but it was actually dumb. If Billy had been really smart, he would have kept those two phones *together*, so as to make it appear that the men were still with each other, and attach them to a car that did not have a pattern that was so easy to identify. And, Passaro noted to himself, by separating the phones at

Paul Reeves's house, Bill had effectively identified that it was here he had killed the two Libyans.

As far as Passaro was concerned, everyone, every single human being, had committed at least one crime, and it was simply a function of law enforcement's curiosity as to whether that crime was worth the trouble to be solved and prosecuted. Most crimes were not worth bothering with. But this one was. The Major Case Squad didn't usually work homicides, but Bobby had been around a long time and more or less pursued the cases he wanted. The phone techs were now running a check on all the calls made by the two Libyans. But Passaro already knew where that would lead. Why? Because the phone data on the Libyans had showed they had spent time that day in an office building on Eighth Avenue that was filled with marginal overseas businesses. The building was already quite interesting to the NYPD and to the FBI because of the volume of overseas calls and e-mails that came out of it, especially to China, and in addition to bugging certain offices, the investigators had set up a continuous surveillance camera inside the EXIT sign in the building's lobby. It had yielded a lot of mostly useless information, capturing patterns of low-level drug deliveries, attempts by homeless men to use the bathroom, and an elderly man with Alzheimer's undressing in search of lice bites. But of particular interest to Passaro, the camera had captured the two beefy Libyans entering the building, twelve hours before the estimated time that they were killed, followed by an unidentified man, shorter, balding, who looked Middle Eastern, and, in complete clarity, Ahmed Mehraz—tall, elegant, rich, and, most relevant, the husband of the woman Bill Wilkerson had been boffing prior to his murder.

Oh, Mr. Mehraz, Passaro whispered to himself, *I do believe you are mine.*

38

Tunnels scared him, always had. When he was a skinny boy selling oranges, he would be paid to walk through the smugglers' long tunnels with a flashlight before an operation to see if there had been a collapse, or if the Mexican police were hiding down there, and he had never wanted to but always had done so, because the men who worked for El Chapo were known to kill anybody for anything, at any time. In Hector's town, they had killed three policemen eating breakfast, they had killed a priest, they had killed the mayor at his daughter's wedding, not to mention the uncountable people who they thought had betrayed them. So Hector had always said sí, okay, jefe, taken his crate of oranges and placed it a few feet inside the entrance of the tunnel and walked the length of it with the flashlight, run it, really, sometimes two miles, until he got to the opening on the other side, where a man would hand him the bent top of a beer bottle. Then, clutching the beer cap tightly, he would run back, trying not to smell the fetid, earthy air or feel the roots touching his head like long bony fingers, and when he emerged into the dusty sunlight on the other side, or the darkness, if it was night, he would hand the men the bent beer bottle top as proof that he had gone the whole way and back. The men usually ate some of his oranges while they waited for him, but they always paid him. One time he was running the tunnel and suddenly lights flashed on and there were five policemen down there with guns drawn and they fired at him, hitting his shoulder, knocking him down, and he got back up and ran back the way he had come as they chased him, and he exploded out of the tunnel yelling policía! And they had thrown him, a bleeding ten-year-old boy, into their van and sped away, talking on the radio. At the doctor's office, they told him he had done a good job and that he was part of them now. And he was. Soon it had been Hector paying the local boys to check the tunnels, and one time one of the boys didn't come back because the tunnel's roof had collapsed on him. There were many tunnels after that, ones with bodies, others that stored millions of dollars of heroin and ecstasy, and he hated going into them and asked if they would train him to be a bodyguard. Which led to him carrying a gun, and that of course led to everything else. First a body-guard then a soldier on jobs, then a hunter of men.

Now, waiting in the subway tunnel for the Arab man named Hassan Mehraz, he checked his watch. Mehraz had agreed to pay $20,000, but Hector knew there was more. It was two a.m. Hector's bulk was obscured by a long coat, his face partly hidden by a blond wig sewn into a base-ball cap. He was also wearing sunglasses. Of course he looked ridicu-lous; that was the idea, yo.

A very old man with a cane, carrying a cloth bag, eased down to the platform. Hector took three steps toward him, saying nothing, but was surprised how feeble the man looked. The light of the train appeared at the end of the tunnel, reflected along the two rails ahead of it. They had agreed to get on and make the handoff inside.

At that hour the train was nearly deserted. They stepped on, Mehraz unsteady when the train jolted to a start.

"Sit," said Hector. "Give me the bag."

Mehraz handed it to him. Hector looked inside. All new bills, in stacks of a thousand dólares, held tight by red rubber bands. Easy to count. "Good," he said as they rocketed along. He put the bag into his backpack. "Now I have some questions."

"What are they? I flew here right away, I've given you the money."

"Why did you want this Wilkerson killed?" pressed Hector behind his sunglasses and wig.

The old man shook his head. "A private matter."

"I want to be told the answer, okay? Who you working for?"

"I am working for nobody."

Hector reached out and squeezed Hassan's arm, so thin his fingers wrapped around the biceps easily. "I killed a good man. A true soldier. He suffered. I want to know why I was to kill him. When I was in México I always knew why. The bosses, they explained it to us. So we understand, sí?"

The old man just shook his head again. There's something I do not get here, thought Hector. This Hassan seems tired, even depressed. His coat is rumpled, but his shoes are muy expensive. He is argumentative, yet does everything I ask.

"I would like to get off at the next stop," said Hassan, "like we agreed."

"Not yet," said Hector. "You leave when I say okay."

When one rides the New York subway, one submits to cartography. Newcomers invariably check the color-coded maps mounted inside the cars, and those who have taken the subway for years nonetheless operate with an internal map of the subway lines veining below the grid of the city. One may easily visualize the urban canyonland that is rushing past a hundred feet overhead, the numbered blocks flicking by if one is headed uptown or downtown, as most do. If one is cognizant of the sway and press of the subway car, then it's clear the operator is taking the motorized beast through a curve and, recalling the subway map, one can imagine the train transecting the grid on a perpendicular angle, sweeping from, say, an east–west orientation to a north–south one. In fact, the comfort that many visitors feel in Manhattan is the subliminal security of always being on a grid easy to locate oneself within, and the anxiety that misinforms the many people who fear Brooklyn, Queens, and the Bronx derives from those boroughs' broken and rebroken grids of their streets, like pieces of torn graph paper dropped at random on one another, and the way that the subways writhe through this crazy maze, which itself is snaked over by endless tangles of highways and expressways inflicted upon it in the name of progress. Some are particularly troubled by the long transit beneath the East River as the N train tunnels from Manhattan to Brooklyn—long minutes under the many billions of gallons of water—but this extended interval was exactly what Hector was waiting for. No stations. No stops. No witnesses.

"We are getting up and going through," he told the old man, meaning the door that led into the dark space between the train cars.

Hassan hesitated. But Hector lifted him with one arm and pushed him toward the door. "Tell me who you are working for, old man. Who has all this money to pay me and to send you across the country?"

"It's me, just me."

"Come on, walk, old man! Keep moving! I don't believe you. There is someone else."

Holding the old man with one hand, Hector opened the sliding door at the end of the car. They stood in the racketing space between the two cars, dark and noisy with the walls rushing by and the track bed below them. "Give me your phone," he said.

Mehraz pulled the phone from his pocket as the train lurched, and just as quickly it fell from his fingers into the dark space between the two rushing cars.

"What?" Enraged, Hector pushed the old man back and bent to see if the phone might have gotten caught on the ridged bumper of the car. *Gone.* As he stood, Hassan's arm flashed forward at him, darting inside his coat, and Hector felt the sharp sting of something like a needle being pressed into his stomach.

"What the—?" He grabbed Hassan's hand, which clutched a stainless-steel thumb knife with an injector device. His stomach burned strangely. With his other hand he punched the old man once, very hard in fury, and he slumped backward, dazed. Hector caught him by the coat.

"Who sent you? Who ordered you to kill me?"

"No one, I tell you."

"Who?" Hector screamed.

The old man smiled. "Allah!"

Hector lifted him by the arms over the safety chain that blocked access to the gaping space between the subway cars, the track rushing loudly below. The old man struggled feebly. The cars were designed to not quite touch, but they lurched back and forth with the movement of the train around turns. The old man was saying something, yelling, even calling loudly, eyes bugged out. Hector lowered the old man feetfirst into the gap between the cars, and as the train moved through a turn, the cars' curved bumpers drew closer, trapping and crushing him at the torso. Blood rivered out of his mouth and down his chin. The whites of his eyes popped red as the blood vessels in them burst. The train straightened out, and the bumpers pulled away from each other, revealing a belly of meat compressed to a blooded thickness of only a few inches. Blood spattered onto Hector's pants and shoes. He dropped the nearly severed torso into the clacking void beneath the cars. Then he checked back through the window of the car; no one was watching, no one had seen.

His stomach burned and he felt a strange heat behind his eyes. Some kind of poison? He pulled off his baseball cap and wig and sunglasses, and threw them all into the darkness. Then he removed his long coat, carefully wiped some blood from the bumper, and dropped it to the side. He then removed his red, tearaway sweatpants, revealing paint-stained jeans. Next went the shoes, which he replaced with sandals from his backpack. A whole different look now. He continued through the next car and the next, making no eye contact with anyone along the way. He put on another pair of clear-lensed glasses. The problem was that there were cameras on all the platforms, and he was sure one had captured him getting on the train. He was running southbound to Brooklyn. When the body was discovered within the hour, the police would run the videos, figure out the station where the old man had boarded, and see which train he'd gotten on and who else had gotten on the same train. Well, maybe they would find him, maybe they would not. Hector had been hunted for years now, by the cartel, for crimes of betrayal both imagined and committed, and they hadn't found him yet. In the Court Street station, the first stop in Brooklyn, he slipped up the stairs, one finger pressed firmly against the tiny injection point in his stomach, his mind ignited by fear and fury. *Somebody else*, Hector muttered feverishly, *somebody else needs to be killed now.*

39

It really should never snow in New York in late October, but thanks to global warming, it can. Paul had lived in the city his whole life, knew its seasons and skies and weather; this was absurd. Four wet inches, dumped overnight. The day was bright; the snow would be gone by nighttime. He trudged up and down the rows of blanketed vehicles, clicking the key fob every few steps. The snow was in his shoes now. On the third row he heard a horn beep, and he turned and saw a snow-blanketed pickup truck five parking spots away. Now he remembered the spot. He beeped the fob again and the horns and lights responded. At last, Bill's truck.

He unlocked the driver's door, pulled it open, and climbed up into the cab, yanking the door shut. For a moment he could see almost nothing. But then he switched his sunglasses for his regular ones and let his eyes adjust—

The inside of the cab was covered with photos of Jennifer. Glued with obsessive care to the roof, the inside of the sunshades, the dashboard, even the interior windshield posts. Jennifer as a baby, a toddler, a five-year-old on her tricycle, a girl, an older teenager; he could see the pretty bright baby becoming the woman. And there were school reports and handwritten notes and ephemera usually kept in scrapbooks or boxes. How had Bill gotten this stuff? Had she given it to him when they were younger? From her mother? The cab's interior felt like nothing so much as the inside of Bill Wilkerson's Jennifer-obsessed brain itself, the light filtering through the snow-buried windshield milky and opaque, buried twice over, a cocoon of memory. It will take hours to look at all this, Paul thought.

He put the key in the ignition and started the engine. It turned over smoothly, and he ran the windshield defroster. After a minute the space warmed and he started to look around more carefully. Behind the front seats were folded clean clothes, a spare pair of boots marked WILKERSON. Then a toolbox, every chromed socket wrench spotless. A box of papers. A plastic bin filled with vitamins, protein bars, caffeine drinks, toiletries, a dozen-odd stacks of new fifty-dollar bills with a band around them. Supplies for a long siege. He found a plastic folder with a note affixed: *The document inside this folder was removed from the body of Tarek al-Badri, one of two men who attacked me inside the residence at*—my house! Paul thought—*and who I was forced to fight in order to defend myself.* Paul opened the folder; inside, kept safely in a clear plastic envelope, was what looked like a folded piece of paper soaked in dried blood. Wincing in his effort to be sure he didn't actually touch the piece of paper, he used the tip of the truck key to gently lift the folded edge; the paper was a hand-drawn map, clearly a map of Brooklyn and the southern edge of Queens, showing the Beltway and the Marine Parkway bridge to the Rockaways. He'd been there a million times as a kid. The paper had a number of words written in Arabic, he guessed, with regular Arabic numerals, perhaps times or addresses. Another section of the paper, a detailed area, showed the intersection and the address of Paul's own house.

Breathing rapidly, telling himself to calm down, Paul carefully photographed the bloodstained document in whole and close-up, returned it to its clear envelope and plastic folder, and photographed Bill's note. I have to get out of here, he told himself, so he gunned the engine, wiped the windshield off with the wipers, and pulled out. The truck was large, but drove smoothly. At the exit booth, an Indian man in a striped uniform said, "That will be five hundred and fifty-eight dollars."

"For a parking bill?"

"Look at your ticket, sir. Your vehicle has been parked with us for more than a month. It's eighteen dollars a day."

"Let me see that."

Paul took the ticket. Bill had told him he was parked in a long-term lot the night Paul had taken him to his house. "Okay," he said, and handed the clerk a credit card. "Wait," he said, "give me that back."

"Sir?"

"I'm going to pay cash."

"That's a lot of cash, sir."

"I know." He found one of the stacks of fifty-dollar bills. It's okay, he told himself, Bill isn't going to miss the money.

A moment later Paul was headed toward Manhattan, the snow on the hood blowing upward and sliding wetly off the windshield. I need to understand what really happened, he thought. Of course he should tell Detective Passaro about the truck. Of course! But Paul didn't feel like doing that, not yet, anyway.

40

Ghosts don't drive old trucks, but real people do. Hector wiped his forehead and watched the icon on his phone travel away from JFK airport up the Van Wyck Expressway and then west on the Long Island Expressway. Taking the red pickup truck to Manhattan, he bet. He might be able to catch up with it, he realized. Just *possibly*. The tiny puncture wound in his stomach had already turned a strange color, tinges of streaky green and yellow. Infected, maybe. And it *hurt*. And he had a fever and felt weird.

But he needed to get to that truck. He gulped five or six Aleve pills to help with the fever and hurried into his garage, where he had to choose which motorcycle to ride. He picked the dumpy little orange Yamaha. A piece of junk, but much less noticeable than the Harley road hog. His biker's leather jacket had a big interior pocket for his Tec-9 semiauto pistol. He pulled on a yellow helmet and gloves, didn't bother with anything else, and started to zigzag through the snowy streets toward the LIE. Yellow helmet, orange bike, I look like a piece of candy, he realized.

Luckily he knew what he was searching for, a big red Ford pickup with extended bed and crew cab. He stuck his phone in the clip on his left handlebar and glanced at it from time to time as he buzzed his way over the on-ramp to the LIE. If the driver knew anything about anything, he'd be taking the truck to a lot, not to a garage, which would be tough to park inside. All Hector needed was to get behind the truck, and luckily the westbound LIE was slow and he wove quite illegally along the slushy service lane until he saw it five cars ahead.

He hung back as the Manhattan skyline loomed and they passed the posters for all the new movies no one would remember in a month and headed toward the Midtown Tunnel. He could tell that the driver wasn't used to driving a big pickup, for he wove a little in the lane as he calibrated the truck's width. Once on the other side of the tunnel the truck headed straight to the West Side Highway. So easy to follow! It stayed in the right lane, driving conservatively, and Hector drew too close once when the light suddenly turned red in front of the truck. Ten blocks north, the pickup pulled into a parking lot just west of the theater district, one of those operations that accommodated luxury SUVs from Jersey in for a show. Hector lingered down the street, straddling the rumbling bike. The driver parked and got out. Did he glance Hector's way? Maybe. Probablemente. But then he handed his keys to the attendant and headed to the street. Hector eased along the pocked roadway to get a better look. A tall, older guy. Much older, maybe late forties, early fifties. Looked like an hombre who had money, real money. This was the guy who was going to pay Hector. Why? Because *this* was the shithead who had wanted Bill Wilkerson dead, Hector was sure of it. How else would he have the keys to Wilkerson's truck? This was the guy who had hired old Hassan as a go-between. The trick would be to get him isolated, one-on-one. Hector pulled the bike up between two parked cars, locked it, threw the helmet into a gym bag, and replaced it with a baseball cap. He followed the man as he walked east on Forty-ninth, then into the uptown 1 train, three stops to West Sixty-sixth Street. From there, he walked west to an apartment building on the south side of the street and then straight inside, not bothering to look back, not concerned someone was following him. Hector's head was hot and he was sweating, but he felt good knowing where the man lived. *You are my amigo now,* Hector thought, *my very good friend.*

41

In his office, with the door closed, Paul downloaded an Arabic–English dictionary to his office computer. After much trial and error, he identified the words on the map as avenues and streets, and a variety of reminders:

> *House of Paul Reeves Number 204B, 14th Street (get BW here*
> *10 p.m. Tues night)*
> *AM drive to Fort Tilden, Queens, Ahmed there 6:30 am.*
> *We arrive at 6:10.*
> *Wilkerson is tall white man, over six feet tall, drive a truck*
> *Do not call Ahmed only call Amir cell*
> *Cash lane toll no E-Z pass*

He had kept the document in its sleeve and consulted his cell phone photos. There was another thing he needed to do, and he called Rollie, the document restorer who had opened the envelope containing the papers from the Ocean City attorney.

"Rollie," Paul asked, "how good is your super hi-res document scanner?"

"You don't want to know."

"I do, actually."

"It makes the surface irregularities in old rag paper look as defined as a rumpled bedsheet. All the old repairs show up. Faked signatures, all that stuff."

"Can you see fingerprints on it?"

"Yup, if we use fluorescent imaging."

"Can you *compare* fingerprints?"

"If we have two good samples."

"I had no idea you did all this stuff, Rollie."

"You never asked. I assume I'll see you soon?"

"Indeed, Rollie, you will see me soon," said Paul.

Next, Paul called James Marone, the disaffected young associate at Gracken and Rothstein, the boutique firm that competed with him.

"Wow, I wasn't expecting to hear from you so fast," said Marone.

"Life sometimes moves quickly."

"I guess."

"Hey, is one of the lawyers there named Roger Metcalfe?" This was the New York City immigration attorney mentioned in the letter to Ahmed from the Ocean City, Maryland, attorney.

"Yes, he's a partner. Knows his stuff. I do work for him sometimes."

It took a moment for Paul to appreciate the enormity of this fact. He was going by feel here, working a hunch based on his years of immigration law practice. "You guys have fully digitized records?"

"We're always talking about that. Yes, back to about 1994 or something. It's all paper before that, in some storage facility."

"Okay, James, listen up. Metcalfe has an old client there whose last name is Mehraz. M-E-H-R-A-Z. First name is Ahmed. Metcalfe did immigration work for him maybe ten years ago. When he was at his previous firm. I'm betting he brought Mehraz with him as a client when he came to Gracken and Rothstein. Can you search the firm's filings?"

"Sure. I mean, the paralegals and the first-years mostly do that."

"I want *you* to search for *me*."

Marone's voice became slow and somber. "We are getting into some deeply gray area here, counselor."

"Last name is Mehraz, first name Ahmed. Please find his immigration filing."

"Hang on a minute."

Paul waited at the window. He watched a tugboat push a barge up the East River.

"Okay, got it," said Marone. "Pretty typical."

"Is there a citizenship application, form N-400?"

"Hang on . . . Yes."

"Scroll to page fourteen, I think, part twelve, question twenty-three."

"Hmmm, yes, the arrest-record question?"

"Don't tell me what the answer is."

"Okay, I got it," said Marone.

"Remember, don't tell me the answer yet."

"I haven't *offered* to tell you."

"I know," said Paul. "I'm about to do something unethical."

"I got that feeling," said Marone.

"Which makes you vulnerable, too."

"Yes."

"We can agree that the chances someone will discover that you have accessed this file are not great."

"System records every file opened, but thousands are opened every day, yes."

"Of course," said Paul. "Okay, James, I am offering you a job at my firm as soon as you would like to start at one hundred and ten percent of your current salary. We can talk about the bonus and the perks later. My only condition is that you need to tell me the answer to question twenty-three, which is either a yes or a no."

"I tell that to you and I have a firm job offer?"

"Correct."

"You want to know just the answer to this single question?"

"Yes. And I want you to take a photo of the answer with your phone and send it to me."

"That's a little more of a problem."

"Why?"

"The metadata on that photo will show I took it. Make your offer one hundred and twenty percent and you have a deal."

Paul watched the barge make progress upriver. I don't care about the money, he thought, not really. He knew Marone was a hard worker.

"Okay. One-twenty."

"Fine, I'm taking the photo."

Paul told him his cell number.

"Okay, sending."

A moment later the photo arrived, nice and crisp, showing the question on part 12, question 23, of form N-400, which asked, "Have you EVER been arrested, cited, or detained by any law enforcement officer for any reason?" And it showed the answer given by Ahmed Mehraz on his application for U.S. citizenship: *No.* And that, as Paul knew, was a stone-cold lie.

"James, thank you very much. I assume you will want to mull this offer?"

"No, no, I will take it."

"Good!" And Paul did feel glad.

"I could start at the first of the month, after I get some stuff wrapped up."

"Sounds good. Call my assistant tomorrow and we will get it all done. Come around next week and I'll introduce you to some people and show you your new office."

They hung up. Paul stared at the photograph. *No!* the answer to question 23 on part 12 of form N-400 protested. *No, I, Ahmed Mehraz, have never been arrested, cited, or detained by any law enforcement officer.* But that, alas, was not true, as the packet of papers sent by the Ocean City attorney to Ahmed detailed. Of course Ahmed knew he had been arrested! One did not forget such an experience. But how had Ahmed lied with such confidence, given that all arrests in the United States were supposedly reported to the FBI? The system depended upon local compliance. And local compliance was not always thorough, folks. Somehow that local lawyer had stuck his hand into the bureaucracy and stopped a certain document from being automatically submitted.

Paul went back to the window. I can now mess with Ahmed, he realized. And I know just *how* to do it. Most people did not understand that becoming a naturalized citizen of the United States of America was not *necessarily* permanent. The government could revoke the citizenship of a naturalized person, and although "denaturalization" was rare, it happened. And when that happened, it was a devastating event. Once denaturalized, a person was considered by law to have *never been* a citizen of the United States. This status had far-reaching consequences, ranging from the sudden inability to live or work in the United States to tax issues, property ownership, Social Security benefits, voting rights— the list went on. There were four basic grounds for denaturalization. Three were comparatively rare: 1) receiving a dishonorable discharge from the U.S. military after serving less than five years; 2) being a member of a "subversive organization," such as a Nazi, communist, or terrorist group, especially within five years of becoming naturalized (such membership constituted a violation of the oath of allegiance to the United States), with a "subversive organization" defined as one that planned or aided others in activities to overthrow the U.S. government, especially through violence or force, or to harm U.S. government officials; or 3) refusing to testify before a committee of the U.S. Congress formed to investigate the citizen's membership in the subversive organization. Those were the three rare grounds, and they tended to be very difficult to appeal.

The much broader category for denaturalization was for falsification or concealment of important facts on the original application for naturalization. Most of these cases revolved around lying about past criminal activity, one's correct name, or the length of time one had been in the United States. The U.S. Citizenship and Immigration Services took a *very* tough position on these cases. Once its lawyers decided to pursue denaturalization, they filed suit in the federal district court where the citizen lived. In the case of Ahmed, that would be the U.S. Southern District Court in downtown Manhattan, which was perhaps the most visible and well-known federal district court in the country. At any given time, the court was the site for high-profile criminal cases and civil trials. Anything of interest going through the court's docket was discovered by members of the press, and a high-flying Iranian-American corporate chieftain with a beautiful blond wife would not escape notice. Moreover, court officials had been known to tip journalists off to be sure to create public exposure. It was New York City, after all. Defendants were given notice of the suit and served with a copy of the complaint. The government had to file an "affidavit of good cause," explaining exactly why it was trying to revoke citizenship. The defendant had sixty days to answer the complaint and refute the government's charges. Paul had written the answers to a complaint and it was not an easy thing to do, because the government's lawyers were dedicated, well-disciplined, and came out of all the best law schools. Smart and tough and committed. Because of the cost of each prosecution, their internal thresholds of evidence were high; they sought to maximize their risk/return ratios, which was also to say they expected to win nearly every case.

The question before Paul was whether or not the U.S. Citizenship and Immigration Services lawyers would decide to pursue a "denaturalization" case against Ahmed on the basis of a relatively old factual discrepancy on his application. If the current policy in the office was zero tolerance, then of course the answer would be yes. But in his experience there was no such thing as zero tolerance. Moreover, Ahmed would hire an attorney who would begin to massage the case. First, it would be pointed out what a successful and currently law-abiding businessman Ahmed was, and that he had donated large sums to charity for years. His prosecution could easily be painted as idiotic overzealousness by U.S. officials, and with the concurrent hiring of one of New York's excellent public relations firms, sympathetic reporters could be found and encouraged to write about the case. If, however, the federal judge was informed that Ahmed was a genuine person of interest in *the murder of a decorated American serviceman*, then that would paint a very different picture. The federal officers would have no option but to arrest him.

Elauriana came in. "This was just messengered to you," she said.

Marone had sent him a printout of the complete original Mehraz file, which he hadn't been asked to do. But Paul would take it. He inspected all the pages of form N-400, including the one in question. At the end of the document was Ahmed's signature attesting that all statements were true. This document, Paul knew, had been filed in at least six different locations within the U.S. government.

Elauriana buzzed him. "There's a New York City detective on the line asking if you like oysters."

"Tell him I'm not crazy about them," said Paul.

"You better speak to him. I don't like talking to the po-lice."

Paul picked up the phone. "So here's the deal," said Passaro. "You buy me a *nice* dinner at the Oyster Bar and I tell you stuff I shouldn't tell you."

"I'll take that deal."

"Meet me in that back room at six."

Paul needed to get to Rollie's restoration studio in Williamsburg first and then back.

"Seven."

"Fine," said Passaro. "I might be there already, eating many delicious oysters you are buying."

"Knock yourself out, baby."

"I plan to, but do you know why?"

"Because life is short, why else?"

A pause. Then Passaro answered, his tone utterly changed. "Yeah. That would be correct."

42

China wanted to eat Hong Kong. If Hong Kong was a box of chocolate bonbons, China was a fat boy who had tasted several and wanted all of them now, and was waiting until no one saw him cram them into his mouth. Month by month, China probed deeper into the former British colony, biting, nibbling, sucking, eager to finally crush the sweet in its mandible.

This was Amir's revelation as he took the jetfoil to Macau, the one-time Portuguese colony peaceably returned to China in 1999. He had heard the casinos were beyond imagining and that at a certain hour each evening, hookers streamed in by the dozens, parading in their shimmery miniskirts and high heels. That sounded fun. And he needed as much fun as he could get, given the misery and isolation he felt. That morning, when he had stopped at the birdcage shop on Ning Po Street near the night market in Kowloon, the affable shopkeeper who usually handed Amir his weekly fat envelope of Hong Kong dollars had said, "No more money. Nobody give me your money."

He'd been instructed not to call home. But now there was a problem. I have to call, Amir told himself. So he bought a pre-paid cell phone and anxiously dialed his uncle Hassan, couldn't get him, then called the house and spoke with Rosie, the housekeeper. Is he there, Amir asked. Panicked by what she told him, he dialed Ahmed.

"You aren't fucking supposed to call!" Ahmed snarled.

"I have to! I have no money!"

"What about our uncle?"

"He doesn't answer. So I called the house. They said they don't know where he is. He hasn't called. But they said he left days ago for New York. They thought maybe to see you."

"Here?" was Ahmed's alarmed response. "Days ago?"

"You don't know where he is?"

"I have no idea."

"Can you send me money?"

"No!" came Ahmed's voice, then a click.

43

The place always made him miss his father. He had taken
Paul there when he was a boy, and he had pointed out the commuters,
the drunks, the loners at the bar. "This doesn't look like a church," his
father had told him, "but it is one. The city has lots of places like this,
places where people go to feel good, feel like they are part of things."
Paul hadn't understood it then but he completely understood it now.
The Oyster Bar hadn't changed at all, which was just fine. The dark
wood, the huge swordfish over the bar. The ancient waiters with the
daily paper menus that showed every kind of fresh fish possible. You
had to have places in the city like that, places that didn't change, or
you didn't know who you were anymore.

Passaro shambled in and sat down without bothering to shake
hands with Paul. "The girl behind the bar wants to fuck me, but she's
not my type."

Paul looked over. "You're getting pretty picky for a fat old guy."

Passaro lifted up the long paper menu, pushed his glasses down his
nose. They ordered from a waiter in a white shirt and black vest who
appeared to have already spent quite a bit of time in his eighth decade.

"That guy makes me look *good*," Passaro noted. "So, okay, anyway,
that girl cop from upstate called me this morning and we had a long
talk. First thing I want to say is that I should have listened to you the

first time. It wouldn't have made any difference *for Billy*, but still, I got to say it. The second thing is, I don't think this murder is going to be solved very easily."

"Why?"

He pulled a file out of his briefcase. "The local PD up there sent me the digitized report. Photos and everything. The reason the barrel was found was that there was enormous flooding in that area from the hurricane we had. The lake was inundated. Went well beyond its banks. They had fishing shacks getting washed away, docks being torn up. People found their belongings five and six miles away. That barrel was sealed up pretty tight by whoever the killer was and ended up at the base of an apple orchard. Just resting there. So it's impossible to say where it was originally, where it started. Also, here, look at these pictures"— Passaro showed him a couple of printed computer photos that focused on Bill Wilkerson's chest—"see how sort of red the skin is? Somebody splashed his body with bleach, which destroys all genetic information. Burns up the proteins in DNA. So no fingerprints, no hair sample of the killer, nothing like that. Do you want to see some more photos? They aren't pretty."

Paul nodded. Passaro looked up and signaled the barmaid.

"Hi, Bobby P.," she said.

"Jasmine, I'm showing my good friend here some things and I don't want anybody coming back here near our table for five minutes, okay?"

"Got it."

"I mean, *you* can come back here anytime. But if you do, then I have to flirt with you and I won't remember to do my job."

She smiled, having heard all the lines by all the guys before. "Five minutes."

"Thanks, sweetheart."

Passaro spread out his photos. "Here we have the barrel in the field as it was discovered. See all the debris washed against it? The whole field was like that. Here is what the barrel looked like as it was being opened, you can see his feet. There was water in the barrel by this point and he was butt-side down, more or less submerged. They think the barrel was sealed up well enough to float away, then slowly filled up with water and got stuck there. Here is the barrel on the police truck, here it is in the lab they have up there. They take a lot of pictures up there, stuff like this doesn't happen too often. So then . . . here we are in the lab. They decided to cut open the barrel in pieces because he was so jammed in. They drained all the water out, by the way. Nothing really in there, some kind of tiny little dead fish that got trapped in there looking for breakfast. So here he is on the table. Naked. It took a while to straighten him out. Someone smart identified the barrel. But that won't help . . . See this photo? It was a spray-painted state highway department code that went out of use maybe fifteen years ago. This was probably from a local dump site that had hundreds of barrels, but that's hard to prove. There are *thousands* of these barrels all over New York. No one knows how many or where they are exactly. There is no central registry in the Department of Highways, and that way somebody can keep ordering new barrels from his brother's barrel-making company and get paid. All it tells you is that he probably didn't come out of New York City in the barrel. But we could have guessed this. *You* guessed that. So here are the rest of the photos, here he is laid out. He has two wounds, one in the thigh, which was very serious but not fatal, and this one . . . in the neck, which killed him. These are not exactly stabbing wounds, probably. They are too regular, they go straight in. He probably went into hypovolemic shock and bled out in a minute or two. His body was devoid of sixty-two percent of the normal amount of blood expected for his body size. That's a lot, too much. We lose consciousness when we've lost about thirty percent. There are no other major wounds. What was weird was that there were high-quality surgical bandages on the wounds, which suggests that he was moved just after being killed and they didn't want him leaking all over something. Which suggests, more than anything else, that this was a planned hit, right? Somebody knew exactly what he was doing. What else? Bill's stomach was almost empty. He had no alcohol or drugs in his system, based on preliminary testing. Nothing. His heart and liver and lungs were normal and clean. He had old shrapnel wounds on his backside and was missing the two small toes on his left foot, which his military records say were from an improvised explosive device that went off but was deflected by a wall. He healed up and went back to action, by the way. That was years ago." Passaro looked at Paul. "But there was one other wound I forgot to mention."

"What?"

"More like a sexual mutilation."

Paul studied Passaro's face. "Do I need to know about this?"

"No, I guess not, but I'm going to tell you anyway. The killer cut his balls off."

"What?"

"Yeah, sliced them right out of the scrotum. Knew how to do it, too."

Paul watched a waiter carry a steaming swordfish steak past him, and felt odd. "So where do you go from here?"

Passaro shook his head. "Nowhere. We don't have witnesses, we don't have a murder site, we don't have an exact dumping site, we have a barrel that is one of thousands, we have no other DNA evidence from his assailants. We have no murder weapon, except that it was sharp and entered his body at high speed. Exact hour of death is hard to pin down because the body was in the water for a few days."

"What about Ahmed Mehraz? Can you question him?"

Passaro frowned. "For what? Being a jealous husband? Welcome to the human race. He's been in Geneva, Paris, Istanbul, Tokyo, London, and other places in the last six weeks. He moves around. Good luck placing him anywhere near this murder."

Paul was unconvinced. He knows something he isn't telling me, he thought. "What about Jennifer?"

"We'll talk to her when we can."

"What do you think happened?"

"I think Bill Wilkerson got jumped or surprised somewhere remote, an empty street, a lot, then stabbed very deeply and bled to death, then was loaded up and taken out of the city, probably at night. Maybe they drove him upstate in an older car that doesn't have GPS, without using E-Z Pass. Every car going through tolls is photographed, but we don't know what car to look for. And, anyway, you can get upstate without going through tolls if you plan ahead. But I haven't even begun to go into some of the things they could have done, like switch cars a few times, change directions, stuff like that."

"Except for that flooded lake, the barrel might never have been found?"

"Could have been years, anyway."

"What am I supposed to do now?"

"You? Nothing. You're a civilian. You collect nice old maps. You've told us what you know. We will talk to Jennifer Mehraz when she shows up, sooner or later. We can look into her husband. He has a big family out in Los Angeles. They know a lot of people. The two men who were killed in Brooklyn are being investigated."

"What's your gut feeling?"

"That the wife had no idea this was happening and that the husband is not so stupid as to get involved with this kind of thing." Passaro waved at the waitress to return.

Why don't I believe him, wondered Paul. "So we're kind of nowhere?"

"Kind of exactly nowhere. This is the type of case that doesn't get solved until some weird little piece of information flutters down from heaven. It could be soon, could be years from now. Could be never. Tell you one thing, the guy or guys who killed him tracked him down, planned ahead, killed him, and then maybe dragged him a couple hundred miles away."

"This is pretty fucking depressing."

"Sorry."

Should he tell Passaro that he had the keys to Bill's truck and what he had found inside it? Yes, of course I should, Paul thought. But an idea had suddenly come to him, a notion, an absurd gambit, and telling Passaro about the truck would prohibit that possibility.

Their fish arrived, steaming. "You *really* have no leads?" said Paul.

"Nope," Passaro answered. "I've got nothing. I have a feeling whoever did it is not going to be caught."

"Tell me you are lying."

"I'm not," said Passaro. "Sometimes the bad guys just get away with it, hate to break it to you."

44

Just knock, Paul told himself. And he did. The door opened. Ahmed stood there in a suit, an impressive man about to go to work.

"Ahmed," Paul said slowly.

"Paul, good morning!" Ahmed smiled widely, hale and confident.

"Ahmed, I have something you want."

"I don't get it."

Paul waited until Ahmed had marked his silence. "Let's sit down a moment. In my apartment." Which isn't bugged, he thought.

"I'm kind of in a hurry here, Paul."

"This is the most important meeting of your day, Ahmed."

That was a pointed statement, even a declaration of aggression, and Ahmed nodded silently.

Paul turned to head back to his apartment, and Ahmed followed from a distance. They sat down on the stools in Paul's kitchen. There was a pile of papers to one side of the counter.

"I have a map," began Paul, "with your name on it, a good bit of Arabic writing, with directions from our apartment building to a deserted place out in Queens." Paul watched Ahmed's response, which seemed controlled. "There is also blood on it. My suspicion is that the blood belongs to the Libyan man who was carrying it, one of two men killed in Brooklyn a few weeks ago."

Ahmed frowned. "Paul, I have no idea what you are talking about."

"The two men who were killed by Bill Wilkerson."

Ahmed stared at Paul. Worry flew across his forehead, for just a moment. "Who is that?" he said.

"The American serviceman Jennifer has been seeing, who is dead now."

"I *truly* have zero idea what you are talking about."

"No? Come on. I think you do. We're not fucking around here, guy."

Paul watched Ahmed restrain himself, torn between physically attacking Paul out of fury, coolly denying any knowledge of Wilkerson, and asking about the map Paul had offered.

"You been talking to Jennifer?"

"Yes, we talk and talk." Paul waited for a response. "Look, Ahmed, Bill Wilkerson's father found me. He gave me the keys to his son's truck and said to contact him if I found it. Then he left."

"What does this have to do with me?"

"I happened to know where the truck was. And when I was in the truck, I found a crudely drawn map." He reached toward the pile of paper on the counter and lifted the top sheet. "This is a very good color copy."

Ahmed held out his hand. He took the map and studied it. "A copy, you say?"

Paul nodded. "The original is elsewhere."

The men sat there. The kitchen was full of knives, of course. Paul watched Ahmed scrutinize the map, then look up.

"What do you want?"

"This." Paul lifted up the next piece of paper from the pile and showed Ahmed the photo he'd taken of the Ratzer map. "I want this map a great deal. It's known as the Stassen-Ratzer map. It is a Revolutionary-era map of the city of New York. The owner is a woman who wants to use it to decorate her barn in the Hamptons. Her name is Hillary Larabee Morton. Her third husband is a guy named Bernie Gunston."

"Some kind of fashion photographer, if I remember correctly."

"Yes."

"The map belongs to his wife, Hillary Morton?"

Yes, nodded Paul. "She or her husband will sell you that map for about one million dollars."

"What are you suggesting?"

"I'm not *suggesting* anything, Ahmed. I'm saying I want *that* map. You want *this* map. I'll trade you. That sometimes happens between collectors, when the value is equal. I think Gunston or his wife will sell that map to you. But get a record of sale, please, so that there is a chain of ownership, in case there is any question later."

"And then?"

Ahmed was containing himself, Paul saw. "You will sell the map to me for one dollar and 'valuable consideration.' The valuable consideration will be the map that your hired goons used to tell you where to go to meet Bill Wilkerson. We will meet in my law offices, where I will have the transaction witnessed and notarized. We will not refer to the other map, *your* map, in any way. But I will hand it to you in an unmarked manila envelope, and you can do with it what you wish. I don't care about your personal life, Ahmed, I care about maps. I will, however, place a statement with my lawyer that if I die of any unusual circumstances—being hit by a truck, poison in my rice pudding, anything—then the transaction will be revealed and you will be identified as the person who would have wanted me to die. Are we clear on this? Do you have any questions?"

Ahmed said, "If in fact this map is what you say it is, then you are tampering with evidence."

"It's only evidence if they know about it. Oh, there's another thing. Your fingerprints are on that map. There are other fingerprints, but yours are on it."

"How do you know?"

Paul reached into his bag and pulled out his laptop. "The technology for scanning documents has changed the way collectors look at maps. Now there is a lot of information we never had before. You can see stains, blood, minute particles of dirt, impressions. The old rag wool paper sucked up everything. But the scanners have infrared and UV modes. They can pick up the swirl of fingerprints on any piece of paper that is porous. Here, look."

He turned the computer around so that Ahmed could look at the screen. It showed a number of fingerprints, some with numbered red boxes around them. "I took the liberty of removing several old copies of *The Wall Street Journal* you had outside your apartment for the recycling pickup. There were plenty of impressions." He pushed a key and an image of a newspaper page appeared, with red-boxed prints identified as matching the ones identified on the map, all thanks to Rollie and his scanners. "I'm surprised you still get the paper version."

Ahmed pushed the computer back to Paul. "I'm leaving on an international business trip tomorrow evening."

"Where?"

"Paris, then Berlin."

"Well, you have the contact information for the map's owners."

"I said, I'm leaving the country *tomorrow*."

Paul closed the laptop and stood to end the conversation. "Let's be clear. Get me the map I want and I will hand you the map that *you* want in a protective sleeve, one that preserves all the many fingerprints you left when you consulted this map, when you studied it, expecting to meet Bill Wilkerson."

"How will I know it's the original?"

"Because if you are smart you will take it on the plane with you and have it tested in some document facility in Paris or Berlin."

"And if it *is* the original?" Ahmed stood.

"What you do with it is your business."

"And if it is faked?" he said, his voice rising in frustration and anger. "A fucking copy?"

"Well, then you know where to find me. Right here. But remember that the bloodstain on the map is from a man dead and gone, though I'm sure the city's medical examiner's office has typed his blood. I could *perhaps* pay for an expensive fake to be made, Ahmed, a fake map with fake blood that could be very convincing. But you wouldn't know until you had some forensic testing done."

"My flight is at eight in the evening. I need to leave for the airport at *five*."

"Then I will see you tomorrow in my office in midtown at four forty-five, or not."

"Have you made any more copies?"

"Yes."

"Where are they?"

"At my office."

"Why?"

"So that you would realize it was useless to try to steal the map from me."

"Where is it, may I ask?" insisted Ahmed in frustration. "Where the *fuck* is the original?"

"Not in my apartment." Now Paul was alarmed.

"But where is it?"

"Where I can get it easily enough."

Ahmed was rapidly figuring out all the questions he needed to ask, all the angles. "Have you mentioned this map to anyone?"

"Nope. And yes, I will dispose of the copies later."

"How the hell can I be sure of that?"

"You can't, Ahmed, you just *can't*, just like Bill Wilkerson can no longer stick his cock into your wife's pussy while she kisses him and tells him she's always loved him and always will."

Ahmed stared at Paul, eyes burning, lips tight. He seemed to be suffering jolts of electricity running through him, his head jerking forward and backward ever so subtly.

Paul went on. "I saw them fucking with my own eyes, Ahmed, right through the window, in your bedroom."

Ahmed stepped forward.

Paul pulled open a drawer and withdrew a very sharp carving knife. "Don't think about it, Ahmed, don't even *think* about it! You could tear this place apart and you would never find *your* map."

"You are—"

"Ahmed, you seem *eager* to leave the country. Don't you *want* to take your map with you, the one that belongs to you?"

The answer was yes, of course, but Ahmed didn't reply, only seethed palpably before he turned to leave, a man who needed to get things done in a hurry now.

"Everyone has his own fetish!" laughed Bernie Gunston into the phone. "I mean, I know *you* do! He just *called* up this morning, he knew my wife had bought it for the most ridiculous, insane, infuriating amount of money and he said he would *match* what she paid, plus the costs. Oh my god, I said yes, I will meet you right *now* at the restoration place, right this very minute! Can you believe it? I checked him out, he is this powerful investment guy. He must be a collector. Who else would be willing to pay so much? I *really* should have asked for more. But I didn't, and so there it is. Instant wire transfer, please bring all my banking information, he says! Does something like this *ever* happen? No, of course not! But it makes me so happy. I can do the house over in Bridgehampton. And my beautiful boyfriend and I can take another little trip. So thrilling! Okay, here I am, more later, baby doll."

Gunston jumped out at Mulberry Street Restoration and a young woman who told him her name was Enid was there at the door. Inside, a tall, elegant man introduced himself as Ahmed Mehraz.

"Mr. Mehraz, you have made my day and my week and my month. Let's do this!"

They went into the restoration space and gazed at the silly old map.

Enid looked on. "As I understand it, Mr. Mehraz, you are paying for all the accrued restoration and reframing and shipping costs."

"Yes. I need this map messengered uptown *now*."

"Well, our delivery guys are out on a—"

"Get them back," he ordered coldly. "I will *pay*."

She nodded in tongue-biting disgust.

"Now then," Gunston said. "Shall we sit?"

They sat in the reception area with a bill of sale Mr. Mehraz had brought with him. "I have *all* the bank information here."

"Let me see it."

Mr. Mehraz typed furiously into his phone, which afforded Gunston the opportunity to study his thick hair, his sweeping forehead, the taper of his nose, just slightly beaked. Now Mr. Mehraz turned his phone to show him.

"I push send and this money appears in your account, okay? Then you call your banker, double-check everything, then sign this bill of sale."

"Perfect," Gunston said, noticing Mr. Mehraz's watch. "Is that an Audemars Piguet?"

"Yes."

"*So* lovely. Congratulations."

"Here I go, okay?"

"Yes, please."

Then the deed was done, the money moving at the speed of light and Mr. Mehraz showing Gunston his screen, demonstrating the transfer from his acccount was successful, and then Gunston calling his banker just to double-double-*triple*-check, because it *was* a lot of money, really. Yes, said the banker, the money is here. You can start spending it now, if you want.

Which he was going to do! So happy! He shook hands with the hunk-a-dunk and gave him an *If ever you want to try something different* smile, found a cab magically, and was soon back on his way uptown! He'd gotten rid of the stupid old map his ridiculous wife had bought! So exciting!

46

The fevers were getting worse, making him pant and hear muffled thunder as the edge of his vision flickered and throbbed. Like going into a dark tunnel. Can't go into the tunnel, no more tunnels for me, Mami. He drank water every few minutes. But I am doing this the wrong way, Hector decided. Waiting around in his apartment like a man who is half muerto. That is wrong! I am going to beat this, he told himself. The old Arab tried to poison me, but I am más stronger than the veneno. Yo soy el asesino! The assassin! He stood before the mirror without his shirt; still jacked, still strong, Mami! He had a lot of pills in a shoe box in the refrigerator and started looking through them. "Necesito medicine," he muttered feverishly. "I got some good pills in here." He stopped at the dimethylamylamine, or DMAA, which body-builders used to look shredded. My assassin heart can take this, Hector thought, I need to *burn* the poison out of my system. The only way to do it. He drank a quart of protein sauce, then popped three of the DMAA pills. Then another, Mami! Then four slow-release caffeine pills, just to be sure, to keep the high chemically complicated. He took a long swig of vodka, just for good measure. That was it, that was *good*. He could feel it already. Burn the poison, asesino! He felt saliva in his mouth, he felt the blood hit his groin, he felt strong. He needed a woman, he needed to ride the Harley, he needed to pump iron . . . This ride was going to last for hours, mi hermano, and he would be godlike at last.

47

The exchange took no more than three minutes. The Ratzer map, swathed in conservator's plastic and carefully protected by cardboard corners and bubble wrap, lay on Paul's conference table. Looking Ahmed in the eye, Paul carefully slit away the plastic and exposed the corner of the frame. Then he cut further and slid the plastic off one foot or so. Yes, that was it. Perfect. His! This almost belongs to me, he told himself.

"I'm in a hurry," said Ahmed. He handed Paul the bill of sale provided him by Gunston and then signed a new bill of sale for one dollar and valuable consideration. Both men were lawyers. They knew what such documents looked like.

Paul handed Ahmed a dollar and he crumpled it into his pocket.

"Where is it?" he asked.

Paul opened a file on his desk and lifted out the Libyan's hand-drawn map, kept in its protective sleeve. "Here you go."

Then he called toward the doorway. "Elauriana?"

She was a sworn notary and now witnessed the transaction, affixing her signature and her stamp on the bill of sale. Then she left.

Ahmed inspected the hand-drawn map closely.

"It's the real thing," Paul said.

Ahmed looked up at him, distrustful, unconvinced.

"But I suggest you not take my word for that."

Ahmed snapped open his briefcase and dropped the plastic sleeve inside. "If I find out it's fake, I will—"

"When is your plane?" Paul asked innocently enough, even though Ahmed had told him the time the day before in his kitchen.

"Eight, but I have to get through the traffic and security."

"Right."

"Done," Ahmed muttered hatefully. And then he left.

Paul picked up his phone.

"Passaro, if you happen to be looking for Ahmed, you will find that he is flying out of the country this evening."

"Leaving the country?"

"Yes. Flying to Paris, then Berlin."

"Fuck! Once he is inside the EU, he can move around without being tracked. I can't hold him. There's no paperwork, no charge."

"Yes, you can."

"How?"

"He could have a little passport problem."

"I don't get it."

"You probably have contacts at Homeland Security?"

"Of course."

"I suggest you tell them there was a serious irregularity on his citizenship application some years ago."

"No statute of limitations on those."

"Nope. Federal law. All that got rewritten after the towers went down."

"He went straight to the airport?"

"Going now," said Paul. "He probably had a car waiting for him. But the traffic will be terrible."

"What was the irregularity?"

"He lied about a previous arrest."

"Not good. What was he arrested for?"

"Assaulting a police officer in Ocean City, Maryland. The form asks, have you ever been arrested, and he said no, but I have paperwork showing the arrest. Names, charges, everything."

"Okay, I'm really listening now."

"Also, he'll probably have a document with him at the airport."

"Really?"

"It looks like this. Give me your cell number."

Paul texted the photo to Passaro. It took a moment or two to go through.

"Where did you get this?"

"It was in Billy's truck. I had the keys. There's blood on it that I bet matches one of the Libyan guys."

"He has this? You just gave it to him?"

"Yes."

"It's original?"

"It's in a protective plastic sleeve."

"You are a complete asshole! Fucking A! He could tear it up into little pieces and dribble it out the car window!"

"Yes, but the driver might notice."

"He could throw it into the trash at the airport."

"Cameras everywhere."

"He could wait until he got on board the aircraft, let it take off, and then at some point flush it down the vacuum toilet, where it would be destroyed in whatever chemical treatment they—"

"He won't do that. I can explain."

"I'm going to the airport. Wait, where is the truck?"

"It's in a lot a few blocks from here."

"You are driving me there while I talk on the phone! You need to explain everything."

"You're kidding."

"No, I'm not, and it would be considered a constructive gesture, Paul Reeves, considering you fucking tampered with evidence by removing the truck from where it was."

"I'll be there."

"Hurry up!" barked Passaro.

They met at the lot ten minutes later. Figuring for the terrible Friday traffic and the fact that Ahmed had to get to the flight two hours before departure gave them some time to catch up with him.

"Wow," said Passaro when Paul opened up the truck. All the photos of Jennifer. "That's the woman?"

"Yup."

As soon as they were moving Passaro was on the phone with his contacts at Homeland Security.

"Technically I'm supposed to go through the Port Authority Police," he said between calls, "but fuck them."

"Belt Parkway or the Van Wyck Expressway?" asked Paul. "I mean, those are the main ways, unless you want to cut through Brooklyn."

"I vote the Belt. Even if the traffic is slow we are next to the water."

And that is what they did, although getting into Brooklyn took an endless amount of time; the tunnel was clogged, Canal Street was a nightmare. Forty-five minutes, an hour to cross to Brooklyn? Could that really be true? Well, yes. Passaro chattered into his phone constantly. "Okay, so that map you sent me, I sent on, and the guys have already matched the handwriting to the dead guy. Your screengrabs of the fingerprints are very pretty, but we can't use them. But we have some other— Oh, wait." Passaro listened. "Okay, so they know he's in the security line now. But they are going to let him through, because it's better if he actually gets on the plane. Then you can charge him for attempted flight from the country. Another charge. We have just enough time. Maybe you will get to see him again."

I don't really need to see Ahmed, thought Paul. I'll just drop off Passaro. It was then he noticed a motorcycle behind him. Orange bike with yellow helmet.

"That's weird," he said.

"What?"

"The last time I drove the truck, from JFK into Manhattan, that same motorcycle was behind me. And the guy followed me, maybe, to the parking lot."

Passaro awkwardly turned around. "Fucking crap racing bike."

The motorcycle came close. Right behind the truck.

"This guy is genuinely crazy," Paul said.

Passaro was watching carefully. "That guy is also seriously muscular under the leather."

Now the bike came up alongside Paul, and the rider pulled a gun out of his jacket and pointed it at Paul, ordering him to pull over.

"Well, we seem to have a new best friend," said Passaro calmly. "I want you to speed up, *fast.*"

This Paul did. Soon the truck was going seventy, which was dangerously fast for the Belt Parkway. The orange motorcycle followed closely, easily accelerating behind the truck. The rider pulled up on the right-hand side of the pickup and threatened again with his gun, which was connected to a strap around his neck.

"That's a fucking Tec-9," said Passaro. "This is some kind of attempted kidnapping."

"What do I do?" hollered Paul, trying to dodge traffic.

"Pull ahead and get in the right lane!"

Paul jammed the accelerator and the powerful truck shot forward into the far right lane. The maniac on the bike pulled up close behind them, and fired one shot that hit the tailgate.

"Hit the brake!" Passaro ordered.

"Hard?"

"Hard!" Passaro yelled, looking back.

So Paul jammed the brakes for all he was worth, making the tires squeal madly, and instantly feeling the seat belt pull tightly against his chest and in the same moment a jolting impact as the motorcyclist hit the rear bumper at seventy-five miles an hour and was flung forward off his motorcycle, only to smack hard against the cab of the pickup, even as the orange motorcycle was tearing itself to pieces as it skidded and spun along the rough pavement and was hit by traffic. The helmeted rider lay facedown in the bed of the truck, barely moving.

"He's in the truck!"

"I know!" said Passaro. "He's dazed, I think."

But dazed or not, the rider rose to his knees in the truck bed, holding his head. A battered Chinese delivery van with three men in the front had drawn close behind to watch the action, then changed lanes.

"Don't slow down!" commanded Passaro. "Keep going fast!"

Paul glanced in the rearview mirror, then back at the road. The truck was all over the place, hitting potholes at high speed. "Look!"

They did and saw that the man had found the gun strapped to his neck. As he lifted it to fire through the window, Paul instinctively lurched to his left, pulling the truck across the highway in front of the same Chinese delivery van, throwing the man off balance. But he fired anyway, shots audible over the noise of the engine, a machine-gun-like *dunk-dunk-dunk-dunk*, and the bullets exploded through the back window of the cab and whizzed out the windshield in front of Paul, leaving spiderwebbed bull's-eyes of cracked glass. Now the man was standing in a crouch, trying to steady himself to fire again, but before he did, Passaro rotated his corpulent bulk just enough to poke the snubby barrel of his modest service revolver through the shattered cab window and shoot, shocking Paul with the sound of it and making him jolt in fear. Passaro fired three times, the gun's smoke blown away instantly by the air rushing through the blasted windshield. Paul watched through the rearview mirror as the muscular cyclist, hit square in the chest, staggered backward on his feet until the inside of the tailgate hit his legs and flipped him violently back off the end of the truck, boot heels over his yellow helmet—and though he landed feet-down, like a gymnast sticking the dismount, the same trailing Chinese delivery van, later revealed to be packed with three-dozen broken washers and dryers to be sold for scrap, briskly ran over his neck, first with the left front wheel and then, irrevocably, with the heavier rear one.

Smart people studied the future. Looked at the trends, prognosticated, checked the numbers. Global warming changed rainfall, which set countries fighting over water, which created refugee crises that destabilized governments. And so on. Yes, you were obligated to do so, Ahmed thought, watching the people getting up to board the plane. What did that mean? China ascendant, America like an old prizefighter, bloated and weakened yet always dangerous, always willing to lash out, then India, ever more crowded, prosperous, and polluted. Then Russia, weakening, population shrinking, but in conflict with its neighbors, Europe growing browner every year, with the Turks, and Pakis, and Africans eventually working their way up through the system, into government, and then the entire Middle East, a place he had never wanted to live, left in flames.

They called for the first-class passengers to board and he stood in line, feeling relief. He'd have his lawyer follow up with the police. No one had told him he couldn't exit the country, after all. The Swissair desk attendant scanned his boarding pass, and he proceeded down the gangway to the plane, an Airbus 330, according to his ticket. At his seat he slid his bag beneath him and sat down. So far as his office was concerned, he was taking a brief trip. He texted Jennifer to say he hoped that she would be waiting for him when he returned. As if.

Ahmed pondered his problem. He could stay in the United States but maybe be arrested for murder consiracy. But what was the proof? There was the meeting with the Libyans. The four people at the meeting had been Ahmed, Amir, now in the Far East, and the two dead men. There was the hand-drawn map, now in his possession. It *looked* real, but he needed to have an expert examine it in Paris. Could Paul *really* have given him the original? Hard to say, but he would know in a few days. In any case, that meeting alone could perhaps be developed into a kidnapping conspiracy charge, assuming the police found Amir and got him to talk. But the meeting had *not* led directly to the murder of William Wilkerson. The murder conspiracy meeting had been with Uncle Hassan in the Monkey Bar. But who was the hired killer? Ahmed didn't know! And yet the two meetings were of a piece; one led to the next, which led to a dead William Wilkerson. And now Uncle Hassan had disappeared. What did that mean?

He closed his eyes as the passengers filed past him.

"Mr. Mehraz?" came a polite voice.

He opened his eyes. "Yes?"

Three young men in respectable suits stood over him. One leaned forward and slipped handcuffs over his left wrist.

"Mr. Mehraz, we are federal air marshals with the Transportation Security Administration. You are being detained in connection with an ongoing NYPD police investigation as well as for certain potential immigration violations."

He stood at their command, both his hands now suddenly cuffed behind his back. They patted him down for weapons. The other passengers gawked. One started to record the scene with his phone.

"Is he a terrorist?" shrieked a woman. "Is there a bomb?"

"No, ma'am," barked one of the marshals. "Routine matter. There's no need for concern."

"Wait, wait," answered another passenger. "This is racial profiling!"

The larger marshal turned to the passenger. "Sir, shall we arrest you, right here, right now, for interfering with federal law enforcement activities?"

The passengers were silent, but three or four used their phones to record the incident. The marshals retrieved Ahmed's bag—oh, how he wished he had discarded or destroyed that map—and ushered him away, off the plane, either toward a murder investigation or a problem with his citizenship. Which was worse? He didn't know.

A blue and white Homeland Security cart was waiting with three other officers. Ahmed was seated in the back, with men to either side of him. Forty minutes later he had traveled by unmarked elevator down three floors and sat in JFK's detention facility, a small jail with individual cells. They had used a magnetic wand to check for hidden weapons, photographed him, done a retinal scan, taken his fingerprints, and removed his passport, cell phone, wallet, belt, and shoelaces. They had performed a full body-cavity search in a professional, respectful way that left a residue of lubricant between his butt cheeks.

He had said nothing in protest, had not complained or resisted or threatened legal reprisal in any manner. Why? Because he was thinking, thinking very hard. He did not understand how he could be charged with immigration law violations. But, come on, he should be able to figure it out. He had, after all, gone to law school at Harvard. And as his mind frantically sifted and sorted facts, he fixed on one piece of information: the package he had recently received from his old lawyer in Ocean City, Maryland, that referred to his arrest when he was a college student one summer. He had opened it, scanned its contents, thrown away the envelope, then filed the documents in his home office, eager that Jennifer not discover this small but ugly incident from his past. It was, seemingly, a forgotten matter. The local lawyer's wife, Ahmed recalled, was the clerk of the court in the municipality. She *alone* oversaw the registration of county arrest data into the FBI system. That was why the arrest had never appeared in the central archive. This had all been explained to him by Uncle Hassan. Corruption in the system, as old as time. A bit of money, a bribe, graft, grease, *baksheesh*— originally a Persian word, in fact. The way things often needed to get done. All to get over on the system. But this was old news, and relevant only in respect to his application of citizenship, in which he had lied about ever having been arrested. And now here he was, in the jail at JFK, courtesy of Homeland Security, the immigration police. There was something he wasn't . . . A human being was needed, of course, a person who had connected the anomaly between the old legal papers that had been sent to him recently and Ahmed's actual application for citizenship, a person who would understand those pieces of paper, be familiar with the federal regulations . . . an immigration attorney, of course, *yes*, one such as Paul Reeves, who lived *across the hall*. Paul Reeves, who coincidentally had also supplied him with the apparently genuine blood-soaked map that Ahmed had slipped into his carry-on bag, a map that had cost Ahmed more than *one million dollars* to obtain—a map that, no doubt, had already been discovered.

Trapped two ways at once, Ahmed realized, trapped by a mere immigration attorney.

49

Paper is so interesting. Simple but so powerful when it re-cords information. There would be no civilization without it, Passaro thought, standing in the apartment where Hector Ruiz had lived. By now his full history had come forth from the Mexican authorities. Hit man for El Chapo, the notorious drug lord. A contract put out on him by El Chapo himself years back had resulted in the three hired hit men all dead, killed by hunting arrows, of all things, and left in the desert. Suspected in the killings of nineteen men, total, in Mexico. Hector had somehow made it across the border and reached New York City, as so many do. Passaro flipped through the bills and envelopes on the kitchen table. Hector was organized; you had to give him that. All the protein mixes and supplements lined up in his refrigerator, a separate room stocked with motorcycle parts in carefully labeled boxes, and in the middle of the garage an enormous Harley-Davidson. With buddy pegs. Passaro had sat on the bike, let his hands rest on the grips. What a beast.

Paper. They'd found a slip of paper in Hector's workout bag. The red truck. Instructions. On the back of the slip was the address of a garage in Queens. A comparison of phone records showed that Hector had gotten a call from an intermediary who worked at the garage named Lorenzo, and a brief interrogation by Passaro made him give up Omar, who was the one contacted by Hassan Mehraz. Omar, it turned out, had, in addition to a wife and two girls, a lot of other problems, and he was happy to tell them what he knew. How he had told Hector about Hassan and told Hassan about Hector. So it all fell together. Poor old Hassan, found clutching a thumb knife with a poison injector, the exact kind that the CIA had provided SAVAK, the Iranian security service, decades ago. But it hadn't worked; the poison was too old. The injector pin matched an infected puncture wound in Hector's stomach discovered during the autopsy. Hassan had failed at killing Hector, and that was why he became the mangled body discovered in the N train subway tunnel, an older man who happened to be, yes, the uncle of Ahmed Mehraz. A murder charge was going to be hard to make stick, Passaro knew, but not murder conspiracy and attempted kidnapping. Ahmed was going down.

50

I am morally suspect, Paul told himself. He had, after all, taken advantage of a tragic situation, to procure the Ratzer map. He had cleverly and perhaps illegally manipulated Ahmed's vulnerability; on the other hand, it was the artifice that had guaranteed his capture before he left the country. And if Paul hadn't done what he had done, then Ahmed might well be somewhere very far from the reach of justice, with ample resources to elude the reckoning he probably deserved. Plus, Paul reminded himself, I would not have this map in my hands! He set the heavy framed map down and measured its dimensions in its paper outer wrapping and then set the height of the slat wall hangers, which were suspended from reinforced grooves in the wall, the same as used in many museums. Each hook was rated for 150 pounds, but he always felt better having two. Then he slipped the map from its wrapping and lifted it up; together, frame, glass, matting, and map were perhaps sixty pounds or so. With practiced grace, he dropped the hanging wire over one hook and then another, let the map down until the hooks took the weight. This was the moment that the map was suddenly displayed. He slid off the protective conservator's plastic and stepped back.

Fabulous? No, not yet! It was ever so slightly off dead level, and with a practiced eye he edged it sideways along the hooks one inch to the left, then dropped his hands. Perfect. He took five steps back to the opposite wall, found the dimmer switch that controlled the recessed lights in the ceiling, switched them on, and then—finally—he looked.

Magnificent, the Ratzer. A map used by George Washington to defend the new republic in a time when America was more an idea than anything else and the island of Manhattan a town of a mere twelve thousand souls living in shingled and clapboard wood houses, with the occasional old farmhouse. When what would be called Texas belonged to the Mexicans, when Iran was Persia, when Paul's forebears were Irish potato farmers who collected horse droppings for their gardens. But even as the lines on the map denoted the contours of the ancient green fish-shaped island, all else had spun forward and changed. This was the inescapable sadness of maps on paper, for while they held the past they were locked within it; their moment of creation was also the instant they perished as the newest depiction of their inscribed world. He stared at the fine lines tracing the Manhattan shoreline, the waters around it, and felt an echo of melancholy. Here he had lived, here he would die.

He heard a knocking on his door, and a voice.

"Paul? Paul?"

He opened the door to see Jennifer standing there; she collapsed against him, crying. "I came back to say goodbye. They let me up."

He led her to the living room.

"Billy is gone," she cried. "And I will never see him again."

"What are you going to do?" he asked, sitting on the sofa across from her.

Jennifer shook her head at the tears. "I have some decisions to make. It's really that simple."

As before, he got out some wine and pulled together a bit of food for them. Some cheese Rachel had bought, some crackers and a spread. When he returned to the living room he saw that Jennifer was carefully holding the glass box of burnt scraps. She seemed happy to be distracted by it. "What is this?"

"That, alas, is the reason Rachel stormed out of here furious at me the other night."

"Really?"

"Yup."

"What happened?"

"She wanted to know the story behind it."

"Did you tell her?"

"No."

"Oh." She considered the scraps. "Why?"

He sat back with his drink and looked out his window at the lights running down the avenue. The events on the Belt Parkway—the stopping of the truck, the inspection of the mangled body of the motorcyclist, the police sirens, Passaro taking charge of the crime scene—had loosened him up, turned a forgotten key in a lonesome lock in his head, made him feel the slippage of years. The sad, incomprehensible nature of time, the way it fooled you and brought you around to the old places in yourself that felt lost. Why *hadn't* he told Rachel? *Someone* had to know his history, no? "Well, Brooklyn is really where I am from, you know. My dad was a New York City fireman who wanted to go to college and study history. But he knocked up my mother, and she insisted he marry her, which is what one usually did back then."

"Right," Jennifer said, eager for the story.

"His uncle, a building inspector, helped him get on the fire department, and for several years his life centered around the firehouse just west of the corner of Union Street and Seventh Avenue in Park Slope, which was pretty run-down then, not the swanky neighborhood it is now."

"Go on."

So he did. "My dad was a regular fireman. At this time, back in the early 1960s, the docks of Brooklyn had fallen into disrepair." What had once been the eastern half of the economically most productive harbor in the western hemisphere had sunk into the doldrums as the harbor silted up and container ships became larger. The warehouses near the docks lost their value and were abandoned. Eventually their roofs rotted. "Many of them were burned down for their insurance money, in fact. On a November night when I was only one, my father's company responded to a six-alarm blaze at what had been the National Refrigeration

Supply Company." Paul remembered his father telling him years later how the men were hauling hoses alongside the burning building when a cry went out and they looked up—just as a jet of superheated air blew out an immense window. Uncountable shards of glass, wood, and burning paint chips blasted the men. "The pieces went down their throats or into their eyes. Of the five men injured, three died within several days, their lungs scorched and punctured, one was instantly blinded in one eye but otherwise unhurt, and the last, my father, lingered between death and life for weeks."

Paul paused. It had been decades since he had discussed the accident.

"And?" whispered Jennifer.

"He was saved by a former army surgeon who had learned his craft in the Korean War. He sucked nearly a hundred pieces of glass, metal, wood, and carbonized lead paint from my father's lungs."

"The box? That's what they are?"

He nodded, choking a bit at the thought of it, almost feeling those sharp pieces in his throat. "The surgeon saved some of the pieces to show him. My dad was finally able to leave the hospital, but it was clear his days as a fireman were over. With a disability pension, he was able to get a mortgage to buy a three-story row house on Fourteenth Street near Fifth Avenue. This was my home growing up."

"I thought you had grown up *rich*," Jennifer said.

"Nope, not at all. My dad had been a strapping man, you know, six-foot-two, and well over two hundred and thirty pounds, but with his injuries, he was, ah, permanently stooped, and he became prematurely old, and as a teenager I felt ashamed that he could not throw a ball with me on the street."

"I'm sorry."

"When I complained to my mother, she asked me when was the last time I had seen my father's back. I didn't understand the question, but later I watched him put on his T-shirt and realized that he couldn't throw a ball to me because the surgeon had cut through his back muscles to operate on his lungs, leaving masses of scar tissue and dead nerves . . .

"He decided to attend Brooklyn College and get a bachelor's degree in history. From there he was able to find a job teaching at a local private girls' school, the Berkeley Institute. The pay wasn't very good, but he liked it. He became a pretty good teacher of American history for almost thirty years."

His mother, meanwhile, was profoundly traumatized by his father's accident and the long, agonizing climb back it required. She never quite recovered, her anxiety over him crystallizing into a permanent structure of worry about everything and a related fury that she was imprisoned by his disability and meager earnings. "She turned into an angry person," Paul said. "Many of the wives of firemen my father's age saw their husbands receive full pensions after twenty years and then go on to start new jobs selling cars or real estate or insurance, fleeing Brooklyn to the seemingly idyllic suburbs of Long Island and New Jersey. She used to say, 'We never got out of Brooklyn,' shaking her head. My dad was able to make it to my law school graduation, even though he was failing."

Jennifer's eyes looked away into the distance, perhaps pondering her own path. "Keep telling it."

"After the ceremony, he took me around to his bar on Fifth Avenue and introduced me to them as his son, the law school graduate. Then we sat down and he ordered boilermakers for us. I remember he said, 'Paul, I want to tell you a couple of things, okay? What I want to tell you is that I am immensely proud of you, but your mother doesn't really understand you now. She's a Brooklyn girl who married a dopey Brooklyn fireman, right? She never really got much of a life. I know she's tough on you, but I want you to promise me you'll take care of her. The only thing she loves as much as you is the rotten little house we live in. Keep her in it until she dies, if you can.' He made me promise. I did. Then he drained his boilermaker, his cheeks ruddier than I'd seen them in a long time. You know, I wonder if I have ever loved someone like I loved him. Maybe that's been my problem."

"I don't think that's a problem, Paul. I never knew my father, and when you never know your father, it causes all kinds of trouble."

Outside, the few taxis stopped at the red lights on the street below, waited, then flowed south. If she had known her father, actually had a father, Paul thought, she might not have married Ahmed. It was ridiculous to be so reductive, yet maybe it was true.

"You were saying about your father?" Jennifer asked.

"He was dead seven weeks later from a lung hemorrhage. The old scar tissue. He got up from his reading chair to get a glass of water, and just went over. I was playing basketball in the park. My mother was destroyed by grief. I guess I eventually became a better son, and I made sure she never left that rotten little house on Fourteenth Street." He'd paid for a new roof twice, windows, boiler, carpeting, paint, plumbing, rewiring. In time he'd come to see that the cramped little structure on Fourteenth Street was the one true place he *knew*, the place where he had been a boy and where he had learned who his father was. "When my mother died I realized that I could never sell the place. It meant too much to me. So, Jennifer, that's what those little scraps are in that glass box. Relics, I guess."

She was crying softly, maybe for Billy more than anything.

"Okay, Jennifer, listen, I think I told you that story for a reason."

She came over and sat next to him on the couch. "Billy didn't have to die, you know," she said. "I could've told him to leave without me or I could have gone with him. It's my fault, Paul." She looked into his face—her eyes so blue, so young, he realized.

"You couldn't have possibly known where it was all going," he responded, trying to comfort her. "That being said, you are going to have to be stronger and smarter in the future."

She curled against him, sobbing quietly. After a time, he stroked her back. "So, look," he finally said, "I want to tell you something, one thing, then give you a kiss on your cheek, and then I want you to go get a cab back to your hotel."

But she didn't want to leave, he could see. "We could—" she began, taking his hand in hers. "Paul, do you—"

He shook his head gently. "That's not the right thing here."

Jennifer blinked, but was perhaps relieved. "Okay, Paul, okay."

"We lose everybody," he told her. "One way or another, they all get taken away from us." He stared into her young face. "So hold on when you can. Don't let the people get away from you."

She nodded her head tearfully, distraught but somehow smiling at him. He led her back into the kitchen and found her coat.

"Button this up," he said. "It's cold out there."

And so she did, her fingers pushing the big top button through its hole. Before she opened the door, she said, "I'll take that kiss now."

He bent and kissed her lightly on the cheek, smelling her perfume. "You know where you have to go now, right?" he whispered. "Somebody needs you, right?"

Eyes closed, she nodded yes.

He gave her a tight hug to send her on her way. "The city will always be here, Jennifer, when you want to come back."

51

These chicks are blow-out *junkies*, Rachel thought, looking around at the long row of hairdressing stations where a dozen women sat, eagerly and excitedly having their hair shampooed, conditioned, dried, and "blown out," that is, styled for that evening's important date or dinner or charity event. After work on a Friday the place was *jammed*, every appointment taken, the women having the styling done feeling, *Oh, yeah, I'm getting it together, having my look polished*, enjoying the lemon-infused water that came by on trays, and why shouldn't they feel that way, given that a whole treatment plus a selection of the exclusive branded products sold there could set you back a couple of hundred dollars? But it was worth it, wasn't it? Yes, it had to be. The place was all very cool, very LA in NYC. A certain kind of woman patronized the place, a certain—

But even though her hair was going to look totally great, she wasn't being cheered up, not really, not if she was going to be honest about it. She missed Paul, so much, and felt stupid and terrible about everything. She blamed herself, actually—or mostly, anyway. In any case, feeling she had nothing to lose, she called him.

"Hello?" she said, surprised when he answered.

"Rachel?"

"Yup," she said, glad he recognized her voice. "I was hoping something?"

"What?" said Paul.

"That you might miss me at least one-millionth of how much I miss you."

There was a pause. "A million is a very high number," he answered.

"I know!" she cried happily.

"Some maps even cost a million dollars."

"I *know*," she said, making sure he heard how sad she was that he hadn't gotten the big, beautiful Stassen-Ratzer map after all. "I'm sorry."

Her words just hung there, and she wondered if he had gotten her meaning.

"But," Paul finally said, "some maps that cost a million dollars sometimes can be traded for another map."

"Really?" exclaimed Rachel.

"Yes," said Paul, "really. It's a long story. Pretty complicated, too."

"You got it?"

He laughed easily. "The map is hanging right here. If not for you, I wouldn't have it."

"I guess so," she said, not sure why she should receive any credit.

"Big beautiful map. The most spectacular one I will ever own."

She heard the happiness in Paul's voice.

"I'm glad!" Rachel said. And she was. But she also wanted to say that—

"How about you come over and see?"

52

I don't know where I am, Jennifer told herself, oddly thrilled at the idea. But the GPS unit on the rental car told her she was close now. She'd called them from the San Antonio airport. Billy's mother answered. "You come on, and we'll see you soon," she'd said in a husked-out voice. Matter-of-fact, not giving away anything. I've got no standing in this situation, Jennifer realized, nothing except the simple fact of who I am. And who that was, exactly, she wasn't sure.

Before flying she had chosen clothes that didn't seem too expensive, too fancy or New York. These are regular people, she told herself, you know these kinds of people.

She had tearfully told Detective Passaro everything she knew about what Billy had been doing in New York, or more exactly what she had been doing with Billy in New York, the sex, everything, as well as all she could tell him about what Ahmed may or may not have done. The detective had said it seemed likely that Billy had killed two Libyan men hired by Ahmed to kidnap him, but now all three of them were dead, and there were no witnesses, no possible resolution. "Did Billy say anything about that?" Detective Passaro had asked. And her answer had been no. "Did he ever talk about his activities in the U.S. military?" No, she'd said, he wouldn't talk about it. Maybe mentioned something in Somalia, drone strikes. But he had never gone into any detail. The detective had just nodded. "Well, it seems he was very handy with a knife," he noted. The man who had killed Billy, a Mexican drug cartel enforcer, had been hired, somehow, through another man, though it appeared Ahmed's uncle Hassan had been involved, before he, too, had been killed, by the Mexican man. It was all a little confusing to her, confusing in the facts of the matter, though she knew she could understand them if she really wanted to, but more deeply confusing in that all this violence had come from the simple fact that she and Billy had been seeing each other. Well, not just that, but from Ahmed, too. It had all led to the whole bloody chain reaction. The detective had said that a charge of murder would not stick to Ahmed because there were too many unknowns, but a charge of attempted kidnapping or conspiracy to commit murder would, because they had good physical evidence they had found on Ahmed as he tried to leave the country. Moreover, they were confident his cousin Amir, also part of the plot, could be successfully extradited from Hong Kong. But meanwhile, Ahmed's citizenship was in danger of being revoked, because of some paperwork from his past that had come to light.

What she did know was that he was living now in a legal no-man's-land. If he stayed in the U.S. he might serve prison time, and if he left the U.S., it might be difficult for him ever to return. In any case, once the story of him being hauled off the airplane hit the news, he was summarily fired from his job. She had spoken to him only once.

"You had Billy killed," she'd said.

"I didn't."

"Nothing you can say will make me change my mind."

"I got that."

"We're done," she said.

"Yes, totally and completely done. You destroyed my life, Jennifer."

"It's not that—"

"Basically it *is* that simple," Ahmed snapped bitterly. "In any case, you can't come to the apartment, because I'm selling it, I've taken you off all the bank accounts, and your phone will die in a few days. All your credit cards are dead. You will never get a fucking dime from me.

Understand? I don't want to hear from you ever again. You will sign some divorce papers and after that it'd be fine with me if you would just *die*, okay?

"And by the way, I'll be fine. You won't know where I am, but I will be just fine. Wherever you are, whatever you are doing, just know that I will be fine and that I don't miss you, that I never want to see you, that you are dead to me, Jennifer."

She hated him with all of her essence, but even so, hearing these words had torn at her, made her sad about everything. She wasn't sure if she had ever loved Ahmed, but she had certainly admired him. She wished she had told him about Henry, just to hurt him, but she was glad she hadn't. It was better that way. Only Henry was pure in all of this.

Jennifer cried as she drove, feeling her old life falling away, replaced by anxious questions about the future. But then the robotic female voice coming out of the dashboard told her which county road to turn down, and she slowed to take in the hill country, the rolling expanses, so much greener than she'd expected. She saw the mailbox. The ranch gate arced high over the gravel road with a sheet metal design of a steer, and it was open. She could see that the driveway went back quite a ways. She made the turn off the road, then stopped to fix her makeup. I can't show up here looking like I was crying, she told herself. She opened the window and felt the dry, cooler air enter. Thanksgiving was coming, she realized as she put the car back into gear.

After a minute, a ranch house appeared with two barns in the back. She saw him riding a green bicycle over the dusty road and she stopped the car right there, not trusting herself to drive anymore. He wore a dirty T-shirt and blue jeans. His blond hair was cut short and she could feel the curve of his neck in her hands. *I had no idea,* she began to tell herself, *if I had ever—* She remembered to put the car in park and stepped out onto the gravel, aware of how awkward her steps were in heels. But she went forward. The boy saw her now, stopped near a barn, and stood astride his green bicycle. As she neared, Billy's parents stepped out into the sunlight; his mother was watchful, while his father, tall and slender like Billy, stepped down to greet Jennifer. They both looked old, depleted by time and yet more suffering. There was an immediate need for the intervening generation. The boy laid down his bike and ran over to his grandfather to take his hand, waiting to be told the name of the pretty young woman who had just arrived from New York City.

ACKNOWLEDGMENTS

As you write a book, people help you along the way, knowingly or not. It's a pleasure to thank them.

My editor at Farrar, Straus and Giroux, Sarah Crichton, was patient beyond measure as the months and then years rolled by. When the manuscript arrived, in chunks, she scrutinized it thoughtfully and made innumerable large and small suggestions as to how it could and should be improved. Sarah possesses that rare mix of editorial acuity, humor, and deep generosity. I am forever indebted to her.

I am also beholden to her many excellent colleagues at FSG: Jonathan Galassi, Jeff Seroy, Lottchen Shivers, Rodrigo Corral, Tyler Comrie, Abby Kagan, Debra Helfand, Kate Sanford, and Rob Sternitzky, whose attention to the text was absolutely stellar. Up in Nova Scotia, John McGhee gave the manuscript a bracing, skeptical copyedit.

My agent, Kris Dahl at ICM Partners, was a stalwart supporter, as always, and a perceptive reader. I am also indebted, one way or another, to Carolyn Reidy, Susan Moldow, Nan Graham, Roz Lippel, Kevin Hanson, Sarah Goldberg, Katrina Diaz, Brian and Diana DeCubellis, John Glusman, Steve Klinsky, Will Levith, Jofie Farrari-Adler, Sloan Harris, Richard Snow, Carol Sklenicka, Marko Maglich, Bob Vitalo, and Darren Von Stein, who not only is probably the best map framer in New York City but deeply knowledgeable about its history.

My wife, Kathryn, was supportive of the long gestation of the book, even as our children grew up, graduated, and weren't kids anymore. They have all been extraordinarily tolerant of my obsession with maps of New York City and the mess of papers the writing of this book generated.

My brother, Dana Harrison, and I spent many weekends out on the East End of Long Island, clearing an overgrown field using chain saws and woodchippers, often in freezing temperatures with snow on the ground. This shared activity was of great benefit to me when it was time to work on the book.

Certain individuals shared their stories with me during the writing of this book. They shall go unnamed, but they know who they are, and that I am grateful.

A Note About the Author

Colin Harrison is the author of eight novels, seven of which are set in New York City. He serves as the editor in chief at Scribner, an imprint of Simon & Schuster. A graduate of Haverford College and the University of Iowa Writers' Workshop, he is married to the writer Kathryn Harrison and lives in Brooklyn, New York, and Jamesport, Long Island.

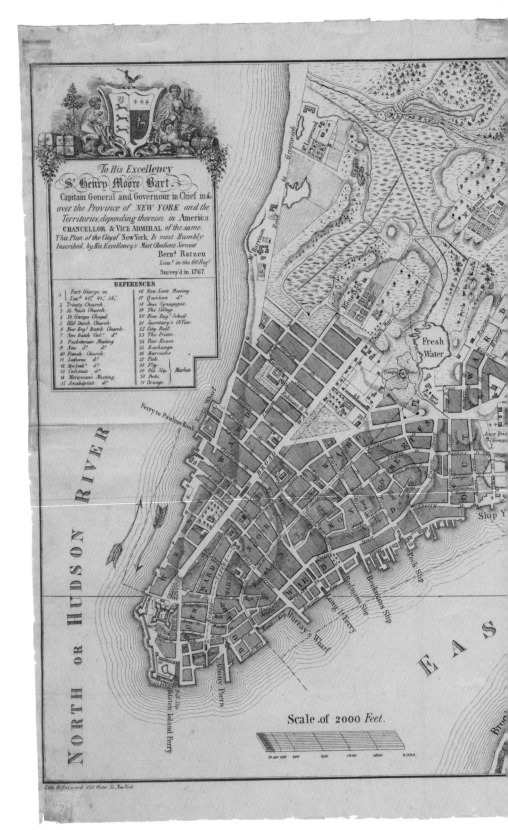

To His Excellency
Sr. Henry Moore Bart.
Capitam General and Governour in Chief in &
over the Province of NEW-YORK and the
Territories, depending thereon in America
CHANCELLOR & VICE ADMIRAL, of the same.
This Plan of the City of New York, Is most Humbly
Inscribed, by His Excellency's Most Obedient Servant
Bernd. Ratzen.
Lieut. in the 60 Regt.
Survey'd in 1767.

REFERENCES

1 Fort George in
   Latd. 40° 41′ 58″.
2 Trinity Church.
3 St. Pauls Church.
4 St. Georges Chapel.
5 Old Dutch Church.
6 New Engd. Dutch Church.
7 New Dutch Cal.l do.
8 Presbiterian Meeting
9 Ann. do.
10 French Church.
11 Lutheran do.
12 Roe Luth. do.
13 Calvinist do.
14 Moravians Meeting
15 Anabaptist do.
16 New Scots Meeting.
17 Quakers do.
18 Jews Synagogue
19 The College
20 Free Engl. School.
21 Secretary's Office
22 City Hall
23 The Prison
24 Poor House
25 Exchange
26 Barracks
27 Fish.   Market
28 Fly.
29 Old Slip.
30 Pecks.
31 Oswego.

North Gouvenour

Fresh Water

Ferry to Paulus Hook

NORTH OR HUDSON RIVER

EAS...

Ship Y...

Scale of 2000 Feet.

50 100 200 500   800   1200   1600   2000.